THOMAS HARRIS

HANNIBAL

arrow books

Reissued by Arrow Books in 2009

1 3 5 7 9 10 8 6 4 2

Copyright © Yazoo Fabrications, Inc 1999

First published in Great Britain in 1999 by
William Heinemann

Arrow Books
Random House, 20 Vauxhall Bridge Road,
London SW1V 2SA

www.rbooks.co.uk

Addresses for companies within The Random House Group Limited can
be found at: www.randomhouse.co.uk/offices.htm

The Random House Group Limited Reg. No. 954009

A CIP catalogue record for this book
is available from the British Library

ISBN 9780099532941

The Random House Group Limited supports the Forest Stewardship
Council (FSC), the leading international forest certification organisation.
All our titles that are printed on Greenpeace approved FSC certified
paper carry the FSC logo. Our paper procurement policy can be found at
www.rbooks.co.uk/environment

Typeset by Palimpsest Book Production Limited,
Polmont, Stirlingshire
Printed in theUK by CPI Bookmarque, Croydon, CR0 4TD

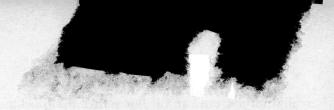

Praise for *Hannibal*

"Is this the best novel of the year? . . . a masterpiece . . . chillingly brilliant . . . *Hannibal* grips like a vice, from its brilliantly realised opening to its horrifying and delight-fully whimsical conclusion . . . [the book] grabs you by the ear, the eye, the throat and drags the reader helplessly around a switchback-cum-maze of narrative ingenuity . . . I sat skewered to my seat until the last page . . . Every line of *Hannibal* is suffused with the sense of a titanic struggle with evil in its blackest form . . . It contains writing of which our best writers would be proud . . . In *Hannibal*, Harris has surpassed himself. It has wit, erudition, golden dialogue and it does that thing that most novels can't do: it describes almost constant action. I'm prepared to bet that *Observer* readers won't pick up a more compelling novel this year." Robert McCrum, *Observer*

"Well if this novel isn't the number one bestseller by this time next week, I'll eat my tongue . . . [it] is quite simply a compelling and brilliant thriller . . . it seems all too real and quite terrifying. Thomas Harris is a brilliantly clever author . . . Sentence for sentence there is nobody to match him . . . It is an incredible achievement . . . absorbing" *Mirror*

"The readers who have been waiting for *Hannibal* only want to know if it is as good as *Red Dragon* and *The Silence of the Lambs* . . . It is a pleasure to reply in the negative. No, not as good. This one is better. It is, in fact, one of the two most frightening popular novels of our time, the other being *The Exorcist* . . . *Hannibal* is

really not a sequel at all, but rather the third and most satisfying part of one very long and scary ride through the haunted palace of abnormal psychiatry . . . I hope with all my heart that [Harris] will write again, and sooner rather than later—novels that bravely and cleverly erase the line between popular fiction and literature are very much to be prized." Stephen King, *New York Times Book Review*

"No panting fan—waiting these 11 years for the three Thomas Harrises to become four—could have hoped for more. Tense, dark, allusive and alert to the state of the nation, *Hannibal* is a great popular novel and a plausible candidate for the Pulitzer Prize. The last two decades of 19th century popular fiction were dominated by Conan Doyle and Sherlock Holmes. A century on, suspense literature has achieved their equals in Thomas Harris and Hannibal Lecter." *Guardian*

"[*Hannibal*] ought to have been a flop—*The Silence of the Lambs* should have been an impossible act to follow. But the opposite is the case: it is a gut-churning, nail-biting, skin-crawling, often lyrical triumph—addictive on every level . . . If there's a better book this year, with truth, fantasy and a touch of erudition combined in prose which really does leap off the page, I'll eat my hat." Francis Fyfield, *Express*

"Astonishing . . . *Hannibal* grips from the very beginning like a crazed dog on Mason Verger's face. And while it's the devilish detail which makes this book a delight to read, the revelations concerning Lecter's own psychology, and that of Clarice Starling, make it imperative that you get to the end. The tension between my desire to savour this story and find out what happens was deliciously awful . . . Harris is that most unusual of things, a genre writer who supersedes and transfigures the genre he chose to write in. I raise my glass of Château d'Yquem to him." Will Self, *Independent on Sunday*

"There is no book more unputdownable this summer . . . The thrills, horror, sly erudition and sheer exquisite writing make this so much more than another serial killer novel . . . [It] reaches almost sublime levels of gothic grandeur at its conclusion. If only all bestsellers were so rewarding" *Guardian*

"An absolutely holiday must. Quite simply this is the best-written thriller to dominate the market in years . . . in the wit, erudition and sheer style of the eponymous Dr Lecter, we have not only a world-class villain but a literary evocation of the diabolical to compare with Goethe and Gogol. Honestly" *The Times*

"So does *Hannibal* live up to the expectations raised by a wait of ten years? Yes. Or rather, no, it exceeds them. *Hannibal* is a momentous achievement . . . the reader is held in a ferocious grip. He lies at the author's mercy . . . *Hannibal* works faultlessly as a thriller . . . no sooner have you finished it than you want to go through it again . . . *Hannibal* is the work of a real writer, following his own path, despite the pressures of fame. He's not doing it for money and there won't be another Lecter novel. We're lucky to have this." *Evening Standard*

"On paper Lecter is wittier, more complex and more frightening than any actor could convey on screen" *Daily Telegraph*

"Impeccably researched, marvellously written and peppered with Harris's dark humour . . . blackly, bizarrely funny, horrific, emotionally wrenching . . . confirms Harris's status as a master of the genre" *Irish Times*

"Beautifully written . . . there is not a single ugly or dead sentence here . . . Lecter is a superbly seductive creation" *Sunday Times*

"Insanely readable . . . No thriller writer is better attuned than Thomas Harris to the rhythms of suspense. No horror writer is more adept at making the stomach churn . . . compelling . . . truly shocking . . . a brilliant book" Craig Brown, *Mail on Sunday*

"It has taken Harris the better part of a decade to produce this, only his fourth novel. It has been worth the wait . . . Harris's writing bears the hallmarks of honed perfection . . . This piece of literature is popular fiction only in the sense that it will sell. And sell . . . Look no further for the chiller of the year: Hannibal walks among us." Peter Millar, *The Times*

"Terrific . . . *Hannibal* confirms our worst fears and will spur many nightmares this summer. It's that good. What can one say but: pig out" *Scotland on Sunday*

"A master breaks his own mould. Edgar Allan Poe for today" *Evening Standard*

"Masterful . . . disturbing . . . a fine novel, deep and intriguing, worthy of its bald, bold language and biblical allusion . . . Lecter's power as a character of fiction is that he lives to haunt us, to exist in the reader's imagination outside the novel, to stand beside the other monsters lingering in the shadows: the Beast with his Beauty, Grendel, Bluebeard and Dracula." *The Times*

"Gets off to a flying start, and barely relents for near on 500 pages. You will be sleeping with the lights on" *Harpers & Queen*

"Harris is a superb writer, clean, economical and witty: as razor sharp in plot and character as Hannibal's rib-tickling knife" *Scotland on Sunday*

"While Harris twists the plot with his usual ease, few will foresee the final outcome which is exactly how a Harris novel should be . . . shows you how psychological horror should be done" *List*

"This is superior craftsmanship, beautifully written and filled with strikingly elegant prose shot through with a coal-black wit, every sentence honed to perfection, making this novel a masterpiece of contemporary fiction" *Uncut*

"Hannibal Lecter is back at his deadliest best . . . for sheer heart-stopping suspense he's hard to beat in a deliriously sadistic dance with death which will grip you to its eerie, unexpected climax" *Big Issue*

"The most significant sequel since *Paradise Regained*" *Independent*

"Reading *Hannibal* and trying to figure out why Harris is so much better than other writers at this sort of thing is a bit like watching a magician . . . Not even the most astute reader will be able to foresee where Harris is leading, but few will be disappointed to get there. And where he takes us in the end is all the more shocking for the calm tones in which it is related." *New York Post*

"Deliciously frightening . . . interested in getting the hell

scared out of you? Buy this book on a Friday. Plan a weekend of easy-to-identify meals. Lock all doors and windows. And by Monday, God and That Guy willing, you just might be able to sleep without a night-light."
Newsday

"486 fast-paced pages, in which every respite is but a prelude to further furious action . . . a tale that is endlessly terrifying . . . *Hannibal* speaks to the imagination, to the feelings, to the passions, to exalted senses and to debased ones. Harris's voice will be heard for awhile."
Los Angeles Times

"Diabolically clever plotting . . . Harris serves up a feast in *Hannibal* . . . Harris writes like an angel with the devil's sense of humor . . . The hypnotic blend of horror story and psychological thriller lifts crime fiction to sublime . . . *Hannibal* is ghoulishly good fare." *Boston Herald*

"A work of art . . . You'll eat up *Hannibal* . . . There isn't a wasted word . . . the last 100 pages are the best I've ever read in the thriller genre." *USA Today*

"[A] devilish tale . . . eerily realistic and chillingly vivid from beginning to end. As Harris sketches his hideous scenarios, he allows us to color them in with our imaginations. But not overdoing it, he draws us in, practically making us conspirators in his macabre fantasy." *New York Post*

"A truly scary book . . . As deep and disturbing a thriller as has ever been written." *People*

"[A] page-turner . . . I have read every word of *Hannibal*, most of them only twice, but some as many as five or six times." *New York Magazine*

HANNIBAL

A native of Mississippi, Thomas Harris began his writing career covering crime in the United States and Mexico, and was a reporter and editor for the Associated Press in New York City. His first novel, *Black Sunday*, was published in 1975, followed by *Red Dragon* in 1981, *The Silence of the Lambs* in 1988, *Hannibal* in 1999 and most recently, *Hannibal Rising*, in 2006.

HANNIBAL

I

WASHINGTON, D.C.

1

You would think that such a day
would tremble to begin . . .

CLARICE STARLING'S Mustang boomed up the entrance
ramp at the Bureau of Alcohol, Tobacco and Firearms
on Massachusetts Avenue, a headquarters rented from
the Reverend Sun Myung Moon in the interest of
economy.

The strike force waited in three vehicles, a battered
undercover van to lead and two black SWAT vans
behind it, manned and idling in the cavernous garage.

Starling hoisted the equipment bag out of her car
and ran to the lead vehicle, a dirty white panel van
with MARCELL'S CRAB HOUSE signs stuck on the sides.

Through the open back doors of the van, four men
watched Starling coming. She was slender in her
fatigues and moving fast under the weight of her equipment, her hair shining in the ghastly fluorescent lights.

"Women. Always late," a D.C. police officer said.

BATF Special Agent John Brigham was in charge.

"She's not late—I didn't beep her until we got the
squeal," Brigham said. "She must have hauled ass from
Quantico—Hey, Starling, pass me the bag."

3

She gave him a fast high five. "Hey, John."

Brigham spoke to the scruffy undercover officer at the wheel and the van was rolling before the back doors closed, out into the pleasant fall afternoon.

Clarice Starling, a veteran of surveillance vans, ducked under the eyepiece of the periscope and took a seat in the back as close as possible to the hundred-fifty-pound block of dry ice that served as air-conditioning when they had to lurk with the engine turned off.

The old van had the monkey-house smell of fear and sweat that never scrubs out. It had borne many labels in its time. The dirty and faded signs on the doors were thirty minutes old. The bullet holes plugged with Bond-O were older.

The back windows were one-way mirror, appropriately tarnished. Starling could watch the big black SWAT vans following. She hoped they wouldn't spend hours buttoned down in the vans.

The male officers looked her over whenever her face was turned to the window.

FBI Special Agent Clarice Starling, thirty-two, always looked her age and she always made that age look good, even in fatigues.

Brigham retrieved his clipboard from the front passenger seat.

"How come you always catch this crap, Starling?" he said, smiling.

"Because you keep asking for me," she said.

"For this I need you. But I see you serving warrants on jump-out squads for Christ's sake. I don't ask, but somebody at Buzzard's Point hates you, I think. You should come to work with me. These are my guys,

4

Agents Marquez Burke and John Hare, and this is Officer Bolton from the D.C. Police Department."

A composite raid team of the Bureau of Alcohol, Tobacco and Firearms, the Drug Enforcement Administration SWAT teams and the FBI was the force-fit product of budget constraints in a time when even the FBI Academy was closed for lack of funding.

Burke and Hare looked like agents. The D.C. policeman, Bolton, looked like a bailiff. He was about forty-five, overweight and yeasty.

The Mayor of Washington, anxious to appear tough on drugs after his own drug conviction, insisted the D.C. police share credit for every major raid in the city of Washington. Hence, Bolton.

"The Drumgo posse's cooking today," Brigham said.

"Evelda Drumgo, I knew it," Starling said without enthusiasm.

Brigham nodded. "She's opened an ice plant beside the Feliciana Fish Market on the river. Our guy says she's cooking a batch of crystal today. And she's got reservations to Grand Cayman tonight. We can't wait."

Crystal methamphetamine, called "ice" on the street, provides a short powerful high and is murderously addictive.

"The dope's DEA business but we need Evelda on interstate transportation of Class Three weapons. Warrant specifies a couple of Beretta submachine guns and some MAC 10s, and she knows where a bunch more are. I want you to concentrate on Evelda, Starling. You've dealt with her before. These guys will back you up."

"We got the easy job," Officer Bolton said with some satisfaction.

"I think you better tell them about Evelda, Starling," Brigham said.

Starling waited while the van rattled over some railroad tracks. "Evelda will fight you," she said. "She doesn't look like it—she was a model—but she'll fight you. She's Dijon Drumgo's widow. I arrested her twice on RICO warrants, the first time with Dijon.

"This last time she was carrying a nine-millimeter with three magazines and Mace in her purse and she had a balisong knife in her bra. I don't know what she's carrying now.

"The second arrest, I asked her very politely to give it up and she did. Then in D.C. detention, she killed an inmate named Marsha Valentine with a spoon shank. So you don't know . . . her face is hard to read. Grand jury found self-defense.

"She beat the first RICO count and pled the other one down. Some weapons charges were dropped because she had infant children and her husband had just been killed in the Pleasant Avenue drive-by, maybe by the Spliffs.

"I'll ask her to give it up. I hope she will—we'll give her a show. But—listen to me—if we have to subdue Evelda Drumgo, I want some real help. Never mind watching my back, I want some weight on her. Gentlemen, don't think you're going to watch me and Evelda mud-wrestling."

There was a time when Starling would have deferred to these men. Now they didn't like what she was saying, and she had seen too much to care.

"Evelda Drumgo is connected through Dijon to the Trey-Eight Crips," Brigham said. "She's got Crip security, our guy says, and the Crips are distributing on the coast. It's security against the Spliffs, mainly. I don't know what the Crips will do when they see it's us. They don't cross the G if they can help it."

"You should know—Evelda's HIV positive," Starling said. "Dijon gave it to her off a needle. She found out in detention and flipped out. She killed Marsha Valentine that day and she fought the guards in jail. If she's not armed and she fights, you can expect to get hit with whatever fluid she has to throw. She'll spit and bite, she'll wet and defecate on you if you try to pat her down, so gloves and masks are SOP. If you put her in a patrol car, when you put your hand on her head, watch out for a needle in her hair and secure her feet."

Burke's and Hare's faces were growing long. Officer Bolton appeared unhappy. He pointed with his wattled chin at Starling's main sidearm, a well-worn Colt .45 Government Model with a strip of skateboard tape on the grip, riding in a Yaqui slide behind her right hip. "You go around with that thing cocked all the time?" he wanted to know.

"Cocked and locked, every minute of my day," Starling said.

"Dangerous," Bolton said.

"Come out to the range and I'll explain it to you, Officer."

Brigham broke it up. "Bolton, I coached Starling when she was interservice combat pistol champion three years straight. Don't worry about her weapon. Those guys from the Hostage Rescue Team, the Velcro Cowboys, what did they call you after you beat their ass, Starling? Annie Oakley?"

"Poison Oakley," she said, and looked out the window.

Starling felt pierced and lonesome in this goat-smelling surveillance van crowded with men. Chaps, Brut, Old Spice, sweat and leather. She felt some fear, and it tasted like a penny under her tongue. *A mental image: her father, who smelled of tobacco and strong soap, peeling an orange with his pocketknife, the tip of the blade broken off square, sharing the orange with her in the kitchen. The taillights of her father's pickup disappearing as he went off on the night-marshal patrol that killed him. His clothes in the closet. His square-dancing shirt. Some nice stuff in her closet now she never got to wear. Sad party clothes on hangers, like toys in the attic.*

"About another ten minutes," the driver called back.

Brigham looked out the windshield and checked his watch. "Here's the layout," he said. He had a crude diagram drawn hastily with a Magic Marker, and a blurry floor plan faxed to him by the Department of Buildings. "The fish market building is in a line of stores and warehouses along the riverbank. Parcell Street dead-ends into Riverside Avenue in this small square in front of the fish market.

"See, the building with the fish market backs on the water. They've got a dock back there that runs all along the back of the building, right here. Beside the fish market on the ground floor, that's Evelda's lab. Entrance here in front, just beside the fish market awning. Evelda will have the watchers out while she's cooking the dope, at least three blocks around. They've tipped her before in time for her to flush her stuff. So—a regular DEA incursion team in the third van is going in from a fishing boat on the dock side at fifteen hundred hours. We can get closer than anybody in this van, right up to the stret door a couple of minutes before the raid. If Evelda comes out the front, we get her. If she stays in, we hit this streetside door right after they hit the other side. Second van's our backup, seven guys, they come in at fifteen hundred unless we call first."

"We're doing the door how?" Starling said.

Burke spoke up. "If it sounds quiet, the ram. If we hear flash-bangs or gunfire, it's 'Avon calling.'" Burke patted his shotgun.

Starling had seen it done before—"Avon calling" is a three-inch magnum shotgun shell loaded with fine powdered lead to blow the lock out without injuring people inside.

"Evelda's kids? Where are they?" Starling said.

"Our informant saw her drop them off at day care," Brigham said. "Our informant's close to the family situation, like, he's very close, as close as you can get with safe sex."

Brigham's radio chirped in his earphone and he searched the part of the sky he could see out the back window. "Maybe he's just doing traffic," he said into his throat microphone. He called to the driver, "Strike Two saw a news helicopter a minute ago. You seen anything?"

"No."

"He better be doing traffic. Let's saddle up and button up."

One hundred and fifty pounds of dry ice will not keep five humans cool in the back of a metal van on a warm day, especially when they are putting on body armor. When Bolton raised his arms, he demonstrated that a splash of Canoe is not the same as a shower.

Clarice Starling had sewn shoulder pads inside her fatigue shirt to take the weight of the Kevlar vest, hopefully bulletproof. The vest had the additional weight of a ceramic plate in the back as well as the front.

Tragic experience had taught the value of the plate in the back. Conducting a forcible entry raid with a team you do not know, of people with various levels of training, is a dangerous enterprise. Friendly fire can smash your spine as you go in ahead of a green and frightened column.

Two miles from the river, the third van dropped off to take the DEA incursion team to a rendezvous with their fishing boat, and the backup van dropped a discreet distance behind the white undercover vehicle.

The neighborhood was getting scruffy. A third of the buildings were boarded up, and burned-out cars rested on crates beside the curbs. Young men idled on the corners in front of bars and small markets. Children played around a burning mattress on the sidewalk.

If Evelda's security was out, it was well concealed among the regulars on the sidewalk. Around the liquor stores and in the grocery parking lots, men sat in cars talking.

A low-rider Impala convertible with four young African-American men in it pulled into the light traffic and cruised along behind the van. The low-riders hopped the front end off the pavement for the benefit of the girls they passed and the thump of their stereo buzzed the sheet metal in the van.

Watching through the one-way glass of the back

window, Starling could see the young men in the convertible were not a threat—a Crip gunship is almost always a powerful, full-sized sedan or station wagon, old enough to blend into the neighborhood, and the back windows roll all the way down. It carries a crew of three, sometimes four. A basketball team in a Buick can look sinister if you don't keep your mind right.

While they waited at a traffic light, Brigham pulled the cover off the eyepiece of the periscope and tapped Bolton on the knee.

"Look around and see if there are any local celebrities on the sidewalk," Brigham said.

The objective lens of the periscope is concealed in a roof ventilator. It only sees sideways.

Bolton made a full rotation and stopped, rubbing his eyes. "Thing shakes too much with the motor running," he said.

Brigham checked by radio with the boat team. "Four hundred meters downstream and closing," he repeated to his crew in the van.

The van caught a red light a block away on Parcell Street and sat facing the market for what seemed a long time. The driver turned as though checking his right mirror and talked out of the corner of his mouth to Brigham. "Looks like not many people buying fish. Here we go."

The light changed and at 2:57 P.M., exactly three minutes before zero hour, the battered undercover van stopped in front of the Feliciana Fish Market, in a good spot by the curb.

In the back they heard the ratchet as the driver set the hand brake.

Brigham relinquished the periscope to Starling. "Check it out."

Starling swept the periscope across the front of the building. Tables and counters of fish on ice glittered beneath a canvas awning on the pavement. Snappers up from the Carolina banks were arranged artfully in schools on the shaved ice, crabs moved their legs in open crates and lobsters climbed over one another in a tank. The smart fishmonger had moisture pads over the eyes of his bigger fish to keep them bright until the evening wave of cagey Caribbean-born housewives came to sniff and peer.

Sunlight made a rainbow in the spray of water from the fish-cleaning table outside, where a Latin-looking man with big forearms cut up a mako shark with graceful strokes of his curved knife and hosed the big fish down with a powerful handheld spray. The bloody water ran down the gutter and Starling could hear it running under the van.

Starling watched the driver talk to the fishmonger, ask him a question. The fishmonger looked at his watch, shrugged, pointed out a local lunch place. The driver poked around the market for a minute, lit a cigarette and walked off in the direction of the café.

A boom box in the market was playing "La Macarena" loud enough for Starling to hear it clearly in the van; she would never again in her life be able to endure the song.

The door that mattered was on the right, a double metal door in a metal casement with a single concrete step.

Starling was about to give up the periscope when the

door opened. A large white man in a luau shirt and sandals came out. He had a satchel across his chest. His other hand was behind the satchel. A wiry black man came out behind him carrying a raincoat.

"Heads up," Starling said.

Behind the two men, with her long Nefertiti neck and handsome face visible over their shoulders, came Evelda Drumgo.

"Evelda's coming out behind two guys, looks like they're both packing," Starling said.

She couldn't give up the periscope fast enough to keep Brigham from bumping her. Starling pulled on her helmet.

Brigham was on the radio. "Strike One to all units. Showdown. Showdown. She's out this side, we're moving.

"Put 'em on the ground as quietly as we can," Brigham said. He racked the slide on his riot gun. "Boat's here in thirty seconds, let's do it."

Starling first out on the ground, Evelda's braids flying out as her head spun toward her. Starling conscious of the men beside her, guns out, barking "Down on the ground, down on the ground!"

Evelda stepping out from between the two men.

Evelda was carrying a baby in a carrier slung around her neck.

"Wait, wait, don't want any trouble," she said to the men beside her. "Wait, wait." She strode forward, posture regal, holding the baby high in front of her at the extent of the sling, blanket hanging down.

Give her a place to go. Starling holstered her weapon by touch, extended her arms, hands open. "Evelda!

13

Give it up. Come to me." Behind Starling, the roar of a big V8 and squeal of tires. She couldn't turn around. *Be the backup.*

Evelda ignoring her, walking toward Brigham, the baby blanket fluttered as the MAC 10 went off behind it and Brigham went down, his face shield full of blood.

The heavy white man dropped the satchel. Burke saw his machine pistol and fired a puff of harmless lead dust from the Avon round in his shotgun. He racked the slide, but not in time. The big man fired a burst, cutting Burke across the groin beneath his vest, swinging toward Starling as she came up from the leather and shot him twice in the middle of his hula shirt before he could fire.

Gunshots behind Starling. The wiry black man dropped the raincoat off his weapon and ducked back in the building, as a blow like a hard fist in the back drove Starling forward, drove breath out of her. She spun and saw the Crip gunship broadside in the street, a Cadillac sedan, windows open, two shooters sitting Cheyenne-style in the offside windows firing over the top and a third from the backseat. Fire and smoke from three muzzles, bullets slamming the air around her.

Starling dived between two parked cars, saw Burke jerking in the road. Brigham lay still, a puddle spreading out of his helmet. Hare and Bolton fired from between cars someplace across the street and over there auto glass powdered and clanged in the road and a tire exploded as automatic fire from the Cadillac pinned them down. Starling, one foot in the running gutter, popped out to look.

Two shooters sitting up in the windows firing across

14

the car roof, the driver firing a pistol with his free hand. A fourth man in the backseat had the door open, was pulling Evelda in with the baby. She carried the satchel. They were firing at Bolton and Hare across the street, smoke from the Cadillac's back tires and the car began to roll. Starling stood up and swung with it and shot the driver in the side of the head. Fired twice at the shooter sitting up in the front window and he went over backward. She dropped the magazine out of the .45 and slammed another one in before the empty hit the ground without taking her eyes off the car.

The Cadillac sideswiped a line of cars across the street and came to a grinding stop against them.

Starling was walking toward the Cadillac now. A shooter still sat in the back window, his eyes wild and hands pushing against the car roof, his chest compressed between the Cadillac and a parked car. His gun slid off the roof. Empty hands appeared out of the near back window. A man in a blue bandana do-rag got out, hands up, and ran. Starling ignored him.

Gunfire from her right and the runner pitched forward, sliding on his face, and tried to crawl under a car. Helicopter blades blatting above her.

Someone yelling in the fish market, "Stay down. Stay down." People under the counters and water at the abandoned cleaning table showering into the air.

Starling advancing on the Cadillac. Movement in the back of the car. Movement in the Cadillac. The car rocking. The baby screaming in there. Gunfire and the back window shattered and fell in.

Starling held up her arm and yelled without turning

15

around. 'HOLD IT. Hold your fire. Watch the door. Behind me. Watch the fish house door."

"Evelda." Movement in the back of the car. The baby screaming in there. "Evelda, put your hands out the window."

Evelda Drumgo was coming out now. The baby was screaming. "La Macarena" pounding on the speakers in the fish market. Evelda was out and walking toward Starling, her fine head down, her arms wrapped around the baby.

Burke twitched on the ground between them. Smaller twitches now that he had about bled out. "La Macarena" jerked along with Burke. Someone, moving low, scuttled to him and, lying beside him, got pressure on the wound.

Starling had her weapon pointed at the ground in front of Evelda. "Evelda, show me your hands, come on, please, show me your hands."

A lump in the blanket. Evelda, with her braids and dark Egyptian eyes, raised her head and looked at Starling.

"Well, it's you, Starling," she said.

"Evelda, don't do this. Think about the baby."

"Let's swap body fluids, bitch."

The blanket fluttered, air slammed. Starling shot Evelda Drumgo through the upper lip and the back of her head blew out.

Starling was somehow sitting down with a terrible stinging in the side of her head and the breath driven out of her. Evelda sat in the road too, collapsed forward over her legs, blood gouting out of her mouth and over the baby, its cries muffled by her body. Starling crawled

16

over to her and plucked at the slick buckles of the baby harness. She pulled the balisong out of Evelda's bra, flicked it open without looking at it and cut the harness off the baby. The baby was slick and red, hard for Starling to hold.

Starling, holding it, raised her eyes in anguish. She could see the water spraying in the air from the fish market and she ran over there carrying the bloody child. She swept away the knives and fish guts and put the child on the cutting board and turned the strong hand-spray on him, this dark child lying on a white cutting board amid the knives and fish guts and the shark's head beside him, being washed of HIV positive blood, Starling's own blood falling on him, washing away with Evelda's blood in a common stream exactly salty as the sea.

Water flying, a mocking rainbow of God's Promise in the spray, sparkling banner over the work of His blind hammer. No holes in this man-child that Starling could see. On the speakers "La Macarena" pounding, a strobe light going off and off and off until Hare dragged the photographer away.

A CUL-DE-SAC in a working-class neighborhood in Arlington, Virginia, a little after midnight. It is a warm fall night after a rain. The air moves uneasily ahead of a cold front. In the smell of wet earth and leaves, a cricket is playing a tune. He falls silent as a big vibration reaches him, the muffled boom of a 5.0-liter Mustang with steel tube headers turning into the cul-de-sac, followed by a federal marshal's car. The two cars pull into the driveway of a neat duplex and stop. The Mustang shudders a little at idle. When the engine goes silent, the cricket waits a moment and resumes his tune, his last before the frost, his last ever.

A federal marshal in uniform gets out of the driver's seat of the Mustang. He comes around the car and opens the passenger door for Clarice Starling. She gets out. A white headband holds a bandage over her ear. Red-orange Betadine stains her neck above the green surgical blouse she wears instead of a shirt.

She carries her personal effects in a plastic zip-lock

bag—some mints and keys, her identification as a Special Agent of the Federal Bureau of Investigation, a speed-loader containing five rounds of ammunition, a small can of Mace. With the bag she carries a belt and empty holster.

The marshal hands her the car keys.

"Thank you, Bobby."

"You want me and Pharon to come in and sit with you awhile? Would you rather I get Sandra? She waits up for me. I'll bring her over a little while, you need some company . . ."

"No, I'll just go in now. Ardelia will be home after a while. Thank you, Bobby."

The marshal gets in the waiting car with his partner and when he sees Starling safely inside the house, the federal car leaves.

The laundry room in Starling's house is warm and smells of fabric softener. The washing machine and clothes dryer hoses are clamped in place with plastic handcuff strips. Starling puts down her personal effects on top of the washing machine. The car keys make a loud clank on the metal top. She takes a load of wash out of the washing machine and stuffs it into the dryer. She takes off her fatigue pants and throws them in the washer and the surgical greens and her bloodstained bra and turns on the machine. She is wearing socks and underpants and a .38 Special with a shrouded hammer in an ankle holster. There are livid bruises on her back and ribs and an abrasion on her elbow. Her right eye and cheek are puffed.

The washing machine is warming and starting to slosh. Starling wraps herself in a big beach towel and pads into the living room. She comes back with two inches of Jack Daniel's neat in a tumbler. She sits down on the rubber mat before the washing machine and leans back against it in the dark as the warm machine throbs and sloshes. She sits on the floor with her face turned up and sobs a few dry sobs before the tears come. Scalding tears on her cheeks, down her face.

Ardelia Mapp's date brought her home about 12:45 A.M. after a long drive down from Cape May, and she told him good night at the door. Mapp was in her bathroom when she heard the water running, the thud in the pipes as the washing machine advanced its cycle.

She went to the back of the house and turned on the lights in the kitchen she shared with Starling. She could see into the laundry room. She could see Starling sitting on the floor, the bandage around her head.

"*Starling!* Oh, baby." Kneeling beside her quickly. "What is it?"

"I got shot through the ear, Ardelia. They fixed it at Walter Reed. Don't turn the light on, okay?"

"Okay. I'll make you something. I haven't heard— we were playing tapes in the car—tell me."

"John's dead, Ardelia."

"*Not Johnny Brigham!*" Mapp and Starling had both had crushes on Brigham when he was gunnery instructor at the FBI Academy. They had tried to read his tattoo through his shirtsleeve.

Starling nodded and wiped her eyes with the back of her hand like a child. "Evelda Drumgo and some Crips.

Evelda shot him. They got Burke too, Marquez Burke from BATF. We all went in together. Evelda was tipped ahead and the TV news got there the same time we did. Evelda was mine. She wouldn't give it up, Ardelia. She wouldn't give it up and she was holding the baby. We shot each other. She's dead."

Mapp had never seen Starling cry before.

"Ardelia, I killed five people today."

Mapp sat on the floor beside Starling and put her arm around her. Together they leaned back against the turning washing machine. "What about Evelda's baby?"

"I got the blood off him, he didn't have any breaks in his skin I could see. The hospital said physically he's all right. They're going to release him to Evelda's mother in a couple of days. You know the last thing Evelda said to me, Ardelia? She said, 'Let's swap body fluids, bitch.'"

"Let me fix you something," Mapp said.

"What?" Starling said.

CHAPTER

3

WITH THE gray dawn came the newspapers and the
early network news.

Mapp came over with some muffins when she heard
Starling stirring around and they watched together.

CNN and the other networks all bought the copy-
righted film from WFUL-TV's helicopter camera. It
was extraordinary footage from directly overhead.

Starling watched once. She had to see that Evelda
shot first. She looked at Mapp and saw anger in her
brown face.

Then Starling ran to throw up.

"That's hard to watch," Starling said when she came
back, shaky-legged and pale.

As usual, Mapp got to the point at once. "Your
question is, how do I feel about you killing that African-
American woman holding that child. This is the answer.
She shot you first. I want you to be alive. But Starling,
think about who's making this insane policy here. What
kind of dumb-ass thinking put you and Evelda Drumgo
together in that sorry place so you could solve the drug

problem between you with some damn guns? How smart is that? I hope you'll think about whether you want to be their cat's paw anymore." Mapp poured some tea for punctuation. "You want me to stay with you? I'll take a personal day."

"Thanks. You don't need to do that. Call me."

The *National Tattler*, prime beneficiary of the tabloid boom in the nineties, put out an extra that was extraordinary even by its own standards. Someone threw it at the house at midmorning. Starling found it when she went to investigate the thump. She was expecting the worst, and she got it:

"*DEATH ANGEL: CLARICE STARLING, THE FBI'S KILLING MACHINE,*" screamed the *National Tattler*'s headline in seventy-two-point Railroad Gothic. The three front-page photos were: Clarice Starling in fatigues firing a .45-caliber pistol in competition, Evelda Drumgo bent over her baby in the road, her head tilted like that of a Cimabue Madonna, with the brains blown out, and Starling again, putting a brown naked baby on a white cutting board amid knives and fish guts and the head of a shark.

The caption beneath the pictures says, "*FBI Special Agent Clarice Starling, slayer of serial killer Jame Gumb, adds at least five notches to her gun. Mother with babe in arms and two police officers among the dead after botched drug raid.*"

The main story covered the drug careers of Evelda and Dijon Drumgo, and the appearance of the Crip gang on the war-torn landscape of Washington, D.C. There was a brief mention of fallen officer John Brigham's military service, and his decorations were cited.

Starling was treated to an entire sidebar, beneath a candid photo of Starling in a restaurant wearing a scoop-necked dress, her face animated.

Clarice Starling, FBI Special Agent, had her fifteen minutes of fame when she shot to death serial murderer Jame Gumb, the "Buffalo Bill" killer, in his basement seven years ago. Now she may face departmental charges and civil liabilities in the death Thursday of a Washington mother accused of manufacturing illegal amphetamines. (See main story Page 1.)

"This may be the end of her career," said one source at the Bureau of Alcohol, Tobacco and Firearms, the FBI's sister agency. "We don't know all the details of how it went down, but John Brigham should be alive today. This is the last thing the FBI needs after Ruby Ridge," said the source, who declined to be identified.

Clarice Starling's colorful career began soon after she arrived at the FBI Academy as a trainee. An honors graduate of the University of Virginia in psychology and criminology, she was assigned to interview the lethal madman Dr Hannibal Lecter, dubbed by this newspaper "Hannibal the Cannibal," and received information from him that was important in the search for Jame Gumb and the rescue of his hostage, Catherine Martin, daughter of the former U.S. senator from Tennessee.

Agent Starling was the interservice combat pistol champion for three years running before she withdrew from competition. Ironically, Officer Brigham, who died at her side, was firearms instructor at Quantico when Starling trained there and was her coach in competition.

An FBI spokesman said Agent Starling will be

*relieved of field duties with pay pending the outcome of
the FBI's internal investigation. A hearing is expected
later this week before the Office of Professional Responsibility, the FBI's own dread inquisition.*

*Relatives of the late Evelda Drumgo said they will
seek civil damages from the U.S. government and from
Starling personally in wrongful-death suits.*

*Drumgo's three-month-old son, seen in his mother's
arms in the dramatic pictures of the shoot-out, was not
injured.*

*Attorney Telford Higgins, who has defended the
Drumgo family in numerous criminal proceedings,
alleged that Special Agent Starling's weapon, a modified Colt .45 semiautomatic pistol, was not approved for
use in law enforcement in the city of Washington. "It
is a deadly and dangerous instrument not suitable for
use in law enforcement," Higgins said. "Its very use
constitutes reckless endangerment of human life," the
noted defense attorney said.*

The *Tattler* had bought Clarice Starling's very home
phone number from one of her informants and rang it
until Starling left it off the hook, and used her FBI cell
phone to talk to the office.

Starling did not have a great deal of pain in her ear and
the swollen side of her face as long as she did not touch
the bandage. At least she didn't throb. Two Tylenol
held her. She didn't need the Percocet the doctor had
prescribed. She dozed against the headboard of the bed,
the *Washington Post* sliding off the spread onto the floor,
gunpowder residue in her hands, dried tears stiff on her
cheeks.

You fall in love with the Bureau, but the
Bureau doesn't fall in love with you.
——MAXIM IN FBI SEPARATION COUNSELING

THE FBI gymnasium in the J. Edgar Hoover Building
was almost empty at this early hour. Two middle-aged
men ran slow laps on the indoor track. The clank of
a weight machine in a far corner and the shouts and
impacts of a racquetball game echoed in the big room.

The voices of the runners did not carry. Jack Crawford
was running with FBI Director Tunberry at the director's request. They had gone two miles and were
beginning to puff.

"Blaylock at ATF has to twist in the wind for Waco. It
won't happen right now, but he's done and he knows it,"
the director said. "He might as well give the Reverend
Moon notice he's vacating the premises." The fact that
the Bureau of Alcohol, Tobacco and Firearms rents
office space in Washington from the Reverend Sun
Myung Moon is a source of amusement to the FBI.

"And Farriday is out for Ruby Ridge," the director
continued.

"I can't see that," Crawford said. He had served in

New York with Farriday in the 1970s when the mob was picketing the FBI field office at Third Avenue and 69th Street. "Farriday's a good man. He didn't set the rules of engagement."

"I told him yesterday morning."

"He going quietly?" Crawford asked.

"Let's just say he's keeping his benefits. Dangerous times, Jack."

Both men were running with their heads back. Their pace quickened a little. Out of the corner of his eye, Crawford saw the director sizing up his condition.

"You're what, Jack, fifty-six?"

"That's right."

"One more year to mandatory retirement. Lot of guys get out at forty-eight, fifty, while they can still get a job. You never wanted that. You wanted to keep busy after Bella died."

When Crawford didn't answer for half a lap, the director saw he had misspoken.

"I don't mean to be light about it, Jack. Doreen was saying the other day, how much—"

"There's still some stuff to do at Quantico. We want to streamline VICAP on the Web so any cop can use it, you saw it in the budget."

"Did you ever want to be director, Jack?"

"I never thought it was my kind of job."

"It's not, Jack. You're not a political guy. You could never have been director. You could never have been an Eisenhower, Jack, or an Omar Bradley." He motioned for Crawford to stop, and they stood wheezing beside the track. "You could have been a Patton, though, Jack. You can lead 'em through hell and make 'em love you.

It's a gift that I don't have. I have to drive them."
Tunberry took a quick look around him, picked up his
towel off a bench and draped it around his shoulders
like the vestment of a hanging judge. His eyes were
bright.

Some people have to tap their anger to be tough,
Crawford reflected as he watched Tunberry's mouth
move.

"In the matter of the late Mrs Drumgo with her MAC
10 and her meth lab, shot to death while holding her
baby: Judiciary Oversight wants a meat sacrifice. Fresh,
bleating meat. And so do the media. DEA has to throw
them some meat. ATF has to throw them some meat.
And we have to throw them some. But in our case, they
just might be satisfied with poultry. Krendler thinks
we can give them Clarice Starling and they'll leave us
alone. I agree with him. ATF and DEA take the rap
for planning the raid. Starling pulled the trigger."

"On a cop killer who shot her first."

"It's the pictures, Jack. You don't get it, do you? The
public didn't see Evelda Drumgo shoot John Brigham.
They didn't see Evelda shoot at Starling first. You
don't see it if you don't know what you're looking at.
Two hundred million people, a tenth of whom vote,
saw Evelda Drumgo sitting in the road in a protective
posture over her baby, with her brains blown out. Don't
say it, Jack—I know you thought for a while Starling
would be your protégée. But she's got a smart mouth,
Jack, and she got off to the wrong start with certain
people—"

"Krendler is a pissant."

"Listen to me and don't say anything until I finish.

28

Starling's career was flat-lining anyway. She'll get an administrative discharge without prejudice, the paperwork won't look any worse than a time-and-attendance rap—she'll be able to get a job. Jack, you've done a great thing in the FBI, the Behavioral Science. A lot of people think if you'd pushed your own interests a little better you'd be a lot more than a section chief, that you deserve a lot more. I'll be the first one to say it. Jack, you're going to retire a deputy director. You have that from me."

"You mean if I stay out of this?"

"In the normal course of events, Jack. With peace all over the kingdom, that's what will happen. Jack, look at me."

"Yes, Director Tunberry?"

"I'm not asking you, I'm giving you a direct order. Stay out of this. Don't throw it away, Jack. Sometimes you've just got to turn your face away. I've done it. Listen, I know it's hard, believe me I know how you feel."

"How I feel? I feel like I need a shower," Crawford said.

STARLING WAS an efficient housekeeper, but not a meticulous one. Her side of the duplex was clean and she could find everything, but stuff tended to pile up— clean unsorted laundry, more magazines than places to put them. She was a world-class last-minute ironer and she didn't need to primp, so she got by.

When she wanted order, she went through the shared kitchen to Ardelia Mapp's side of the duplex. If Ardelia was there, she had the benefit of her counsel, which was always useful, though sometimes closer to the bone than she might wish. If Ardelia was not there, it was understood that Starling could sit in the absolute order of Mapp's dwelling to think, as long as she didn't *leave* anything. There she sat today. It is one of those residences that always contains its occupant whether she's there or not.

Starling sat looking at Mapp's grandmother's life insurance policy, hanging on the wall in a handmade frame, just as it had hung in the grandmother's farm tenant house and in the Mapp's project apartment during Ardelia's childhood. Her grandmother had sold garden vegetables and flowers and saved the dimes to pay the premiums, and she had been able to borrow against the paid-up policy to help Ardelia over the last hump when she was working her way through college. There was a picture, too, of the tiny old woman, making no attempt to smile above her starched white collar, ancient knowlege shining in the black eyes beneath the rim of her straw boater.

Ardelia felt her background, found strength in it every day. Now Starling felt for hers, tried to gather herself. The Lutheran Home at Bozeman had fed and clothed her and given her a decent model of behavior, but for what she needed now, she must consult her blood.

What do you have when you come from a poor-white background? And from a place where Reconstruction didn't end until the 1950s. If you came from people often referred to on campuses as crackers and rednecks or, condescendingly, as blue-collar or poor-white Appalachians. If even the uncertain gentility of the South, who accord physical work no dignity at all, refer to your people as peckerwoods—in what tradition do you find an example? That we whaled the piss out of them that first time at Bull Run? That Great-granddaddy did right at Vicksburg, that a corner of Shiloh is forever Yazoo City?

There is much honor and more sense in having succeeded with what was left, making something with the damned forty acres and a muddy mule, but you have to be able to see that. No one will tell you.

Starling had succeeded in FBI training because she

had nothing to fall back on. She survived most of her life in institutions, by respecting them and playing hard and well by the rules. She had always advanced, won the scholarship, made the team. Her failure to advance in the FBI after a brilliant start was a new and awful experience for her. She batted against the glass ceiling like a bee in a bottle.

She had had four days to grieve for John Brigham, shot dead before her eyes. A long time ago John Brigham had asked her something and she said no. And then he asked her if they could be friends, and meant it, and she said yes, and meant it.

She had to come to terms with the fact that she herself had killed five people at the Feliciana Fish Market. She flashed again and again on the Crip with his chest crushed between the cars, clawing at the car top as his gun slid away.

Once, for relief, she went to the hospital to look at Evelda's baby. Evelda's mother was there, holding her grandchild, preparing to take him home. She recognized Starling from the newspapers, handed the baby to the nurse and, before Starling realized what she was about, she slapped Starling's face hard on the bandaged side.

Starling didn't strike back, but pinned the older woman against the maternity ward window in a wrist-lock until she stopped struggling, her face distorted against the foam and spit-smeared glass. Blood ran down Starling's neck and the pain made her dizzy. She had her ear restitched in the emergency room, and declined to file charges. An emergency room aide tipped the *Tattler* and got three hundred dollars.

She had to go out twice more—to make John Brigham's final arrangements and to attend his funeral at Arlington National Cemetery. Brigham's relatives were few and distant and in his written final requests, he named Starling to take care of him.

The extent of his facial injuries required a closed casket, but she had seen to his appearance as well as she could. She laid him out in his perfect Marine dress blues, with his Silver Star and ribbons for his other decorations.

After the ceremony, Brigham's commanding officer delivered to Starling a box containing John Brigham's personal weapons, his badges, and some items from his ever-cluttered desk, including his silly weather bird that drank from a glass.

In five days Starling faced a hearing that could ruin her. Except for one message from Jack Crawford, her work phone had been silent, and there was no Brigham to talk to anymore.

She called her representative in the FBI Agent's Association. His advice was to not wear dangly earrings or open-toed shoes to the hearing.

Every day television and the newspapers seized the story of Evelda Drumgo's death and shook it like a rat.

Here in the absolute order of Mapp's house, Starling tried to think.

The worm that destroys you is the temptation to agree with your critics, to get their approval.

A noise was intruding.

Starling tried to remember her exact words in the undercover van. Had she said more than was necessary? A noise was intruding.

Brigham told her to brief the others on Evelda. Did she express some hostility, say some slur—

A noise was intruding.

She came to herself and realized she was hearing her doorbell next door. A reporter probably. She was also expecting a civil subpoena. She moved Mapp's front curtain and peeked out to see the mailman returning to his truck. She opened Mapp's front door and caught him, turning her back to the press car across the street with the telephoto lens as she signed for the express mail. The envelope was mauve, with silky threads in the fine linen paper. Distracted as she was, it reminded her of something. Back inside, out of the glare, she looked at the address. A fine copperplate hand.

Above the constant droning note of dread in Starling's mind, a warning went off. She felt the skin on her belly quiver as though she had dripped something cold down her front.

Starling took the envelope by the corners and carried it into the kitchen. From her purse, she took the everpresent white evidence-handling gloves. She pressed the envelope on the hard surface of the kitchen table and felt it carefully all over. Though the paper stock was heavy, she would have detected the lump of a watch battery ready to fire a sheet of C-4. She knew she should take it to a fluoroscope. If she opened it she might get in trouble. Trouble. Right. Balls.

She slit the envelope with a kitchen knife and took out the single, silky sheet of paper. She knew at once, before she glanced at the signature, who had written to her.

Dear Clarice,

I have followed with enthusiasm the course of your disgrace and public shaming. My own never bothered me, except for the inconvenience of being incarcerated, but you may lack perspective.

In our discussions down in the dungeon, it was apparent to me that your father, the dead night watchman, figures large in your value system. I think your success in putting an end to Jame Gumb's career as a couturier pleased you most because you could imagine your father doing it.

Now you are in bad odour with the FBI. Have you always imagined your father ahead of you there, have you imagined him a section chief, or—better even than Jack Crawford—a DEPUTY DIRECTOR, watching your progress with pride? And now do you see him shamed and crushed by your disgrace? Your failure? The sorry, petty end of a promising career? Do you see yourself doing the menial tasks your mother was reduced to, after the addicts busted a cap on your DADDY? Hmmmm? Will your failure reflect on them, will people forever wrongly believe that your parents were trailer camp tornado bait white trash? Tell me truly, Special Agent Starling.

Give it a moment before we proceed.

Now I will show you a quality you have that will help you: You are not blinded by tears, you have the onions to read on.

Here's an exercise you might find useful. I want you physically to do this with me:

Do you have a black iron skillet? You are a southern mountain girl, I can't imagine you would not.

Put it on the kitchen table. Turn on the overhead lights.

Mapp had inherited her grandmother's skillet and used it often. It had a glassy black surface that no soap ever touched. Starling put it in front of her on the table.

Look into the skillet, Clarice. Lean over it and look down. If this were your mother's skillet, and it well may be, it would hold among its molecules the vibrations of all the conversations ever held in its presence. All the exchanges, the petty irritations, the deadly revelations, the flat announcements of disaster, the grunts and poetry of love.

Sit down at the table, Clarice. Look into the skillet. If it is well cured, it's a black pool, isn't it? It's like looking down a well. Your detailed reflection is not in the bottom, but you loom there, don't you? The light behind you, there you are in blackface, with a corona like your hair on fire.

We are elaborations of carbon, Clarice. You and the skillet and Daddy dead in the ground, cold as the skillet. It's all still there. Listen. How did they really sound, and live—your struggling parents. The concrete memories, not the imagi that swell your heart.

Why was your father not a deputy sheriff, in tight with the courthouse crowd? Why did your mother clean motels to keep you, even if she failed to keep you all together until you were grown?

What is your most vivid memory of the kitchen? Not the hospital, the kitchen.

My mother washing the blood out of my father's hat.

What is your best memory in the kitchen?

My father peeling oranges with his old pocketknife with the tip broken off, and passing the sections to us.

Your father, Clarice, was a night watchman. Your mother was a chambermaid.

Was a big federal career your hope or theirs? How much would your father bend to get along in a stale bureaucracy? How many buttocks would he kiss? Did you ever in your life see him toady or fawn?

Have your supervisors demonstrated any values, Clarice? How about your parents, did they demonstrate any? If so, are those values the same?

Look into the honest iron and tell me. Have you failed your dead family? Would they want you to suck up? What was their view on fortitude? You can be as strong as you wish to be.

You are a warrior, Clarice. The enemy is dead, the baby safe. You are a warrior.

The most stable elements, Clarice, appear in the middle of the periodic table, roughly between iron and silver.

Between iron and silver. I think that is appropriate for you.

Hannibal Lecter

P.S. You still owe me some information, you know.

Tell me if you still wake up hearing the lambs. On any Sunday place an ad in the agony column of the national edition of the Times, *the* International Herald-Tribune, *and the* China Mail. *Address it to A. A. Aaron so it will be first, and sign it Hannah.*

Reading, Starling heard the words in the same voice that had mocked her and pierced her, probed her life and enlightened her in the maximum security ward of the insane asylum, when she had to trade the quick of her life to Hannibal Lecter in exchange for his vital knowledge of Buffalo Bill. The metallic rasp of that seldom-used voice still sounded in her dreams.

There was a new spiderweb in the corner of the kitchen ceiling. Starling stared at it while her thoughts tumbled. Glad and sorry, sorry and glad. Glad of the help, glad she saw a way to heal. Glad and sorry that Dr Lecter's remailing service in Los Angeles must be hiring cheap help—they had used a postal meter this time. Jack Crawford would be delighted with the letter, and so would the postal authorities and the lab.

THE CHAMBER where Mason spends his life is quiet, but it has its own soft pulse, the hiss and sigh of the respirator that finds him breath. It is dark except for the glow of the big aquarium where an exotic eel turns and turns in an endless figure eight, its cast shadow moving like a ribbon over the room.

Mason's plaited hair lies in a thick coil on the respirator shell covering his chest on the elevated bed. A device of tubes, like panpipes, is suspended before him.

Mason's long tongue slides out from between his teeth. He scrolls his tongue around the end pipe and puffs with the next pulse of the respirator.

Instantly a voice responds from a speaker on the wall. "Yes, sir."

"The *Tattler*." The initial *t*'s are lost, but the voice is deep and resonant, a radio voice.

"Page one has—"

"Don't read to me. Put it up on the elmo." The *d* and *m* and the *p* are lost from Mason's speech.

The large screen of an elevated monitor crackles. Its

blue-green glow goes pink as the red masthead of the *Tattler* appears.

"*DEATH ANGEL: CLARICE STARLING, THE FBI'S KILLING MACHINE,*" Mason reads, through three slow breaths of his respirator. He can zoom on the pictures.

Only one of his arms is out from under the covers of his bed. He has some movement in the hand. Like a pale spider crab the hand moves, more by the motion of the fingers than the power of his wasted arm. Since Mason cannot turn his head much to see, the index and middle fingers feel ahead like antennae as the thumb, ring and little fingers scuttle the hand along. It finds the remote, where he can zoom and turn the pages.

Mason reads slowly. The goggle over his single eye makes a tiny hiss twice a minute as it sprays moisture on his lidless eyeball, and often fogs the lens. It takes him twenty minutes to get through the main article and the sidebar.

"Put up the X ray," he said when he had finished.

It took a moment. The large sheet of X ray film required a light table to show up well on the monitor. Here was a human hand, apparently damaged. Here was another exposure, showing the hand and the entire arm. A pointer pasted on the X ray showed an old fracture in the humerus about halfway between the elbow and the shoulder.

Mason looked at it through many breaths. "Put up the letter," he said at last.

Fine copperplate appeared on the screen, the handwriting absurdly large in magnification.

Dear Clarice, Mason read, *I have followed with*

enthusiasm the course of your disgrace and public shaming.
. . . The very rhythm of the voice excited in him old
thoughts that spun him, spun his bed, spun his room,
tore the scabs off his unspeakable dreams, raced his
heart ahead of his breath. The machine sensed his
excitement and filled his lungs ever faster.

He read it all, at his painful rate, reading over the
moving machine, like reading on horseback. Mason
could not close his eye, but when he had finished
reading, his mind went away from behind his eye for
a while to think. The breathing machine slowed down.
Then he puffed on his pipe.

"Yes, sir."

"Punch up Congressman Vellmore. Bring me the
headphone. Turn off the speakerphone.

"Clarice Starling," he said to himself with the next
breath the machine permitted him. The name has no
plosive sounds and he managed it very well. None of
the sounds was lost. While he waited for the telephone,
he dozed a moment, the shadow of the eel crawling over
his sheet and his face and his coiled hair.

BUZZARD's POINT, the FBI's field office for Washington and the District of Columbia, is named for a gathering of vultures at a Civil War hospital on the site.

The gathering today is of middle-management officials of the Drug Enforcement Administration, the Bureau of Alcohol, Tobacco and Firearms and the FBI to discuss Clarice Starling's fate.

Starling stood alone on the thick carpet of her boss's office. She could hear her pulse thump beneath the bandage around her head. Over her pulse she heard the voices of the men, muffled by the frosted-glass door of an adjoining conference room.

The great seal of the FBI with its motto, "Fidelity, Bravery, Integrity," is rendered handsomely in gold leaf on the glass.

The voices behind the seal rose and fell with some passion; Starling could hear her name when no other word was clear.

The office has a fine view across the yacht basin to Fort McNair, where the accused Lincoln assassination conspirators were hanged.

Starling flashed on photos she had seen of Mary Surratt, walking past her own casket and mounting the gallows at Fort McNair, standing hooded on the trap, her skirts tied around her legs to prevent immodesty as she dropped through to the loud crunch and the dark.

Next door, Starling heard the chairs scrape back as the men got to their feet. They were filing into this office now. Some of the faces she recognized. Jesus, there was Noonan, the A/DIC over the whole investigation division.

And there was her nemesis, Paul Krendler from Justice, with his long neck and his round ears set high on his head like the ears of a hyena. Krendler was a climber, the gray eminence at the shoulder of the Inspector General. Since she caught the serial killer Buffalo Bill ahead of him in a celebrated case seven years ago, he had dripped poison into her personnel file at every opportunity, and whispered close to the ears of the Career Board.

None of these men had ever been on the line with her, served a warrant with her, been shot at with her or combed the glass splinters out of their hair with her.

The men did not look at her until they all looked at once, the way a sidling pack turns its attention suddenly on the cripple in the herd.

"Have a chair, Agent Starling." Her boss, Special Agent Clint Pearsall, rubbed his thick wrist as though his watch hurt him.

Without meeting her eyes, he gestured toward an armchair facing the windows. The chair in an interrogation is not the place of honor.

43

The seven men remained standing, their silhouettes black against the bright windows. Starling could not see their faces now, but below the glare, she could see their legs and feet. Five were wearing the thick-soled tasseled loafers favored by country slicksters who have made it to Washington. A pair of Thom McAn wing tips with Corfam soles and some Florsheim wing tips rounded out the seven. A smell in the air of shoe polish warmed by hot feet.

"In case you don't know everybody, Agent Starling, this is Assistant Director Noonan, I'm sure you know who *he* is; this is John Eldredge from DEA, Bob Sneed, BATF, Benny Holcomb is assistant to the mayor and Larkin Wainwright is an examiner from our Office of Professional Responsibility," Pearsall said. "Paul Krendler—you know Paul—came over unofficially from the Inspector General's Office at Justice. Paul's here as a favor to us, he's here and he's not here, just to help us head off trouble, if you follow me."

Starling knew what the saying was in the service: a federal examiner is someone who arrives at the battlefield after the battle is over and bayonets the wounded.

The heads of some of the silhouettes bobbed in greeting. The men craned their necks and considered the young woman they were gathered over. For a few beats, nobody spoke.

Bob Sneed broke the silence. Starling remembered him as the BATF spin doctor who tried to deodorize the Branch Davidian disaster at Waco. He was a crony of Krendler's and considered a climber.

"Agent Starling, you've seen the coverage in the papers and on television, you've been widely identified as the shooter in the death of Evelda Drumgo. Unfortunately, you've been sort of demonized."

Starling did not reply.

"Agent Starling?"

"I have nothing to do with the news, Mr Sneed."

"The woman had the baby in her arms, you can see the problem that creates."

"Not in her arms, in a sling across her chest and her arms and hands were beneath it, under a blanket, where she had her MAC 10."

"Have you seen the autopsy protocol?" Sneed asked.

"No."

"But you've never denied being the shooter."

"Do you think I'd deny it because you haven't recovered the slug?" She turned to her bureau chief. "Mr Pearsall, this is a friendly meeting, right?"

"Absolutely."

"Then why is Mr Sneed wearing a wire? Engineering Division quit making those tiepin microphones years ago. He's got an F-Bird in his breast pocket just recording away. Are we wearing wires to one another's offices now?"

Pearsall's face turned red. If Sneed was wired, it was the worst kind of treachery, but nobody wanted to be heard on tape telling Sneed to turn it off.

"We don't need any attitude from you or accusations," Sneed said, pale with anger. "We're all here to help you."

"To help me do what? Your agency called this office and got me assigned to help *you* on this raid. I gave

Evelda Drumgo two chances to surrender. She was holding a MAC 10 under the baby blanket. She had already shot John Brigham. I wish she had given up. She didn't. She shot me. I shot her. She's dead. You might want to check your tape counter right there, Mr Sneed."

"You had *foreknowledge* Evelda Drumgo would be there?" Eldredge wanted to know.

"Foreknowledge? Agent Brigham told me in the van going over that Evelda Drumgo was cooking in a guarded meth lab. He assigned me to deal with her."

"Remember, Brigham is dead," Krendler said, "and so is Burke, damn fine agents, both of them. They're not here to confirm or deny anything."

It turned Starling's stomach to hear Krendler say John Brigham's name.

"I'm not likely to forget John Brigham is dead, Mr Krendler, and he *was* a good agent, and a good friend of mine. The fact is he asked me to deal with Evelda."

"Brigham gave you that assignment even though you and Evelda Drumgo had had a run-in before," Krendler said.

"Come on, Paul," Clint Pearsall said.

"What run-in?" Starling said. "A peaceful arrest. She had fought other officers before at arrests. She didn't fight me when I arrested her before, and we talked a little—she was smart. We were civil to each other. I hoped I could do it again."

"Did you make the verbal statement that you would 'deal with her?'" Sneed said.

"I acknowledged my instructions."

Holcomb from the mayor's office and Sneed put their heads together.

Sneed shot his cuffs. "Ms Starling, we have information from Officer Bolton of the Washington PD that you made inflammatory statements about Ms Drumgo in the van on the way to the confrontation. Want to comment on that?"

"On Agent Brigham's instructions I explained to the other officers that Evelda had a history of violence, she was usually armed and she was HIV positive. I said we would give her a chance to surrender peacefully. I asked for physical help in subduing her if it came to that. There weren't many volunteers for the job, I can tell you."

Clint Pearsall made an effort. "After the Crip shooters' car crashed and one perp fled, you could see the car rocking and you could hear the baby crying inside the car?"

"Screaming," Starling said. "I raised my hand for everybody to stop shooting and I came out of cover."

"That's against procedure right there," Eldredge said.

Starling ignored him. "I approached the car in the ready position, weapon out, muzzle depressed. Marquez Burke was dying on the ground between us. Somebody ran out and got a compress on him. Evelda got out with the baby. I asked her to show me her hands, I said something like 'Evelda, don't do this.'"

"She shot, you shot. Did she go right down?"

Starling nodded. "Her legs collapsed and she sat down in the road, leaning over the baby. She was dead."

"You grabbed up the baby and ran to the water. Exhibited concern," Pearsall said.

"I don't know what I exhibited. He had blood all over him. I didn't know if the baby was HIV positive or not, I knew she was."

"And you thought your bullet might have hit the baby," Krendler said.

"No. I knew where the bullet went. Can I speak freely, Mr Pearsall?"

When he did not meet her eyes, she went on.

"This raid was an ugly mess. It put me in a position where I had a choice of dying or shooting a woman holding a child. I chose, and what I had to do burns me. I shot a female carrying an infant. The lower *animals* don't even do that. Mr Sneed, you might want to check your tape counter again, right there where I admit it. I resent the hell out of being put in that position. I resent the way I feel now." She flashed on Brigham lying facedown in the road and she went too far. "Watching you all run from it makes me sick at my stomach."

"Starling—" Pearsall, anguished, looked her in the face for the first time.

"I know you haven't had a chance to write your 302 yet," Larkin Wainwright said. "When we review—"

"Yes, sir, I have," Starling said. "A copy's on the way to the Office of Professional Responsibility. I have a copy with me if you don't want to wait. I have everything I did and saw in there. See, Mr Sneed, you had it all the time."

Starling's vision was a little too clear, a danger sign she recognized, and she consciously lowered her voice.

"This raid went wrong for a couple of reasons. BATF's snitch lied about the baby's location because the snitch was desperate for the raid to go down—before his federal grand jury date in Illinois. And Evelda Drumgo knew we were coming. She came out with the money in one bag and the meth in another. Her beeper still showed the number for WFUL-TV. She got the beep five minutes before we got there. WFUL's helicopter got there with us. Subpoena WFUL's phone tapes and see who leaked. It's somebody whose interests are local, gentlemen. If BATF had leaked, like they did in Waco, or DEA had leaked, they'd have done it to national media, not the local TV."

Benny Holcomb spoke for the city. "There's no evidence anybody in city government or the Washington police department leaked anything."

"Subpoena and see," Starling said.

"Do you have Drumgo's beeper?" Pearsall asked.

"It's under seal in the property room at Quantico."

Assistant Director Noonan's own beeper went off. He frowned at the number and excused himself from the room. In a moment, he summoned Pearsall to join him outside.

Wainwright, Eldredge and Holcomb looked out the window at Fort McNair, hands in their pockets. They might have been waiting in an intensive care unit. Paul Krendler caught Sneed's eye and urged him toward Starling.

Sneed put his hand on the back of Starling's chair and leaned over her. "If your testimony at a hearing is that, while you were on TDY assignment from the FBI, your weapon killed Evelda Drumgo, BATF is prepared to sign off on a statement that Brigham asked you to pay . . . special attention to Evelda in order to take her into custody peacefully. Your weapon killed her, that's where your service has to carry the can. There will be no interagency pissing contest over rules of engagement and we won't have to bring in any inflammatory or hostile statements you made in the van about what sort of person she was."

Starling saw Evelda Drumgo for an instant, coming out of the doorway, coming out of the car, saw the carriage of her head and, despite the foolishness and waste of Evelda's life, saw her decision to take her child and front her tormenters and not run from it.

Starling leaned close to the microphone on Sneed's tie and said clearly, "I'm perfectly happy to acknowledge the sort of person she was, Mr Sneed: She was better than you."

Pearsall came back into the office without Noonan and closed the door. "Assistant Director Noonan has gone back to his office. Gentlemen, I'm going to call a halt to this meeting, and I'll get back to you individually by telephone," Pearsall said.

Krendler's head came up. He was suddenly alert at the scent of politics.

"We've got to decide some things," Sneed began.

"No, we don't."

"But—"

"Bob, believe me, we don't have to decide anything. I'll get back to you. And, Bob?"

"Yeah?"

Pearsall grabbed the wire behind Sneed's tie and pulled down hard, popping buttons off Sneed's shirt and snatching tape loose from his skin. "You come to me with a wire again and I'll put my foot in your ass."

None of them looked at Starling as they left, except Krendler.

Moving toward the door, sliding his feet so he would not have to look where he was going, he used the extreme articulation of his long neck to turn his face to her, as a hyena would shuffle at the fringe of a herd, peering in at a candidate. Mixed hungers crossed his face; it was Krendler's nature to both appreciate Starling's leg and look for the hamstring.

BEHAVIORAL SCIENCE is the FBI section that deals with serial murder. Down in its basement offices, the air is cool and still. Decorators with their color wheels have tried in recent years to brighten the subterranean space. The result is no more successful than funeral home cosmetics.

The section chief's office remains in the original brown and tan with the checked café curtains on its high windows. There, surrounded by his hellish files, Jack Crawford sat writing at his desk.

A knock, and Crawford looked up to a sight that pleased him—Clarice Starling stood in his doorway.

Crawford smiled and rose from his chair. He and Starling often talked while standing; it was one of the tacit formalities they had come to impose on their relationship. They did not need to shake hands.

"I heard you came to the hospital," Starling said. "Sorry I missed you."

"I was just glad they let you go so fast," he said. "Tell me about your ear, is it okay?"

"It's fine if you like cauliflower. They tell me it'll go down, most of it." Her ear was covered by her hair. She did not offer to show him.

A little silence.

"They had me taking the fall for the raid, Mr Crawford. For Evelda Drumgo's death, all of it. They were like hyenas and then suddenly it stopped and they slunk away. Something drove them off."

"Maybe you have an angel, Starling."

"Maybe I do. What did it cost you, Mr Crawford?"

Crawford shook his head. "Close the door, please, Starling." Crawford found a wadded Kleenex in his pocket and polished his spectacles. "I would have done it if I could. I didn't have the juice by myself. If Senator Martin was still in office, you'd have had some cover. . . . They wasted John Brigham on that raid—just threw him away. It would have been a shame if they wasted you like they wasted John. It felt like I was stacking you and John across a Jeep."

Crawford's cheeks colored and she remembered his face in the sharp wind above John Brigham's grave. Crawford had never talked to her about his war.

"You did *something*, Mr Crawford."

He nodded. "I did something. I don't know how glad you'll be. It's a job."

A job. *Job* was a good word in their private lexicon. It meant a specific and immediate task and it cleared the air. They never spoke if they could help it about the troubled central bureaucracy of the Federal Bureau of Investigation. Crawford and Starling were like medical missionaries, with little patience for theology, each concentrating hard on the one baby before them, knowing and not saying that God wouldn't do a goddamned thing to help. That for fifty thousand Ibo infant lives, He would not bother to send rain.

"Indirectly, Starling, your benefactor is your recent correspondent."

"Dr Lecter." She had long noted Crawford's distaste for the spoken name.

"Yes, the very same. For all this time he'd eluded us—he was away clean—and he writes you a letter. Why?"

It had been seven years since Dr Hannibal Lecter, known murderer of ten, escaped from custody in Memphis, taking five more lives in the process.

It was as though Lecter had dropped off the earth. The case remained open at the FBI and would remain open forever, or until he was caught. The same was true in Tennessee and other jurisdictions, but there was no task force assigned to pursue him anymore, though relatives of his victims had wept angry tears before the Tennessee state legislature and demanded action.

Whole tomes of scholarly conjecture on his mentality were available, most of it authored by psychologists who had never been exposed to the doctor in person. A few works appeared by psychiatrists he had skewered in the professional journals, who apparently felt that it was safe to come out now. Some of them said his aberrations would inevitably drive him to suicide and that it was likely he was already dead.

In cyberspace at least, interest in Dr Lecter remained very much alive. The damp floor of the Internet sprouted Lecter theories like toadstools and sightings of the doctor rivaled those of Elvis in number. Impostors plagued the chat rooms and in the phosphorescent swamp of the Web's dark side, police photographs of his outrages were bootlegged to collectors of hideous arcana. They were second in popularity only to the execution of Fou-Tchou-Li.

One trace of the doctor after seven years—his letter to Clarice Starling when she was being crucified by the tabloids.

The letter bore no fingerprints, but the FBI felt reasonably sure it was genuine. Clarice Starling was certain of it.

"Why did he do it, Starling?" Crawford seemed almost angry at her. "I've never pretended to understand him any more than these psychiatric jackasses do. You tell me."

"He thought what happened to me would . . . destroy, would *disillusion* me about the Bureau, and he enjoys seeing the destruction of faith, it's his favorite thing. It's like the church collapses he used to collect. The pile of rubble in Italy when the church collapsed on all the grandmothers at that special Mass and somebody stuck a Christmas tree in the top of the pile, he loved that. I amuse him, he toys with me. When I was interviewing him he liked to point out holes in my education, he thinks I'm pretty naïve."

Crawford spoke from his own age and isolation when he said, "Have you ever thought that he might like you, Starling?"

"I think I amuse him. Things either amuse him or they don't. If they don't . . ."

"Ever *felt* that he liked you?" Crawford insisted on the distinction between thought and feeling like a Baptist insists on total immersion.

"On really short acquaintance he told me some things about myself that were true. I think it's easy to mistake understanding for empathy—we want empathy so badly. Maybe learning to make that distinction is part of growing up. It's hard and ugly to know somebody can understand you without even liking you. When you see understanding just used as a predator's tool, that's the worst. I . . . I have no idea how Dr Lecter feels about me."

"What sort of thing did he tell you, if you don't mind."

"He said I was an ambitious, hustling little rube and my eyes shined like cheap birthstones. He told me I wore cheap shoes, but I had some taste, a little taste."

"That struck you as true?"

"Yep. Maybe it still is. I've improved my shoes."

"Do you think, Starling, he might have been interested to see if you'd rat him out when he sent you a letter of encouragement?"

"He knew I'd rat him out, he'd better know it."

"He killed six after the court committed him," Crawford said. "He killed Miggs in the asylum for throwing semen in your face, and five in his escape. In the present political climate, if the doctor's caught he'll get the needle." Crawford smiled at the thought. He had pioneered the study of serial murder. Now he was facing mandatory retirement and the monster who had tried him the most remained free. The prospect of death for Dr Lecter pleased him mightily.

Starling knew Crawford mentioned Miggs's act to goose her attention, to put her back in those terrible days when she was trying to interrogate Hannibal the

Cannibal in the dungeon at the Baltimore State Hospital for the Criminally Insane. When Lecter toyed with her while a girl crouched in Jame Gumb's pit, waiting to die. Usually Crawford heightened your attention when he was coming to the point, as he did now.

"Did you know, Starling, that one of Dr Lecter's early victims is still alive?"

"The rich one. The family offered a reward."

"Yes, Mason Verger. He's on a respirator in Maryland. His father died this year and left him the meat-packing fortune. Old Verger also left Mason a U.S. congressman and a member of the House Judiciary Oversight Committee who just couldn't make ends meet without him. Mason says he's got something that might help us find the doctor. He wants to speak with you."

"With *me*."

"You. That's what Mason wants and suddenly everyone agrees it's a really good idea."

"That's what Mason wants after you suggested it to him?"

"They were going to throw you away, Starling, clean up with you like you were a rag. You would have been wasted just like John Brigham. Just to save some bureaucrats at BATF. Fear. Pressure. That's all they understand anymore. I had somebody drop a dime to Mason and tell him how much it would hurt the hunt for Lecter if you got canned. Whatever else happened, who Mason might have called after that, I don't want to know, probably Representative Vollmer."

A year ago, Crawford would not have played this way. Starling searched his face for any of the short-timer craziness that sometimes comes over imminent retirees. She didn't see any, but he did look weary.

"Mason's not pretty, Starling, and I don't just mean his face. Find out what he's got. Bring it here, we'll work with it. At last."

Starling knew that for years, ever since she graduated from the FBI Academy, Crawford had tried to get her assigned to Behavioral Science.

Now that she was a veteran of the Bureau, veteran of many lateral assignments, she could see that her early triumph in catching the serial murderer Jame Gumb was part of her undoing in the Bureau. She was a rising star that stuck on the way up. In the process of catching Gumb, she had made at least one powerful enemy and excited the jealousy of a number of her male contemporaries. That, and a certain cross-grainedness, had led to years of jump-out squads, and reactive squads rolling on bank robberies and years of serving warrants, seeing Newark over a shotgun barrel. Finally, deemed too irascible to work with groups, she was a tech agent, bugging the telephones and cars of gangsters and child pornographers, keeping lonesome vigils over Title Three wiretaps. And she was forever on loan, when a sister agency needed a reliable hand in a raid. She had wiry strength and she was fast and careful with the gun.

Crawford saw this as a chance for her. He assumed she had always wanted to chase Lecter. The truth was more complicated than that.

Crawford was studying her now. "You never got that gunpowder out of your cheek."

Grains of burnt powder from the revolver of the

late Jame Gumb marked her cheekbone with a black spot.

"Never had time," Starling said.

"Do you know what the French call a beauty spot, a *mouche* like that, high on the cheek? Do you know what it stands for?" Crawford owned a sizeable library on tattoos, body symbology, ritual mutilation.

Starling shook her head.

"They call that one 'courage,' " Crawford said. "You can wear that one. I'd keep it if I were you."

THERE IS a witchy beauty about Muskrat Farm, the Verger family's mansion near the Susquehanna River in northern Maryland. The Verger meatpacking dynasty bought it in the 1930s when they moved east from Chicago to be closer to Washington, and they could well afford it. Business and political acumen has enabled the Vergers to batten on U.S. Army meat contracts since the Civil War.

The "embalmed beef" scandal in the Spanish-American War hardly touched the Vergers. When Upton Sinclair and the muckrakers investigated dangerous packing-plant conditions in Chicago, they found that several Verger employees had been rendered into lard inadvertently, canned and sold as Durham's Pure Leaf Lard, a favorite of bakers. The blame did not stick to the Vergers. The matter cost them not a single government contract.

The Vergers avoided these potential embarrassments and many others by giving money to politicians—their single setback being passage of the Meat Inspection Act of 1906.

Today the Vergers slaughter 86,000 cattle a day, and approximately 36,000 pigs, a number that varies slightly with the season.

The new-mown lawns of Muskrat Farm, the riot of its lilacs in the wind, smell nothing at all like the stockyard. The only animals are ponies for the visiting children and amusing flocks of geese grazing on the lawns, their behinds wagging, heads low to the grass. There are no dogs. The house and barn and grounds are near the center of six square miles of national forest, and will remain there in perpetuity under a special exemption granted by the Department of the Interior.

Like many enclaves of the very rich, Muskrat Farm is not easy to find the first time you go. Clarice Starling went one exit too far on the expressway. Coming back along the service road, she first encountered the trade entrance, a big gate secured with chain and padlock in the high fence enclosing the forest. Beyond the gate, a fire road disappeared into the overarching trees. There was no call box. Two miles farther along she found the gatehouse, set back a hundred yards along a handsome drive. The uniformed guard had her name on his clipboard.

An additional two miles of manicured roadway brought her to the farm.

Starling stopped her rumbling Mustang to let a flock of geese cross the drive. She could see a file of children on fat Shetlands leaving a handsome barn a quarter-mile from the house. The main building before her was a Stanford White-designed mansion handsomely set among low hills. The place looked solid and fecund, the province of pleasant dreams. It tugged at Starling.

The Vergers had had sense enough to leave the house as it was, with the exception of a single addition, which Starling could not yet see, a modern wing that sticks out from the eastern elevation like an extra limb attached in a grotesque medical experiment.

Starling parked beneath the central portico. When the engine was off she could hear her own breathing. In the mirror she saw someone coming on a horse. Now hooves clopped on the pavement beside the car as Starling got out.

A broad-shouldered person with short blond hair swung down from the saddle, handed the reins to a valet without looking at him. "Walk him back," the rider said in a deep scratchy voice. "I'm Margot Verger." At close inspection she was a woman, holding out her hand, arm extended straight from the shoulder. Clearly Margot Verger was a bodybuilder. Beneath her corded neck, her massive shoulders and arms stretched the mesh of her tennis shirt. Her eyes had a dry glitter and looked irritated, as though she suffered from a shortage of tears. She wore twill riding breeches and boots with no spurs.

"What's that you're driving?" she said. "An old Mustang?"

"It's an '88."

"Five-liter? It sort of hunkers down over its wheels."

"Yes. It's a Roush Mustang."

"You like it?"

"A lot."

"What'll it do?"

"I don't know. Enough, I think."

"Scared of it?"

"Respectful of it. I'd say I use it respectfully," Starling said.

"Do you know about it, or did you just buy it?"

"I knew enough about it to buy it at a dope auction when I saw what it was. I learned more later."

"You think it would beat my Porsche?"

"Depends on which Porsche. Ms Verger, I need to speak with your brother."

"They'll have him cleaned up in about five minutes. We can start up there." The twill riding breeches whistled on Margot Verger's big thighs as she climbed the stairs. Her cornsilk hair had receded enough to make Starling wonder if she took steroids and had to tape her clitoris down.

To Starling, who spent most of her childhood in a Lutheran orphanage, the house felt like a museum, with its vast spaces and painted beams above her, and walls hung with portraits of important-looking dead people. Chinese cloisonné stood on the landings and long Moroccan runners lined the halls.

There is an abrupt shear in style at the new wing of the Verger mansion. The modern functional structure is reached through frosted glass double doors, incongruous in the vaulted hall.

Margot Verger paused outside the doors. She looked at Starling with her glittery, irritated gaze.

"Some people have trouble talking with Mason," she said. "If it bothers you, or you can't take it, I can fill you in later on whatever you forget to ask him."

There is a common emotion we all recognize and have not yet named—the happy anticipation of being able to

63

feel contempt. Starling saw it in Margot Verger's face. All Starling said was "Thank you."

To Starling's surprise, the first room in the wing was a large and well-equipped playroom. Two African-American children played among oversized stuffed animals, one riding a Big Wheel and the other pushing a truck along the floor. A variety of tricycles and wagons were parked in the corners and in the center was a large jungle gym with the floor heavily padded beneath it.

In a corner of the playroom, a tall man in a nurse's uniform sat on a love seat reading *Vogue*. A number of video cameras were mounted on the walls, some high, others at eye level. One camera high in the corner tracked Starling and Margot Verger, its lens rotating to focus.

Starling was past the point where the sight of a brown child pierced her, but she was keenly aware of these children. Their cheerful industry with the toys was pleasant to see as she and Margot Verger passed through the room.

"Mason likes to watch the kids," Margot Verger said. "It scares them to see him, all but the littlest ones, so he does it this way. They ride ponies after. They're day-care kids out of child welfare in Baltimore."

Mason Verger's chamber is approached only through his bathroom, a facility worthy of a spa that takes up the entire width of the wing. It is institutional-looking, all steel and chrome and industrial carpet, with wide-doored showers, stainless-steel tubs with lifting devices over them, coiled orange hoses, steam rooms and vast glass cabinets of unguents from the Farmacia of Santa Maria Novella in Florence. The air in the bathroom was still steamy from recent use and the scents of balsam and wintergreen hung in the air.

Starling could see light under the door to Mason Verger's chamber. It went out as his sister touched the doorknob.

A seating area in the corner of Mason Verger's chamber was severely lit from above. A passable print of William Blake's "The Ancient of Days" hung above the couch—God measuring with his calipers. The picture was draped with black to commemorate the recent passing of the Verger patriarch. The rest of the room was dark.

From the darkness came the sound of a machine working rhythmically, sighing at each stroke.

"Good afternoon, Agent Starling." A resonant voice mechanically amplified, the fricative *f* lost out of *afternoon*.

"Good afternoon, Mr Verger," Starling said into the darkness, the overhead light hot on the top of her head. Afternoon was someplace else. Afternoon did not enter here.

"Have a seat."

Going to have to do this. Now is good. Now is called for.

"Mr Verger, the discussion we'll have is in the nature of a deposition and I'll need to tape-record it. Is that all right with you?"

"Sure." The voice came between the sighs of the machine, the sibilant *s* lost from the word. "Margot, I think you can leave us now."

Without a look at Starling, Margot Verger left in a whistle of riding pants.

"Mr Verger, I'd like to attach this microphone to your—clothing or your pillow if you're comfortable with that, or I'll call a nurse to do it if you prefer."

"By all means," he said, minus the *b* and the *m*. He waited for power from the next mechanical exhalation. "You can do it yourself, Agent Starling. I'm right over here."

There were no light switches Starling could find at once. She thought she might see better with the glare out of her eyes and she went into the darkness, one hand before her, toward the smell of wintergreen and balsam.

She was closer to the bed than she thought when he turned on the light.

Starling's face did not change. Her hand holding the clip-on microphone jerked backward, perhaps an inch.

Her first thought was separate from the feelings in her chest and stomach; it was the observation that his speech anomalies resulted from his total lack of lips. Her second thought was the recognition that he was not blind. His single blue eye was looking at her through a sort of monocle with a tube attached that kept the eye damp, as it lacked a lid. For the rest, surgeons years ago had done what they could with expanded skin grafts over bone.

Mason Verger, noseless and lipless, with no soft tissue on his face, was all teeth, like a creature of the deep, deep ocean. Inured as we are to masks, the shock in seeing him is delayed. Shock comes with the recognition that this is a human face with a mind behind it. It churns you with its movement, the articulation of the jaw, the turning of the eye to see you. To see your normal face.

Mason Verger's hair is handsome and, oddly, the hardest thing to look at. Black flecked with gray, it is plaited in a ponytail long enough to reach the floor if it is brought back over his pillow. Today his plaited hair is in a big coil on his chest above the turtle-shell respirator. Human hair beneath the blue-john ruin, the plaits shining like lapping scales.

Under the sheet, Mason Verger's long-paralyzed body tapered away to nothing on the elevated hospital bed.

Before his face was the control that looked like panpipes or a harmonica in clear plastic. He curled his tongue tubelike around a pipe end and puffed with the next stroke of his respirator. His bed responded with a hum, turned him slightly to face Starling and increased the elevation of his head.

"I thank God for what happened," Verger said. "It was my salvation. Have you accepted Jesus, Miss Starling? Do you have faith?"

"I was raised in a close religious atmosphere, Mr Verger. I have whatever that leaves you with," Starling said. "Now, if you don't mind, I'm just going to clip this to the pillowcase. It won't be in the way here, will it?" Her voice sounded too brisk and nursey to suit her.

Her hand beside his head, seeing their two fleshes together, did not aid Starling, nor did his pulse in the vessels grafted over the bones of his face to feed it blood; their regular dilation was like worms swallowing.

Gratefully, she paid out cord and backed to the table and her tape recorder and separate microphone.

"This is Special Agent Clarice M. Starling, FBI

number 5143690, deposing Mason R. Verger, Social Security number 475989823, at his home on the date stamped above, sworn and attested. Mr Verger understands that he has been granted immunity from prosecution by the U.S. Attorney for District Thirty-six, and by local authorities in a combined memorandum attached, sworn and attested.

"Now, Mr Verger—"

"I want to tell you about camp," he interrupted with his next exhalation. "It was a wonderful childhood experience that I've come back to, in essence."

"We can get to that, Mr Verger, but I thought we'd—"

"Oh, we can get to it *now*, Miss Starling. You see, it all comes to bear. It was how I met Jesus, and I'll never tell you anything more important than that." He paused for the machine to sigh. "It was a Christian camp my father paid for. He paid for the whole thing, all one hundred twenty-five campers on Lake Michigan. Some of them were unfortunates and they would do anything for a candy bar. Maybe I took advantage of it, maybe I was rough with them if they wouldn't take the chocolate and do what I wanted—I'm not holding anything back, because it's all okay now."

"Mr Verger, let's look at some material with the same—"

He was not listening to her, he was only waiting for the machine to give him breath. "I have immunity, Miss Starling, and it's all okay now. I've got a grant of immunity from Jesus, I've got immunity from the U.S. Attorney, I've got immunity from the DA in

Owings Mills, Hallelujah. I'm free, Miss Starling, and it's all okay now. I'm right with Him and it's all okay now. He's the Risen Jesus, and at camp we called him The Riz. Nobody beats The Riz. We made it contemporary, you know, The Riz. I served him in Africa, Hallelujah, I served him in Chicago, praise His name, and I serve Him now and He will raise me up from this bed and He will smite mine enemies and drive them before me and I will hear the lamentations of their women, and it's all okay now." He choked on saliva and stopped, the vessels on the front of his head dark and pulsing.

Starling rose to get a nurse, but his voice stopped her before she reached the door.

"I'm fine, it's all okay now."

Maybe a direct question would be better than trying to lead him. "Mr Verger, had you ever seen Dr Lecter before the court assigned you to him for therapy? Did you know him socially?"

"No."

"You were both on the board of the Baltimore Philharmonic."

"No, my seat was just because we contribute. I sent my lawyer when there was a vote."

"You never gave a statement in the course of Dr Lecter's trial." She was learning to time her questions so he would have breath to answer.

"They said they had enough to convict him six times, nine times. And he beat it all on an insanity plea."

"The court found him insane. Dr Lecter did not plead."

"Do you find that distinction important?" Mason asked.

With the question, she first felt his mind, prehensile and deep-sleeved, different from the vocabulary he used with her.

The big eel, now accustomed to the light, rose from the rocks in his aquarium and began the tireless circle, a rippling ribbon of brown beautifully patterned with irregular cream spots.

Starling was ever aware of it, moving in the corner of her vision.

"It's a *Muraena Kidako*," Mason said. "There's an even bigger one in captivity in Tokyo. This one is second biggest.

"Its common name is the Brutal Moray, would you like to see why?"

"No," Starling said, and turned a page in her notes. "So in the course of your court-ordered therapy, Mr Verger, you invited Dr Lecter to your home."

"I'm not ashamed anymore. I'll tell you about anything. It's all okay now. I got a walk on those trumped-up molestation counts if I did five hundred hours of community service, worked at the dog pound and got therapy from Dr Lecter. I thought if I got the doctor involved in something, he'd have to cut me some slack on the therapy and wouldn't violate my parole if I didn't show up all the time, or if I was a little stoned at my appointments."

"This was when you had the house in Owings Mills."

"Yes. I had told Dr Lecter everything, about Africa and Idi and all, and I said I'd show him some of my stuff."

"You'd show him . . . ?"

"Paraphernalia. Toys. In the corner there, that's the little portable guillotine I used for Idi Amin. You can throw it in the back of a Jeep, go anywhere, the most remote village. Set up in fifteen minutes. Takes the condemned about ten minutes to cock it with a windlass, little longer if it's a woman or a kid. I'm not ashamed of any of that, because I'm cleansed."

"Dr Lecter came to your house."

"Yes. I answered the door in some leather, you know. Watched for some reaction, didn't see any. I was concerned he'd be afraid of me, but he didn't seem to be. *Afraid* of me—that's funny now. I invited him upstairs. I showed him, I had adopted some dogs from the shelter, two dogs that were friends, and I had them in a cage together with plenty of fresh water, but no food. I was curious about what would eventually happen.

"I showed him my noose setup, you know, autoerotic asphyxsia, you sort of hang yourself but not really, feels good while you—you follow?"

"I follow."

"Well, he didn't seem to follow. He asked me how it worked and I said, you're an odd psychiatrist not to know that, and he said, and I'll never forget his smile, he said, 'Show me.' I thought, *I've got you now!*"

"And you showed him."

"I am not ashamed of that. We grow by our mistakes. I'm cleansed."

"Please go on, Mr Verger."

"So I pulled down the noose in front of my big

mirror and put it on and had the release in my hand, and I was beating off with the other hand watching for his reaction, but I couldn't tell anything. Usually I can read people. He was sitting in a chair over in the corner of the room. His legs were crossed and he had his fingers locked over his knee. Then he stood up and reached in his jacket pocket, all elegant, like James Mason reaching for his lighter, and he said, 'Would you like an amyl popper?' I thought, *Wow!*— he gives me one now and he's got to give them to me forever to keep his license. Prescription city. Well, if you read the report, you know it was a lot more than amyl nitrite."

"Angel Dust and some other methamphetamines and some acid," Starling said.

"I mean *whoa*! He went over to the mirror I looked at myself in, and kicked the bottom of it and took out a shard. I was flying. He came over and gave me the piece of glass and looked me in the eyes and suggested I might like to peel off my face with it. He let the dogs out. I fed them my face. It took a long time to get it all off, they say. I don't remember. Dr Lecter broke my neck with the noose. They got my nose back when they pumped the dogs' stomachs at the animal shelter, but the graft didn't take."

Starling took longer than she needed to in rearranging the papers on the table.

"Mr Verger, your family posted the reward after Dr Lecter escaped from custody in Memphis."

"Yes, a million dollars. One million. We advertised worldwide."

"And you also offered to pay for any kind of relevant

information, not just the usual apprehension and conviction. You were supposed to share that information with us. Have you always done that?"

"Not exactly, but there was never anything good to share."

"How do you know that? Did you follow up on some leads yourself?"

"Just far enough to know they were worthless. And why shouldn't we—you people never told us anything. We had a tip from Crete that was nothing and one from Uruguay that we could never confirm. I want you to understand, this is not a revenge thing, Miss Starling. I have forgiven Dr Lecter just as Our Savior forgave the Roman soldiers."

"Mr Verger, you indicated to my office that you might have something now."

"Look in the drawer of the end table."

Starling took the white cotton gloves out of her purse and put them on. In the drawer was a large manila envelope. It was stiff and heavy. She pulled out an X ray and held it to the bright overhead light. The X ray was of a left hand that appeared to be injured. She counted the fingers. Four plus the thumb.

"Look at the metacarpals, do you know what I'm talking about?"

"Yes."

"Count the knuckles."

Five knuckles. "Counting the thumb, this person had six fingers on his left hand. Like Dr Lecter."

"Like Dr Lecter."

The corner where the X ray's case number and origin should be was clipped off.

"Where did it come from, Mr Verger?"

"Rio de Janeiro. To find out more, I have to pay. A lot. Can you tell me if it's Dr Lecter? I need to know if I should pay."

"I'll try, Mr Verger. We'll do our best. Do you have the package the X ray came in?"

"Margot has it in a plastic bag, she'll give it to you. If you don't mind, Miss Starling, I'm rather tired and I need some attention."

"You'll hear from my office, Mr Verger."

Starling had not been out of the room long when Mason Verger tooted the endmost pipe and said, "Cordell?" The male nurse from the playroom came in and read to him from a folder marked DEPARTMENT OF CHILD WELFARE, CITY OF BALTIMORE.

"*Franklin*, is it? Send *Franklin* in," Mason said, and turned out his light.

The little boy stood alone under the bright overhead light of the seating area, squinting into the gasping darkness.

Came the resonant voice, "Are you *Franklin*?"

"Franklin," the little boy said.

"Where do you stay, *Franklin*?"

"With Mama and Shirley and Stringbean."

"Does Stringbean stay there all the time?

"He in and out."

"Did you say 'He in and out'?"

"Yeah."

"'Mama' is not your real mama, is she, *Franklin*?"

"She my foster."

74

"She's not the first foster you've had, is she?"

"Nome."

"Do you like it at your house, *Franklin*?"

He brightened. "We got Kitty Cat. Mama make patty-cake in the stove."

"How long have you been there, at Mama's house?"

"I don't know."

"Have you had a birthday there?"

"One time I did. Shirley make Kool-Aid."

"Do you like Kool-Aid?"

"Strawberry."

"Do you love Mama and Shirley?"

"I love, um hum, and Kitty Cat."

"Do you want to live there? Do you feel safe when you go to bed?"

"Um hum. I sleep in the room with Shirley. Shirley, she a big girl."

"*Franklin*, you can't live there anymore with Mama and Shirley and the Kitty Cat. You have to go away."

"Who say?"

"The government say. Mama has lost her job and her approval as a foster home. The police found a marijuana cigarette in your house. You can't see Mama anymore after this week. You can't see Shirley anymore or Kitty Cat after this week."

"No," Franklin said.

"Or maybe they just don't want you anymore, *Franklin*. Is there something wrong with you? Do you have a sore on you or something nasty? Do you think your skin is too dark for them to love you?"

Franklin pulled up his shirt and looked at his small brown stomach. He shook his head. He was crying.

"Do you know what will happen to Kitty Cat? What is Kitty Cat's name?"

"She call Kitty Cat, that her name."

"Do you know what will happen to Kitty Cat? The policemen will take Kitty Cat to the pound and a doctor there will give her a shot. Did you get a shot at day care? Did the nurse give you a shot? With a shiny needle? They'll give Kitty Cat a shot. She'll be so scared when she sees the needle. They'll stick it in and Kitty Cat will hurt and die."

Franklin caught the tail of his shirt and held it up beside his face. He put his thumb in his mouth, something he had not done for a year after Mama asked him not to.

"Come here," said the voice from the dark. "Come here and I'll tell you how you can keep Kitty Cat from getting a shot. Do you want Kitty Cat to have the shot, *Franklin*? No? Then come here, *Franklin*."

Franklin, eyes streaming, sucking his thumb, walked slowly forward into the dark. When he was within six feet of the bed, Mason blew into his harmonica and the lights came on.

From innate courage, or his wish to help Kitty Cat, or his wretched knowledge that he had no place to run to anymore, Franklin did not flinch. He did not run. He held his ground and looked at Mason's face.

Mason's brow would have furrowed if he had a brow, at this disappointing result.

"You can save Kitty Cat from getting the shot if you give Kitty Cat some rat poison yourself," Mason said. The plosive *p* was lost, but Franklin understood.

Franklin took his thumb out of his mouth.

76

"You a mean old doo-doo," Franklin said. "An you ugly too." He turned around and walked out of the chamber, through the hall of coiled hoses, back to the playroom.

Mason watched him on video.

The nurse looked at the boy, watched him closely while pretending to read his *Vogue*.

Franklin did not care about the toys anymore. He went over and sat under the giraffe, facing the wall. It was all he could do not to suck his thumb.

Cordell watched him carefully for tears. When he saw the child's shoulders shaking, the nurse went to him and wiped the tears away gently with sterile swatches. He put the wet swatches in Mason's martini glass, chilling in the playroom's refrigerator beside the orange juice and the Cokes.

FINDING MEDICAL information about Dr Hannibal
Lecter was not easy. When you consider his utter
contempt for the medical establishment and for most
medical practitioners, it is not surprising that he never
had a personal physician.

The Baltimore State Hospital for the Criminally
Insane, where Dr Lecter was kept until his disastrous
transfer to Memphis, was now defunct, a derelict
building awaiting demolition.

The Tennessee State Police were the last custodians of Dr Lecter before his escape, but they claimed
they never received his medical records. The officers
who brought him from Baltimore to Memphis, now
deceased, had signed for the prisoner, not for any
medical records.

Starling spent a day on the telephone and the computer, then physically searched the evidence storage
rooms at Quantico and the J. Edgar Hoover Building.
She climbed around the dusty and malodorous bulky
evidence room of the Baltimore Police Department

for an entire morning, and spent a maddening afternoon dealing with the uncatalogued Hannibal Lecter Collection at the Fitzhugh Memorial Law Library, where time stands still while the custodians try to locate the keys.

At the end, she was left with a single sheet of paper—the cursory physical examination Dr Lecter received when he was first arrested by the Maryland State Police. No medical history was attached.

Inelle Corey had survived the demise of the Baltimore State Hospital for the Criminally Insane and gone on to better things at the Maryland State Board of Hospitals. She did not want to be interviewed by Starling in the office, so they met in a ground-floor cafeteria.

Starling's practice was to arrive early for meetings and observe the specific meeting point from a distance. Corey was punctual to the minute. She was about thirty-five years old, heavy and pale, without makeup or jewelry. Her hair was almost to her waist, as she had worn it in high school, and she wore white sandals with Supp-Hose.

Starling collected sugar packets at the condiment stand and watched Corey seat herself at the agreed table.

You may labor under the misconception that all Protestants look alike. Not so. Just as one Caribbean person can often tell the specific island of another, Starling, raised by the Lutherans, looked at this woman and said to herself, *Church of Christ, maybe a Nazarene at the outside*.

Starling took off her jewelry, a plain bracelet and a gold stud in her good ear, and put them in her bag.

Her watch was plastic, okay. She couldn't do much about the rest of her appearance.

"Inelle Corey? Want some coffee?" Starling was carrying two cups.

"It's pronounced *Eyenelle*. I don't drink coffee."

"I'll drink both of them, want something else? I'm Clarice Starling."

"I don't care for anything. You want to show me some picture ID?"

"Absolutely," Starling said. "Ms Corey—may I call you Inelle?"

The woman shrugged.

"Inelle, I need some help on a matter that really doesn't involve you personally at all. I just need guidance in finding some records from the Baltimore State Hospital."

Inelle Corey speaks with exaggerated precision to express righteousness or anger.

"We have went through this with the state board at the time of closure, Miss—"

"Starling."

"Miss Starling. You will find that not a patient went out of that hospital without a folder. You will find that not a folder went out of that hospital that was not approved by a supervisor. As for as the deceased go, the Health Department did not need their folders, the Bureau of Vital Statistics did not want their folders, and as for as I know, the dead folders, that is the folders of the deceased, remained at the Baltimore State Hospital past my separation date and I was about the last one out. The elopements went to the city police and the sheriff's department."

"Elopements?"

"That's when somebody runs off. Trusties took off sometimes."

"Would Dr Hannibal Lecter be carried as an elopement? Do you think his records might have gone to law enforcement?"

"He was *not* an elopement. He was never carried as *our* elopement. He was not in our custody when he took off. I went down there to the bottom and looked at Dr Lecter one time, showed him to my sister when she was here with the boys. I feel sort of nasty and cold when I think about it. He stirred up one of those other ones to throw some"—she lowered her voice—"*jism* on us. Do you know what that is?"

"I've heard the term," Starling said. "Was it Mr Miggs, by any chance? He had a good arm."

"I've shut it out of my mind. I remember *you*. You came to the hospital and talked to Fred—Dr Chilton—and went down there in that basement with Lecter, didn't you?"

"Yes."

Dr Frederick Chilton was the director of the Baltimore State Hospital for the Criminally Insane who went missing while on vacation after Dr Lecter's escape.

"You know Fred disappeared."

"Yes, I heard that."

Ms Corey developed quick, bright tears. "He was my fiancé," she said. "He was gone, and then the hospital closed, it was just like the roof had fell in on me. If I hadn't had my church I could not have got by."

"I'm sorry," Starling said. "You have a good job now."

"But I don't have Fred. He was a fine, fine man. We shared a love, a love you don't find everday. He was voted Boy of the Year in Canton when he was in high school."

"Well, I'll be. Let me ask you this, Inelle, did he keep the records in his office, or were they out in reception where your desk—"

"They were in the wall cabinets in his office and then they got so many we got big filing cabinets out in the reception area. They was always locked, of course. When we moved out, they moved in the methadone clinic on a temporary basis and a lot of stuff was moved around."

"Did you ever see and handle Dr Lecter's file?"

"Sure."

"Do you remember any X rays in it? Were X rays filed with the medical reports or separate?"

"With. Filed with. They were bigger than the files and that made it clumsy. We had an X ray but no full-time radiologist to keep a separate file. I honestly don't remember if it was one with his or not. There was an electrocardiogram tape Fred used to show to people, Dr Lecter—I don't even want to call him a *doctor*— was all wired up to the electrocardiograph when he got the poor nurse. See, it was freakish—his pulse rate didn't even go up much when he attacked her. He got a separated shoulder when all the orderlies, you know, grabbed aholt of him and pulled him off of her. They'd of had to X-ray him for that. They'd have give him plenty more than a separated shoulder if I'd had something to say about it."

"If anything occurs to you, any place the file might be, would you call me?"

82

"We'll do what we call a global search?" Ms Corey said, savoring the term, "but I don't think we'll find anything. A lot of stuff just got abandoned, not by us, but by the methadone people."

The coffee mugs had the thick rims that dribble down the sides. Starling watched Inelle Corey walk heavily away like hell's own option and drank half a cup with her napkin tucked under her chin.

Starling was coming back to herself a little. She knew she was weary of something. Maybe it was tackiness, worse than tackiness, stylelessness maybe. An indifference to things that please the eye. Maybe she was hungry for some style. Even snuff-queen style was better than nothing, it was a statement, whether you wanted to hear it or not.

Starling examined herself for snobbism and decided she had damn little to be snobbish about. Then, thinking of style, she thought of Evelda Drumgo, who had plenty of it. With the thought, Starling wanted badly to get outside herself again.

AND SO, Starling returned to the place where it all began for her, the Baltimore State Hospital for the Criminally Insane, now defunct. The old brown building, house of pain, is chained and barred, marked with graffiti and awaiting the wrecking ball.

It had been going downhill for years before the disappearance on vacation of its director, Dr Frederick Chilton. Subsequent revelations of waste and mismanagement and the decrepitude of the building itself soon caused the legislature to choke off its funds. Some patients were moved to other state institutions, some were dead and a few wandered the streets of Baltimore as Thorazine zombies in an ill-conceived outpatient program that got more than one of them frozen to death.

Waiting in front of the old building, Clarice Starling realized she had exhausted the other possibilities first because she did not want to go in this place again.

The caretaker was forty-five minutes late. He was a stocky older man with a built-up shoe that clopped, and an eastern European haircut that may have been done at home. He wheezed as he led her to a side door, a few steps down from the sidewalk. The lock had been punched out by scavengers and the door secured with a chain and two padlocks. There were fuzzy webs in the links of the chain. Grass growing in the cracks of the steps tickled Starling's ankles as the caretaker fumbled with his keys. The late afternoon was overcast, the light grainy and without shadows.

"I am not knowing this building well, I just check the fire alarums," the man said.

"Do you know if any papers are stored here? Any filing cabinets, any records?"

He shrugged. "After the hospital, they had the methadone clinic here, a few months. They put everything in the basement, some bads, some linens, I don't know what it was. It's bed in there for my asthma, the mold, very bed mold. The mattresses on the bads were moldy, bed mold on the bads. I kint breed in dere. The stairs are hal on my leck. I would show you, but—?"

Starling would have been glad of some company, even his, but he would slow her down. "No, go on. Where's your office?"

"Down the block there where the driver's license bureau was before."

"If I'm not back in an hour—"

He looked at his watch. "I'm supposed to be off in a half hour."

That's just about E goddamned nuff. "What you're going to do for me, sir, is wait for your keys in your office. If I'm not back in an hour, call this number here on the card and show them where I

85

went. If you aren't there when I come out—if you have closed up and gone home, I will personally go to see your supervisor in the morning to report you. In addition—in addition you will be audited by the Internal Revenue Service and your situation reviewed by the Bureau of Immigration and . . . and Naturalization. Do you understand? I'd appreciate a reply, sir."

"I would have waited for you, of course. You don't have to say these things."

"Thank you very much, sir," Starling said.

The caretaker put his big hands on the railing to pull himself up to sidewalk level and Starling heard his uneven gait trail off to silence. She pushed open the door and went in to a landing on the fire stairs. High, barred windows in the stairwell admitted the gray light. She debated whether to lock the door behind her and settled on tying the chain in a knot inside the door so she could open it if she lost the key.

On Starling's previous trips to the asylum, to interview Dr Hannibal Lecter, she came through the front entrance and now it took her a moment to orient herself.

She climbed the fire stairs to the main floor. The frosted windows further cut the failing daylight and the room was in semidarkness. With her heavy flashlight, Starling found a switch and turned on the overhead light, three bulbs still burning in a broken fixture. The raw ends of the telephone wires lay on top of the receptionist's desk.

Vandals with spray cans of paint had been in the building. An eight-foot phallus and testicles decorated

the reception room wall, along with the inscription
FARON MAMA JERK ME OF.

The door to the director's office was open. Starling
stood in the doorway. It was here she came on her
first FBI assignment, when she was still a trainee,
still believed everything, still thought that if you
could do the job, if you could cut it, you would
be accepted, regardless of race, creed, color, national
origin or whether or not you were a good old boy. Of
all this, there remained to her one article of faith. She
believed that she could cut it.

Here Hospital Director Chilton had offered his greasy
hand, and come on to her. Here he had traded secrets
and eavesdropped and, believing he was as smart as
Hannibal Lecter, had made the decisions that allowed
Lecter to escape with so much bloodshed.

Chilton's desk remained in the office, but there was
no chair, it being small enough to steal. The drawers
were empty except for a crushed Alka-Seltzer. Two
filing cabinets remained in the office. They had simple
locks and former technical agent Starling had them
open in less than a minute. A desiccated sandwich in
a paper bag and some office forms for the methadone
clinic were in a bottom drawer, along with breath
freshener and a tube of hair tonic, a comb and some
condoms.

Starling thought about the dungeonlike basement
level of the asylum where Dr Lecter had lived for eight
years. She didn't want to go down there. She could use
her cell phone and ask for a city police unit to go down
there with her. She could ask the Baltimore field office
to send another FBI agent with her. It was late on the

gray afternoon and there was no way, even now, she could avoid the rush-hour traffic in Washington. If she waited, it would be worse.

She leaned on Chilton's desk in spite of the dust and tried to decide. Did she really think there might be files in the basement, or was she drawn back to the first place she ever saw Hannibal Lecter?

If Starling's career in law enforcement had taught her anything about herself, it was this: She was not a thrill seeker, and she would be happy never to feel fear again. But there *might* be files in the basement. She could find out in five minutes.

She could remember the clang of the high-security doors behind her when she went down there years ago. In case one should close behind her this time, she called the Baltimore field office and told them where she was and made an arrangement to call back in an hour to say she was out.

The lights worked in the inside staircase, where Chilton had walked her to the basement level years ago. Here he had explained the safety procedures used in dealing with Hannibal Lecter, and here he had stopped, beneath this light, to show her his wallet photograph of the nurse whose tongue Dr Lecter had eaten during an attempted physical examination. If Dr Lecter's shoulder had been dislocated as he was subdued, surely there must be an X ray.

A draft of air on the stairs touched her neck, as though there were a window open somewhere.

A McDonald's hamburger box was on the landing, and scattered napkins. A stained cup that had held beans. Dumpster food. Some ropey turds and napkins in the corner. The light ended at the bottom floor landing, before the great steel door to the violent ward, now standing open and hooked back against the wall. Starling's flashlight held five D-cells and cast a good wide beam.

She shined it down the long corridor of the former maximum security unit. There was something bulky at the far end. Eerie to see the cell doors standing open. The floor was littered with bread wrappers and cups. A soda can, blackened from use as a crack pipe, lay on the former orderly's desk.

Starling flipped the light switches behind the orderly station. Nothing. She took out her cell phone. The red light seemed very bright in the gloom. The phone was useless underground, but she spoke into it loudly. "Barry, back the truck up to the side entrance. Bring a floodlight. You'll need some dollies to move this stuff up the stairs . . . yeah, come on down."

Then Starling called into the dark, "Attention in there. I'm a federal officer. If you are living here illegally, you are free to leave. I will not arrest you. I am not interested in you. If you return after I complete my business, it's of no interest to me. You can come out now. If you attempt to interfere with me you will suffer severe personal injury when I bust a cap in your ass. Thank you."

Her voice echoed down the corridor where so many had ranted their voices down to croaks and gummed the bars when their teeth were gone.

Starling remembered the reassuring presence of the big orderly, Barney, when she had come to interview Dr Lecter. The curious courtesy with which Barney and Dr

Lecter treated each other. No Barney now. Something from school bumped at her mind and, as a discipline, she made herself recall it:

> *Footfalls echo in the memory*
> *Down the passage which we did not take*
> *Towards the door we never opened*
> *Into the rose garden.*

Rose Garden, right. This was damn sure not the rose garden.

Starling, who had been encouraged in recent editorials to hate her gun as well as herself, found the touch of the weapon not at all hateful when she was uneasy. She held the .45 against her leg and started down the hall behind her flashlight. It is hard to watch both flanks at once, and imperative not to leave anyone behind you. Water dripped somewhere.

Bed frames disassembled and stacked in the cells. In others, mattresses. The water stood in the center of the corridor floor and Starling, ever mindful of her shoes, stepped from one side of the narrow puddle to the other as she proceeded. She remembered Barney's advice from years ago when all the cells were occupied. *Stay in the middle as you go down.*

Filing cabinets, all right. In the center of the corridor all the way down, dull olive in her flashlight beam.

Here was the cell that had been occupied by Multiple Miggs, the one she had hated most to pass. Miggs, who whispered filth to her and threw body fluids. Miggs, whom Dr Lecter killed by instructing him to swallow his vile tongue. And when Miggs was dead, Sammie lived in the cell. Sammie, whose poetry Dr Lecter encouraged with startling effect on the poet. Even now she could hear Sammie howling his verse:

> *I WAN TO GO TO JESA*
> *I WAN TO GO WIV CRIEZ*
> *I CAN GO WIV JESA*
> *EF I AC RELL NIZE.*

She still had the labored crayon text, somewhere.

The cell was stacked with mattresses now, and bales of bed linens tied up in sheets.

And at last, Dr Lecter's cell.

The sturdy table where he read was still bolted to the floor in the middle of the room. The boards were gone from the shelves that had held his books, but the brackets still stuck out of the walls.

Starling should turn to the cabinets, but she was fixed on the cell. Here she had had the most remarkable encounter of her life. Here she had been startled, shocked, surprised.

Here she had heard things about herself so terribly true her heart resounded like a great deep bell.

She wanted to go inside. She wanted to go in, wanting it as we want to jump from balconies, as the glint of the rails tempts us when we hear the approaching train.

Starling shined her light around her, looked on the back side of the row of filing cabinets, swept her light through the nearby cells.

Curiosity carried her across the threshold. She stood in the middle of the cell where Dr Hannibal Lecter had spent eight years. She occupied his space, where she had seen him standing, and expected to tingle, but she did not. Put her pistol and her flashlight on his table, careful that the flashlight didn't roll, and put her hands flat on his table, and beneath her hands felt only crumbs.

Overall, the affect was disappointing. The cell was as empty of its former occupant as a snake's shed skin. Starling thought then that she came to understand something: Death and danger do not have to come with trappings. They can come to you in the sweet breath of your beloved. Or on a sunny afternoon in a fish market with "La Macarena" playing on a boom box.

To business. There were about eight feet of filing cabinets, four cabinets in all, chin-high. Each had five drawers, secured by a single four-pin lock beside the top drawer. None of them was locked. All were full of files, some of them fat, all of them in folders. Old marbleized paper folders gone limp with time, and newer ones in manila folders. The files on the health of dead men, dating back to the hospital's opening in 1932. They were roughly alphabetical, with some material piled flat behind the folders in the long drawers. Starling skipped quickly along, holding her heavy flashlight on her shoulder, walking the fingers of her free hand through the files, wishing she had brought a small light she could hold in her teeth. As soon as she had some sense of the files she could skip whole drawers, through the *J*'s, very few *K*'s, on to the *L*'s and bam: Lecter, Hannibal.

Starling pulled out the long manila folder, felt it at once for the stiffness of an X ray negative, laid the folder on top of the other files and opened it to find the health history of the late I. J. Miggs. Goddammit. Miggs was going to plague her from the grave. She put the file on top of the cabinet and raced ahead into the *M*'s. Miggs's own manila folder was there, in alphabetical order. It was empty. Filing error? Did someone accidentally put Miggs's records in Hannibal Lecter's jacket? She went through all the *M*'s looking for a file without a jacket. She went back to the *J*'s. Aware of an increasing annoyance. The smell of the place was bothering her more. The caretaker was right, it was hard to breathe in this place. She was halfway through the *J*'s when she realized the stench was . . . increasing rapidly.

A small splash behind her and she spun, flashlight cocked for a blow, hand fast beneath her blazer to the gun butt. A tall man in filthy rags stood in the beam of her light, one of his outsize swollen feet in the water. One of his hands was spread from his side. The other hand held a piece of a broken plate. One of his legs and both of his feet were bound with strips of sheet.

"Hello," he said, his tongue thick with thrush. From five feet Starling could smell his breath. Beneath her jacket, her hand moved from the pistol to the Mace.

"Hello," Starling said. "Would you please stand over there against the bars?"

The man did not move. "Are you Jesa?" he asked.

"No," Starling said. "I'm not Jesus." The voice. Starling remembered the voice.

"Are you Jesa!" His face was working.

That voice. Come on, think. "Hello, Sammie," she said. "How are you? I was just thinking about you."

What about Sammie? The information, served up fast, was not exactly in order. *Put his mother's head in the collection plate while the congregation was singing*

"Give of Your Best to the Master." Said it was the nicest thing he had. Highway Baptist Church somewhere. Angry, Dr Lecter said, because Jesus is so late.

"Are you Jesa?" he said, plaintive this time. He reached in his pocket and came out with a cigarette butt, a good one more than two inches long. He put it on his shard of plate and held it out in offering.

"Sammie, I'm sorry, I'm not. I'm—"

Sammie suddenly livid, furious that she is not Jesus, his voice booming in the wet corridor:

I WAN TO GO WIV JESA
I WAN TO GO WIV CRIEZ!

He raised the plate shard, its sharp edge like a hoe, and took a step toward Starling, both his feet in the water now and his face contorted, his free hand clutching the air between them.

She felt the cabinets hard at her back.

"YOU CAN GO WITH JESUS . . . IF YOU ACT REAL NICE," Starling recited, clear and loud as though she called to him in a far place.

"Uh huh," Sammie said calmly and stopped.

Starling fished in her purse, found her candy bar. "Sammie, I have a Snickers. Do you like Snickers?"

He said nothing.

She put the Snickers on a manila folder and held it out to him as he had held out the plate.

He took the first bite before he removed the wrapper, spit out the paper and bit again, eating half the candy bar.

"Sammie, has anybody else been down here?"

He ignored her question, put the remainder of the candy bar on his plate and disappeared behind a pile of mattresses in his old cell.

"What the hell is this?" A woman's voice. "Thank you, Sammie."

"Who are you?" Starling called.

"None of your damn business."

"Do you live here with Sammie?"

"Of course not. I'm here on a date. Do you think you could leave us alone?"

"Yes. Answer my question. How long have you been here?"

"Two weeks."

"Has anybody else been here?"

"Some bums Sammie run out."

"Sammie protects you?"

"Mess with me and find out. I can walk good. I get stuff to eat, he's got a safe place to eat it. Lot of people have deals like that."

"Is either one of you in a program someplace? Do you want to be? I can help you there."

"He done all that. You go out in the world and do all that shit and come back to what you know. What are you looking for? What do you want?"

"Some files."

"If it ain't here, somebody stole it, how smart do you have to be to figure that out?"

"Sammie?" Starling said. "Sammie?"

Sammie did not answer. "He's asleep," his friend said.

"If I leave some money out here, will you buy some food?" Starling said.

"No, I'll buy liquor. You can *find* food. You can't find liquor. Don't let the doorknob catch you in the butt on the way out."

"I'll put the money on the desk," Starling said. She felt like running, remembered leaving Dr Lecter, remembered holding on to herself as she walked toward what was then the calm island of Barney's orderly station.

In the light of the stairwell, Starling took a twenty-dollar bill out of her wallet. She put the money on Barney's scarred, abandoned desk, and weighted it with an empty wine bottle. She unfolded a plastic shopping bag and put in it the Lecter file jacket containing Miggs's records and the empty Miggs jacket.

"Good-bye. 'Bye, Sammie," she called to the man who had circled in the world and come back to the hell he knew. She wanted to tell him she hoped Jesus would come soon, but it sounded too silly to say.

Starling climbed back into the light, to continue her circle in the world.

12

IF THERE are depots on the way to Hell, they must resemble the ambulance entrance to Maryland-Misericordia General Hospital. Over the sirens' dying wail, wails of the dying, clatter of the dripping gurneys, cries and screams, the columns of manhole steam, dyed red by a great neon EMERGENCY sign, rise like Moses' own pillar of fire in the darkness and change to cloud in the day.

Barney came out of the steam, shrugging his powerful shoulders into his jacket, his cropped round head bent forward as he covered the broken pavement in long strides east toward the morning.

He was twenty-five minutes late getting off work— the police had brought in a stoned pimp with a gunshot wound who liked to fight women, and the head nurse had asked him to stay. They always asked Barney to stay when they took in a violent patient.

Clarice Starling peered out at Barney from the deep hood of her jacket and let him get a half-block lead on the other side of the street before she hitched her tote bag on her shoulder and followed. When he passed both the parking lot and the bus stop, she was relieved. Barney would be easier to follow on foot. She wasn't sure where he lived and she needed to know before he saw her.

The neighborhood behind the hospital was quiet, blue-collar and mixed racially. A neighborhood where you put a Chapman lock on your car but you don't have to take the battery in with you at night, and the kids can play outside.

After three blocks, Barney waited for a van to clear the crosswalk and turned north onto a street of narrow houses, some with marble steps and neat front gardens. The few empty storefronts were intact with the windows soaped. Stores were beginning to open and a few people were out. Trucks parked overnight on both sides of the street blocked Starling's view for half a minute and she walked up on Barney before she realized that he had stopped. She was directly across the street when she saw him. Maybe he saw her too, she wasn't sure.

He was standing with his hands in his jacket pockets, head forward, looking from under his brows at something moving in the center of the street. A dead dove lay in the road, one wing flapped by the breeze of passing cars. The dead bird's mate paced around and around the body, cocking an eye at it, small head jerking with each step of its pink feet. Round and round, muttering the soft dove mutter. Several cars and a van passed, the surviving bird barely dodging the traffic with short last-minute flights.

Maybe Barney glanced up at her, Starling couldn't be positive. She had to keep going or be spotted. When she looked over her shoulder, Barney was squatting in the middle of the road, arm raised to the traffic.

She turned the corner out of sight, pulled off her hooded jacket, took a sweater, a baseball cap and a gym bag out of her tote bag, and changed quickly, stuffing her jacket and the tote into the gym bag, and her hair into the cap. She fell in with some homeward-bound cleaning women and turned the corner back onto Barney's street.

He had the dead dove in his cupped hands. Its mate flew with whistling wings up to the overhead wires and watched him. Barney laid the dead bird in the grass of a lawn and smoothed down its feathers. He turned his broad face up to the bird on the wire and said something. When he continued on his way, the survivor of the pair dropped down to the grass and continued circling the body, pacing through the grass. Barney didn't look back. When he climbed the steps of an apartment house a hundred yards farther on and reached for keys, Starling sprinted a half-block to catch up before he opened the door.

"Barney. Hi."

He turned on the stairs in no great haste and looked down at her. Starling had forgotten that Barney's eyes were unnaturally far apart. She saw the intelligence in them and felt the little electronic pop of connection.

She took her cap off and let her hair fall. "I'm Clarice Starling. Remember me? I'm—"

"The G," Barney said, expressionless.

Starling put her palms together and nodded. "Well, yes, I *am* the G. Barney, I need to talk with you. It's just informal, I need to ask you some stuff."

Barney came down the steps. When he was standing on the sidewalk in front of Starling, she still had to look up at his face. She was not threatened by his size, as a man would be.

"Would you agree for the record, Officer Starling, that I have not been read my rights?" His voice was high and rough like the voice of Johnny Weismuller's Tarzan.

"Absolutely. I have not Mirandized you. I acknowledge that."

"How about saying it into your bag?"

Starling opened her bag and spoke down into it in a loud voice as though it contained a troll. "I have not Mirandized Barney, he is unaware of his rights."

"There's some pretty good coffee down the street," Barney said. "How many hats have you got in that bag?" he asked as they walked.

"Three," she said.

When the van with handicap plates passed by, Starling was aware that the occupants were looking at her, but the afflicted are often horny, as they have every right to be. The young male occupants of a car at the next crossing looked at her too, but said nothing because of Barney. Anything extended from the windows would have caught Starling's instant attention—she was wary of Crip revenge—but silent ogling is to be endured.

When she and Barney entered the coffee shop, the van backed into an alley to turn around and went back the way it came.

They had to wait for a booth in the crowded ham and egg place while the waiter yelled in Hindi to the cook, who handled meat with long tongs and a guilty expression.

"Let's eat," Starling said when they were seated. "It's on Uncle Sam. How's it going, Barney?"

"The job's okay."

"What is it?"

"Orderly, LPN."

"I figured you for an RN by now, or maybe medical school."

Barney shrugged and reached for the creamer. He looked up at Starling. "They jam you up for shooting Evelda?"

"We'll have to see. Did you know her?"

"I saw her once, when they brought in her husband, Dijon. He was dead, he bled out on them before they ever got him in the ambulance. He was leaking clear IV when he got to us. She wouldn't let him go and tried to fight the nurses. I had to . . . you know . . . Handsome woman, strong too. They didn't bring her in after—"

"No, she was pronounced at the scene."

"I would think so."

"Barney, after you turned over Dr Lecter to the Tennessee people—"

"They weren't civil to him."

"After you—"

"And they're all dead now."

"Yes. His keepers managed to stay alive for three days. You lasted eight years keeping Dr Lecter."

"It was six years—he was there before I came."

"How'd you do it, Barney? If you don't mind my asking, how'd you manage to last with him? It wasn't just being civil."

Barney looked at his reflection in his spoon, first convex and then concave, and thought a moment. "Dr Lecter had perfect manners, not stiff, but easy and elegant. I was working on some correspondence courses and he shared his mind with me. That didn't mean he wouldn't *kill* me any second if he got the chance—one quality in a person doesn't rule out any other quality. They can exist side by side, good and terrible. Socrates said it a lot better. In maximum lock-down you can't afford to forget that, ever. If you keep it in mind, you're all right. Dr Lecter may have been sorry he showed me Socrates." To Barney, lacking the disadvantage of formal schooling, Socrates was a fresh experience, with the quality of an encounter.

"Security was separate from conversation, a whole other thing," he said. "Security was never personal, even when I had to shut off his mail or put him in restraints."

"Did you talk with Dr Lecter a lot?"

"Sometimes he went months without saying anything, and sometimes we'd talk, late at night when the crying died down. In fact—I was taking these courses by mail and I knew diddly—and he showed me a whole world, literally, of stuff—Suetonius, Gibbon, all that." Barney picked up his cup. He had a streak of orange Betadine on a fresh scratch across the back of his hand.

"Did you ever think when he escaped that he might come after you?"

Barney shook his huge head. "He told me once that, whenever it was 'feasible,' he preferred to eat the rude. 'Free-range rude,' he called them." Barney laughed, a rare sight. He has little baby teeth and his amusement seems a touch maniacal, like a baby's glee when he blows his pablum in a goo-goo uncle's face.

Starling wondered if he had stayed underground with the loonies too long.

"What about you, did you ever feel . . . creepy after he got away? Did you think he might come after you?" Barney asked.

"No."

"Why?"

"He said he wouldn't."

This answer seemed oddly satisfactory to them both.

The eggs arrived. Barney and Starling were hungry and they ate steadily for a few minutes. Then . . .

"Barney, when Dr Lecter was transferred to Memphis, I asked you for his drawings out of his cell and you brought them to me. What happened to the rest of the stuff—books, papers? The hospital doesn't even have his medical records."

"There was this big upheaval." Barney paused, tapping the salt shaker against his palm. "There was a big upheaval, you know at the hospital. I got laid off, a lot of people got laid off, and stuff just got scattered. There's no telling—"

"*Excuse* me?" Starling said, "I couldn't hear what you said for the racket in here. I found out last night that Dr Lecter's annotated and signed copy of Alexandre Dumas' *Dictionary of Cuisine* came up at a private auction in New York two years ago. It went to a private collector for sixteen thousand dollars. The seller's affidavit of ownership was signed 'Cary Phlox.' You know 'Cary Phlox,' Barney? I hope you do because he did the handwriting on your employment application at the hospital where you're working but he signed it 'Barney.' Made out your tax return too. Sorry I missed what you were saying before. Want to start over? What did you get for the book, Barney?"

"Around ten," Barney said, looking straight at her.

Starling nodded. "The receipt says ten-five. What did you get for that interview with the *Tattler* after Dr Lecter escaped?"

"Fifteen G's."

"Cool. Good for you. You made up all that bull you told those people."

"I knew Dr Lecter wouldn't mind. He'd be disappointed if I didn't jerk them around."

"He attacked the nurse before you got to Baltimore State?"

"Yes."

"His shoulder was dislocated."

"That's what I understand."

"Was there an X ray taken?"

"Most likely."

"I want the X ray."

"Ummmm."

"I found out Lecter autographs are divided into two groups, the ones written in ink, or preincarceration, and crayon or felt-tip writing from the asylum. Crayon's worth more, but I expect you know that. Barney, I think you have all that stuff and you figure on parceling it out over the years to the autograph trade."

Barney shrugged and said nothing.

"I think you're waiting for him to be a hot topic again. What do you *want*, Barney?"

"I want to see every Vermeer in the world before I die."

"Do I need to ask who got you started on Vermeer?"

"We talked about a lot of things in the middle of the night."

"Did you talk about what he'd like to do if he was free?"

"No. Dr Lecter has no interest in hypothesis. He doesn't believe in syllogism, or synthesis, or any absolute."

"What does he believe in?"

"Chaos. And you don't even have to believe in it. It's self-evident."

Starling wanted to indulge Barney for the moment.

"You say that like you believe it," she said, "but your whole job at Baltimore State was maintaining order. You were the chief *orderly*. You and I are both in the order business. Dr Lecter never got away from you."

"I explained that to you."

"Because you never let your guard down. Even though in a sense you fraternized—"

"I did not *fraternize*," Barney said. "He's nobody's brother. We discussed matters of mutual interest. At least the stuff was interesting to me when I found out about it."

"Did Dr Lecter ever make fun of you for not knowing something?"

"No. Did he make fun of you?"

"No," she said to save Barney's feelings, as she recognized for the first time the compliment implied in the monster's ridicule. "He could have made fun of me if he'd wanted to. Do you know where the stuff is, Barney?"

"Is there a reward for finding it?"

Starling folded her paper napkin and put it under the edge of her plate. "The reward is my not charging you with obstruction of justice. I gave you a walk before when you bugged my desk at the hospital."

"That bug belonged to the late Dr Chilton."

"*Late?* How do you know he's the *late* Dr Chilton?"

"Well, he's seven years late anyway," Barney said. "I'm not expecting him anytime soon. Let me ask you, what would satisfy *you*, Special Agent Starling?"

"I want to see the X ray. I want the X ray. If there are books of Dr Lecter's, I want to see them."

"Say we came upon the stuff, what would happen to it afterward?"

"Well, the truth is I can't be sure. The U.S. Attorney might seize all the material as evidence in the investigation of the escape. Then it'll molder in his Bulky Evidence Room. If I examine the stuff and find nothing useful in the books, and I say so, you could claim that Dr Lecter gave them to you. He's been *in absentia* seven years, so you might exercise a civil claim. He has no known relatives. I would recommend that any innocuous material be handed over to you. You should know my recommendation is at the low end of the totem pole. You wouldn't ever get the X ray back probably or the medical report, since they weren't his to give."

"And if I explain to you that I don't have the stuff?"

"Lecter material will become really hard to sell because we'll put out a bulletin on it and advise the market that we'll seize and prosecute for receiving and possession. I'll exercise a search and seizure warrant on your premises."

"Now that you know where my premises is. Or is it premises *are*?"

"I'm not sure. I *can* tell you, if you turn the material over, you won't get any grief for having taken it, considering what would have happened to it if you'd left it in place. As far as promising you'd get it back, I can't promise for sure." Starling rooted in her purse for punctuation. "You know, Barney, I have the feeling you haven't gotten an advanced medical degree because maybe you can't get bonded. Maybe you've got a prior somewhere. See? Now look at that—I never pulled a rap sheet on you, I never checked."

"No, you just looked at my tax return and my job application is all. I'm touched."

"If you've got a prior, maybe the USDA in that jurisdiction could drop a word, get you expunged."

Barney mopped his plate with a piece of toast. "You about finished? Let's walk a little."

"I saw Sammie, remember he took over Miggs's cell? He's still living in it," Starling said when they were outside.

"I thought the place was condemned."

"It is."

"Is Sammie in a program?"

"No, he just lives there in the dark."

"I think you ought to blow the whistle on him. He's a brittle diabetic, he'll die. Do you know why Dr Lecter made Miggs swallow his tongue?"

"I think so."

"He killed him for offending you. That was just the

specific thing. Don't feel bad—he might have done it anyway."

They continued past Barney's apartment house to the lawn where the dove still circled the body of its dead mate. Barney shooed it with his hands. "Go on," he said to the bird. "That's long enough to grieve. You'll walk around until the cat gets you." The dove flew away whistling. They could not see where it lit.

Barney picked up the dead bird. The smooth-feathered body slid easily into his pocket.

"You know, Dr Lecter talked about you a little, once. Maybe the last time I talked to him, one of the last times. The bird reminds me. You want to know what he said?"

"Sure," Starling said. Her breakfast crawled a little, and she was determined not to flinch.

"We were talking about inherited, hardwired behavior. He was using genetics in roller pigeons as an example. They go way up in the air and roll over and over backwards in a display, falling toward the ground. There are shallow rollers and deep rollers. You can't breed two deep rollers or the offspring will roll all the way down, crash and die. What he said was 'Officer Starling is a deep roller, Barney. We'll hope one of her parents was not.'"

Starling had to chew on that. "What'll you do with the bird?" she asked.

"Pluck it and eat it," Barney said. "Come on to the house and I'll give you the X ray and the books."

Carrying the long package back toward the hospital and her car, Starling heard the surviving mourning dove call once from the trees.

CHAPTER
13

THANKS TO the consideration of one madman and the obsession of another, Starling now had for the moment what she always wanted, an office on the storied subterranean corridor at Behavioral Science. It was bitter to get the office this way.

Starling never expected to go straight to the elite Behavioral Science section when she graduated from the FBI Academy, but she had believed that she could earn a place there. She knew she would spend several years in field offices first.

Starling was good at the job, but not good at office politics, and it took her years to see that she would never go to Behavioral Science, despite the wishes of its chief, Jack Crawford.

A major reason was invisible to her until, like an astronomer locating a black hole, she found Deputy Assistant Inspector General Paul Krendler by his influence on the bodies around him. He had never forgiven her for finding the serial killer Jame Gumb ahead of him, and he could not bear the press attention it brought her.

Once Krendler called her at home on a rainy winter

night. She answered the telephone in a robe and bunny slippers with her hair up in a towel. She would always remember the date exactly because it was the first week of Desert Storm. Starling was a tech agent then and she had just returned from New York, where she had replaced the radio in the Iraqi U.N. Mission's limousine. The new radio was just like the old one, except it broadcast conversations in the car to a Defense Department satellite overhead. It had been a dicey maneuver in a private garage and she was still edgy.

For a wild second, she thought Krendler had called to say she'd done a good job.

She remembered the rain against the windows and Krendler's voice on the phone, speech a little slurred, bar noises in the background.

He asked her out. He said he could come by in half an hour. He was married.

"I think not, Mr Krendler," she said and pushed the record button on her answering machine, it making the requisite legal beep, and the line went dead.

Now, years later in the office she had wanted to earn, Starling penciled her name on a piece of scrap paper and Scotch-taped it to the door. That wasn't funny and she tore it off again and threw it in the trash.

There was one piece of mail in her in-tray. It was a questionnaire from *The Guinness Book of World Records*, which prepared to list her as having killed more criminals than any other female law enforcement officer in United States history. The term *criminals* was being used advisedly, the publisher explained, as all of the deceased had multiple felony convictions and three had outstanding warrants. The questionnaire

110

went into the trash along with her name.

She was in her second hour of pecking away at the computer workstation, blowing stray strands of hair out of her face, when Crawford knocked on the door and stuck his head inside.

"Brian called from the lab, Starling. Mason's X ray and the one you got from Barney are a match. It's Lecter's arm. They'll digitize the images and compare them, but he says there's no question. We'll post everything to the secure Lecter VICAP folder."

"What about Mason Verger?"

"We tell him the truth," Crawford said. "You and I both know he won't share, Starling, unless he gets something he can't move on himself. But if we try to take over his lead in Brazil at this point, it'll evaporate."

"You told me to leave it alone and I did."

"You were doing *something* in here."

"Mason's X ray came by DHL Express. DHL took the bar code and label information and pinpointed the pickup location. It's in the Hotel Ibarra in Rio." Starling raised her hand to forestall interruption. "This is all New York sources, now. No inquiries at all in Brazil.

"Mason does his phone business, a lot of it, through the switch-board of a sports book in Las Vegas. You can imagine the volume of calls they take."

"Do I want to know how you found that out?"

"Strictly legit," Starling said. "Well, pretty much legit—I didn't leave anything in his house. I've got the codes to look at his phone bill, that's all. All the tech agents have them. Let's say he obstructs justice. With his influence, how long would we have to beg for a warrant to trap and trace? What could you do to him anyway if he was convicted? But he's using a *sports* book."

"I see it," Crawford said. "The Nevada Gaming Commission could either tap the phone or squeeze the sports book for what we need to know, which is where the calls go."

She nodded. "I left Mason alone just like you said."

"I can see that," Crawford said. "You can tell Mason we expect to help through Interpol and the embassy. Tell him we need to move people down there and start the framework for extradition. Lecter's probably committed crimes in South America, so we better extradite before the Rio police start looking in their files under *Cannibalismo*. If he's in South America at all. Starling, does it make you sick to talk to Mason?"

"I have to get in the mode. You walked me through it when we did that floater in West Virginia. What am I saying, 'floater.' She was a *person* named Fredericka Bimmel, and, yes, Mason makes me sick. A lot of stuff makes me sick lately, Jack."

Starling surprised herself into silence. She had never before addressed Section Chief Jack Crawford by his first name, she had never planned to call him "Jack" and it shocked her. She studied his face, a face famously hard to read.

He nodded, his smile wry and sad. "Me too, Starling. Want a couple of these Pepto-Bismol tablets to chew before you talk to Mason?"

Mason Verger did not bother to take Starling's call. A secretary thanked her for the message and said he'd return her call. But he didn't get back to her personally. To Mason, several places higher on the notification list than Starling, the X ray match was old news.

MASON KNEW that his X ray was truly of Dr Lecter's arm well before Starling was told, because Mason's sources within the Justice Department were better than hers.

Mason was told in an E-mail message signed with the screen name Token287. That is the second screen name of U.S. Representative Parton Vellmore's assistant on the House Judiciary Committee. Vellmore's office had been E-mailed by Cassius199, the second screen name of the Justice Department's own Paul Krendler.

Mason was excited. He did not think Dr Lecter was in Brazil, but the X ray proved that the doctor now had the normal number of fingers on his left hand. That information meshed with a new lead from Europe on the doctor's whereabouts. Mason believed the tip came from within Italian law enforcement and it was the strongest whiff of Lecter he had had in years.

Mason had no intention of sharing his lead with the FBI. Owing to seven years of relentless effort, access to confidential federal files, extensive leafleting, no international restrictions and large expenditures of money, Mason was ahead of the FBI in the pursuit of Lecter. He only shared information with the Bureau when he needed to suck its resources.

To keep up appearances, he instructed his secretary to pester Starling for developments anyway. Mason's tickler file prompted the secretary to call her at least three times a day.

Mason immediately wired five thousand dollars to his informant in Brazil to pursue the source of the X ray. The contingency fund he wired to Switzerland was much larger and he was prepared to send more when he had hard information in hand.

He believed that his source in Europe had found Dr Lecter, but Mason had been cheated on information many times and he had learned to be careful. Soon proof would come. Until it did, to relieve the agony of waiting Mason concerned himself with what would happen after the doctor was in his hands. These arrangements had also been long in the making, for Mason was a student of suffering . . .

God's choices in inflicting suffering are not satisfactory to us, nor are they understandable, unless innocence offends Him. Clearly He needs some help in directing the blind fury with which He flogs the earth.

Mason came to understand his role in all of this in the twelfth year of his paralysis, when he was no longer sizeable beneath his sheet and knew that he would never rise again. His quarters at the Muskrat Farm mansion were completed and he had means, but not unlimited means, because the Verger patriarch, Molson, still ruled.

It was Christmas in the year of Dr Lecter's escape. Subject to the quality of feelings that commonly attend Christmas, Mason was wishing bitterly that he had arranged for Dr Lecter to be murdered in the asylum; Mason knew that somewhere Dr Lecter was going to and fro in the earth and walking up and down in it, and very likely having a good time.

Mason himself lay under his respirator, a soft blanket covering all, a nurse standing by, shifting on her feet, wishing she could sit down. Some poor children had been bussed to Muskrat Farm to carol. With the doctor's permission, Mason's windows were opened briefly to the crisp air and, beneath the windows, holding candles in their cupped hands, the children sang.

The lights were out in Mason's room and in the black air above the farm the stars hung close.

"O little town of Bethlehern, how still we see thee lie!"

How still we see thee lie.
How still we see thee lie.

The mockery of the line pressed down on him. *How still we see thee lie, Mason!*

The Christmas stars outside his window maintained their stifling silence. The stars said nothing to him when he looked up to them with his pleading, goggled eye, gestured to them with the fingers he could move. Mason did not think that he could breathe. If he were suffocating in space, he thought, the last thing he would see would be the beautiful silent airless stars. He was suffocating now, he thought, his respirator could not keep up, he had to *wait for breath* the lines of his vital signs Christmas-green on the scopes and spiking, little evergreens in the black forest night of the scopes. Spike of his heartbeat, systolic spike, diastolic spike.

The nurse frightened, about to push the alarm button, about to reach for the adrenaline.

Mockery of the lines, *how still we see thee lie, Mason.*

An Epiphany then at Christmas. Before the nurse could ring, or reach for medication, the first coarse bristles of Mason's revenge brushed his pale and seeking, ghost crab of a hand, and began to calm him.

At Christmas communions around the earth, the devout believe that, through the miracle of transubstantiation, they eat the actual body and blood of Christ. Mason began the preparations for an even more impressive ceremony with no transubstantiation necessary. He began his arrangements for Dr Hannibal Lecter to be eaten alive.

MASON'S EDUCATION was an odd one, but perfectly fitted to the life his father envisioned for him and to the task before him now.

As a child he attended a boarding school, to which his father contributed heavily, where Mason's frequent absences were excused. For weeks at a time the elder Verger conducted Mason's real education, taking the boy with him to the stockyards and slaughterhouses that were the basis of his fortune.

Molson Verger was a pioneer in many areas of livestock production, particularly in the area of economy. His early experiments with cheap feed rank with those of Batterham fifty years before. Molson Verger adulterated the pigs' diet with hog hair meal, mealed chicken feathers and manure to an extent considered daring at the time. He was regarded as a reckless visionary in the 1940s when he first took away the pigs' fresh drinking water and had them drink ditch liquor, made of fermented animal waste, to hasten weight gain. The laughter stopped when his profits rolled in, and his competitors hurried to copy him.

Molson Verger's leadership in the meatpacking industry did not stop there. He fought bravely and with his own funds against the Humane Slaughter Act, strictly from the standpoint of economy, and managed to keep face branding legal though it cost him dearly in legislative compensation. With Mason at his side, he supervised large-scale experiments in the problems of lairage, determining how long you could deprive animals of food and water before slaughter without significant weight losses.

It was Verger-sponsored genetic research that finally achieved the heavy double-muscling of the Belgian swine breeds without the concomitant drip losses that plagued the Belgians. Molson Verger bought breeding stock worldwide and sponsored a number of foreign breeding programs.

But slaughterhouses are at base a people business and nobody understood that better than Molson Verger. He managed to cow the leadership of the unions when they tried to encroach on his profits with wage and safety demands. In this area his solid relationships with organized crime served him well for thirty years.

Mason bore a strong resemblance to his father then, with dark shiny eyebrows above pale blue butcher's eyes, and a low hairline that slanted across his forehead, descending from his right to his left. Often, affectionately, Molson Verger liked to take his son's head in his hands and just feel it, as though he were confirming the son's paternity through physiognomy, just as he could feel the face of a pig and tell by the bone structure its genetic makeup.

Mason learned well and, even after his injuries confined him to his bed, he was able to make sound business decisions to be implemented by his minions. It was Son Mason's idea to have the U.S. government and the United Nations slaughter all the native pigs in Haiti, citing the danger from them of African swine flu. He was then able to sell the government great white American pigs to replace the native swine. The great sleek swine, when faced with Haitian conditions, died as soon as possible and had to be replaced again and again from Mason's stock until the Haitians replaced their own pigs with hardy little rooters from the Dominican Republic.

Now, with a lifetime of knowledge and experience, Mason felt like Stradivarius approaching the worktable as he built the engines of his revenge.

What a wealth of information and resources Mason had in his faceless skull! Lying in his bed, composing in his mind like the deaf Beethoven, he remembered walking the swine fairs with his father, checking out the competition, Molson's little silver knife ever ready to slip out of his waistcoat and into a pig's back to check the depth of back fat, walking away from the outraged squeal, too dignified to be challenged, his hand back in his pocket, thumb marking the place on the blade.

Mason would have smiled if he had lips, remembering his father sticking a 4-H contestant pig who thought everyone was his friend, the child who owned it crying. The child's father coming over furious, and Molson's thugs taking him outside the tent. Oh, there were some good, funny times.

At the swine fairs Mason had seen exotic pigs from

all over the world. For his new purpose, he brought together the best of all that he had seen.

Mason began his breeding program immediately after his Christmas Epiphany and centered it in a small pig-breeding facility the Vergers owned in Sardinia, off the coast of Italy. He chose the place for its remoteness and its convenience to Europe.

Mason believed—correctly—that Dr Lecter's first stop outside the United States after his escape was in South America. But he had ever been convinced that Europe was where a man of Dr Lecter's tastes would settle—and he had watchers yearly at the Salzburg Music Festival and other cultural events.

This is what Mason sent to his breeders in Sardinia to prepare the theater of Dr Lecter's death:

The giant forest pig, *Hylochoerus meinertzhageni*, six teats and thirty-eight chromosomes, a resourceful feeder, an opportunistic omnivore, like man. Two meters in length in the highland families, it weighs about two hundred seventy-five kilograms. The giant forest pig is Mason's ground note.

The classic European wild boar, *S. scrofa scrofa*, thirty-six chromosomes in its purest form, no facial warts, all bristles and great ripping tusks, a big fast and fierce animal that will kill a viper with its sharp hooves and eat the snake like it was a Slim Jim. When aroused or rutting, or protecting its piglets, it will charge anything that threatens. Sows have twelve teats and are good mothers. In *S. scrofa scrofa*, Mason found his theme and the facial appearance appropriate to provide Dr Lecter a last, hellish vision of himself consumed. (See *Harris on the Pig, 1881*.)

He bought the Ossabaw Island pig for its aggressiveness, and the Jiaxing Black for high estradiol levels.

A false note when he introduced a Babirusa, *Babyrousa babyrussa*, from Eastern Indonesia, known as the hog-deer for the exaggerated length of its tusks. It was a slow breeder with only two teats, and at one hundred kilograms it cost him too much in size. No time was lost, as there were other, parallel litters that did not include the Babirusa.

In dentition, Mason had little variety to choose from. Almost every species had teeth adequate to the task, three pairs of sharp incisors, one pair of elongated canines, four pairs of premolars, and three crushing pairs of molars, upper and lower, for a total of forty-four teeth.

Any pig will eat a dead man, but to get him to eat a live one some education is required. Mason's Sardinians were up to the task.

Now, after an effort of seven years and many litters, the results were . . . remarkable.

C H A P T E R

16

WITH ALL the actors except Dr Lecter in place in the Gennargentu Mountains of Sardinia, Mason turned his attention toward recording the doctor's death for posterity and his own viewing pleasure. His arrangements had long been made, but now the alert must be given.

He conducted this sensitive business on the telephone through his legitimate sports book switchboard near the Castaways in Las Vegas. His calls were tiny lost threads in the great volume of weekend action there.

Mason's radio quality voice, minus plosives and fricatives, bounced from the National Forest near the Chesapeake shore to the desert and back across the Atlantic, first to Rome:

In an apartment on the seventh floor of a building on the Via Archimede, behind the hotel of the same name, the telephone is ringing, the hoarse double-rumpf of a telephone ringing in Italian. In the darkness, sleepy voices.

"Cosa? Cosa c'è?"

"Accendi la luce, idiòta."

The bedside lamp comes on. Three people are in the bed. The young man nearest the phone picks up the receiver and hands it to a portly older man in the middle. On the other side is a blond girl in her twenties. She raises a sleepy face to the light, then subsides again.

"*Pronto, chi? Chi parla?*"

"Oreste, my friend. It's Mason."

The heavy man gets himself together, signals to the younger man for a glass of mineral water.

"Ah, Mason my friend, excuse me, I was asleep, what time is it there?"

"It's late everywhere, Oreste. Do you remember what I said I would do for you and what you must do for me?"

"Well, of course."

"The time has come, my friend. You know what I want. I want a two-camera setup, I want better quality sound than your sex films have, and you have to make your own electricity, so I want the generator a long way from the set. I want some nice nature footage too for when we edit, and birdcalls. I want you to check out the location tomorrow and set it up. You can leave the stuff there, I'll provide security and you can come back to Rome until the shoot. But be ready to roll on two hours' notice. Do you understand that, Oreste? A draft is waiting for you in Citibank at the EUR, got it?"

"Mason, in this moment, I am making—"

"Do you want to do this, Oreste? You *said* you were tired of making hump movies and snuff movies and historical crap for the RAI. Do you seriously want to make a feature, Oreste?"

"Yes, Mason."

"Then go today. The cash is at Citibank. I want you to go."

"Where, Mason?"

"Sardinia. Fly to Cagliari, you'll be met."

The next call went to Porto Torres on the east coast of Sardinia. The call was brief. There was not a lot to say because the machinery there was long established and as efficient as Mason's portable guillotine. It was sounder too, ecologically, but not as quick.

II

FLORENCE

17

Night in the heart of Florence, the old city artfully lighted.

The Palazzo Vecchio rising from the dark piazza, floodlit, intensely medieval with its arched windows and battlements like jack-o'-lantern teeth, bell tower soaring into the black sky.

Bats will chase mosquitoes across the clock's glowing face until dawn, when the swallows rise on air shivered by the bells.

Chief Investigator Rinaldo Pazzi of the Questura, raincoat black against the marble statues fixed in acts of rape and murder, came out of the shadows of the Loggia and crossed the piazza, his pale face turning like a sunflower to the palace light. He stood on the spot where the reformer Savonarola was burned and looked up at the windows where his own forebear came to grief.

There, from that high window, Francesco de' Pazzi was thrown naked with a noose around his neck, to die writhing and spinning against the rough wall. The archbishop hanged beside Pazzi in all his holy vestments provided no spiritual comfort; eyes bulging, wild as he choked, the archbishop locked his teeth in Pazzi's flesh.

The Pazzi family were all brought low on that Sunday, 26 April, 1478, for killing Giuliano de' Medici and trying to kill Lorenzo the Magnificent in the cathedral at Mass.

Now Rinaldo Pazzi, a Pazzi of the Pazzi, hating the government as much as his ancestor ever did, disgraced and out of fortune, listening for the whisper of the axe, came to this place to decide how best to use a singular piece of luck:

Chief Investigator Pazzi believed that he had found Hannibal Lecter living in Florence. He had a chance to regain his reputation and enjoy the honors of his trade by capturing the fiend. Pazzi also had a chance to sell Hannibal Lecter to Mason Verger for more money than he could imagine—if the suspect was indeed Lecter. Of course, Pazzi would be selling his own ragged honor as well.

Pazzi did not head the Questura investigation division for nothing—he was gifted and in his time he had been driven by a wolfish hunger to succeed in his profession. He also carried the scars of a man who, in the haste and heat of his ambition, once seized his gift by the blade.

He chose this place to cast his lot because he once experienced a moment of epiphany here that made him famous and then ruined him.

The Italian sense of irony was strong in Pazzi: How fitting that his fateful revelation came beneath this window, where the furious spirit of his forebear might still spin against the wall. In this same place, he could forever change the Pazzi luck.

It was the hunt for another serial killer, *Il Mostro*, that made Pazzi famous and then let the crows peck at his heart. That experience made possible his new discovery. But ending of the *Il Mostro* case was bitter ashes in Pazzi's mouth and inclined him now toward a dangerous game outside the law.

Il Mostro, the Monster of Florence, preyed on lovers in Tuscany for seventeen years in the 1980s and 1990s. The Monster crept up on couples as they embraced in the many Tuscan lovers' lanes. It was his custom to kill the lovers with a small-caliber pistol, arrange them in a careful tableau with flowers and expose the woman's left breast. His tableaux had an odd familiarity about them, they left a sense of déjà vu.

The Monster also excised anatomical trophies, except in the single instance when he slew a long-haired German homosexual couple, apparently by mistake.

The public pressure on the Questura to catch *Il Mostro* was intense, and drove Rinaldo Pazzi's predecessor out of office. When Pazzi took over as chief investigator, he was like a man fighting bees, with the press swarming through his office whenever they were allowed, and photographers lurking in the Via Zara behind Questura headquarters, where he had to drive out.

Tourists to Florence during the period will remember plastered everywhere the posters with the single watching eye that warned couples against the Monster.

Pazzi worked like a man possessed.

He called on the American FBI's Behavioral Science section for help in profiling the killer and read everything he could find on FBI profiling methods.

He used proactive measures: Some lovers' lanes and cemetery trysting places had more police than lovers sitting in pairs in the cars. There were not enough women officers to go around. During hot weather male couples took turns wearing a wig and many mustaches were sacrificed. Pazzi set an example by shaving off his own mustache.

The Monster was careful. He struck, but his needs did not force him to strike often.

Pazzi noticed that in years past there were long periods when the Monster did not strike at all—one gap of eight years. Pazzi seized on this. Painstakingly, laboriously, dragooning clerical help from every agency he could threaten, confiscating his nephew's computer to use along with the Questura's single machine, Pazzi listed every criminal in northern Italy whose periods of imprisonment coincided with the time gaps in *Il Mostro*'s series of murders. The number was ninety-seven.

Pazzi took over an imprisoned bank robber's fast, comfortable old Alfa-Romeo GTV and, putting more than five thousand kilometers on the car in a month, he personally looked at ninety-four of the convicts and had them interrogated. The others were disabled or dead.

There was almost no evidence at the scenes of the crimes to help him narrow down the list. No body fluids of the perpetrator, no fingerprints.

A single shell casing was recovered from a murder scene at Impruneta. It was a .22 Winchester-Western rimfire with extractor marks consistent with a Colt semiautomatic pistol, possibly a Woodsman.

The bullets in all the crimes were .22s from the same gun. There were no wipe marks on the bullets from a silencer, but a silencer could not be ruled out.

Pazzi was a Pazzi and above all things ambitious, and he had a young and lovely wife with an ever-open beak. His efforts ground twelve pounds off his lean frame. Younger members of the Questura privately remarked on his resemblance to the cartoon character Wile E. Coyote.

When some young smart alecks put a morph program in the Questura computer that changed the Three Tenors' faces into those of a jackass, a pig and a goat, Pazzi stared at the morph for minutes and felt his own face changing back and forth into the countenance of the jackass.

The window of the Questura laboratory is garlanded with garlic to keep out evil spirits. With the last of his suspects visited and grilled to no effect, Pazzi stood at this window looking out on the dusty courtyard and despaired.

He thought of his new wife, and her good hard ankles and the patch of down in the small of her back. He thought of how her breasts quivered and bounced when she brushed her teeth and how she laughed when she saw him watching. He thought of the things he wanted to give her. He imagined her opening the gifts. He thought of his wife in visual terms; she was fragrant and wonderful to touch as well, but the visual was first in his memory.

He considered the way he wanted to appear in her eyes. Certainly not in his present role as butt of the press—Questura headquarters in Florence is located in a former mental hospital, and the cartoonists were taking full advantage of that fact.

Pazzi imagined that success came as a result of inspiration. His visual memory was excellent and, like many people whose primary sense is sight, he thought of revelation as the development of an image, first blurred and then coming clear. He ruminated the way most of us look for a lost object: We review its image in our minds and compare that image to what we see, mentally refreshing the image many times a minute and turning it in space.

Then a political bombing behind the Uffizi museum took the public's attention, and Pazzi's time, away from the case of *Il Mostro* for a short while.

Even as he worked the important museum bomb case, *Il Mostro*'s created images stayed in Pazzi's mind. He saw the Monster's tableaux peripherally, as we look beside an object to see it in the dark. Particularly he dwelt on the couple found slain in the bed of a pickup truck in Impruneta, the bodies carefully arranged by the Monster, strewn and garlanded with flowers, the woman's left breast exposed.

Pazzi had left the Uffizi museum one early afternoon and was crossing the nearby Piazza Signoria, when an image jumped at him from the display of a postcard vendor.

Not sure where the image came from, he stopped just at the spot where Savonarola was burned. He turned and looked around him. Tourists were thronging the piazza. Pazzi felt cold up his back. Maybe it was all in his head, the image, the pluck at his attention. He retraced his steps and came again.

There it was: a small, fly-specked, rain-warped poster of Botticelli's painting "Primavera." The original painting was behind him in the Uffizi museum. "Primavera." The garlanded nymph on the right, her left breast exposed, flowers streaming from her mouth as the pale Zephyrus reached for her from the forest.

There. The image of the couple dead in the bed of the pickup, garlanded with flowers, flowers in the girl's mouth. Match. Match.

Here, where his ancestor spun choking against the wall, came the idea, the master image Pazzi sought, and it was an image created five hundred years ago by Sandro Botticelli—the same artist who had for forty florins painted the hanged Francesco de' Pazzi's image on the wall of the Bargello prison, noose and all. How could Pazzi resist this inspiration, with its origin so delicious?

He had to sit down. All the benches were full. He was reduced to showing his badge and commandeering a place on a bench from an old man whose crutches he honestly did not see until the old veteran was up on his single foot and very loud and rude about it too.

Pazzi was excited for two reasons. To find the image *Il Mostro* used was a triumph, but much more important, Pazzi had seen a copy of "Primavera" in his rounds of the criminal suspects.

He knew better than to flog his memory; he leaned and loafed and invited it. He returned to the Uffizi and stood before the original "Primavera," but not too long. He walked to the straw market and touched the snout of the bronze boar "Il Porcellino," drove out to the Ippocampo and, leaning against the hood of his dusty car, the smell of hot oil in his nose, watched the children playing soccer . . .

He saw the staircase first in his mind, and the landing above, the top of the "Primavera" poster appearing first as he climbed the stairs; he could go back and see the entrance doorframe for a second, but nothing of the street, and no faces.

Wise in the ways of interrogation, he questioned himself, going to the secondary senses:

When you saw the poster, what did you hear? . . . Pots rattling in a ground-floor kitchen. When you went up on the landing and stood before the poster, what did you hear? The television. A television in a sitting room. Robert Stack playing Eliot Ness in Gli intoccabili. *Did you smell cooking? Yes, cooking. Did you smell anything else? I saw the poster—NO, not what you saw. Did you smell anything else? I could still smell the Alfa, hot inside, it was still in my nose, hot oil smell, hot from . . . the Raccordo, going fast on the Raccordo Autostrada to where? San Casciano. I heard a dog barking too, in San Casciano, a burglar and rapist named Girolamo something.*

In that moment when the connection is made, in that synaptic spasm of completion when the thought drives through the red fuse, is our keenest pleasure. Rinaldo Pazzi had had the best moment of his life.

In an hour and a half, Pazzi had Girolamo Tocca in custody. Tocca's wife threw rocks after the little convoy that took her husband away.

CHAPTER

18

TOCCA WAS a dream suspect. As a young man, he had
served nine years in prison for the murder of a man he
caught embracing his fiancée in a lovers' lane. He had
also faced charges of sexually molesting his daughters
and other domestic abuse, and had served a prison
sentence for rape.

The Questura nearly destroyed Tocca's house trying
to find evidence. In the end Pazzi himself, searching
Tocca's grounds, came up with a cartridge case that
was one of the few pieces of physical evidence the
prosecution submitted.

The trial was a sensation. It was held in a high-security
building called the Bunker where terrorist trials were
held in the seventies, across from the Florence offices
of the newspaper *La Nazione*. The sworn and besashed
jurors, five men and five women, convicted Tocca on
almost no evidence except his character. Most of the
public believed him innocent, but many said Tocca
was a jerk and well jailed. At the age of sixty-five, he
received a sentence of forty years at Volterra.

The next months were golden. A Pazzi had not been so celebrated in Florence for the last five hundred years, since Pazzo de' Pazzi returned from the First Crusade with flints from the Holy Sepulchre.

Rinaldo Pazzi and his beautiful wife stood beside the archbishop in the Duomo when, at the traditional Easter rite, these same holy flints were used to ignite the rocket-powered model dove, which flew out of the church along its wire to explode a cart of fireworks for a cheering crowd.

The papers hung on every word Pazzi said as he dispensed credit, within reason, to his subordinates for the drudgery they had performed. Signora Pazzi was sought for fashion advice, and she did look wonderful in the garments designers encouraged her to wear. They were invited to stuffy teas in the homes of the powerful, and had dinner with a count in his castle with suits of armor standing all around.

Pazzi was mentioned for political office, praised over the general noise in the Italian parliament and given the brief to head Italy's co-operative effort with the American FBI against the Mafia.

That brief, and a fellowship to study and take part in criminology seminars at Georgetown University, brought the Pazzis to Washington, D.C. The chief inspector spent much time at Behavioral Science in Quantico and dreamed of creating a Behavioral Science division in Rome.

Then, after two years, disaster: In a calmer atmosphere, an appellate court not under public pressure agreed to review Tocca's conviction. Pazzi was brought home to face the investigation. Among the former colleagues he had left behind, the knives were out for Pazzi.

An appellate panel overthrew Tocca's conviction and reprimanded Pazzi, saying the court believed he had planted evidence.

His former supporters in high places fled him as they would a bad smell. He was still an important official of the Questura, but he was a lame duck and everyone knew it. The Italian government moves slowly, but soon the axe would fall.

19

IT WAS in the awful searing time while Pazzi waited for
the axe that he first saw the man known among scholars
in Florence as Dr Fell. . . .

Rinaldo Pazzi, climbing the stairs in the Palazzo
Vecchio on a menial errand, one of many found for
him by his former subordinates at the Questura as they
enjoyed his fall from grace. Pazzi saw only the toes of his
own shoes on the cupped stone and not the wonders of
art around him as he climbed beside the frescoed wall.
Five hundred years ago, his forebear had been dragged
bleeding up these stairs.

At a landing, he squared his shoulders like the man he
was, and forced himself to meet the eyes of the people in
the frescoes, some of them kin to him. He could already
hear the wrangling from the Salon of Lilies above him
where the directors of the Uffizi Gallery and the Belle
Arti Commission were meeting in joint session.

Pazzi's business today was this: The longtime curator
of the Palazzo Capponi was missing. It was widely
believed the old fellow had eloped with a woman or

someone's money or both. He had failed to meet with his governing body here in the Palazzo Vecchio for the last four monthly meetings.

Pazzi was sent to continue the investigation. Chief Inspector Pazzi, who had sternly lectured these same gray-faced directors of the Uffizi and members of the rival Belle Arti Commission on security following the museum bombing, must now appear before them in reduced circumstances to ask questions about a curator's love life. He did not look forward to it.

The two committees were a contentious and prickly assembly—for years they could not even agree on a venue, neither side willing to meet in the other's offices. They met instead in the magnificent Salon of Lilies in the Palazzo Vecchio, each member believing the beautiful room suitable to his own eminence and distinction. Once established there, they refused to meet anywhere else, even though the Palazzo Vecchio was undergoing one of its thousand restorations, with scaffolding and drop cloths and machinery underfoot.

Professor Ricci, an old schoolmate of Rinaldo Pazzi, was in the hall outside the salon with a sneezing fit from the plaster dust. When he had recovered sufficiently, he rolled his streaming eyes at Pazzi.

"*La solita arringa*," Ricci said, "they are arguing as usual. You've come about the missing Capponi curator? They're fighting over his job right now. Sogliato wants the job for his nephew. The scholars are impressed with the temporary one they appointed months ago, Dr Fell. They want to keep him."

Pazzi left his friend patting his pockets for tissues, and went into the historic chamber with its ceiling of gold lilies. Hanging drop cloths on two of the walls helped to soften the din.

The nepotist, Sogliato, had the floor, and was holding it by dint of volume:

"The Capponi correspondence goes back to the thirteenth century. Dr Fell might hold in his hand, in his *non-Italian* hand, a note from Dante Alighieri himself. Would he recognize it? I think *not*. You have examined him in medieval Italian, and I will not deny his language is admirable. For a *straniero*. But is he familiar with the personalities of pre-Renaissance Florence? I think *not*. What if he came upon a note in the Capponi library from—from Guido de' Cavalcanti for instance? Would he recognize it? I think *not*. Would you care to address that, Dr Fell?"

Rinaldo Pazzi scanned the room and did not see anyone he recognized as Dr Fell, even though he had examined a photograph of the man not an hour before. He did not see Dr Fell because the doctor was not seated with the others. Pazzi heard his voice first, then located him.

Dr Fell stood very still beside the great bronze statue of Judith and Holofernes, giving his back to the speaker and the crowd. He spoke without turning around and it was hard to know which figure the voice came from—Judith, her sword forever raised to strike the drunken king, or Holofernes, gripped by the hair, or Dr Fell, slender and still beside Donatello's bronze figures. His voice cut through the din like a laser through smoke and the squabbling men fell silent.

"Cavalcanti replied publicly to Dante's first sonnet in *La Vita Nuova*, where Dante describes his strange dream of Beatrice Portinari," Dr Fell said. "Perhaps Cavalcanti commented privately as well. If he wrote to a Capponi, it would be to Andrea, he was more literary than his brothers." Dr Fell turned to face the group in his own time, after an interval uncomfortable to everyone but him. "Do you know Dante's first sonnet, Professor Sogliato? *Do* you? It fascinated Cavalcanti and it's worth your time. In part it says:

"The first three hours of night were almost spent
The time that every star shines down on us
When Love appeared to me so suddenly
That I still shudder at the memory.
Joyous Love seemed to me, the while he held
My heart within his hands, and in his arms
My lady lay asleep wrapped in a veil.
He woke her then and trembling and obedient
She ate that burning heart out of his hand;
Weeping I saw him then depart from me.

"Listen to the way he makes an instrument of the Italian vernacular, what he called the *vulgari eloquentia* of the people:

"Allegro mi sembrava Amor tenendo
Meo core in mano, e ne le braccia avea
Madonna involta in un drappo dormendo.
Poi la svegliava, e d'esto core ardendo
Lei paventosa umilmente pascea
Appreso gir lo ne vedea piangendo."

Even the most contentious Florentines could not

resist the verse of Dante ringing off these frescoed walls in Dr Fell's clear Tuscan. First applause, and then by wet-eyed acclamation, the memberships affirmed Dr Fell as master of the Palazzo Capponi, leaving Sogliato to fume. If the victory pleased the doctor, Pazzi could not tell, for he turned his back again. But Sogliato was not quite through.

"If he is such an expert on Dante, let him lecture on Dante, *to the Studiolo*." Sogliato hissed the name as though it were the Inquisition. "Let him face them *extempore*, next Friday if he can." The Studiolo, named for an ornate private study, was a small, fierce group of scholars who had ruined a number of academic reputations and met often in the Palazzo Vecchio. Preparing for them was regarded as a considerable chore, appearing before them a peril. Sogliato's uncle seconded his motion and Sogliato's brother-in-law called for a vote, which his sister recorded in the minutes. It passed. The appointment stood, but Dr Fell must satisfy the Studiolo to keep it.

The committees had a new curator for the Palazzo Capponi, they did not miss the old curator, and they gave the disgraced Pazzi's questions about the missing man short shrift. Pazzi held up admirably.

Like any good investigator, he had sifted the circumstances for profit. Who would benefit from the old curator's disappearance? The missing curator was a bachelor, a well-respected quiet scholar with an orderly life. He had some savings, nothing much. All he had was his job and with it the privilege of living in the attic of the Palazzo Capponi.

Here was the new appointee, confirmed by the board

after close questioning on Florentine history and archaic Italian. Pazzi had examined Dr Fell's application forms and his National Health affidavits.

Pazzi approached him as the board members were packing their briefcases to go home.

"Dr Fell."

"Yes, *Commendatore*?"

The new curator was small and sleek. His glasses were smoked in the top half of the lenses and his dark clothing beautifully cut, even for Italy.

"I was wondering if you ever met your predecessor?" An experienced policeman's antennae are tuned to the bandwidth of fear. Watching Dr Fell carefully, Pazzi registered absolute calm.

"I never met him. I read several of his monographs in the *Nuova Antologia*." The doctor's conversational Tuscan was as clear as his recitation. If there was a trace of an accent, Pazzi could not place it.

"I know that the officers who first investigated checked the Palazzo Capponi for any sort of note, a farewell note, a suicide note, and found nothing. If you come upon anything in the papers, anything personal, even if it's trivial, would you call me?"

"Of course, *Commendator* Pazzi."

"Are his personal effects still at the Palazzo?"

"Packed in two suitcases, with an inventory."

"I'll send—I'll come by and pick them up."

"Would you call me first, *Commendatore*? I can disarm the security system before you arrive, and save you time."

The man is too calm. Properly, he should fear me a little. He asks me to call him before coming by.

The committee had ruffled Pazzi's feathers. He could do nothing about that. Now he was piqued by this man's presumption. He piqued back.

"Dr Fell, may I ask you a personal question?"

"If your duty requires it, *Commendatore*."

"You have a relatively new scar on the back of your left hand."

"And you have a new wedding ring on yours: *La Vita Nuova*?" Dr Fell smiled. He has small teeth, very white. In Pazzi's instant of surprise, before he could decide to be offended, Dr Fell held up his scarred hand and went on: "Carpal tunnel syndrome, *Commendatore*. History is a hazardous profession."

"Why didn't you declare carpal tunnel syndrome on your National Health forms when you came to work here?"

"My impression was, *Commendatore*, that injuries are relevant only if one is receiving disability payments; I am not. Nor am I disabled."

"The surgery was in Brazil, then, your country of origin."

"It was not in Italy, I received nothing from the Italian government," Dr Fell said, as though he believed he had answered completely.

They were the last to leave the council room. Pazzi had reached the door when Dr Fell called to him.

"*Commendator* Pazzi?"

Dr Fell was a black silhouette against the tall windows. Behind him in the distance rose the Duomo.

"Yes?"

"I think you are a Pazzi of the Pazzi, am I correct?"

"Yes. How did you know that?" Pazzi would consider

a reference to recent newspaper coverage rude in the extreme.

"You resemble a figure from the Della Robbia rondels in your family's chapel at Santa Croce."

"Ah, that was Andrea de' Pazzi depicted as John the Baptist," Pazzi said, a small slick of pleasure on his acid heart.

When Rinaldo Pazzi left the slender figure standing in the council room, his lasting impression was of Dr Fell's extraordinary stillness.

He would add to that impression very soon.

NOW THAT ceaseless exposure has calloused us to the lewd and the vulgar, it is instructive to see what still seems wicked to us. What still slaps the clammy flab of our submissive consciousness hard enough to get our attention?

In Florence it was the exposition called Atrocious Torture Instruments, and it was here that Rinaldo Pazzi next encountered Dr Fell.

The exhibit, featuring more than twenty classic instruments of torture with extensive documentation, was mounted in the forbidding Forte di Belvedere, a sixteenth-century Medici stronghold that guards the city's south wall. The expo opened to enormous, unexpected crowds; excitement leaped like a trout in the public trousers.

The scheduled run was a month; Atrocious Torture Instruments ran for six months, equaling the draw of the Uffizi Gallery and outdrawing the Pitti Palace Museum.

The promoters, two failed taxidermists who formerly got along by eating offal from the trophies they mounted, became millionaires and made a triumphal tour of Europe with their show, wearing their new tuxedos.

The visitors came in couples, mostly, from all over Europe, taking advantage of the extended hours to file among the engines of pain, and read carefully in any of four languages the provenance of the devices and how to use them. Illustrations by Dürer and others, along with contemporary diaries, enlightened the crowds on matters such as the finer points of wheeling.

The English from one placard:

The Italian princes preferred to have their victims broken on the ground with the use of the iron-tired wheel as the striking agent and blocks beneath the limbs as shown, while in northern Europe the popular method was to lash the victim to the wheel, break him or her with an iron bar, and then lace the limbs through the spokes around the periphery of the wheel, compound fractures providing the requisite flexibility, with the still-noisy head and trunk in the center. The latter method was a more satisfactory spectacle, but the recreation might be cut short if a piece of marrow went to the heart.

The exposition of Atrocious Torture Instruments could not fail to appeal to a connoisseur of the worst in mankind. But the essence of the worst, the true asafoetida of the human spirit, is not found in the Iron Maiden or the whetted edge; Elemental Ugliness is found in the faces of the crowd.

In the semidarkness of this great stone room, beneath the lit, hanging cages of the damned, stood Dr Fell, connoisseur of facial cheeses, holding his spectacles in his scarred hand, the tip of an ear-piece against his lips, his face rapt as he watched the people file through.

Rinaldo Pazzi saw him there.

Pazzi was on his second menial errand of the day. Instead of having dinner with his wife, he was pushing through the crowd to post new warnings to couples about the Monster of Florence, whom he had failed to catch. Such a warning poster was prominent over his own desk, placed there by his new superiors, along with other wanted posters from around the world.

The taxidermists, watching the box office together, were happy to add a bit of contemporary horror to their show, but asked Pazzi to put up the poster himself, as neither seemed willing to leave the other alone with the cash. A few locals recognized Pazzi and hissed him from the anonymity of the crowd.

Pazzi pushed pins through the corners of the blue poster, with its single staring eye, on a bulletin board near the exit where it would attract the most attention, and turned on a picture light above it. Watching the couples leaving, Pazzi could see that many were in estrus, rubbing against each other in the crowd at the exit. He did not want to see another tableau, no more blood and flowers.

Pazzi did want to speak to Dr Fell—it would be convenient to pick up the missing curator's effects while he was this near the Palazzo Capponi. But when Pazzi turned from the bulletin board, the doctor was gone. He was not in the crowd at the exit. There was only the stone wall where he had stood, beneath the hanging starvation cage with its skeleton in a fetal curve still pleading to be fed.

Pazzi was annoyed. He pushed through the crowd until he was outside, but did not find the doctor.

The guard at the exit recognized Pazzi and said nothing when he stepped over the rope and walked off the path, onto the dark grounds of the Forte di Belvedere. He went to the parapet, looking north across the Arno. Old Florence was at his feet, the great hump of the Duomo, the tower of the Palazzo Vecchio rising in light.

Pazzi was a very old soul, writhing on a spike of ridiculous circumstance. His city mocked him.

The American FBI had given the knife a final twist in Pazzi's back, saying in the press that the FBI profile of *Il Mostro* had been nothing like the man Pazzi arrested. *La Nazione* added that Pazzi had "rail-roaded Tocca off to prison."

The last time Pazzi had put up the blue *Il Mostro* poster was in America; it was a proud trophy he hung on the wall of Behavioral Science, and he had signed it at the request of the American FBI agents. They knew all about him, admired him, invited him. He and his wife had been guests on the Maryland shore.

Standing at the dark parapet, looking over his ancient city, he smelled the salt air off the Chesapeake, saw his wife on the shore in her new white sneakers.

There was a picture of Florence in Behavioral Science at Quantico, shown him as a curiosity. It was the same view he was seeing now, old Florence from the Belvedere, the best view there is. But not in color. No, a pencil drawing, shaded with charcoal. The drawing was in a photograph, in the background of a photograph. It was a photograph of the American serial murderer, Dr Hannibal Lecter. Hannibal the Cannibal. Lecter had drawn Florence from memory and the drawing was hanging in his cell in the asylum, a place as grim as this.

When did it fall on Pazzi, the ripening idea? Two images, the real Florence lying before him, and the drawing he recalled. Placing the poster of *Il Mostro* minutes ago. Mason Verger's poster of Hannibal Lecter on his own office wall with its huge reward and its advisories:

DR LECTER WILL HAVE TO CONCEAL HIS LEFT HAND AND MAY ATTEMPT TO HAVE IT SURGICALLY ALTERED, AS HIS TYPE OF POLYDACTYLY, THE APPEARANCE OF PERFECT EXTRA FINGERS, IS EXTREMELY RARE AND INSTANTLY IDENTIFIABLE.

Dr Fell holding his glasses to his lips with his scarred hand.

A detailed sketch of this view on the wall of Hannibal Lecter's cell.

Did the idea come to Pazzi while he was looking at the city of Florence beneath him, or out of the swarming dark above the lights? And why was its harbinger a scent of the salt breeze off the Chesapeake?

Oddly for a visual man, the connection arrived with a sound, the sound a drop would make as it lands in a thickening pool.

Hannibal Lecter had fled to Florence.
plop
Hannibal Lecter was Dr Fell.

Rinaldo Pazzi's inner voice told him he might have gone mad in the cage of his plight; his frenzied mind might be breaking its teeth on the bars like the skeleton in the starvation cage.

With no memory of moving, he found himself at the Renaissance gate leading from the Belvedere into the steep Costa di San Giorgio, a narrow street that winds and plunges down to the heart of Old Florence in less than half a mile. His steps seemed to carry him down the steep cobbles without his volition, he was going faster than he wished, looking always ahead for the man called Dr Fell, for this was the way home for him—halfway down Pazzi turned in to the Costa Scarpuccia, always descending until he came out on the Via de' Bardi, near the river. Near the Palazzo Capponi, home of Dr Fell.

Pazzi, puffing from his descent, found a place shadowed from the streetlight, an apartment entrance across from the palazzo. If someone came along he could turn and pretend to press a bell.

The palazzo was dark. Pazzi could make out above the great double doors the red light of a surveillance camera. He could not be sure if it worked full-time, or served only when someone rang the bell. It was well within the covered entrance. Pazzi did not think it could see along the façade.

He waited a half-hour, listening to his own breath, and the doctor did not come. Perhaps he was inside with no lights on.

The street was empty. Pazzi crossed quickly and stood close against the wall.

Faintly, faintly a thin sound from within. Pazzi leaned his head against the cold window bars to listen. A clavier, Bach's *Goldberg Variations* well played.

Pazzi must wait, and lurk and think. This was too soon to flush his quarry. He must decide what to do. He did not want to be a fool again. As he backed into the shadow across the street, his nose was last to disappear.

CHAPTER
21

THE CHRISTIAN martyr San Miniato picked up his severed head from the sand of the Roman amphitheater in Florence and carried it beneath his arm to the mountainside across the river where he lies in his splendid church, tradition says.

Certainly San Miniato's body, erect or not, passed en route along the ancient street where we now stand, the Via de' Bardi. The evening gathers now and the street is empty, the fan pattern of the cobbles shining in a winter drizzle not cold enough to kill the smell of cats. We are among the palaces built six hundred years ago by the merchant princes, the kingmakers and connivers of Renaissance Florence. Within bow-shot across the Arno River are the cruel spikes of the Signoria, where the monk Savonarola was hanged and burned, and that great meat house of hanging Christs, the Uffizi museum.

These family palaces, pressed together in an ancient street, frozen in the modern Italian bureaucracy, are prison architecture on the outside, but they contain

153

great and graceful spaces, high silent halls no one ever sees, draped with rotting, rain-streaked silk where lesser works of the great Renaissance masters hang in the dark for years, and are illuminated by the lightning after the draperies collapse.

Here beside you is the palazzo of the Capponi, a family distinguished for a thousand years, who tore up a French king's ultimatum in his face and produced a pope.

The windows of the Palazzo Capponi are dark now, behind their iron grates. The torch rings are empty. In that pane of crazed old glass is a bullet hole from the 1940s. Go closer. Rest your head against the cold iron as the policeman did and listen. Faintly you can hear a clavier. Bach's *Goldberg Variations* played, not perfectly, but exceedingly well, with an engaging understanding of the music. Played not perfectly, but exceedingly well; there is perhaps a slight stiffness in the left hand.

If you believe you are beyond harm, will you go inside? Will you enter this palace so prominent in blood and glory, follow your face through the web-spanned dark, toward the exquisite chiming of the clavier? The alarms cannot see us. The wet policeman lurking in the doorway cannot see us. Come . . .

Inside the foyer the darkness is almost absolute. A long stone staircase, the stair rail cold beneath our sliding hand, the steps scooped by the hundreds of years of footfalls, uneven beneath our feet as we climb toward the music.

The tall double doors of the main salon would squeak and howl if we had to open them. For you, they are open. The music comes from the far, far corner, and from the corner comes the only light, light of many candles pouring reddish through the small door of a chapel off the corner of the room.

Cross to the music. We are dimly aware of passing large groups of draped furniture, vague shapes not quite still in the candlelight, like a sleeping herd. Above us the height of the room disappears into darkness.

The light glows redly on an ornate clavier and on the man known to Renaissance scholars as Dr Fell, the doctor elegant, straight-backed as he leans into the music, the light reflecting off his hair and the back of his quilted silk dressing gown with a sheen like pelt.

The raised cover of the clavier is decorated with an intricate scene of banquetry, and the little figures seem to swarm in the candlelight above the strings. He plays with his eyes closed. He has no need of the sheet music. Before him on the lyre-shaped music rack of the clavier is a copy of the American trash tabloid the *National Tattler*. It is folded to show only the face on the front page, the face of Clarice Starling.

Our musician smiles, ends the piece, repeats the saraband once for his own pleasure and as the last quill-plucked string vibrates to silence in the great room, he opens his eyes, each pupil centered with a red pinpoint of light. He tilts his head to the side and looks at the paper before him.

He rises without sound and carries the American tabloid into the tiny, ornate chapel, built before the discovery of America. As he holds it up to the light of the candles and unfolds it, the religious icons above the altar seem to read the tabloid over his shoulder, as they would in a grocery line. The type is seventy-two-point Railroad Gothic. It says "*DEATH ANGEL: CLARICE STARLING, THE FBI'S KILLING MACHINE.*"

Faces painted in agony and beatitude around the altar fade as he snuffs the candles. Crossing the great hall he has no need of light. A puff of air as Dr Hannibal Lecter passes us. The great door creaks, closes with a thud we can feel in the floor. Silence.

Footsteps entering another room. In the resonances of this place, the walls feel closer, the ceiling still high—sharp sounds echo late from above—and the still air holds the smell of vellum and parchment and extinguished candlewicks.

The rustle of paper in the dark, the squeak and scrape of a chair. Dr Lecter sits in a great armchair in the fabled Capponi Library. His eyes reflect light redly, but they do not glow red in the dark, as some of his keepers have sworn they do. The darkness is complete. He is considering . . .

It is true that Dr Lecter created the vacancy at the Palazzo Capponi by removing the former curator—a simple process requiring a few seconds' work on the old man and a modest outlay for two bags of cement—but once the way was clear he won the job fairly, demonstrating to the Belle Arti Committee an extraordinary linguistic capability, sight-translating medieval Italian and Latin from the densest Gothic black-letter manuscripts.

He has found a peace here that he would preserve—he has killed hardly anybody, except his predecessor, during his residence in Florence.

His appointment as translator and curator of the

Capponi Library is a considerable prize to him for several reasons:

The spaces, the height of the palace rooms, are important to Dr Lecter after his years of cramped confinement. More important, he feels a resonance with the palace; it is the only private building he has ever seen that approaches in dimension and detail the memory palace he has maintained since youth.

In the library, this unique collection of manuscripts and correspondence going back to the early thirteenth century, he can indulge a certain curiosity about himself.

Dr Lecter believed, from fragmentary family records, that he was descended from a certain Giuliano Bevisangue, a fearsome twelfth-century figure in Tuscany, and from the Machiavelli as well as the Visconti. This was the ideal place for research. While he had a certain abstract curiosity about the matter, it was not ego-related. Dr Lecter does not require conventional reinforcement. His ego, like his intelligence quota, and the degree of his rationality, is not measurable by conventional means.

In fact, there is no consensus in the psychiatric community that Dr Lecter should be termed a man. He has long been regarded by his professional peers in psychiatry, many of whom fear his acid pen in the professional journals, as something entirely Other. For convenience they term him "monster."

The monster sits in the black library, his mind painting colors on the dark and a medieval air running in his head. He is considering the policeman.

Click of a switch and a low lamp comes on.

Now we can see Dr Lecter seated at a sixteenth-century refectory table in the Capponi Library. Behind him is a wall of pigeonholed manuscripts and great canvas-covered ledgers going back eight hundred years. A fourteenth-century correspondence with a minister of the Republic of Venice is stacked before him, weighted with a small casting Michelangelo did as a study for his horned Moses, and in front of the inkstand, a laptop computer with on-line research capability through the University of Milan.

Bright red and blue among the dun and yellow piles of parchment and vellum is a copy of the *National Tattler*. And beside it, the Florence edition of *La Nazione*.

Dr Lecter selects the Italian newspaper and reads its latest attack on Rinaldo Pazzi, prompted by an FBI disclaimer in the case of *Il Mostro*. "Our profile never matched Tocca," an FBI spokesman said.

La Nazione cited Pazzi's background and training in America, at the famous Quantico academy, and said he should have known better.

The case of *Il Mostro* did not interest Dr Lecter at all, but Pazzi's background did. How unfortunate that he should encounter a policeman trained at Quantico, where Hannibal Lecter was a textbook case.

When Dr Lecter looked into Rinaldo Pazzi's face at the Palazzo Vecchio, and stood close enough to smell him, he knew for certain that Pazzi suspected nothing, even though he had asked about the scar on Dr Lecter's hand. Pazzi did not even have any serious interest in him regarding the curator's disappearance.

The policeman saw him at the exposition of torture

instruments. Better to have encountered him at an orchid show.

Dr Lecter was well aware that all the elements of epiphany were present in the policeman's head, bouncing at random with the million other things he knew.

Should Rinaldo Pazzi join the late curator of the Palazzo Vecchio down in the damp? Should Pazzi's body be found after an apparent suicide? *La Nazione* would be pleased to have hounded him to death.

Not now, the monster reflected, and turned to his great rolls of vellum and parchment manuscripts.

Dr Lecter does not worry. He delighted in the writing style of Neri Capponi, banker and emissary to Venice in the fifteenth century, and read his letters, aloud from time to time, for his own pleasure late into the night.

BEFORE DAYLIGHT Pazzi had in his hands the photographs taken for Dr Fell's state work permit, attached with the negatives to his *permesso di soggiorno* in the files of the Carabinieri. Pazzi also had the excellent mug shots reproduced on Mason Verger's poster. The faces were similar in shape, but if Dr Fell was Dr Hannibal Lecter, some work had been done on the nose and cheeks, maybe collagen injections.

The cars looked promising. Like Alphonse Bertillon a hundred years before, Pazzi pored over the ears with his magnifying glass. They seemed to be the same.

On the Questura's outdated computer, he punched in his Interpol access code to the American FBI's Violent Criminal Apprehension Program and called up the voluminous Lecter file. He cursed his slow modem and tried to read the fuzzy text off the screen until the letters jumped in his vision. He knew most of the case. Two things made him catch his breath. One old and one new. The most recent update cited an X ray indicating Lecter probably had had surgery on his hand. The old item, a scan of a hand-printed Tennessee police report, noted that while he killed his guards in Memphis, Hannibal Lecter played a tape of the *Goldberg Variations*.

The poster circulated by the rich American victim, Mason Verger, dutifully encouraged an informant to call the FBI number provided. It gave the standard warning about Dr Lecter being armed and dangerous. A private telephone number was provided as well—just below the paragraph about the huge reward.

Airfare from Florence to Paris is ridiculously expensive and Pazzi had to pay it out of his own pocket. He did not trust the French police to give him a phone patch without meddling, and he knew no other way to get one. From an American Express phone cabin near the Opera, he telephoned the private number on Mason's poster. He assumed the call would be traced. Pazzi spoke English well enough, but he knew his accent would betray him as Italian.

The voice was male, American, very calm.

"Would you state your business please?"

"I may have information about Hannibal Lecter."

"Yes, well, thank you for calling. Do you know where he is now?"

"I believe so. Is the reward in effect?"

"Yes, it is. What hard evidence do you have that it's him? You have to understand we get a lot of crank calls."

"I'll tell you he's undergone plastic surgery on his face and had an operation on his left hand. He can still play the *Goldberg Variations*. He has Brazilian papers."

A pause. Then, "Why haven't you called the police? I'm required to encourage you to do that."

"Is the reward in effect in all circumstances?"

"The reward is for information leading to the arrest and conviction."

"Would the reward be payable in . . . special circumstances?"

"Do you mean a bounty on Dr Lecter? Say, in the case of someone who might not ordinarily be eligible to accept a reward?"

"Yes."

"We are both working toward the same goal. So stay on the telephone please, while I make a suggestion. It is against international convention and U.S. law to offer a bounty for someone's death, sir. Stay on the telephone please. May I ask if you're calling from Europe?"

"Yes, I am, and that's all I'm telling you."

"Good, hear me out—I suggest you contact an attorney to discuss legality of bounties and not to undertake any illegal action against Dr Lecter. May I recommend an attorney? There's one in Geneva who is excellent in these matters. May I give you the toll-free number? I encourage you strongly to call him and to be frank with him."

Pazzi bought a prepaid telephone card and made his next call from a booth in the Bon Marché department store. He spoke to a person with a dry Swiss voice. It took less than five minutes.

Mason would pay one million United States dollars for Dr Hannibal Lecter's head and hands. He would pay the same amount for information leading to arrest. He would privately pay three million dollars for the doctor alive, no questions asked, discretion guaranteed. The terms included one hundred thousand dollars in advance. To qualify for the advance, Pazzi would have to provide a positively identifiable fingerprint from Dr Lecter, the print *in situ* on an object. If he did that, he could see the rest of the cash in an escrowed safe deposit locker in Switzerland at his convenience.

Before he left Bon Marché for the airport, Pazzi bought a peignoir for his wife in peach silk moiré.

How DO you behave when you know the conventional
honors are dross? When you have come to believe with
Marcus Aurelius that the opinion of future generations
will be worth no more than the opinion of the current
one? Is it possible to behave well then? Desirable to
behave well then?

Now Rinaldo Pazzi, a Pazzi of the Pazzi, chief inspector of the Florentine Questura, had to decide what his
honor was worth, or if there is a wisdom longer than
considerations of honor.

He returned from Paris by dinnertime, and slept a
little while. He wanted to ask his wife, but he could
not, though he did take comfort in her. He lay awake
for a long time afterward, after her breathing was quiet.
Late in the night he gave up on sleep and went out to
walk and think.

Avarice is not unknown in Italy, and Rinaldo Pazzi
had imbibed plenty with his native air. But his natu-
ral acquisitiveness and ambition had been whetted in
America, where every influence is felt more quickly,

including the death of Jehovah and the incumbency of Mammon.

When Pazzi came out of the shadows of the Loggia and stood in the spot where Savonarola was burned in the Piazza Signoria, when he looked up at the window in the floodlit Palazzo Vecchio where his ancestor died, he believed that he was deliberating. He was not. He had already decided piecemeal.

We assign a moment to decision, to dignify the process as a timely result of rational and conscious thought. But decisions are made of kneaded feelings; they are more often a lump than a sum.

Pazzi had decided when he got on the plane to Paris. And he had decided an hour ago, after his wife in her new peignoir had been only dutifully receptive. And minutes later when, lying in the dark, he reached over to cup her cheek and give her a tender good night kiss, and he felt a tear beneath his palm. Then, unaware, she ate his heart.

Honors again? Another chance to endure the archbishop's breath while the holy flints were struck to the rocket in the cloth dove's ass? More praise from the politicians whose private lives he knew too well? What was it worth to be known as the policeman who caught Dr Hannibal Lecter? For a policeman, credit has a short half-life. Better to SELL HIM.

The thought pierced and pounded Rinaldo, left him pale and determined, and when the visual Rinaldo cast his lot he had two scents mixed in his mind, his wife and the Chesapeake shore.

SELL HIM. SELL HIM. SELL HIM. SELL HIM. SELL HIM. SELL HIM.

Francesco de' Pazzi did not stab harder in 1478 when he had Giuliano on the cathedral floor, when in his frenzy he stabbed himself through the thigh.

24

Dr Hannibal Lecter's fingerprint card is a curiosity and something of a cult object. The original is framed on the wall of the FBI's Identification Section. Following the FBI custom in printing people with more than five fingers, it has the thumb and four adjacent fingers on the front side of the card, and the sixth finger on the reverse.

Copies of the fingerprint card went around the earth when the doctor first escaped, and his thumbprint appears enlarged on Mason Verger's wanted poster with enough points marked on it for a minimally trained examiner to make a hit.

Simple fingerprinting is not a difficult skill and Pazzi could do a workmanlike job of lifting prints, and could make a coarse comparison to reassure himself. But Mason Verger required a fresh fingerprint, *in situ* and unlifted, for his experts to examine independently; Mason had been cheated before with old fingerprints lifted years ago at the scenes of Dr Lecter's early crimes.

But how to get Dr Fell's fingerprints without alerting him? Above all, he must not alarm the doctor. The man could disappear too well, and Pazzi would be left with nothing.

The doctor did not often leave the Palazzo Capponi, and it would be a month before the next meeting of the Belle Arti. Too long to wait to plant a water glass at his place, at all the places, as the committee never furnished such amenities.

Once he had decided to sell Hannibal Lecter to Mason Verger, Pazzi had to work alone. He could not afford to bring the attention of the Questura to Dr Fell by getting a warrant to enter the Palazzo, and the building was too well defended with alarms for him to break in and take fingerprints.

Dr Fell's refuse can was much cleaner and newer than the others on the block. Pazzi bought a new can and in the dead of night switched lids with the Palazzo Capponi can. The galvanized surface was not ideal and, in an all-night effort, Pazzi came out with a pointillist's nightmare of prints that he could never decipher.

The next morning he appeared red-eyed at the Ponte Vecchio. In a jewelry shop on the old bridge he bought a wide, highly polished silver bracelet and the velvet-covered stand that held it for display. In the artisan sector south of the Arno, in the narrow streets across from the Pitti Palace, he had another jeweler grind the maker's name off the bracelet. The jeweler offered to apply an antitarnish coating to the silver, but Pazzi said no.

* * *

Dread Sollicciano, the Florentine jail on the road to Prato.

On the second floor of the women's division, Romula Cjesku, leaning over a deep laundry sink, soaped her breasts, washing and drying carefully before she put on a clean, loose cotton shirt. Another Gypsy, returning from the visiting room, spoke in the Romany language to Romula in passing. A tiny line appeared between Romula's eyes. Her handsome face kept its usual solemn set.

She was allowed off the tier at the customary 8:30 A.M., but when she approached the visitor's room, a turnkey intercepted her and steered her aside to a private interview room on the prison's ground floor. Inside, instead of the usual nurse, Rinaldo Pazzi was holding her infant boy.

"Hello, Romula," he said.

She went straight up to the tall policeman and there was no question that he would hand over the child at once. The baby wanted to nurse and began to nuzzle at her.

Pazzi pointed with his chin at a screen in the corner of the room. "There's a chair back there. We can talk while you feed him."

"Talk about what, *Dottore*?" Romula's Italian was passable, as was her French, English, Spanish, and Romany. She spoke without affect—her best theatrics had not prevented this three-month term for picking pockets.

She went behind the screen. In a plastic bag concealed in the baby's swaddling clothes were forty cigarettes and sixty-five thousand lire, a little more than

169

forty-one dollars, in ragged notes. She had a choice to make here. If the policeman had frisked the baby, he could charge her when she took out the contraband and have all her privileges revoked. She deliberated a moment, looking up at the ceiling while the baby suckled. Why would he bother? He had the advantage anyway. She took out the bag and concealed it in her underwear. His voice came over the screen.

"You are a nuisance in here, Romula. Nursing mothers in jail are a waste of time. There are legitimately sick people in here for the nurses to take care of. Don't you hate to hand over your baby when the visiting time is up?"

What could he want? She knew who he was, all right—a chief, a *Pezzo da novanta*, bastard .90 caliber.

Romula's business was reading the street for a living, and pick-pocketing was a subset of that. She was a weathered thirty-five and she had antennae like the great luna moth. *This policeman*—she studied him over the screen—*look how neat, the wedding ring, the shined shoes, lived with his wife but had a good maid—his collar stays were put in after the collar was ironed. Wallet in the jacket pocket, keys in the right front trouser, money in the left front trouser folded flat probably with a rubber band around. His dick between. He was flat and masculine, a little cauliflower in the ear and a scar at the hairline from a blow. He wasn't going to ask her for sex—if that was the idea, he wouldn't have brought the baby. He was no prize, but she didn't think he would have to take sex from women in jail. Better not to look into his bitter black eyes while the baby was suckling. Why did he bring the baby? Because he wants her to see his power, suggest he could have it taken from her. What does he want? Information? She would tell him anything he wants to hear about fifteen Gypsies who never existed. All right, what can I get out of this? We'll see. Let's show him a bit of the brown.*

She watched his face as she came out from behind the screen, a crescent of aureole showing beside the baby's face.

"It's hot back there," she said. "Could you open a window?"

"I could do better than that, Romula. I could open the *door*, and you know it."

Quiet in the room. Outside the noise of Sollicciano like a constant, dull headache.

"Tell me what you want. I would do something gladly, but not anything." Her instinct told her, correctly, he would respect her for the caveat.

"It's only *la tua solita cosa*, the usual thing you do," Pazzi said, "but I want you to botch it."

171

DURING THE day, they watched the front of the Palazzo Capponi from the high shuttered window of an apartment across the street—Romula, and an older Gypsy woman who helped with the baby and may have been Romula's cousin, and Pazzi, who stole as much time as possible from his office.

The wooden arm that Romula used in her trade waited on a chair in the bedroom.

Pazzi had obtained the daytime use of the apartment from a teacher at the nearby Dante Alighieri School. Romula insisted on a shelf for herself and the baby in the small refrigerator.

They did not have to wait long.

At 9:30 A.M. on the second day, Romula's helper hissed from the window seat. A black void appeared across the street as one of the massive palazzo doors swung inward.

There he was, the man known in Florence as Dr Fell, small and slender in his dark clothing, sleek as a mink as he tested the air on the stoop and regarded the street in both directions. He clicked a remote control to set the alarms and pulled the door shut with its great wrought-iron handle, pitted with rust and impossible to print. He carried a shopping bag.

Seeing Dr Fell for the first time through the crack in the shutters, the older Gypsy gripped Romula's hand as though to stop her, looked Romula in the face and gave her head a quick sharp shake while the policeman was not looking.

Pazzi knew at once where he was going.

In Dr Fell's garbage, Pazzi had seen the distinctive wrapping papers from the fine food store, Vera dal 1926, on the Via San Jacopo near the Santa Trìnita Bridge. The doctor headed in that direction now as Romula shrugged into her costume and Pazzi watched out the window.

"*Dunque*, it's groceries," Pazzi said. He could not help repeating Romula's instructions for the fifth time. "Follow along, Romula. Wait this side of the Ponte Vecchio. You'll catch him coming back, carrying the full bag in his hand. I'll be half a block ahead of him, you'll see me first. I'll stay close by. If there's a problem, if you get arrested, I'll take care of it. If he goes someplace else, come back to the apartment. I'll call you. Put this pass in a taxi windshield and come to me."

"*Eminenza*," Romula said, elevating the honorifics in the Italian ironic style, "if there is a problem and someone else helps me, don't hurt him, my friend won't take anything, let him run."

Pazzi did not wait for the elevator, he raced down the stairs in a greasy boilersuit, wearing a cap. It is hard

173

to tail somebody in Florence because the sidewalks are narrow and your life is worth nothing in the street. Pazzi had a battered *motorino* at the curb with a bundle of a dozen brooms tied to it. The scooter started on the first kick and in a puff of blue smoke the chief investigator started down the cobbles, the little motorbike bouncing over the cobbles like a small burro trotting beneath him.

Pazzi dawdled, was honked at by the ferocious traffic, bought cigarettes, killed time to stay behind, until he was sure where Dr Fell was going. At the end of the Via de' Bardi, the Borgo San Jacopo was one-way coming toward him. Pazzi abandoned the bike on the sidewalk and followed on foot, turning his flat body sideways to slide through the crowd of tourists at the south end of the Ponte Vecchio.

Florentines say Vera dal 1926, with its wealth of cheeses and truffles, smells like the feet of God.

The doctor certainly took his time in there. He was making a selection from the first white truffles of the season. Pazzi could see his back through the windows, past the marvelous display of hams and pastas.

Pazzi went around the corner and came back, he washed his face in the fountain spewing water from its own mustachioed, lion-eared face. "You'd have to shave that to work for me," he said to the fountain over the cold ball of his stomach.

The doctor coming out now, a few light parcels in his bag. He started back down the Borgo San Jacopo toward home. Pazzi moved ahead on the other side of the street. The crowds on the narrow sidewalk forced Pazzi into the street, and the mirror of a passing Carabinieri patrol car banged painfully against his wristwatch. *"Stronzo! Analfabeta!"* the driver yelled out the window, and Pazzi vowed revenge. By the time he reached the Ponte Vecchio he had a forty-meter lead.

Romula was in a doorway, the baby cradled in her wooden arm, her other hand extended to the crowds, her free arm ready beneath her loose clothing to lift another wallet to add to the more than two hundred she had taken in her lifetime. On her concealed arm was the wide and well-polished silver bracelet.

In a moment the victim would pass through the throng coming off the old bridge. Just as he came out of the crowd onto the Via de' Bardi, Romula would meet him, do her business and slip into the stream of tourists crossing the bridge.

In the crowd, Romula had a friend she could depend on. She knew nothing of the victim and she did not trust the policeman to protect her. Giles Prevert, known on some police dossiers as Giles Dumain, or Roger LeDuc, but locally known as Gnocco, waited in the crowd at the south end of the Ponte Vecchio for Romula to make the dip. Gnocco was diminished by his habits and his face beginning to show the skull beneath, but he was still wiry and strong and well able to help Romula if the dip went sour.

In clerk's clothing, he was able to blend with the crowd, popping up from time to time as though the crowd were a prairie dog town. If the intended victim seized Romula and held her, Gnocco could trip, fall all over the victim and remain entangled with him, apologizing profusely until she was well away. He had done it before.

Pazzi passed her, stopped in a line of customers at a juice bar, where he could see.

Romula came out of the doorway. She judged with a practiced eye the sidewalk traffic between her and the slender figure coming toward her. She could move wonderfully well through a crowd with the baby in front of her, supported in her false arm of wood and canvas. All right. As usual she would kiss the fingers of her visible hand and reach for his face to put the kiss there. With her free hand, she would fumble at his ribs near his wallet until he caught her wrist. Then she would pull away from him.

Pazzi had promised that this man could not afford to hold her for the police, that he would want to get away from her. In all her attempts to pick a pocket, no one had ever offered violence to a woman holding a baby. The victim often thought it was someone else beside him fumbling in his jacket. Romula herself had denounced several innocent bystanders as pickpockets to avoid being caught.

Romula moved with the crowd on the sidewalk, freed her concealed arm, but kept it under the false arm cradling the baby. She could see the mark coming through the field of bobbing heads, ten meters and closing.

Madonna! Dr Fell was veering off in the thick of the crowd, going with the stream of tourists *over* the Ponte Vecchio. He was not going home. She pressed into the crowd, but could not get to him. Gnocco's face, still ahead of the doctor, looking to her, questioning. She shook her head and Gnocco let him pass. It would do no good if Gnocco picked his pocket.

Pazzi snarling beside her as though it were her fault. "Go to the apartment. I'll call you. You have the taxi pass for the old town? Go. *Go!*"

Pazzi retrieved his motorbike and pushed it across the Ponte Vecchio, over the Arno opaque as jade. He thought he had lost the doctor, but there he was, on the other side of the river under the arcade beside the Lungarno, peering for a moment over a sketch artist's shoulder, moving on with quick light strides. Pazzi guessed Dr Fell was going to the Church of Santa Croce, and followed at a distance through the hellish traffic.

THE CHURCH of Santa Croce, seat of the Franciscans, its vast interior ringing with eight languages as the hordes of tourists shuffle through, following the bright umbrellas of their guides, fumbling for two-hundred-lire pieces in the gloom so they can pay to light, for a precious minute in their lives, the great frescoes in the chapels.

Romula came in from the bright morning and had to pause near the tomb of Michelangelo while her dazzled eyes adjusted. When she could see that she was standing on a grave in the floor, she whispered, "*Mi dispiace!*" and moved quickly off the slab; to Romula the throng of dead beneath the floor was as real as the people above it, and perhaps more influential. She was daughter and granddaughter of spirit readers and palmists, and she saw the people above the floor, and the people below, as two crowds with the mortal pane between. The ones below, being smarter and older, had the advantage in her opinion.

She looked around for the sexton, a man deeply

prejudiced against Gypsies, and took refuge at the first pillar under the protection of Rossellino's "Madonna del Latte," while the baby nuzzled at her breast. Pazzi, lurking near Galileo's grave, found her there.

He pointed with his chin toward the back of the church where, across the transept, floodlights and forbidden cameras flashed like lightning through the vast high gloom as the clicking timers ate two-hundred-lire pieces and the occasional slug or Australian quarter.

Again and again Christ was born, betrayed, and the nails driven as the great frescoes appeared in brilliant light, and plunged again into a darkness close and crowded, the milling pilgrims holding guidebooks they cannot see, body odor and incense rising to cook in the heat of the lamps.

In the left transept, Dr Fell was at work in the Capponi Chapel. The glorious Capponi Chapel is in Santa Felicità. This one, redone in the nineteenth century, interested Dr Fell because he could look through the restoration into the past. He was making a charcoal rubbing of an inscription in stone so worn that even oblique lighting would not bring it up.

Watching through his little monocular, Pazzi discovered why the doctor had left his house with only his shopping bag—he kept his art supplies behind the chapel altar. For a moment, Pazzi considered calling off Romula and letting her go. Perhaps he could fingerprint the art materials. No, the doctor was wearing cotton gloves to keep the charcoal off his hands.

It would be awkward at best. Romula's technique was designed for the open street. But she was obvious, and the furthest thing from what a criminal would fear. She was the person least likely to make the doctor flee. No. If the doctor seized her, he would give her to the sexton and Pazzi could intervene later.

The man was insane. What if he killed her? What if he killed the baby? Pazzi asked himself two questions. Would he fight the doctor if the situation looked lethal? Yes. Was he willing to risk lesser injury to Romula and her child to get his money? Yes.

They would simply have to wait until Dr Fell took off the gloves to go to lunch. Drifting back and forth along the transept there was time for Pazzi and Romula to whisper. Pazzi spotted a face in the crowd.

"Who's following you, Romula? Better tell me. I've seen his face in the jail."

"My friend, just to block the way if I have to run. He doesn't know anything. Nothing. It's better for you. You don't have to get dirty."

To pass the time, they prayed in several chapels, Romula whispering in a language Rinaldo did not understand, and Pazzi with an extensive list to pray for, particularly the house on the Chesapeake shore and something else he shouldn't think about in church.

Sweet voices from the practicing choir, soaring over the general noise.

A bell, and it was time for the midday closing. Sextons came out, rattling their keys, ready to empty the coin boxes.

Dr Fell rose from his labors and came out from behind Andreotti's *Pietà* in the chapel, removed his gloves and put on his jacket. A large group of Japanese, crowded in the front of the sanctuary, their supply of coins exhausted, stood puzzled in the dark, not yet understanding that they had to leave.

Pazzi poked Romula quite unnecessarily. She knew the time had come. She kissed the top of the baby's head as it rested in her wooden arm.

The doctor was coming. The crowd would force him to pass close to her, and with three long strides she went to meet him, squared in front of him, held her hand up in his vision to attract his eye, kissed her fingers and got ready to put the kiss on his cheek, her concealed arm ready to make the dip.

Lights on as someone in the crowd found a two-hundred-lire piece and at the moment of touching Dr Fell she looked into his face, felt sucked to the red centers of his eyes, felt the huge cold vacuum pull her heart against her ribs and her hand flew away from his face to cover the baby's face and she heard her voice say "*Perdonami, perdonami, signore*," turning and fleeing as the doctor looked after her for a long moment, until the light went out and he was a silhouette again against candles in a chapel, and with quick, light strides he went on his way.

Pazzi, pale with anger, found Romula supporting herself on the font, bathing the baby's head repeatedly with holy water, bathing its eyes in case it had looked at Dr Fell. Bitter curses stopped in his mouth when he looked at her stricken face.

Her eyes were enormous in the gloom. "That is the Devil," she said. "Shaitan, Son of the Morning, I've seen him now."

"I'll drive you back to jail," Pazzi said.

Romula looked in the baby's face and sighed, a

slaughterhouse sigh, so deep and resigned it was terrible to hear. She took off the wide silver cuff and washed it in the holy water.

"Not yet," she said.

IF RINALDO Pazzi had decided to do his duty as an officer of the law, he could have detained Dr Fell and determined very quickly if the man was Hannibal Lecter. Within a half hour he could have obtained a warrant to take Dr Fell out of the Palazzo Capponi and all the palazzo's alarm systems would not have prevented him. On his own authority he could have held Dr Fell without charging him for long enough to determine his identity.

Fingerprinting at Questura headquarters would have revealed within ten minutes if Fell was Dr Lecter. PFLP DNA testing would confirm the identification.

All those resources were denied to Pazzi now. Once he decided to sell Dr Lecter, the policeman became a bounty hunter, outside the law and alone. Even the police snitches under his thumb were useless to him, because they would hasten to snitch on Pazzi himself.

The delays frustrated Pazzi, but he was determined. He would make do with these damned Gypsies . . .

"Would Gnocco do it for you, Romula? Can you

find him?" They were in the parlor of the borrowed apartment on the Via de' Bardi, across from the Palazzo Capponi, twelve hours after the debacle in the Church of Santa Croce. A low table lamp lit the room to waist height. Above the light, Pazzi's black eyes glittered in the semi-dark.

"I'll do it myself, but not with the baby," Romula said. "But you have to give me—"

"No. I can't let him see you twice. Would Gnocco do it for you?"

Romula sat bent over in her long bright dress, her full breasts touching her thighs, with her head almost to her knees. The wooden arm lay empty on a chair. In the corner sat the older woman, possibly Romula's cousin, holding the baby. The drapes were drawn. Peering around them through the smallest crack, Pazzi could see a faint light, high in the Palazzo Capponi.

"I can do this, I can change my look until he would not know me. I can—"

"No."

"Then Esmeralda can do it."

"No." This voice from the corner, the older woman speaking for the first time. "I'll care for your baby, Romula, until I die. I will never touch Shaitan." Her Italian was barely intelligible to Pazzi.

"Sit up, Romula," Pazzi said. "*Look* at me. Would Gnocco do it for you? Romula, you're going back to Sollicciano tonight. You have three more months to serve. It's possible that the next time you get your money and cigarettes out of the baby's clothes you'll be caught . . . I could get you six months additional for that last time you did it. I could easily have you

184

declared an unfit mother. The state would take the baby. But if I get the fingerprints, you get released, you get two million lire and your record disappears, and I help you with Australian visas. Would Gnocco do it for you?"

She did not answer.

"Could you find Gnocco?" Pazzi snorted air through his nose. "*Senti*, get your things together, you can pick up your fake arm at the property room in three months, or sometime next year. The baby will have to go to the foundling hospital. The old woman can call on it there."

"*IT?* Call on *IT, Commendatore*? His name is—" She shook her head, not wanting to say the child's name to this man. Romula covered her face with her hands, feeling the two pulses in her face and hands beat against each other, and then she spoke from behind her hands. "I can find him."

"Where?"

"Piazza Santo Spirito, near the fountain. They build a fire and somebody will have wine."

"I'll come with you."

"Better not," she said. "You'd ruin his reputation. You'll have Esmeralda and the baby here—you know I'll come back."

The Piazza Santo Spirito, an attractive square on the left bank of the Arno gone seedy at night, the church dark and locked at that late hour, noise and steamy food smells from Casalinga, the popular trattoria.

Near the fountain, the flicker of a small fire and the

sound of a Gypsy guitar, played with more enthusiasm than talent. There is one good *fado* singer in the crowd. Once the singer is discovered, he is shoved forward and lubricated with wine from several bottles. He begins with a song about fate, but is interrupted with demands for a livelier tune.

Roger LeDuc, also known as Gnocco, sits on the edge of the fountain. He has smoked something. His eyes are hazed, but he spots Romula at once, at the back of the crowd across the firelight. He buys two oranges from a vendor and follows her away from the singing. They stop beneath a streetlamp away from the fire. Here the light is colder than firelight and dappled by the leaves left on a struggling maple. The light is greenish on Gnocco's pallor, the shadows of the leaves like moving bruises on his face as Romula looks at him, her hand on his arm.

A blade flicks out of his fist like a bright little tongue and he peels the oranges, the rind hanging down in one long piece. He gives her the first one and she puts a section in his mouth as he peels the second.

They spoke briefly in Romany. Once he shrugged. She gave him a cell phone and showed him the buttons. Then Pazzi's voice was in Gnocco's ear. After a moment, Gnocco folded the telephone and put it in his pocket.

Romula took something on a chain off her neck, kissed the little amulet and hung it around the neck of the small, scruffy man. He looked down at it, danced a little, pretending that the holy image burned him, and got a small smile from Romula. She took off the wide bracelet and put it on his arm. It fit easily. Gnocco's arm was no bigger than hers.

"Can you be with me an hour?" Gnocco asked her.

"Yes," she said.

28

NIGHT AGAIN and Dr Fell in the vast stone room of the Atrocious Torture Instruments show at Forte di Belvedere, the doctor leaning at ease against the wall beneath the hanging cages of the damned.

He is registering aspects of damnation from the avid faces of the voyeurs as they press around the torture instruments and press against each other in steamy, goggle-eyed *frottage*, hair rising on their forearms, breath hot on one another's neck and cheeks. Sometimes the doctor presses a scented handkerchief to his face against an overdose of cologne and rut.

Those who pursue the doctor wait outside.

Hours pass. Dr Fell, who has never paid more than passing attention to the exhibits themselves, cannot seem to get enough of the crowd. A few feel his attention, and become uncomfortable. Often women in the crowd look at him with particular interest before the shuffling movement of the line through the exhibit forces them to move on. A pittance paid to the two taxidermists operating the show enables the doctor to lounge at his ease, untouchable behind the ropes, very still against the stone.

Outside the exit, waiting on the parapet in a steady drizzle, Rinaldo Pazzi kept his vigil. He was used to waiting.

Pazzi knew the doctor would not be walking home. Down the hill behind the fort, in a small piazza, Dr Fell's automobile awaited him. It was a black Jaguar Saloon, an elegant thirty-year-old Mark II glistening in the drizzle, the best one that Pazzi had ever seen, and it carried Swiss plates. Clearly Dr Fell did not need to work for a salary. Pazzi noted the plate numbers, but could not risk running them through Interpol.

On the steep cobbled Via San Leonardo between the Forte di Belvedere and the car, Gnocco waited. The ill-lit street was bounded on both sides by high stone walls protecting the villas behind them. Gnocco had found a dark niche in front of a barred gateway where he could stand out of the stream of tourists coming down from the fort. Every ten minutes the cell phone in his pocket vibrated against his thigh and he had to affirm he was in position.

Some of the tourists held maps and programs over their heads against the fine rain as they came by, the narrow sidewalk full, and people spilling over into the street, slowing the few taxis coming down from the fort.

In the vaulted chamber of torture instruments, Dr Fell at last stood away from the wall where he had leaned, rolled his eyes up at the skeleton in the starvation cage above him as though they shared a secret and made his way through the crowd toward the exit.

Pazzi saw him framed in the doorway, and again under a floodlight on the grounds. He followed at a distance. When he was sure the doctor was walking down to his car, he flipped open his cell phone and alerted Gnocco.

The Gypsy's head came up out of his collar like that of a tortoise, eyes sunken, showing, as a tortoise shows, the skull beneath the skin. He rolled his sleeve above the elbow and spit on the bracelet, wiping it dry with a rag. Now that the silver was polished with spit and holy water, he held his arm behind him under his coat to keep it dry as he peered up the hill. A column of bobbing heads was coming. Gnocco pushed through the stream of people out into the street, where he could go against the current and could see better. With no assistant, he would have to do both the bump and the dip himself—not a problem since he wanted to fail at making the dip. There the slight man came—near the curb, thank God. Pazzi was thirty meters behind the doctor, coming down.

Gnocco made a nifty move from the middle of the street. Taking advantage of a coming taxi, skipping as though to get out of the traffic, he looked back to curse the driver and bumped bellies with Dr Fell, his fingers scrambling inside the doctor's coat, and felt his arm seized in a terrific grip, felt a blow, and twisted away, free of the mark, Dr Fell hardly pausing in his stride and gone in the stream of tourists, Gnocco free and away.

Pazzi was with him almost instantly, beside him in the niche before the iron gate, Gnocco bent over briefly, straightening up, breathing hard.

"I got it. He grabbed me right. *Cornuto* tried to hit me in the balls, but he missed," Gnocco said.

Pazzi on one knee carefully working the bracelet off Gnocco's arm, when Gnocco felt hot and wet down his leg and, as he shifted his body, a hot stream of arterial blood shot out of a rent in the front of his trousers, onto Pazzi's face and hands as he tried to remove the bracelet holding it only by the edges. Blood spraying everywhere, into Gnocco's own face as he bent to look at himself, his legs caving in. He collapsed against the gate, clung to it with one hand and jammed his rag against the juncture of his leg and body trying to stop the gouting blood from his split femoral artery.

Pazzi, with the freezing feeling he always had in action, got his arm around Gnocco and kept him turned away from the crowd, kept him spraying through the bars of the gate, eased him to the ground on his side.

Pazzi took his cell phone from his pocket and spoke into it as though calling an ambulance, but did not turn the telephone on. He unbuttoned his coat and spread it like a hawk mantling its prey. The crowd was moving, incurious behind him. Pazzi got the bracelet off Gnocco and slipped it into the small box he carried. He put Gnocco's cell phone in his pocket.

Gnocco's lips moved. "Madonna, *che freddo*."

With an effort of will, Pazzi moved Gnocco's failing hand from the wound, held it as though to comfort him, and let him bleed out. When he was sure Gnocco was dead, Pazzi left him lying beside the gate, his head resting on his arm as though he slept, and stepped into the moving crowd.

In the piazza, Pazzi stared at the empty parking place,

the rain just beginning to wet the cobbles where Dr Lecter's Jaguar had stood.

Dr Lecter—Pazzi no longer thought of him as Dr Fell. He was Dr Hannibal Lecter.

Proof enough for Mason could be in the pocket of Pazzi's raincoat. Proof enough for Pazzi dripped off his raincoat onto his shoes.

THE MORNING star over Genoa was dimmed by the lightening east when Rinaldo Pazzi's old Alfa purred down to the dock. A chilly wind riffled the harbor. On a freighter at an outer mooring someone was welding, orange sparks showering into the black water.

Romula stayed in the car out of the wind with the baby in her lap. Esmeralda was scrunched in the small backseat of the *berlinetta* coupe with her legs sideways. She had not spoken again since she refused to touch Shaitan.

They had thick black coffee in paper cups and *pasticcini*.

Rinaldo Pazzi went into the shipping office. By the time he came out again the sun was well risen, glowing orange on the rust-streaked hull of the freighter *Astra Philogenes*, completing its loading at dockside. He beckoned to the women in the car.

The *Astra Philogenes*, twenty-seven thousand tons, Greek registry, could legally carry twelve passengers without a ship's doctor on its route to Rio. There,

Pazzi explained to Romula, they would transship to Sydney, Australia, the transshipment supervised by the *Astra* purser. Passage was fully paid and emphatically nonrefundable. In Italy, Australia is considered an attractive alternative where jobs can be found, and it has a large Gypsy population.

Pazzi had promised Romula two million lire, about twelve hundred and fifty dollars at the current rate of exchange, and he gave it to her in a fat envelope.

The Gypsies' baggage amounted to very little, a small valise and Romula's wooden arm packed in a French horn case.

The Gypsies would be at sea and incommunicado for most of the next month.

Gnocco is coming, Pazzi told Romula for the tenth time, but he could not come today. Gnocco would leave word for them general delivery at the Sydney main post office. "I'll keep my promise to him, just as I did to you," he told them as they stood together at the foot of the gangway, the early sun sending their long shadows down the rough surface of the dock.

At the moment of parting, with Romula and the baby already climbing the gangway, the old woman spoke for the second and last time in Pazzi's experience.

With eyes as black as Kalamata olives she looked into his face. "You gave Gnocco to Shaitan," she said quietly. "Gnocco is dead." Bending stiffly, as she would bend to a chicken on the block, Esmeralda spit carefully on Pazzi's shadow, and hurried up the gangway after Romula and the child.

CHAPTER

30

THE DHL Express delivery box was well made. The fingerprint technician, sitting at a table under hot lights in the seating area of Mason's room, carefully backed out the screws with an electric screwdriver.

The broad silver bracelet was held on a velvet jeweler's stand braced within the box so the outer surfaces of the bracelet touched nothing.

"Bring it over here," Mason said.

Fingerprinting the bracelet would have been much easier at Baltimore Police Department's Identification Section, where the technician worked during the day, but Mason was paying a very high and private fee in cash, and he insisted the work be done before his eyes. Or before his eye, the technician reflected sourly as he placed the bracelet, stand and all, on a china plate held by a male attendant.

The attendant held the plate in front of Mason's goggle. He could not set it down on the coil of hair over Mason's heart, because the respirator moved his chest constantly, up and down.

The heavy bracelet was streaked and crusted with blood, and flecks of dried blood fell from it onto the china plate. Mason regarded it with his goggled eye. Lacking any facial flesh, he had no expression, but his eye was bright.

"Dust it," he said.

The technician had a copy of the prints off the front of Dr Lecter's FBI fingerprint card. The sixth print on the back and the identification were not reproduced.

He dusted between the crusts of blood. The Dragon's Blood fingerprint powder he preferred was too close in color to the dried blood on the bracelet, so he went to black, dusting carefully.

"We got prints," he said, stopping to mop his head under the hot lights of the seating area. The light was good for photography and he took pictures of the prints *in situ* before he lifted them for microscopic comparison. "Middle finger and thumb of the left hand, sixteen-point match—it would hold up in court," he said at last. "No question, it's the same guy."

Mason was not interested in court. His pale hand was already crawling across the counterpane to the telephone.

SUNNY MORNING in a mountain pasture deep in the Gennargentu Mountains of central Sardinia.

Six men, four Sardinians and two Romans, work beneath an airy shed built of timbers cut from the surrounding forest. Small sounds they make seem magnified in the vast silence of the mountains.

Beneath the shed, hanging from rafters with their bark still peeling, is a huge mirror in a gilt rococo frame. The mirror is suspended over a sturdy livestock pen with two gates, one opening into the pasture. The other gate is built like a Dutch door, so the top and bottom halves can be opened separately. The area beneath the Dutch gate is paved with cement, but the rest of the pen is strewn with clean straw in the manner of an executioner's scaffold.

The mirror, its frame carved with cherubs, can be tilted to provide an overhead view of the pen, as a cooking-school mirror provides the pupils with an overhead view of the stove.

The filmmaker, Oreste Pini, and Mason's Sardinian

foreman, a professional kidnapper named Carlo, disliked each other from the beginning.

Carlo Deogracias was a stocky, florid man in an alpine hat with a boar bristle in the band. He had the habit of chewing the gristle off a pair of stag's teeth he kept in the pocket of his vest.

Carlo was a leading practitioner of the ancient Sardinian profession of kidnapping, and a professional revenger as well.

If you have to be kidnapped for ransom, wealthy Italians will tell you, it's better to fall into the hands of the Sards. At least they are professional and won't kill you by accident or in a panic. If your relatives pay, you might be returned unharmed, unraped and unmutilated. If they don't pay, your relatives can expect to receive you piecemeal in the mail.

Carlo was not pleased with Mason's elaborate arrangements. He was experienced in this field and had actually fed a man to the pigs in Tuscany twenty years before— a retired Nazi and bogus count who imposed sexual relations on Tuscan village children, girls and boys alike. Carlo was engaged for the job and took the man out of his own garden within three miles of the Badia di Passignano and fed him to five large domestic swine on a farm below the Poggio alle Corti, though he had to withhold rations from the pigs for three days, the Nazi struggling against his bonds, pleading and sweating with his feet in the pen, and still the swine were shy about starting on his writhing toes until Carlo, with a guilty twinge at violating the letter of his agreement, fed the Nazi a tasty salad of the pigs' favorite greens and then cut his throat to accommodate them.

Carlo was cheerful and energetic in nature, but the presence of the filmmaker annoyed him—Carlo had taken the mirror from a brothel he owned in Cagliari, on Mason Verger's orders, just to accommodate this pornographer, Oreste Pini.

The mirror was a boon to Oreste, who had used mirrors as a favorite device in his pornographic films and in the single genuine snuff movie he made in Mauritania. Inspired by the admonition printed on his auto mirror, he pioneered the use of warped reflections to make some objects seem larger than they appear to the unaided eye.

Oreste must use a two-camera setup with good sound, as Mason dictated, and he must get it right the first time. Mason wanted a running, uninterrupted close-up of the face, aside from everything else.

To Carlo, he seemed to fiddle endlessly.

"You can stand there jabbering at me like a woman, or you can watch the practice and ask me whatever you can't understand," Carlo told him.

"I want to *film* the practice."

"*Va bene.* Get your shit set up and let's get on with it."

While Oreste placed his cameras, Carlo and the three silent Sardinians with him made their preparations.

Oreste, who loved money, was ever amazed at what money will buy.

At a long trestle table at one side of the shed, Carlo's brother, Matteo, unpacked a bundle of used clothing. He selected from the pile a shirt and trousers, while the other two Sardinians, the brothers Piero and Tommaso Falcione, rolled an ambulance gurney into the shed,

199

pushing it slowly over the grass. The gurney was stained and battered.

Matteo had ready several buckets of ground meat, a number of dead chickens still in their feathers and some spoiled fruit, already attracting flies, and a bucket of beef tripe and intestines.

Matteo laid out a pair of worn khaki trousers on the gurney and began to stuff them with a couple of chickens and some meat and fruit. Then he took a pair of cotton gloves and filled them with ground meat and acorns, stuffing each finger carefully, and placed them at the ends of the trouser legs. He selected a shirt for his ensemble and spread it on the gurney, filling it with tripe and intestines, and improving the contours with bread, before he buttoned the shirt and tucked the tail neatly into the trousers. A pair of stuffed gloves went at the ends of the sleeves. The melon he used for a head was covered with a hairnet, stuffed with ground meat where the face would be along with two boiled eggs for eyes. When he had finished, the result looked like a lumpy mannequin, looked better on the gurney than some jumpers look when they are rolled away. As a final touch, Matteo sprayed some extremely expensive aftershave on the front of the melon and on the gloves at the ends of the sleeves.

Carlo pointed with his chin at Oreste's slender assistant leaning over the fence, extending the boom mike over the pen, measuring its reach.

"Tell your fuckboy, if he falls in, I'm not going in after him."

At last all was ready. Piero and Tommaso dropped

the gurney to its low position with the legs folded and rolled it to the gate of the pen.

Carlo brought a tape recorder from the house and a separate amplifier. He had a number of tapes, some of which he had made himself while cutting the ears off kidnap victims to mail to the relatives. Carlo always played the tapes for the animals while they ate. He would not need the tapes when he had an actual victim to provide the screams.

Two weathered outdoor speakers were nailed to the posts beneath the shed. The sun was bright on the pleasant meadow sloping down to the woods. The sturdy fence around the meadow continued into the forest. In the midday hush Oreste could hear a carpenter bee buzzing under the shed roof.

"Are you ready?" Carlo said.

Oreste turned on the fixed camera himself. "*Giriamo*," he called to his cameraman.

"*Pronti!*" came the reply.

"*Motore!*" The cameras were rolling.

"*Partito!*" Sound was rolling with the film.

"*Azione!*" Oreste poked Carlo.

The Sard pushed the play button on his tape machine and a hellish screaming started, sobbing, pleading. The cameraman jerked at the sound, then steadied himself. The screaming was awful to hear, but a fitting overture for the faces that came out of the woods, drawn to the screams announcing dinner.

ROUND-TRIP to Geneva in a day, to see the money.

The commuter plane to Milan, a whistling Aerospatiale prop jet, climbed out of Florence in the early morning, swinging over the vineyards with their rows wide apart like a developer's coarse model of Tuscany. Something was wrong in the colors of the landscape—the new swimming pools beside the villas of the wealthy foreigners were the wrong blue. To Pazzi, looking out the window of the airplane, the pools were the milky blue of an aged English eye, a blue out of place among the dark cypresses and the silver olive trees.

Rinaldo Pazzi's spirits climbed with the airplane, knowing in his heart that he would not grow old here, dependent on the whim of his police superiors, trying to last in order to get his pension.

He had been terribly afraid that Dr Lecter would disappear after killing Gnocco. When Pazzi spotted Lecter's work lamp again in Santa Croce, he felt something like salvation; the doctor believed that he was safe.

The death of the Gypsy caused no ripple at all in the calm of the Questura and was believed drug-related— fortunately there were discarded syringes on the ground around him, a common sight in Florence, where syringes were available for free.

Going to see the money. Pazzi had insisted on it.

The visual Rinaldo Pazzi remembered sights completely: the first time he ever saw his penis erect, the first time he saw his own blood, the first woman he ever saw naked, the blur of the first fist coming to strike him. He remembered wandering casually into a side chapel of a Sienese church and looking into the face of St Catherine of Siena unexpectedly, her mummified head in its immaculate white wimple resting in a reliquary shaped like a church.

Seeing three million U.S. dollars had the same impact on him.

Three hundred banded blocks of hundred-dollar bills in nonsequential serial numbers.

In a severe little room, like a chapel, in the Geneva Crédit Suisse, Mason Verger's lawyer showed Rinaldo Pazzi the money. It was wheeled in from the vault in four deep lock boxes with brass number plates. The Crédit Suisse also provided a counting machine, a scale and a clerk to operate them. Pazzi dismissed the clerk. He put his hands on top of the money once.

Rinaldo Pazzi was a very competent investigator. He had spotted and arrested scam artists for twenty years. Standing in the presence of this money, listening to the arrangements, he detected no false note; if he gave them Hannibal Lecter, Mason would give him the money.

In a hot sweet rush Pazzi realized that these people

were not fooling around—Mason Verger would actually pay him. And he had no illusions about Lecter's fate. He was selling the man into torture and death. To Pazzi's credit, he acknowledged to himself what he was doing.

Our freedom is worth more than the monster's life. Our happiness is more important than his suffering, he thought with the cold egoism of the damned. Whether the "our" was magisterial or stood for Rinaldo and his wife is a difficult question, and there may not be a single answer.

In this room, scrubbed and Swiss, neat as a wimple, Pazzi took the final vow. He turned from the money and nodded to the lawyer, Mr Konie. From the first box, the lawyer counted out one hundred thousand dollars and handed it to Pazzi.

Mr Konie spoke briefly into a telephone and handed the receiver to Pazzi. "This is a land line, encrypted," he said.

The American voice Pazzi heard had a peculiar rhythm, words rushed into a single breath with a pause between, and the plosives were lost. The sound of it made Pazzi slightly dizzy, as though he were straining for breath along with the speaker.

Without preamble, the question: "Where is Dr Lecter?"

Pazzi, the money in one hand and the phone in the other, did not hesitate. "He is the one who studies the Palazzo Capponi in Florence. He is the . . . curator."

"Would you please show your identification to Mr Konie and hand him the telephone. He won't say your name into the telephone."

Mr Konie consulted a list from his pocket and said

some prearranged code words to Mason, then he handed the phone back to Pazzi.

"You get the rest of the money when he is alive in our hands," Mason said. "You don't have to seize the doctor yourself, but you've got to identify him to us and put him in our hands. I want your documentation as well, everything you've got on him. You'll be back in Florence tonight? You'll get instructions tonight for a meeting near Florence. The meeting will be no later than tomorrow night. There you'll get instructions from the man who will take Dr Lecter. He'll ask you if you know a florist. Tell him all florists are thieves. Do you understand me? I want you to cooperate with him."

"I don't want Dr Lecter in my . . . I don't want him near Florence when . . ."

"I understand your concern. Don't worry, he won't be."

The line went dead.

In a few minutes' paperwork, two million dollars was placed in escrow. Mason Verger could not get it back, but he could release it for Pazzi to claim. A Crédit Suisse official summoned to the meeting room informed Pazzi the bank would charge him a negative interest to facilitate a deposit there if he converted to Swiss francs, and pay three percent compound interest only on the first hundred thousand francs. The official presented Pazzi with a copy of Article 47 of the *Bundesgesetz über Banken und Sparkassen* governing bank secrecy and agreed to perform a wire transfer to the Royal Bank of Nova Scotia or to the Cayman Islands immediately after the release of the funds, if that was Pazzi's wish.

With a notary present, Pazzi granted alternate signature power over the account to his wife in the event of his death. The business concluded, only the Swiss bank official offered to shake hands. Pazzi and Mr Konie did not look at each other directly, though Mr Konie offered a good-bye from the door.

The last leg home, the commuter plane from Milan dodging through a thunderstorm, the propeller on Pazzi's side of the aircraft a dark circle against the dark gray sky. Lightning and thunder as they swung over the old city, the campanile and dome of the cathedral beneath them now, lights coming on in the early dusk, a flash and boom like the ones Pazzi remembered from his childhood when the Germans blew up the bridges over the Arno, sparing only the Ponte Vecchio. And for a flash as short as lightning he remembered seeing as a little boy a captured sniper chained to the Madonna of Chains to pray before he was shot.

Descending through the ozone smell of lightning, feeling the booms of thunder in the fabric of the plane, Pazzi of the ancient Pazzi returned to his ancient city with his aims as old as time.

CHAPTER

33

RINALDO PAZZI would have preferred to maintain constant surveillance on his prize in the Palazzo Capponi,
but he could not.

Instead Pazzi, still rapt from the sight of the money,
had to leap into his dinner clothes and meet his wife
at a long-anticipated concert of the Florence Chamber
Orchestra.

The Teatro Piccolomini, a nineteenth-century half-
scale copy of Venice's glorious Teatro La Fenice, is a
baroque jewel box of gilt and plush, with cherubs flouting
the laws of aerodynamics across its splendid ceiling.

A good thing, too, that the theater is beautiful because
the performers often need all the help they can get.

It is unfair but inevitable that music in Florence
should be judged by the hopelessly high standards
of the city's art. The Florentines are a large and
knowledgeable group of music lovers, typical of Italy,
but they are sometimes starved for musical artists.

Pazzi slipped into the seat beside his wife in the
applause following the overture.

She gave him her fragrant cheek. He felt his heart grow big inside him looking at her in her evening gown, sufficiently décolleté to emit a warm fragrance from her cleavage, her musical score in the chic Gucci cover Pazzi had given her.

"They sound a hundred percent better with the new viola player," she breathed into Pazzi's ear. This excellent *viola da gamba* player had been brought in to replace an infuriatingly inept one, a cousin of Sogliato's, who had gone oddly missing some weeks before.

Dr Hannibal Lecter looked down from a high box, alone, immaculate in white tie, his face and shirtfront seeming to float in the dark box framed by gilt baroque carving.

Pazzi spotted him when the lights went up briefly after the first movement, and in the moment before Pazzi could look away, the doctor's head came round like that of an owl and their eyes met. Pazzi involuntarily squeezed his wife's hand hard enough for her to look round at him. After that Pazzi kept his eyes resolutely on the stage, the back of his hand warm against his wife's thigh as she held his hand in hers.

At intermission, when Pazzi turned from the bar to hand her a drink, Dr Lecter was standing beside her.

"Good evening, Dr Fell," Pazzi said.

"Good evening, *Commendatore*," the doctor said. He waited with a slight inclination of the head, until Pazzi had to make the introduction.

"Laura, allow me to present Dr Fell. Doctor, this is Signora Pazzi, my wife."

Signora Pazzi, accustomed to being praised for her beauty, found what followed curiously charming, though her husband did not.

"Thank you for this privilege, *Commendatore*," the doctor said. His red and pointed tongue appeared for an instant before he bent over Signora Pazzi's hand, his lips perhaps closer to the skin than is customary in Florence, certainly close enough for her to feel his breath on her skin.

His eyes rose to her before his sleek head lifted.

"I think you particularly enjoy Scarlatti, Signora Pazzi."

"Yes, I do."

"It was pleasant to see you following the score. Hardly anyone does it anymore. I hoped that this might interest you." He took a portfolio from under his arm. It was an antique score on parchment, hand-copied. "This is from the Teatro Capranica in Rome, from 1688, the year the piece was written."

"*Meraviglioso!* Look at this, Rinaldo!"

"I marked in overlay some of the differences from the modern score as the first movement went along," Dr Lecter said. "It might amuse you to follow along in the second. Please, take it. I can always retrieve it from Signor Pazzi—is that permissible, *Commendatore?*"

The doctor looking deeply, deeply as Pazzi replied.

"If it would please you, Laura," Pazzi said. A beat of thought. "Will you be addressing the Studiolo, Doctor?"

"Yes, Friday night in fact. Soglioto can't wait to see me discredited."

"I have to be in the old city," Pazzi said. "I'll return

the score then. Laura, Dr Fell has to sing for his supper before the dragons at the Studiolo."

"I'm sure you'll sing *very* well, Doctor," she said, giving him her great dark eyes—within the bounds of propriety, but just.

Dr Lecter smiled, with his small white teeth. "Madame, if I manufactured Fleur du Ciel, I would offer you the Cape Diamond to wear it. Until Friday night, *Commendatore*."

Pazzi made sure the doctor returned to his box, and did not look at him again until they waved good night at a distance on the theater steps.

"I gave you that Fleur du Ciel for your birthday," Pazzi said.

"Yes, and I love it, Rinaldo," Signora Pazzi said. "You have the most marvellous taste."

34

IMPRUNETA IS an ancient Tuscan town where the roof tiles of the Duomo were made. Its cemetery is visible at night from the hilltop villas for miles around because of the lamps forever burning at the graves. The ambient light is low, but enough for visitors to make their way among the dead, though a flashlight is needed to read the epitaphs.

Rinaldo Pazzi arrived at five minutes to nine with a small bouquet of flowers he planned to place on a grave at random. He walked slowly along a gravel path between the tombs.

He felt Carlo's presence, though he did not see him.

Carlo spoke from the other side of a mausoleum more than head high. "Do you know a good florist in the town?"

The man sounded like a Sard. Good, maybe he knew what he was doing.

"Florists are all thieves," Pazzi replied.

Carlo came briskly around the marble structure without peeking.

211

He looked feral to Pazzi, short and round and powerful, nimble in his extremities. His vest was leather and he had a boar bristle in his hat. Pazzi guessed he had three inches reach advantage on Carlo and four inches of height. They weighed about the same, he guessed. Carlo was missing a thumb. Pazzi figured he could find him in the Questura's records with about five minutes' work. Both men were lit from beneath by the grave lamps.

"His house has good alarms," Pazzi said.

"I looked at it. You have to point him out to me."

"He has to speak at a meeting tomorrow night, Friday night. Can you do it that soon?"

"It's good." Carlo wanted to bully the policeman a little, establish his control. "Will you walk with him, or are you afraid of him? You'll do what you're paid to do. You'll point him out to me."

"Watch your mouth. I'll do what I'm paid to do and so will you. Or you can pass your retirement as a fuckboy at Volterra, suit yourself."

Carlo at work was as impervious to insult as he was to cries of pain. He saw that he had misjudged the policeman. He spread his hands. "Tell me what I need to know." Carlo moved to stand beside Pazzi as though they mourned together at the small mausoleum. A couple passed on the path holding hands. Carlo removed his hat and the two men stood with bowed heads. Pazzi put his flowers at the door of the tomb. A smell came from Carlo's warm hat, a rank smell, like sausage from an animal improperly gelded.

Pazzi raised his face from the odor. "He's fast with his knife. Goes low with it."

"Has he got a gun?"

"I don't know. He's never used one, that I know of."

"I don't want to have to take him out of a car. I want him on the open street with not many people around."

"How will you take him down?"

"That's my business." Carlo put a stag's tooth in his mouth and chewed at the gristle, protruding the tooth between his lips from time to time.

"It's my business too," Pazzi said. "How will you do it?"

"Stun him with a beanbag gun, net him, then I can give him a shot. I need to check his teeth fast in case he's got poison under a tooth cap."

"He has to lecture at a meeting. It starts at seven in the Palazzo Vecchio. If he works in the Capponi Chapel at Santa Croce on Friday, he'll walk from there to the Palazzo Vecchio. Do you know Florence?"

"I know it well. Can you get me a vehicle pass for the old city?"

"Yes."

"I won't take him out of the church," Carlo said.

Pazzi nodded. "Better he shows up for the meeting, then he probably won't be missed for two weeks. I have a reason to walk with him to the Palazzo Capponi after the meeting—"

"I don't want to take him in his house. That's his ground. He knows it and I don't. He'll be alert, he'll look around him at the door. I want him on the open sidewalk."

"Listen to me then—we'll come out the front entrance of the Palazzo Vecchio, the Via dei Leoni side will be closed. We'll go along the Via Neri and come across the river on the Ponte alle Grazie. There are trees in front of the Museo Bardini on the other side that block the streetlights. It's quiet at that hour when school is out."

"We'll say in front of the Museo Bardini then, but I may do it sooner if I see a chance, closer to the palazzo, or earlier in the day if he spooks and tries to run. We may be in an ambulance. Stay with him until the beanbag hits him and then get away from him fast."

"I want him out of Tuscany before anything happens to him."

"Believe me, he'll be gone from the face of the earth, *feet first*," Carlo said, smiling at his private joke, sticking the stag's tooth out through the smile.

FRIDAY MORNING. A small room in the attic of the Palazzo Capponi. Three of the whitewashed walls are bare. On the fourth wall hangs a large thirteenth-century Madonna of the Cimabue school, enormous in the little room, her head bent at the signature angle like that of a curious bird, and her almond eyes regarding a small figure asleep beneath the painting.

Dr Hannibal Lecter, veteran of prison and asylum cots, lies still on this narrow bed, his hands on his chest.

His eyes open and he is suddenly, completely awake, his dream of his sister Mischa, long dead and digested, running seamlessly into this present waking: danger then, danger now.

Knowing he is in danger did not disturb his sleep any more than killing the pickpocket did.

Dressed for his day now, lean and perfectly groomed in his dark silk suit, he turns off the motion sensors at the top of the servants' stairs and comes down into the great spaces of the palazzo.

Now he is free to move through the vast silence of the palace's many rooms, always a heady freedom to him after so many years of confinement in a basement cell.

Just as the frescoed walls of Santa Croce or the Palazzo Vecchio are suffused with mind, so the air of the Capponi Library thrums with presence for Dr Lecter as he works at the great wall of pigeonholed manuscripts. He selects rolled parchments, blows dust away, the motes of dust swarming in a ray of sun as though the dead, who now are dust, vie to tell him their fate and his. He works efficiently, but without undue haste, putting a few things in his own portfolio, gathering books and illustrations for his lecture tonight to the Studiolo. There are so many things he would have liked to read.

Dr Lecter opens his laptop computer and, dialing through the University of Milan's criminology department, checks the FBI's home page on the World Wide Web at www.fbi.gov, as any private citizen can do. The Judiciary Subcommittee hearing on Clarice Starling's abortive drug raid has not been scheduled, he learns. He does not have the access codes he would need to look into his own case file at the FBI. On the Most Wanted page, his own former countenance looks at him, flanked by a bomber and an arsonist.

Dr Lecter takes up the bright tabloid from a pile of parchment and looks at the picture of Clarice Starling on the cover, touches her face with his finger. The bright blade appears in his hand as though he had sprouted it to replace his sixth finger. The knife is called a Harpy and it has a serrated blade shaped like a talon. It slices as easily through the *National Tattler* as it sliced through the Gypsy's femoral artery—the blade was in the Gypsy and gone so quickly Dr Lecter did not even need to wipe it.

Dr Lecter cuts out the image of Clarice Starling's face and glues it on a piece of blank parchment.

He picks up a pen and, with a fluid ease, draws on the parchment the body of a winged lioness, a griffon with Starling's face. Beneath it, he writes in his distinctive copperplate, *Did you ever think, Clarice, why the philistines don't understand you? It's because you're the answer to Samson's riddle: You are the honey in the lion.*

Fifteen kilometers away, parked for privacy behind a high stone wall in Impruneta, Carlo Deogracias went over his equipment, while his brother Matteo practiced a series of judo takedowns on the soft grass with the other two Sardinians, Piero and Tommaso Falcione. Both Falciones were quick and very strong—Piero played briefly with the Cagliari professional soccer team. Tommaso had once studied to be a priest, and he spoke fair English. He prayed with their victims, sometimes.

Carlo's white Fiat van with Roman license plates was legally rented. Ready to attach to its sides were signs reading OSPEDALE DELLA MISERICORDIA. The walls and floor were covered with mover's pads in case the subject struggled inside the van.

Carlo intended to carry out this project exactly as Mason wished, but if the plan went wrong and he had to kill Dr Lecter in Italy and abort the filming in

Sardinia, all was not lost. Carlo knew he could butcher Dr Lecter and have his head and hands off in less than a minute.

If he didn't have that much time, he could take the penis and a finger, which with DNA testing would do for proof. Sealed in plastic and packed in ice, they would be in Mason's hands in less than twenty-four hours, entitling Carlo to a reward in addition to his fees.

Neatly stored behind the seats were a small chain saw, long-handled metal shears, a surgical saw, sharp knives, plastic zip-lock bags, a Black & Decker Work Buddy to hold the doctor's arms still, and a DHL Air Express crate with prepaid delivery fee, estimating the weight of Dr Lecter's head at six kilos and his hands at a kilo apiece.

If Carlo had a chance to record an emergency butchery on videotape, he felt confident Mason would pay extra to see Dr Lecter butchered alive, even after he had coughed up the one million dollars for the doctor's head and hands. For that purpose Carlo had provided himself with a good video camera, light source and tripod, and taught Matteo the rudiments of operating it.

His capture equipment got just as much attention. Piero and Tommaso were expert with the net, now folded as carefully as a parachute. Carlo had both a hypodermic and a dart gun loaded with enough of the animal tranquilizer acepromazine to drop an animal of Dr Lecter's size in seconds. Carlo had told Rinaldo Pazzi he would commence with the beanbag gun, which was charged and ready, but if he got a chance to put the hypodermic anywhere in Dr Lecter's buttocks or legs, the beanbag would not be needed.

The abductors only had to be on the Italian mainland with their captive for about forty minutes, the length of time it took to drive to the jetport at Pisa where an ambulance plane would be waiting. The Florence airstrip was closer, but the air traffic there was light, and a private flight more noticeable.

In less than an hour and a half, they would be in Sardinia, where the doctor's reception committee was growing ravenous.

Carlo had weighed it all in his intelligent, malodorous head. Mason was no fool. The payments were weighted so no harm must come to Rinaldo Pazzi—it would cost Carlo money to kill Pazzi and try to claim all the reward. Mason did not want the heat from a dead policeman. Better to do it Mason's way. But it made Carlo itch all over to think what he might have accomplished with a few strokes of the saw if he had found Dr Lecter himself.

He tried his chain saw. It started on the first pull.

Carlo conferred briefly with the others, and left on a small *motorino* for town, armed only with a knife and a gun and a hypodermic.

Dr Hannibal Lecter came in early from the noisome street to the Farmacia di Santa Maria Novella, one of the best-smelling places on Earth. He stood for some minutes with his head back and eyes closed, taking in the aromas of the great soaps and lotions and creams, and of the ingredients in the workrooms. The porter was accustomed to him, and the clerks, normally given to a certain amount of hauteur, had great respect for him. The purchases of the courteous Dr Fell over his months in Florence would not have totaled more than one hundred thousand lire, but the fragrances and essences were chosen and combined with a sensibility startling and gratifying to these scent merchants, who live by the nose.

It was to preserve this pleasure that Dr Lecter had not altered his own nose with any rhinoplasty other than external collagen injections. For him the air was painted with scents as distinct and vivid as colors, and he could layer and feather them as though painting wet-on-wet. Here there was nothing of jail. Here the air was music. Here were pale tears of frankincense awaiting extraction, yellow bergamot, sandalwood, cinnamon and mimosa in concert, over the sustaining ground notes of genuine ambergris, civet, castor from the beaver, and essence of the musk deer.

Dr Lecter sometimes entertained the illusion that he could smell with his hands, his arms and cheeks, that odor suffused him. That he could smell with his face and his heart.

For good, anatomic reasons, scent fosters memory more readily than any other sense.

Here Dr Lecter had fragments and flashes of memory as he stood beneath the soft light of the Farmacia's great Art Deco lamps, breathing, breathing. Here there was nothing from jail. Except—what was that? Clarice Starling, why? Not the l'Air du Temps he caught when she opened her handbag close to the bars of his cage in the asylum. That was not it. Such perfumes were not sold here in the Farmacia. Nor was it her skin lotion. Ah. *Sapone di mandorle*. The Farmacia's famous almond soap. Where had he smelled it? Memphis, when she stood outside his cell, when he briefly touched her finger shortly before his escape. Starling, then. Clean, and rich in textures. Cotton sun-dried and ironed. Clarice Starling, then. Engaging and toothsome. Tedious in her earnestness and absurd in her principles. Quick in her mother wit. Ummmm.

On the other hand, bad memories for Dr Lecter were associated with unpleasant odors, and here in the Farmacia he was perhaps as far as he ever got from the rank black oubliettes beneath his memory palace.

Contrary to his usual practice, Dr Lecter bought quite a lot of soaps and lotions and bath oils on this gray Friday. A few he took with him, and he had the Farmacia ship the rest, making out the shipping labels himself in his distinctive copperplate hand.

"Would the *Dottore* like to include a note?" the clerk asked.

"Why not?" Dr Lecter replied, and slipped the folded drawing of the griffon into the box.

The Farmacia di Santa Maria Novella is attached to a convent in the Via Scala and Carlo, ever devout, removed his hat to lurk beneath an image of the Virgin near the entrance. He had noticed that air pressure from the foyer's inner doors made the exterior doors puff ajar seconds before anyone comes out. This gave him time to conceal himself and peep from hiding each time a customer left.

When Dr Lecter came out with his slim portfolio, Carlo was well concealed behind a card vendor's stall. The doctor started on his way. As he passed the image of the Virgin, his head came up, his nostrils flared as he looked up at the statue and tested the air.

Carlo thought it might be a gesture of devotion. He wondered if Dr Lecter was religious, as crazy men often are. Perhaps he could make the doctor curse God at the end—that might please Mason. He'd have to send the pious Tommaso out of earshot first, of course.

Rinaldo Pazzi in the late afternoon wrote a letter to his wife including his effort at a sonnet, composed early in their courtship, which he had been too shy to give her at the time. He enclosed the codes required to claim the escrowed money in Switzerland, along with a letter for her to mail to Mason if he tried to renege. He put the letter where she would only find it if she were gathering his effects.

At six o'clock, he rode his little *motorino* to the Museo Bardini and chained it to an iron railing where the last students of the day were claiming their bicycles. He saw the white van with ambulance markings parked near the museum and guessed it might be Carlo's. Two men were sitting in the van. When Pazzi turned his back, he felt their eyes on him.

He had plenty of time. The streetlights were already on and he walked slowly toward the river through the black useful shadows under the museum's trees. Crossing over the Ponte alle Grazie, he stared down for a time at the slow-moving Arno and thought the last long thoughts he would have time to entertain. The night would be dark. Good. Low clouds rushed eastward over Florence, just brushing the cruel spike on the Palazzo Vecchio, and the rising breeze swirled the grit and powdered pigeon droppings in the piazza before Santa Croce, where Pazzi now made his way, his pockets heavy with a .380 Beretta, a flat leather sap and a knife to plant on Dr Lecter in case it was necessary to kill him at once.

The church of Santa Croce closes at six P.M., but a sexton let Pazzi in a small door near the front of the church. He did not want to ask the man if "Dr Fell" was working, so he went carefully to see. Candles burning at the altars along the walls gave him enough light. He walked the great length of the church until he could see down the right arm of the cruciform church. It was hard to see, past the votive candles, if Dr Fell was in the Capponi Chapel. Walking quietly down the right transept now. Looking. A great shadow reared up the chapel wall, and for a second Pazzi's breathing stopped. It was Dr Lecter, bent over his lamp on the floor where he worked at his rubbings. The doctor stood up, peered into the dark like an owl, head turning, body still, lit from beneath by his work light, shadow immense behind him. Then the shadow shrank down the chapel wall as he bent to his task again.

Pazzi felt sweat trickle down his back beneath his shirt, but his face was cold.

There was yet an hour before the meeting at the Palazzo Vecchio began and Pazzi wanted to arrive at the lecture late.

In its severe beauty, the chapel which Brunelleschi built for the Pazzi family at Santa Croce is one of the glories of Renaissance architecture. Here the circle and the square are reconciled. It is a separate structure

223

outside the sanctuary of Santa Croce, reached only through an arched cloister.

Pazzi prayed in the Pazzi chapel, kneeling on the stone, watched by his likeness in the Della Robbia rondel high above him. He felt his prayers constricted by the circle of apostles on the ceiling, and thought perhaps the prayers might have escaped into the dark cloister behind him and flown from there to the open sky and God.

With an effort he pictured in his mind some good things he could do with the money he got in exchange for Dr Lecter. He saw himself and his wife handing out coins to some urchins, and some sort of medical machine they would give to a hospital. He saw the waves of Galilee, which looked to him much like the Chesapeake. He saw his wife's shapely rosy hand around his dick, squeezing it to further swell the head.

He looked about him, and seeing no one, said aloud to God, "Thank you, Father, for allowing me to remove this monster, monster of monsters, from your Earth. Thank you on behalf of the souls We will spare of pain." Whether this was the magisterial "We" or a reference to the partnership of Pazzi and God is not clear, and there may not be a single answer.

The part of him that was not his friend said to Pazzi that he and Dr Lecter had killed together, that Gnocco was their victim, since Pazzi did nothing to save him, and was relieved when death stopped his mouth.

There was some comfort in prayer, Pazzi reflected, leaving the chapel—he had the distinct feeling, walking out through the dark cloister, that he was not alone.

* * *

Carlo was waiting under the overhang of the Palazzo Piccolomini, and he fell into step with Pazzi. They said very little.

They walked behind the Palazzo Vecchio and confirmed the rear exit into the Via dei Leone was locked, the windows above it shuttered.

The only open door was the main entrance to the Palazzo.

"We'll come out here, down the steps and around the side to the Via Neri," Pazzi said.

"My brother and I will be on the Loggia side of the piazza. We'll fall in a good distance behind you. The others are at the Museo Bardini."

"I saw them."

"They saw you too," Carlo said.

"Does the beanbag make much noise?"

"Not a lot, not like a gun, but you'll hear it and he'll go down fast." Carlo did not tell him Piero would shoot the beanbag from the shadows in front of the museum while Pazzi and Dr Lecter were still in the light. Carlo did not want Pazzi to flinch away from the doctor and warn him before the shot.

"You have to confirm to Mason that you have him. You have to do that tonight," Pazzi said.

"Don't worry. This prick will spend tonight begging Mason on the telephone," Carlo said, glancing sideways at Pazzi, hoping to see him uncomfortable. "At first he'll beg for Mason to spare him, and after a while he'll beg to die."

NIGHT CAME and the last tourists were shooed out of the Palazzo Vecchio. Many, feeling the loom of the medieval castle on their backs as they scattered across the piazza, had to turn and look up a last time at the jack-o'-lantern teeth of its parapets, high over them.

Floodlights came on, washing the sheer rough stone, sharpening the shadows under the high battlements. As the swallows went to their nests, the first bats appeared, disturbed in their hunting more by the high-frequency squeals of the restorers' power tools than by the light.

Inside the palazzo the endless job of conservation and maintenance would go on for another hour, except in the Salon of Lilies, where Dr Lecter conferred with the foreman of the maintenance crew.

The foreman, accustomed to the penury and sour demands of the Belle Arti Committee, found the doctor both courteous and extremely generous.

In minutes his workers were stowing their equipment, moving the great floor polishers and compressors out of the way against the walls and rolling up their lines and electrical cords. Quickly they set up the folding chairs for the meeting of the Studiolo—only a dozen chairs were needed—and threw open the windows to clear out the smell of their paint and polish and gilding materials.

The doctor insisted on a proper lectern, and one as big as a pulpit was found in the former office of Niccolò Machiavelli adjacent to the salon and brought on a tall hand truck, along with the palazzo's overhead projector.

The small screen that came with the projector did not suit Dr Lecter and he sent it away. Instead he tried showing his images life-sized against one of the hanging canvas drop cloths protecting a refurbished wall. After he had adjusted its fastenings and smoothed out the folds, he found the cloth would serve him very well.

He marked his place in several of the weighty tomes piled on the lectern, and then stood at the window with his back to the room as the members of the Studiolo in their dusty dark suits arrived and seated themselves, the tacit skepticism of the scholars evident as they rearranged their chairs from a semicircle into more of a jury-box configuration.

Looking out the tall windows, Dr Lecter could see the Duomo and Giotto's campanile, black against the west, but not Dante's beloved Baptistry below them. The upturned floodlights prevented him from seeing down into the dark piazza where the assassins awaited him.

As these, the most renowned medieval and Renaissance scholars in the world, settled in their chairs, Dr Lecter composed in his mind his lecture to them. It took him a little more than three minutes to organize the lecture. Its subject was Dante's *Inferno* and Judas Iscariot.

Much in accord with the Studiolo's taste for the pre-Renaissance, Dr Lecter began with the case of Pier della Vigna, Logothete of the Kingdom of Sicily, whose avarice earned him a place in Dante's Hell. For the first half-hour the doctor fascinated them with the real-life medieval intrigues behind della Vigna's fall.

"Della Vigna was disgraced and blinded for his betrayal of the emperor's trust through his avarice," Dr Lecter said, approaching his principal topic. "Dante's pilgrim found him in the seventh level of the Inferno, reserved for suicides. Like Judas Iscariot, he died by hanging.

"Judas and Pier della Vigna and Ahithophel, the ambitious counsellor of Absalom, are linked in Dante by the avarice he saw in them and by their subsequent deaths by hanging.

"Avarice and hanging are linked in the ancient and the medieval mind: St Jerome writes that Judas' very surname, Iscariot, means 'money' or 'price,' while Father Origen says Iscariot is derived from the Hebrew 'from suffocation' and that his name means 'Judas the Suffocated.'"

Dr Lecter glanced up from his podium, looking over his spectacles at the door.

"Ah, *Commendator* Pazzi, welcome. Since you are nearest to the door, would you be kind enough to dim the lights? You will be interested in this, *Commendatore*, as there are two Pazzis already in Dante's *Inferno* . . ."

The professors of the Studiolo cackled dryly. "There is Camicion de' Pazzi, who murdered a kinsman, and he is expecting the arrival of a second Pazzi—but it's not you—it's Carlino, who will be placed even farther down in Hell for treachery and betrayal of the White Guelphs, the party of Dante himself."

A little bat flew in through one of the open windows and circled the room over the heads of the professors for a few laps, a common event in Tuscany and ignored by everyone.

Dr Lecter resumed his podium voice. "Avarice and hanging, then, linked since antiquity, the image appearing again and again in art." Dr Lecter pressed the switch in his palm and the projector came to life, throwing an image on the drop cloth covering the wall. In quick succession further images followed as he spoke:

"Here is the earliest known depiction of the Crucifixion, carved on an ivory box in Gaul about A.D. four hundred. It includes the death by hanging of Judas, his face upturned to the branch that suspends him. And here on a reliquary casket of Milan, fourth century, and an ivory diptych of the ninth century, Judas hanging. He's *still* looking up."

The little bat flickered across the screen, hunting bugs.

"In this plate from the doors of the Benevento Cathedral, we see Judas hanging with his bowels falling out as St Luke, the physician, described him in the Acts of the Apostles. Here he hangs beset by Harpies, above him in the sky is the face of Cain-in-the-Moon; and here he's depicted by your own Giotto, again with pendant viscera.

"And finally, here, from a fifteenth-century edition of the *Inferno*, is Pier della Vigna's body hanging from a bleeding tree. I will not belabor the obvious parallel with Judas Iscariot.

"But Dante needed no drawn illustration: It is the genius of Dante Alighieri to make Pier della Vigna, now in Hell, speak in strained hisses and coughing sibilants as though he is hanging still. Listen to him as he tells of dragging, with the other damned, his own dead body to hang upon a thorn tree:

> *"Surge in vermena e in pianta silvestra:*
> *l'Arpie, pascendo poi de le sue foglie,*
> *fanno dolore, e al dolor fenestra."*

Dr Lecter's normally white face flushes as he creates for the Studiolo the gargling, choking words of the agonal Pier della Vigna, and as he thumbs his remote control, the images of della Vigna and Judas with his bowels out alternate on the large field of the hanging drop cloth.

> *"Come l'altre verrem per nostre spoglie,*
> *ma non però ch'alcuna sen rivesta,*
> *ché non è giusto aver ciò ch'om si toglie.*
>
> *"Qui le strascineremo, e per la mesta*
> *selva saranno i nostri corpi appesi,*
> *ciascuno al prun de l'ombra sua molesta.*

"So Dante recalls, in sound, the death of Judas in the

death of Pier della Vigna for the same crimes of avarice and treachery.

"Ahithophel, Judas, your own Pier della Vigna. Avarice, hanging, self-destruction, with avarice counting as self-destruction as much as hanging. And what does the anonymous Florentine suicide say in his torment at the end of the canto?

"Io fei gibetto a me de le mie case.

"And I—I made my own house be my gallows.

"On the next occasion you might like to discuss Dante's son Pietro. Incredibly, he was the only one of the early writers on the thirteenth canto who links Pier della Vigna and Judas. I think, too, it would be interesting to take up the matter of chewing in Dante. Count Ugolino chewing on the back of the archbishop's head, Satan with his three faces chewing Judas, Brutus and Cassius, all betrayers like Pier della Vigna.

"Thank you for your kind attention."

The scholars applauded him enthusiastically, in their soft and dusty way, and Dr Lecter left the lights down as he said good-bye to them, each by name, holding books in his arms so he would not have to shake their hands. Going out of the soft light of the Salon of Lilies, they seemed to carry the spell of the lecture with them.

Dr Lecter and Rinaldo Pazzi, alone now in the great chamber, could hear wrangling over the lecture break out among the scholars as they descended the stairs.

"Would you say that I saved my job, *Commendatore*?"

"I'm not a scholar, Dr Fell, but anyone can see that you impressed them. Doctor, if it's convenient for you, I'll walk home with you and collect your predecessor's effects."

"They fill two suitcases, *Commendatore*, and you already have your briefcase. Do you want to carry them?"

"I'll have a patrol car come for me at the Palazzo Capponi." Pazzi would insist if necessary.

"Fine," Dr Lecter said. "I'll be a minute, putting things away."

Pazzi nodded and went to the tall windows with his cell phone, never taking his eyes off Lecter.

Pazzi could see that the doctor was perfectly calm. From the floors below came the sounds of power tools.

Pazzi dialed a number and when Carlo Deogracias answered, Pazzi said, "Laura, *amore*, I'll be home very shortly."

Dr Lecter took his books off the podium and packed them in a bag. He turned to the projector, its fan still humming, dust swimming in its beam.

"I should have shown them this one, I can't imagine how I missed it." Dr Lecter projected another drawing, a man naked hanging beneath the battlements of the palace. "This one will interest you, *Commendator* Pazzi, let me see if I can improve the focus."

Dr Lecter fiddled with the machine, and then he approached the image on the wall, his silhouette black on the cloth the same size as the hanged man.

"Can you make this out? It won't enlarge any more. Here's where the archbishop bit him. And beneath him is written his name."

Pazzi did not get close to Dr Lecter, but as he approached the wall he smelled a chemical, and thought for an instant it was something the restorers used.

"Can you make out the characters? It says 'Pazzi' along with a rude poem. This is your ancestor, Francesco, hanging outside the Palazzo Vecchio, beneath these windows," Dr Lecter said. He held Pazzi's eyes across the beam of light between them.

"On a related subject, Signore Pazzi, I must confess to you: I'm giving serious thought to eating your wife."

Dr Lecter flipped the big drop cloth down over Pazzi, Pazzi flailing at the canvas, trying to uncover his head as his heart flailed in his chest, and Dr Lecter behind him fast, seizing him around the neck with terrible strength and clapping an ether-soaked sponge over the canvas covering Pazzi's face.

Rinaldo Pazzi strong and thrashing, feet and arms tangled in the canvas, feet tangled in the cloth, he was still able to get his hand on his pistol as they fell to the floor together, tried to point the Beretta behind him under the smothering canvas, pulled the trigger and shot himself through the thigh as he sank into spinning black . . .

The little .380 going off beneath the canvas did not make much more noise than the banging and grinding on the floors below. No one came up the staircase. Dr Lecter swung the great doors to the Salon of Lilies closed and bolted them . . .

A certain amount of nausea and gagging as Pazzi came

back to consciousness, the taste of ether in his throat and a heaviness in his chest.

He found that he was still in the Salon of Lilies and discovered that he could not move. Rinaldo Pazzi was bound upright with the drop cloth canvas and rope, stiff as a grandfather clock, strapped to the tall hand truck the workers had used to move the podium. His mouth was taped. A pressure bandage stopped the bleeding of the gunshot wound in his thigh.

Watching him, leaning against the pulpit, Dr Lecter was reminded of himself, similarly bound when they moved him around the asylum on a hand truck.

"Can you hear me, Signore Pazzi? Take some deep breaths while you can, and clear your head."

Dr Lecter's hands were busy as he talked. He had rolled a big floor polisher into the room and he was working with its thick orange power cord, tying a hangman's noose in the plug end of the cord. The rubber-covered cord squeaked as he made the traditional thirteen wraps.

He completed the hangman's noose with a tug and put it down on the pulpit. The plug protruded from the coils at the noose end.

Pazzi's gun, his plastic handcuff strips, the contents of his pockets and briefcase were on top of the podium.

Dr Lecter poked among the papers. He slipped into his shirtfront the Carabinieri's file containing his *permesso di soggiorno*, his work permit, the photos and negatives of his new face.

And here was the musical score Dr Lecter loaned Signora Pazzi. He picked up the score now and tapped his teeth with it. His nostrils flared and he breathed in deeply, his face close to Pazzi's. "Laura, if I may call her Laura, must use a wonderful hand cream at night, Signore. Slick. Cold at first and then warm," he said. "The scent of orange blossoms. Laura, *l'orange*. Ummmm. I haven't had a bite all day. Actually, the liver and kidneys would be suitable for dinner right away—tonight—but the rest of the meat should hang a week in the current cool conditions. I did not see the forecast, did you? I gather that means 'no.'

"If you tell me what I need to know, *Commendatore*, it would be convenient for me to leave without my meal; Signora Pazzi will remain unscathed. I'll ask you the questions and then we'll see. You can trust me, you know, though I expect you find trust difficult, knowing yourself.

"I saw at the theater that you had identified me, *Commendatore*. Did you wet yourself when I bent over the Signora's hand? When the police didn't come, it was clear that you had sold me. Was it Mason Verger you sold me to? Blink twice for yes.

"Thank you, I thought so. I called the number on his ubiquitous poster once, far from here, just for fun. Are his men waiting outside? Umm hmmm. And one of them smells like tainted boar sausage? I see. Have you told anyone in the Questura about me? Was that a single blink? I thought so. Now, I want you to think a minute, and tell me your access code for the VICAP computer at Quantico."

Dr Lecter opened his Harpy knife. "I'm going to take your tape off and you can tell me." Dr Lecter held up his knife. "Don't try to scream. Do you think you can keep from screaming?"

Pazzi was hoarse from the ether. "I swear to God I don't know the code. I can't think of the whole thing. We can go to my car, I have papers—"

Dr Lecter wheeled Pazzi around to face the screen and flipped back and forth between his images of Pier della Vigna hanging, and Judas hanging with his bowels out.

"Which do you think, *Commendatore*? Bowels in or out?"

"The code's in my notebook."

Dr Lecter held the book in front of Pazzi's face until he found the notation, listed among telephone numbers.

"And you can log on remotely, as a guest?"

"Yes," Pazzi croaked.

"Thank you, *Commendatore*." Dr Lecter tilted back the hand truck and rolled Pazzi to the great windows.

"*Listen to me!* I have *money*, man! You'll have to have *money* to run. Mason Verger will never quit. He'll never quit. You can't go home for *money*, they're watching your house."

Dr Lecter put two boards from the scaffolding as a ramp over the low windowsill and rolled Pazzi on the hand truck out onto the balcony outside.

The breeze was cold on Pazzi's wet face. Talking quickly now, "You'll never get away from this building alive. I have *money*. I have *one hundred and sixty million lire* in cash, U.S. dollars *one hundred thousand*! Let me telephone my wife. I'll tell her to get the money and put it in my car, and leave the car right in front of the palazzo."

Dr Lecter retrieved his noose from the pulpit and carried it outside, trailing the orange cord behind him. The other end was tight in a series of hitches around the heavy floor polisher.

Pazzi was still talking. "She'll call me on the cell phone when she's outside, and then she'll leave it for you. I have the police pass, she can drive right across the piazza to the entrance. She'll do what I tell her. The car *smokes*, man, you can look down and see it's running, the keys will be in it."

Dr Lecter tilted Pazzi forward against the balcony railing. The railing came to his thighs.

Pazzi could look down at the piazza and make out through the floodlights the spot where Savonarola was burned, where he had sworn to sell Dr Lecter to Mason Verger. He looked up at the clouds scudding low, colored by the floodlights, and hoped, so much, that God could see.

Down is the awful direction and he could not help staring there, toward death, hoping against reason that the beams of the floodlights gave some substance to the air, that they would somehow press on him, that he might snag on the light beams.

The orange rubber cover of the wire noose cold around his neck, Dr Lecter standing so close to him.

"*Arrivederci, Commendatore.*"

Flash of the Harpy up Pazzi's front, another swipe severed his attachment to the dolly and he was tilting, tipped over the railing trailing the orange cord, ground coming up in a rush, mouth free to scream, and inside the salon, the floor polisher rushed across the floor and slammed to a stop against the railing, Pazzi jerked head-up, his neck broke and his bowels fell out.

Pazzi and his appendage swinging and spinning before the rough wall of the floodlit palace, jerking in posthumous spasms but not choking, dead, his shadow thrown huge on the wall by the floodlights, swinging with his bowels swinging below him in a shorter, quicker arc, his manhood pointing out of his rent trousers in a death erection.

Carlo charging out of a doorway, Matteo beside him, across the piazza toward the entrance to the palazzo, knocking tourists aside, two of whom had video cameras trained on the castle.

"It's a trick," someone said in English as he ran by.

"Matteo, cover the back door. If he comes out just kill him and cut him," Carlo said, fumbling with his cell phone as he ran. Into the palazzo now, up the stairs to the first level, then the second.

The great doors of the salon stood ajar. Inside, Carlo swung his gun on the projected figure on the wall, ran out onto the balcony, searched Machiavelli's office in seconds.

With his cell phone he reached Piero and Tommaso, waiting with the van in front of the museum. "Get to his house, cover it front and back. Just kill him and cut him."

Carlo dialed again. "Matteo?"

Matteo's phone buzzed in his breast pocket as he stood, breathing hard, in front of the locked rear exit of the palazzo. He had scanned the roof, and the dark

238

windows, tested the door, his hand under his coat, on the pistol in his waistband.

He flipped open the phone. "*Pronto!*"

"What do you see."

"Door's locked."

"The roof?"

Matteo looked up again, but not in time to see the shutters open on the window above him.

Carlo heard a rustle and a cry in his telephone, and Carlo was running, down the stairs, falling on a landing, up again and running, past the guard before the palace entrance, who now stood outside, past the statues flanking the entrance, around the corner and pounding now toward the rear of the palace, scattering a few couples. Dark back here now, running, the cell phone squeaking like a small creature in his hand as he ran. A figure ran across the street in front of him shrouded in white, ran blindly in the path of a *motorino*, and the scooter knocked it down, the figure up again and crashing into the front of a shop across the narrow street of the palace, ran into the plate glass, turned and ran blindly, an apparition in white, screaming, "Carlo! Carlo," great stains spreading on the ripped canvas covering him, and Carlo caught his brother in his arms, cut the plastic handcuff strip around his neck binding the canvas tight over his head, the canvas a mask of blood. Uncovered Matteo and found him ripped badly, across the face, across the abdomen, deeply enough across the chest for the wound to suck. Carlo left him long enough to run to the corner and look both ways, then he came back to his brother.

With sirens approaching, flashing lights filling the

Piazza Signoria, Dr Hannibal Lecter shot his cuffs and strolled up to a *gelateria* in the nearby Piazza de Giudici. Motorcycles and *motorinos* were lined up at the curb.

He approached a young man in racing leathers starting a big Ducati.

"Young man, I am desperate," he said with a rueful smile. "If I am not at the Piazza Bellosguardo in ten minutes, my wife will kill me," he said, showing the young man a fifty-thousand-lire note. "This is what my life is worth to me."

"That's all you want? A ride?" the young man said.

Dr Lecter showed him his open hands. "A ride."

The fast motorcycle split the lines of traffic on the Lungarno, Dr Lecter hunched behind the young rider, a spare helmet that smelled like hairspray and perfume on his head. The rider knew where he was going, peeling off the Via de' Serragli toward the Piazza Tasso, and out the Via Villani, hitting the tiny gap beside the Church of San Francesco di Paola that leads into the winding road up to Bellosguardo, the fine residential district on the hill overlooking Florence from the south. The big Ducati engine echoed off the stone walls lining the road with a sound like ripping canvas, pleasing to Dr Lecter as he leaned into the curves and coped with the smell of hairspray and inexpensive perfume in his helmet. He had the young man drop him off at the entrance to the Piazza Bellosguardo, not far from the home of Count Montauto, where Nathaniel Hawthorne had lived. The rider tucked his wages in the breast pocket of his leathers and the taillight of the motorcycle receded fast down the winding road.

Dr Lecter, exhilarated by his ride, walked another

forty meters to the black Jaguar, retrieved the keys
from behind the bumper and started the engine. He
had a slight fabric burn on the heel of his hand where
his glove had ridden up as he flung the canvas drop
cloth over Matteo and leaped down on him from the
first-floor palazzo window. He put a dab of the Italian
antibacterial unguent Cicatrine on it and it felt better
at once.

Dr Lecter searched among his music tapes as the
engine warmed. He decided on Scarlatti.

37

THE TURBOPROP air ambulance lifted over the red tile roofs and banked southwest toward Sardinia, the Leaning Tower of Pisa poking above the wing in a turn steeper than the pilot would have made if he carried a living patient.

The stretcher intended for Dr Hannibal Lecter held instead the cooling body of Matteo Deogracias. Older brother Carlo sat beside the corpse, his clothing stiff with blood.

Carlo Deogracias made the medical attendant put on earphones and turn up the music while he spoke on his cell phone to Las Vegas, where a blind encryption repeater relayed his call to the Maryland shore . . .

For Mason Verger, night and day are much the same. He happened to be sleeping. Even the aquarium lights were off. Mason's head was turned on the pillow, his single eye ever open like the eyes of the great eel, which was sleeping too. The only sounds were the regular hiss and sigh of the respirator, the soft bubbling of the aerator in the aquarium.

Above these constant noises came another sound, soft and urgent. The buzzing of Mason's most private telephone. His pale hand walked on its fingers like a crab to push the telephone button. The speaker was under his pillow, the microphone near the ruin of his face.

First Mason heard the airplane in the background and then a cloying tune, *"Gli Innamorati."*

"I'm here. Tell me."

"It's a bloody *casino*," Carlo said.

"Tell me."

"My brother Matteo is dead. I have my hand on him now. Pazzi's dead too. Dr Fell killed them and got away."

Mason did not reply at once.

"You owe two hundred thousand dollars for Matteo," Carlo said. "For his family." Sardinian contracts always call for death benefits.

"I understand that."

"The shit will fly about Pazzi."

"Better to get it out that Pazzi was dirty," Mason said. "They'll take it better if he's dirty. Was he dirty?"

"Except for this, I don't know. What if they trace from Pazzi back to you?"

"I can take care of that."

"I have to take care of *myself*," Carlo said. "This is too much. A chief inspector of the Questura dead, I can't buy out of that."

"You didn't do anything, did you?"

"We did nothing, but if the Questura put my name

in this—*dirty Madonna*! They'll watch me for the rest of my life. Nobody will take fees from me, I won't be able to break wind on the street. What about Oreste? Did he know who he was supposed to film?"

"I don't think so."

"The Questura will have Dr Fell identified by tomorrow or the next day. Oreste will put it together as soon as he sees the news, just from the timing."

"Oreste is well paid. Oreste is harmless to us."

"Maybe to you, but Oreste is facing a judge in a pornography case in Rome next month. Now he has a thing to trade. If you don't know that already you should kick some ass. You got to have Oreste?"

"I'll talk with Oreste," Mason said carefully, the rich tones of a radio announcer coming from his ravaged face. "Carlo, are you still game? You *want* to find Dr Fell now, don't you? You *have* to find him for Matteo."

"Yes, but at your expense."

"Then keep the farm going. Get certified swine flu and cholera inoculations for the pigs. Get shipping crates for them. You have a good passport?"

"Yes."

"I mean a *good* one, Carlo, not some upstairs Trastevere crap."

"I have a good one."

"You'll hear from me."

Ending his connection in the droning airplane, Carlo inadvertently pushed the auto dial on his cell phone. Matteo's telephone beeped loudly in his dead hand, still held in the steely grip of cadaveric spasm. For an instant Carlo thought his brother would raise the telephone to his ear. Dully, seeing that Matteo could not answer, Carlo pushed his hang-up button. His face contorted and the medical attendant could not look at him.

38

THE DEVIL'S Armor with its horned helmet is a splendid suit of fifteenth-century Italian armor that has hung high on the wall in the village church of Santa Reparata south of Florence since 1501. In addition to the graceful horns, shaped like those of the chamois, the pointed gauntlet cuffs are stuck where shoes should be, at the ends of the greaves, suggesting the cloven hooves of Satan.

According to the local legend, a young man wearing the armor took the name of the Virgin in vain as he passed the church, and found that afterward he could not take his armor off until he beseeched the Virgin for forgiveness. He gave the armor to the church as a gift of thanksgiving. It is an impressive presence and it honored its proof marks when an artillery shell burst in the church in 1942.

The armor, its upper surfaces covered with a feltlike coating of dust, looks down on the small sanctuary now as Mass is being completed. Incense rises, passes through the empty visor.

Only three people are in attendance, two elderly women, both dressed in black, and Dr Hannibal Lecter. All three take Communion, though Dr Lecter touches his lips to the cup with some reluctance.

The priest completes the benediction and withdraws. The women depart. Dr Lecter continues his devotions until he is alone in the sanctuary.

From the organ loft, Dr Lecter can just reach over the railing and, leaning between the horns, raise the dusty visor on the helmet of the Devil's Armor. Inside, a fishhook over the lip of the gorget suspends a string and a package hanging inside the cuirass where the heart would be. Carefully, Dr Lecter draws it out.

A package: passports of the best Brazilian manufacture, identification, cash, bankbooks, keys. He puts it under his arm beneath his coat.

Dr Lecter does not indulge much in regret, but he was sorry to be leaving Italy. There were things in the Palazzo Capponi that he would have liked to find and read. He would have liked to play the clavier and perhaps compose; he might have cooked for the Widow Pazzi, when she overcame her grief.

WHILE BLOOD still fell from the hanging body of Rinaldo Pazzi to fry and smoke on the hot floodlights beneath Palazzo Vecchio, the police summoned the fire department to get him down.

The *pompieri* used an extension on their ladder truck. Ever practical, and certain the hanged man was dead, they took their time retrieving Pazzi. It was a delicate process requiring them to boost the dangling viscera up to the body and wrap netting around the whole mass, before attaching a line to lower him to the ground.

As the body reached the upstretched arms of those on the ground, *La Nazione* got an excellent picture that reminded many readers of the great Deposition paintings.

The police left the noose in place until it could be fingerprinted, and then cut the stout electrical cord in the center of the noose to preserve the integrity of the knot.

Many Florentines were determined that the death be a spectacular suicide, deciding that Rinaldo Pazzi bound his own hands in the manner of a jail suicide, and ignoring the fact that the feet were also bound. In the first hour, local radio reported Pazzi had committed hara-kiri with a knife in addition to hanging himself.

The police knew better at once—the severed bonds on the balcony and the hand truck, Pazzi's missing gun, eyewitness accounts of Carlo running into the Palazzo and the bloody shrouded figure running blindly behind the Palazzo Vecchio told them Pazzi was murdered.

Then the Italian public decided *Il Mostro* had killed Pazzi.

The Questura began with the wretched Girolamo Tocca, once convicted of being *Il Mostro*. They seized him at home and drove away with his wife once again howling in the road. His alibi was solid. He was drinking a Ramazzotti at a café in sight of a priest at the time. Tocca was released in Florence and had to return to San Casciano by bus, paying his own fare.

The staff at Palazzo Vecchio were questioned in the first hours, and the questioning spread through the membership of the Studiolo.

The police could not locate Dr Fell. By noon on Saturday close attention was brought to bear on him. The Questura recalled that Pazzi had been assigned to investigate the disappearance of Fell's predecessor.

A clerk at the Carabinieri reported Pazzi in recent days had examined a *permesso di soggiorno*. Fell's records, including his photographs, attached negatives and fingerprints, were signed out to a false name in what appeared to be Pazzi's handwriting. Italy has not yet computerized its records nationwide and the *permessos* are still held at the local level.

Immigration records yielded Fell's passport number, which rang the lemons in Brazil.

Still, the police did not beep to Dr Fell's true identity. They took fingerprints from the coils of the hangman's noose and fingerprints from the podium, the hand truck and from the kitchen at the Palazzo Capponi. With plenty of artists available, a sketch of Dr Fell was prepared in minutes.

By Sunday morning, Italian time, a fingerprint examiner in Florence had laboriously, point by point, determined that the same fingerpritns were on the podium, the noose, and Dr Fell's kitchen utensils at the Palazzo Capponi.

The thumbprint of Hannibal Lecter, on the poster hanging in Questura headquarters, was not examined.

The fingerprints from the crime scene went to Interpol on Sunday night, and arrived as a matter of course at FBI headquarters in Washington, D.C., along with seven thousand other sets of crime scene prints. Submitted to the automated fingerprint classification system, the fingerprints from Florence registered a hit of such magnitude that an audible alarm sounded in the office of the assistant director in charge of the Identification section. The night duty officer watched the face and fingers of Hannibal Lecter crawl out of the printer, and called the assistant director at home, who called the director first, and then Krendler at Justice.

Mason's telephone rang at 1:30 A.M. He acted surprised and interested.

Jack Crawford's telephone rang at 1:35. He grunted several times and rolled over to the empty, haunted side of his marriage bed where his late wife, Bella, used to be. It was cool there and he seemed to think better.

Clarice Starling was the last to know that Dr Lecter had killed again. After she hung up the phone, she lay still for many minutes in the dark and her eyes stung for some reason she did not understand, but she did not cry. From her pillow looking up, she could see his face on the swarming dark. It was Dr Lecter's old face, of course.

40

THE PILOT of the air ambulance would not go into the short, uncontrolled airfield at Arbatax in darkness. They landed at Cagliari, refueled and waited until daylight, and flew up the coast in a spectacular sunrise that gave a false pink cast to Matteo's dead face.

A truck with a coffin was waiting at the Arbatax airstrip. The pilot argued about money and Tommaso stepped in before Carlo slapped his face.

Three hours into the mountains and they were home.

Carlo wandered alone to the rough timber shed he had built with Matteo. All was ready there, the cameras in place to film Lecter's death. Carlo stood beneath the work of Matteo's hands and looked at himself in the great rococo mirror above the animal pen. He looked around at the timbers they had sawn together, he thought of Matteo's great square hands on the saw and a great cry escaped him, a cry from his anguished heart loud enough to ring off the trees. Tusked faces appeared from the brush of the mountain pasture.

Piero and Tommaso, brothers themselves, left him alone.

Birds sang in the mountain pasture.

Came Oreste Pini from the house buttoning his fly with one hand and waving his cell phone with the other. "So you missed Lecter. Bad luck."

Carlo appeared not to hear him.

"Listen, everything is not lost. This can still work out," Oreste Pini said. "I have Mason here. He'll take a *simulado*. Something he can show Lecter when he does catch him. Since we're all set up. We've got a body— Mason says it was just a thug you hired. Mason says we could just, ah, just jerk it around under the fence when the pigs come and just play the canned sound. Here, talk to Mason."

Carlo turned and looked at Oreste as though he had arrived from the moon. Finally he took the cell phone. As he spoke with Mason, his face cleared and a certain peace seemed to settle on him.

Carlo snapped the cell phone shut. "Get ready," he said.

Carlo spoke with Piero and Tommaso, and with the cameraman's help they carried the coffin to the shed.

"You don't want that close enough to get in the frame," Oreste said. "Let's get some footage of the animals milling and then we'll go from there."

Seeing the activity in the shed, the first pigs broke cover.

"*Giriamo!*" Oreste called.

They came running, the wild swine, brown and silver, tall, hip-high to a man, deep in the chest, long-bristled, moving with the speed of a wolf on their little hooves, intelligent little eyes in their hellish faces, massive neck muscles beneath the ridge of standing bristles on their backs capable of lifting a man on their great ripping tusks.

"*Pronti!*" the cameraman called.

They had not eaten in three days, others coming now in an advancing line unfazed by the men behind the fence.

"*Motore!*" Oreste called.

"*Partito!*" the cameraman yelled.

The pigs stopped ten yards short of the shed in a milling, pawing line, a thicket of hooves and tusks, the pregnant sow in the the center. They surged forward and back like linemen, and Oreste framed them with his hands.

"*Azione!*" he yelled at the Sards, and Carlo coming up behind him cut him up the crease of his buttocks and made him scream, gripped him around the hips and hoisted him headfirst into the pen, and the pigs charged. Oreste tried to get to his feet, got to one knee and the sow hit him in the ribs and knocked him sprawling. And they were on him, snarling and squealing, two boars pulling at his face got his jaw off and divided it like a wishbone. And still Oreste nearly made his feet and then he was on his back again with his belly exposed and open, his arms and legs waving above the milling backs, Oreste screaming with his jaw gone, not able to make any words.

Carlo heard a shot and turned. The cameraman had deserted his running camera and tried to flee, but not fast enough to escape Piero's shotgun.

The pigs were settling in now, dragging things away.

"*Azione* my ass," Carlo said, and spit on the ground.

III

TO THE NEW WORLD

A CAREFUL SILENCE surrounded Mason Verger. His
staff treated him as though he had lost a baby. Asked
how he was feeling, he said, "I feel like I just paid a
lot of money for a dead dago."

After a sleep of several hours, Mason wanted children
brought into the playroom outside his chamber, and to
have a talk with one or two of the most troubled ones,
but there were no troubled children to be had immediately, and no time for his supplier in the Baltimore
slums to trouble some for him.

That failing, he had his attendant Cordell cripple
ornamental carp and drop them to the eel until the eel
could eat no more and retreated into its rock, the water
clouded pink and gray and full of iridescent golden
shreds.

He tried to torment his sister Margot, but she retired
to the workout room and for hours ignored his pages.
She was the only person at Muskrat Farm who dared
to ignore Mason.

A short, much-edited piece of tourist's videotape

showing the death of Rinaldo Pazzi was on the television evening news Saturday night, before Dr Lecter was identified as the killer. Blurred areas of the image spared viewers the anatomical details.

Mason's secretary was on the telephone immediately to get the unedited tape. It arrived by helicopter four hours later.

The videotape had a curious provenance:

Of the two tourists who were videotaping the Palazzo Vecchio at the moment of Rinaldo Pazzi's death, one panicked and the camera swung away at the moment of the fall. The other tourist was Swiss and held steady through the entire episode, even panning back up the jerking, swinging cord.

The amateur cameraman, a patent clerk named Viggert, was fearful that the police would seize the videotape and the RAI Italian television would get it free. He called his lawyer in Lausanne at once, made arrangements to copyright the images and sold the rights on a per-broadcast basis to ABC television news after a bidding war. First North American serial rights for print went to the *New York Post*, followed by the *National Tattler*.

The tape instantly took its place among the classic horrific spectacles—Zapruder, the assassination of Lee Harvey Oswald and the suicide of Edgar Bolger—but Viggert would bitterly regret selling so soon, before Dr Lecter was accused of the crime.

This copy of the Viggerts' vacation videotape was complete. We see Swiss family Viggert dutifully orbiting the balls of the David at the Accademia hours before the events at Palazzo Vecchio.

Mason, watching the video with his single goggled eye, had little interest in the expensive piece of meat twitching at the end of the electrical cord. The little history lesson *La Nazione* and *Corriere della Sera* provided on the two Pazzis hanged from the same window five hundred twenty years apart did not interest him either. What held him, what he ran over and over and over, was the pan up the jerking cord to the balcony where a slender figure stood in fuzzy silhouette against the dim light within, waving. Waving to Mason. Dr Lecter waved to Mason from the wrist the way you would wave bye-bye to a child.

"Bye-bye," Mason replied from his darkness. "Bye-bye," the deep radio voice shaking with rage.

THE IDENTIFICATION of Dr Hannibal Lecter as the murderer of Rinaldo Pazzi gave Clarice Starling something serious to do, thank God. She became the de facto low-level liaison between the FBI and the Italian authorities. It was good to make a sustained effort at one task.

Starling's world had changed since the drug raid shoot-out. She and the other survivors of the Feliciana Fish Market were kept in a kind of administrative purgatory pending a Department of Justice report to a minor House Judiciary Subcommittee.

After finding the Lecter X ray, Starling had marked time as a highly qualified temporary, filling in at the National Police Academy, Quantico, for instructors who were ill or on vacation

Through the fall and winter, Washington was obsessed with a scandal in the White House. The frothing reformers used more saliva than did the sad little sin, and the President of the United States publicly ate more than his portion of ordure trying to avoid impeachment.

In this circus, the small matter of the Feliciana Fish Market Massacre was pushed aside.

Each day, inside Starling a grim knowledge grew: The federal service would never be the same for her again. She was marked. Her coworkers had caution in their faces when they dealt with her, as though she had something contagious. Starling was young enough for this behavior to surprise and disappoint her.

It was good to be busy—requests from the Italians for information about Hannibal Lecter were pouring into Behavioral Science, usually in duplicate—one copy being forwarded by the State Department. And Starling replied with a will, stoking the fax lines and E-mailing Lecter files. She was surprised at how much the peripheral material had scattered over the seven years since the doctor's escape.

Her small cubicle in the basement at Behavioral Science was overflowing with paper, inky faxes from Italy, copies of the Italian papers.

What could she send the Italians that would be of value? The item they seized on was the single Questura computer query to the Lecter VICAP file at Quantico a few days before Pazzi's death. The Italian press resurrected Pazzi's reputation with it, claiming he was working in secret to capture Dr Lecter and reclaim his honor.

On the other hand, Starling wondered, what information from the Pazzi crime could be useful here, in case the doctor returned to the United States?

Jack Crawford was not in the office much to advise her. He was in court a lot, and as his retirement approached he was deposed in a lot of open cases.

He took more and more sick days, and when he was in the office he seemed increasingly distant.

The thought of not having his counsel gave Starling flashes of panic.

In her years at the FBI, Starling had seen a great deal. She knew that if Dr Lecter killed again in the United States, the trumpets of flatulence would sound in Congress, an enormous roar of second-guessing would go up from Justice, and the Catch-Me-Fuck-Me would begin in earnest. Customs and Border Patrol would catch it first for letting him in.

The local jurisdiction where the crime occurred would demand everything relating to Lecter and the FBI effort would center around the local line bureau. Then, when the doctor did it again someplace else, everything would move.

If he were caught, the authorities would fight for credit like bears around a bloody seal.

Starling's business was to prepare for the eventuality of his coming, whether he ever came or not, putting aside all the weary knowledge of what would happen around the investigation.

She asked herself a simple question that would have sounded corny to the career climbers inside the Beltway: How could she do exactly what she was sworn to do? How could she protect the citizens and catch him if he came?

Dr Lecter obviously had good papers and money. He was brilliant at concealing himself. Take the elegant simplicity of his first hideout after his escape from Memphis—he checked into a four-star hotel next door to a great plastic surgery facility in St Louis. Half the guests had their faces bandaged. He bandaged his own face and lived high on a dead man's money.

Among her hundreds of scraps of paper, she had his room service receipts from St Louis. Astronomical. A bottle of Bâtard-Montrachet one hundred twenty-five dollars. How good it must have tasted after all those years of jail food.

She had asked for copies of everything from Florence and the Italians obliged. From the quality of the print, she thought they must copy with some kind of soot blower.

There was no order anywhere. Here were Dr Lecter's personal papers from the Palazzo Capponi. A few notes on Dante in his familiar handwriting, a note to the cleaning lady, a receipt from the Florentine fine grocer Vera dal 1926 for two bottles of Bâtard-Montrachet and some *tartufi bianchi*. Same wine again, and what was the other thing?

Starling's *Bantam New College Italian & English Dictionary* told her *tartufi bianchi* were white truffles. She called the chef at a good Washington Italian restaurant and asked him about them. She had to beg off the phone after five minutes as he raved about their taste.

Taste. The wine, the truffles. Taste in all things was a constant between Dr Lecter's lives in America and Europe, between his life as a successful medical practitioner and fugitive monster. His face may have changed but his tastes did not, and he was not a man who denied himself.

Taste was a sensitive area to Starling, because it was in the area of taste that Dr Lecter first touched her in the quick, complimenting her on her pocketbook and making fun of her cheap shoes. What had he called her? A well-scrubbed hustling rube with a little taste.

It was taste that itched at her in the daily round of her institutional life with its purely functional equipment in utilitarian settings.

At the same time her faith in *technique* was dying and leaving room for something else.

Starling was weary of technique. Faith in technique is the religion of the dangerous trades. To go up against an armed felon in a gunfight or to fight him in the dirt you have to believe perfect technique, hard training, will guarantee that you are invincible. This is not true, particularly in firefights. You can stack the odds in your favor, but if you get into enough gunfights, you will be killed in one.

Starling had seen it.

Having come to doubt the religion of technique, where could Starling turn?

In her tribulation, in the gnawing sameness of her days, she began to look at the shapes of things. She began to credit her own visceral reactions to things, without quantifying them or restricting them to words. At about this time she noticed a change in her reading habits. Before, she would have read a caption before she looked at a picture. Not now. Sometimes she did not read captions at all.

For years she had read couture publications on the sly, guiltily as though they were pornography. Now she began to admit to herself that there was something in those pictures that made her hungry. Within the framework of her mind, galvanized by the Lutherans against corrupting rust, she felt as though she were giving in to a delicious perversion.

She would have arrived at her tactic anyway, in time, but she was aided by the sea change inside her: It sped her toward the idea that Dr Lecter's taste for rarified things, things in a small market, might be the monster's dorsal fin, cutting the surface and making him visible.

Using and comparing computerized customer lists, Starling might be able to crack one of his alternate identities. To do this, she had to know his preferences. She needed to know him better than anyone in the world knew him.

What are the things I know he likes? He likes music, wine, books, food. And he likes me.

The first step in the development of taste is to be willing to credit your own opinion. In the areas of food and wine and music, Starling would have to follow the doctor's precedents, looking at what he used in the past, but in one area she was at least his equal. Automobiles. Starling was a car buff, as anyone who saw her car could tell.

Dr Lecter had owned a supercharged Bentley before his disgrace. Supercharged, not turbocharged. Custom supercharged with a Rootes-type positive displacement blower, so it had no turbo lag. She quickly realized that the custom Bentley market is so small, he would entail some risk going back to it.

What would he buy now? She understood the feeling he liked. A blown, big displacement V8, with power down low, and not peaky. What would she buy in the current market?

No question, an XJR Jaguar supercharged sedan.

She faxed the East and West Coast Jaguar distributors asking for weekly sales reports.

What else did Dr Lecter have a taste for, that Starling knew a lot about?

He likes me, she thought.

How quickly he had responded to her plight. Even considering the delay from using a remailing service to write to her. Too bad the postage meter lead fizzled—the meter was in such a public place any thief could use it.

How quickly did the *National Tattler* get to Italy? That's one place he saw Starling's trouble, a copy was found in the Palazzo Capponi. Did the scandal sheet have a Web site? Also, if he had a computer in Italy, he might have read a summary of the gunfight on the FBI's public Web site. What might be learned from Dr Lecter's computer?

No computer was listed among the personal effects at Palazzo Capponi.

Still, she had seen *something*. She got out the photos of the library at the Palazzo Capponi. Here was a picture of the beautiful desk where he wrote to her. Here on the desk was a computer. A Phillips laptop. In subsequent pictures it was gone.

With her dictionary, Starling painfully composed a fax to the Questura in Florence:

Fra le cose personali del dottor Lecter, c'è un computer portatile?

And so, with small steps, Clarice Starling began to pursue Dr Lecter down the corridors of his taste, with more confidence in her footing than was entirely justified.

43

MASON VERGER'S assistant Cordell, with an example posted in a frame on his desk, recognized the distinctive handwriting at once. The stationery was from the Excelsior Hotel in Florence, Italy.

Like an increasing number of wealthy people in the era of the Unabomber, Mason had his own mail fluoroscope, similar to the one at the U.S. Post Office.

Cordell pulled on some gloves and checked the letter. The fluoroscope showed no wires or batteries. In accordance with Mason's strict instructions, he copied the letter and the envelope on the copying machine, handling it with tweezers, and changed gloves before picking up the copy and delivering it to Mason.

In Dr Lecter's familiar copperplate:

Dear Mason,

Thank you for posting such a huge bounty on me. I wish you would increase it. As an early-warning system, the bounty is better than radar. It inclines authorities

267

everywhere to forsake their duty and scramble after me privately, with the results you see.

Actually, I'm writing to refresh your memory on the subject of your former nose. In your inspirational antidrug interview the other day in the Ladies' Home Journal *you claim that you fed your nose, along with the rest of your face, to the pooches, Skippy and Spot, all waggy at your feet. Not so: You ate it yourself, for refreshment. From the crunchy sound when you chewed it up, I would say it had a consistency similar to that of a chicken gizzard—"Tastes just like chicken!" was your comment at the time. I was reminded of the sound in a bistro when a French person tucks into a gésier salad.*

You don't remember that, Mason?

Speaking of chicken, you told me in therapy that, while you were subverting the underprivileged children at your summer camp, you learned that chocolate irritates your urethra. You don't remember that either, do you?

Don't you think it likely you told me all sorts of things you don't remember now?

There is an inescapable parallel between you and Jezebel, Mason. Keen Bible student that you are, you will recall the dogs ate Jezebel's face, along with the rest of her, after the eunuchs threw her out the window.

Your people might have assassinated me in the street. But you wanted me alive, didn't you? From the aroma of your henchmen, it's obvious how you planned to entertain me. Mason, Mason. Since you want to see me so badly, let me give you some words of comfort, and you know I never lie.

Hannibal

> *Before you die you will see my face.*
> > *Sincerely,*
> > > *Hannibal Lecter, MD*

> *P.S. I worry, though, that you won't live that long, Mason. You must avoid the new strains of pneumonia. You're very susceptible, prone as you are (and will remain). I would recommend vaccination immediately, along with immunization shots for hepatitis A and B. Don't want to lose you prematurely.*

Mason seemed somewhat out of breath when he finished reading. He waited, waited and in his own good time said something to Cordell, which Cordell could not hear.

Cordell leaned close and was rewarded with a spray of spit when Mason spoke again:

"Get me Paul Krendler on the phone. And get me the Pigmaster."

44

THE SAME helicopter that brought the foreign news-papers daily to Mason Verger also brought Deputy Assistant Inspector General Paul Krendler to Muskrat Farm.

Mason's malign presence and his darkened chamber with its hissing and sighing machinery and its ever-moving eel would have made Krendler uneasy enough, but he also had to sit through the video of Pazzi's death again and again.

Seven times Krendler watched the Viggerts orbit the David, saw Pazzi plunge and his bowels fall out. By the seventh time, Krendler expected David's bowels to fall out too.

Finally the bright overhead lights came on in the seating area of Mason's room, hot on top of Krendler's head and shining off his scalp through the thinning brush cut.

The Vergers have an unparalleled understanding of piggishness, so Mason began with what Krendler wanted for himself. Mason spoke out of the dark,

270

his sentences measured by the stroke of his respirator.

"I don't need to hear . . . your whole platform . . . how much money will it take?"

Krendler wanted to talk privately with Mason, but they were not alone in the room. A broad-shouldered figure, terrifically muscled, loomed in black outline against the glowing aquarium. The idea of a bodyguard hearing them made Krendler nervous.

"I'd rather it was just us talking, do you mind asking him to leave?"

"This is my sister, Margot," Mason said. "She can stay."

Margot came out of the darkness, her bicycle pants whistling.

"Oh, I'm sorry," Krendler said, half-rising from his chair.

"Hello," she said, but instead of taking Krendler's outstretched hand, Margot picked up two walnuts from the bowl on the table and, squeezing them together in her fist until they cracked loudly, returned to the gloom in front of the aquarium where presumably she ate them. Krendler could hear the hulls dropping to the floor.

"Oookay, let's hear it," Mason said.

"For me to unseat Lowenstein in the twenty-seventh district, ten million dollars minimum." Krendler crossed his legs and looked off somewhere into the dark. He didn't know if Mason could see him. "I'd need that much just for media. But I guarantee you he's vulnerable. I'm in a position to know."

"What's his thing?"

"We'll just say his conduct has—"

"Well, is it money or snatch?"

Krendler didn't feel comfortable saying "snatch" in front of Margot, though it didn't seem to bother Mason. "He's married and he's had a longtime affair with a state court of appeals judge. The judge has ruled in favor of some of his contributors. The rulings are probably coincidence, but when TV convicts him that's all I'll need."

"The judge a woman?" Margot asked.

Krendler nodded. Not sure Mason could see him, he added, "Yes. A woman."

"Too bad," Mason said. "It would be better if he was a *queer*, wouldn't it, Margot? Still, you can't sling that crap yourself, Krendler. It can't come from you."

"We've put together a plan that offers the voters . . ."

"You can't sling the crap yourself," Mason said again.

"I'll just make sure the Judicial Review Board knows where to look, so it'll stick to Lowenstein when it hits him. Are you saying you can help me?"

"I can help you with half of it."

"Five?"

"Let's not just toss it off like 'five.' Let's say it with the respect it deserves—*five million dollars*. The Lord has blessed me with this money. And with it I will do His will: You get it only if Hannibal Lecter falls cleanly into my hands." Mason breathed for a few beats. "If that happens, you'll be Mr Congressman Krendler of the twenty-seventh district, free and clear, and all I'll ever ask you to do is oppose the Humane Slaughter Act. If the FBI gets Lecter, the cops grab him someplace and he gets off with lethal injection, it's been nice to know you."

"I can't help it if a local jurisdiction gets him. Or Crawford's outfit lucks up and catches him, I can't control that."

"How many states with death penalties could Dr Lecter be charged in?" Margot asked. Her voice was scratchy but deep like Mason's from the hormones she had taken.

"Three states, multiple Murder One in each."

"If he's arrested I want him prosecuted at the state level," Mason said. "No kidnapping rap, no civil rights violations, no interstate. I want him to get off with life, I want him in a state prison, not a maximum federal pen."

"Do I have to ask why?"

"Not unless you want me to tell you. It doesn't fall under the Humane Slaughter Act," Mason said, and giggled. Talking had exhausted him. He gestured to Margot.

She carried a clipboard into the light and read from her notes. "We want everything you get and we want it before Behavioral Science sees it, we want Behavioral Science reports as soon as they're filed and we want the VICAP and National Crime Information Center access codes."

"You'd have to use a public phone every time you access VICAP," Krendler said, still talking out into the dark as though the woman wasn't there. "How can you do that?"

"*I* can do it," Margot said.

"She can do it," Mason whispered from the dark.

"She writes workout programs for exercise machines in gyms. It's her little business so she doesn't have to live off of *Brother*."

"The FBI has a closed system and some of it's encrypted. You'll have to sign on from a guest location exactly as I tell you and download to a laptop programmed at the Justice Department," Krendler said. "Then if VICAP hides a tracer cookie on you, it will just come back to Justice. Buy a fast laptop with a fast modem for cash over-the-counter at a volume dealer and don't mail any warranties. Get a zip drive too. Stay off the Net with it. I'll need it overnight and I want it back when you're through. You'll hear from me. Okay, that's it." Krendler stood and gathered his papers.

"That's not *quite* it, Mr Krendler . . ." Mason said. "Lecter doesn't have to come out. He's got the money to hide forever."

"How does he have money?" Margot said.

"He had some very rich old people in his psychiatric practice," Krendler said. "He got them to sign over a lot of money and stocks to him and he hid it good. The IRS hasn't been able to find it. They exhumed the bodies of a couple of his benefactors to see if he'd killed them, but they couldn't find anything. Toxin scans negative."

"So he won't get caught in a stickup, he has cash," Mason said. "We've got to lure him out. Be thinking of ways."

"He'll know where the hit came from in Florence," Krendler said.

"Sure he will."

"So he'll want you."

"I don't know," Mason said. "He likes me like I am. Be thinking, Krendler." Mason began to hum.

All Deputy Assistant Inspector General Krendler heard was humming as he went out the door. Mason often hummed hymns while he was scheming: *You've got the prime bait, Krendler, but we'll discuss it after you've made an incriminating bank deposit—when you belong to me.*

ONLY FAMILY remains in Mason's room, brother and sister.

Soft light and music. North African music, an oud and drums. Margot sits on the couch, head down, elbows on her knees. She might have been a hammer thrower resting, or a weight lifter resting in a gym after a workout. She breathes a little faster than Mason's respirator.

The song ends and she rises, goes to his bedside. The eel pokes his head out of the hole in the artificial rock to see if his wavy silver sky might rain carp again tonight. Margot's raspy voice at its softest. "Are you awake?"

In a moment Mason was present behind his ever-open eye. "Is it time to talk about—a hiss of breath—what *Margot* wants? Sit here on Santa's knee."

"You know what I want."

"Tell me."

"Judy and I want to have a baby. We want to have a Verger baby, our own baby."

"Why don't you buy a Chinese baby? They're cheaper than shoats."

"It's a good thing to do. We might do that too."

"What does Papa's will say . . . *To an heir, confirmed as my descendent in the Cellmark Laboratory or its equivalent by DNA testing, my estate entire upon the passing of my beloved son, Mason.* Beloved son, Mason, that's me. *In the absence of an heir, the sole beneficiary shall be the Southern Baptist Convention with specific clauses concerning Baylor University at Waco, Texas.* You really pissed Papa off with that muff-diving, Margot."

"You may not believe this, Mason, but it's not the money—well, it is a little bit, but don't you want an heir? It would be your heir too, Mason."

"Why don't you find a nice fellow and give him a little nooky, Margot? It's not like you don't know how."

The Moroccan music is building again, the obsessive repetitions of the oud in her ear like anger.

"I've messed myself up, Mason. I shriveled my ovaries with all the stuff I took. And I want Judy to be part of it. She wants to be the birth mother. Mason, you said if I helped you—you promised me some sperm."

Mason's spidery fingers gestured. "Help yourself. If it's still there."

"Mason, there's every chance that you still have viable sperm, and we could arrange to harvest it painlessly—"

"*Harvesting* my *viable sperm?* Sounds like you've been talking to somebody."

"Just the fertility clinic, it's confidential." Margot's face softened, even in the cold light of the aquarium.

"We could be really good to a child, Mason, we've been to parenting classes, Judy comes from a big, tolerant family and there's a support group of women parents."

"You used to be able to make me come when we were kids, Margot. Made me shoot like a belt-fed mortar. And pretty damn fast too."

"You *hurt* me when I was little, Mason. You hurt me and you dislocated my elbow making me do the other—I still can't curl more than eighty pounds with my left arm."

"Well, you wouldn't take the chocolate. I said we'll talk about it, Little Sister, when this job is done."

"Let's just test you now," Margot said. "The doctor can take a painless sample—"

"What *painless*, I can't feel anything down there anyway. You could suck it till you're blue in the face, and it wouldn't be like it was the first time. But I've made people do that already and nothing happens."

"The doctor can take a painless sample, just to see if you've got motile sperm. Judy's taking Clomid already. We're getting her cycle charted, there's a lot of stuff to do."

"I haven't had the pleasure of meeting Judy in all this time. Cordell says she's bowlegged. How long have you two been an *item*, Margot?"

"Five years."

"Why don't you bring her by? We might . . . *work something out*, so to speak."

The North African drums end with a final slap and leave a ringing silence in Margot's ear.

"Why don't you manage your little hookup with the

278

Justice Department by yourself?" she said close to his ear hole. "Why don't you try to get in a phone booth with your fucking laptop. Why don't you pay some more fucking guineas to catch the guy that made dog food out of your face? *You said you'd help me, Mason.*"

"I will. I just have to think about the timing."

Margot crushed two walnuts together and let the shells fall on Mason's sheet. "Don't think too goddamned long, Smiley." Her cycle pants whistled like building steam as she walked out of the room.

ARDELIA MAPP cooked when she felt like it, and when she cooked the result was extremely good. Her heritage was a combination of Jamaican and Gullah, and at the moment she was making jerk chicken, seeding a Scotch bonnet pepper she held carefully by the stem. She refused to pay the premium for cut-up chickens and had Starling busy with the cleaver and the cutting board.

"If you leave the pieces whole, Starling, they won't take the seasoning like they will if you cut them up," she explained, not for the first time. "Here," she said, taking the cleaver and splitting a back with such force bone splinters stuck to her apron. "Like that. What are you doing throwing those necks out? Put that handsome thing back in there."

And a minute later, "I was at the post office today. Mailing the shoes to my mom," Mapp said.

"I was in the post office too, I could have taken them."

"Did you *hear* anything at the post office?"

"Nope."

Mapp nodded, not surprised. "The drum says they're covering your mail."

"Who is?"

"Confidential directive from the Postal Inspector. You didn't know that, did you?"

"No."

"So discover it some other way, we need to cover my post office buddy."

"Okay." Starling put down her cleaver for a moment. "Jesus, Ardelia."

Starling had stood at the post office counter and bought her stamps, reading nothing in the closed faces of the busy postal clerks, most of them African-American, and several of whom she knew. Clearly someone wanted to help her, but it was a big chance to take with criminal penalties and your pension on the line. Clearly that someone trusted Ardelia more than Starling. Along with her anxiety, Starling felt a happy flash at having a favor from the African-American hot line. Maybe it expressed a tacit judgment of self-defense in the shooting of Evelda Drumgo.

"Now, take those green onions and mash them with the knife handle and give them here. Mash the green and all," Ardelia said.

When she had finished the prep work, Starling washed her hands and went into the absolute order of Ardelia's living room and sat down. Ardelia came in in a minute, drying her hands on a dish towel.

"Hell kind of bullshit is this?" Ardelia said.

It was their practice to curse heartily before taking up anything truly ominous, a late-century form of whistling in the dark.

"Be Got Dam if I know," Starling said. "*Who's* the sumbitch looking at my mail, that's the thing."

"PI's office is as far back as my folks can go."

"It's not the shooting, it's not Evelda," Starling said. "If they're looking at my mail, it's got to be about Dr Lecter."

"You turned in every damn thing he ever sent you. You down with Crawford on that."

"Damn straight. If it's the Bureau OPR checking up on me I can find that out, I think. If it's Justice OPR, I don't know."

The Justice Department and its subsidiary, the FBI, have separate Offices of Professional Responsibility, which theoretically cooperate and sometimes collide. Such conflicts are known in-house as pissing contests, and agents caught in the middle sometimes get drowned. In addition, the Inspector General at Justice, a political appointee, can jump in anytime and take over a sensitive case.

"If they know something Hannibal Lecter's up to, if they think he's close, they got to let you know it to protect yourself. Starling, do you ever . . . feel him around you?"

Starling shook her head. "I don't worry about him much. Not that way. I used to go a long time and not even think about it. You know that lead feeling, that heavy gray feeling when you dread something? I don't ever have that. I just think I'd know if I had a problem."

"What would you *do*, Starling? What would you do if you saw him in front of you? All of a sudden? Have you got it set in your mind? Would you throw down on him?"

"Fast as I could grab it out of my *britches*, I'd throw down on his ass."

Ardelia laughed. "And then what?"

Starling's smile went away. "That would be up to him."

"Could you shoot him?"

"To keep my own chitterlings in place, are you kidding me? My *God*, I hope that never happens, Ardelia. I'd be glad if he got back in custody without anybody else getting hurt—including him. I'll tell you though, sometimes I think, if he's ever cornered, I'd want to take the point going in for him."

"Don't even say that."

"With me he'd have a better chance to come out alive. I wouldn't shoot him because I'm scared of him. He's not the wolf man. It would just be up to him."

"Are you scared of him? You better be scared *enough*."

"You know what's scary, Ardelia? It's scary when somebody tells you the truth. I'd like to see him beat the needle. If he can do that, and he's put in an institution, there's enough academic interest in him to keep his treatment pretty good. And he won't have any problem with roommates. If he was in the slams I'd thank him for his note. Can't waste a man that's crazy enough to tell the truth."

"There's a reason somebody's monitoring your mail. They got a court order and it's someplace under seal. We're not staked out yet—we'd have spotted it," Ardelia said. "I wouldn't put it past those sons of bitches to know he's coming and not tell you. You watch out tomorrow."

"Mr Crawford would have told us. They can't mount

much against Lecter without bringing Mr Crawford in on it."

"Jack Crawford is *history*, Starling. You've got a blind spot there. What if they mount something against *you*? For having a wise mouth, for not letting Krendler get in your pants? What if somebody wants to trash you? Hey, I'm serious about covering my source now."

"Is there something we can do for your post office buddy? Do we need to do something?"

"Who do you think is coming to dinner?"

"*All right Ardelia!* . . . Wait a minute, I thought *I* was coming to dinner."

"You can take some home with you."

"I 'preciate it."

"No trouble, girl. My pleasure, in fact."

CHAPTER

47

WHEN STARLING was a child she moved from a clap-
board house that groaned in the wind to the solid
redbrick of the Lutheran Orphanage.

The most ramshackle family dwelling of her early
childhood had had a warm kitchen where she could
share an orange with her father. But death knows
where the little houses are, where people live who
do dangerous work for not much money. Her father
rode away from this house in his old pickup truck on
the night patrol that killed him.

Starling rode away from her foster home on a slaughter horse while they were killing the lambs, and she
found a kind of refuge in the Lutheran Orphanage.
Institutional structures, big and solid, made her feel
safe ever since. The Lutherans might have been short
on warmth and oranges and long on Jesus, but the
rules were the rules and if you understood them you
were okay.

As long as impersonal competitive testing was the
challenge, or doing the job on the street, she knew she

could make her place secure. But Starling had no gift for institutional politics.

Now, as she got out of her old Mustang at the beginning of the day, the high façades of Quantico were no more the great brick bosom of her refuge. Through the crazed air over the parking lot, the very entrances looked crooked.

She wanted to see Jack Crawford, but there was no time. Filming at Hogan's Alley began as soon as the sun was well up.

The investigation of the Feliciana Fish Market Massacre required filmed reenactments made on the Hogan's Alley shooting range at Quantico, with every shot, every trajectory, accounted for.

Starling had to perform her part. The undercover van they used was the original one with body putty, unpainted, plugging the latest bullet holes. Again and again they piled out of the old van, over and over the agent playing John Brigham went down on his face and the one playing Burke writhed on the ground. The process, using noisy blank ammunition, left her wrung out.

They finished in midafternoon.

Starling hung up her SWAT gear and found Jack Crawford in his office.

She was back to addressing him as Mr Crawford now, and he seemed increasingly vague and distant from everyone.

"Want an Alka-Seltzer, Starling?" he said when he saw her in his office door. Crawford took a number of patent medicines in the course of the day. He was also taking Ginkgo Biloba, Saw Palmetto, St John's Wort and baby aspirin. He took them in a certain order from his palm, his head going back as though he were taking a shot of liquor.

In recent weeks, he had started hanging up his suit coat in the office and putting on a sweater his late wife, Bella, had knitted for him. He looked much older now than any memory she had of her own father.

"Mr Crawford, some of my mail is being opened. They're not very good at it. Looks like they're steaming the glue with a teapot."

"You've had mail surveillance since Lecter wrote to you."

"They just fluoroscoped packages. That was fine, but I can read my own personal mail. Nobody's said anything to me."

"It's not our OPR doing it."

"It's not Deputy Dawg either, Mr Crawford—it's somebody big enough to get a Title Three intercept warrant under seal."

"But it looks like amateurs doing the opening?" She was quiet long enough for him to add, "Better if you noticed it that way, is it, Starling?"

"Yes, sir."

He pursed his lips and nodded. "I'll look into it." He arranged his patent medicine bottles in the top drawer of his desk. "I'll speak to Carl Schirmer at Justice, we'll straighten that out."

Schirmer was a lame duck. The grapevine said he'd be retiring at the end of the year—all Crawford's cronies were retiring.

"Thank you, sir."

"Anybody in your cop classes show much promise? Anybody recruiting ought to talk to?"

"In the forensics, I can't tell yet—they're shy with me in sex crimes. There's a couple of pretty good shooters."

"We've got all we need of those." He looked at her quickly. "I didn't mean you."

At the end of this day of playing out his death, she went to John Brigham's grave in Arlington National Cemetery.

Starling put her hand on his stone, still gritty from the chisel. Suddenly she had on her lips the distinct sensation of kissing his forehead, cold as marble and gritty with powder, when she came to his bier the last time and put in his hand, beneath the white glove, her own last medal as Open Combat Pistol Champion.

Now leaves were falling in Arlington, strewing the crowded ground. Starling, with her hand on John Brigham's stone, looking over the acres of graves, wondered how many like him had been wasted by stupidity and selfishness and the bargaining of tired old men.

Whether you believe in God or not, if you are a warrior Arlington is a sacred place, and the tragedy is not to die, but to be wasted.

She felt a bond with Brigham that was no less strong because they were never lovers. On one knee beside his stone she remembered: He asked her something gently and she said no, and then he asked her if they could be friends, and meant it, and she said yes, and meant it.

Kneeling in Arlington, she thought about her father's grave far away. She had not visited it since she graduated first in her college class and went to his grave to tell him. She wondered if it was time to go back.

The sunset through Arlington's black branches was as orange as the orange she shared with her father; the distant bugle shivered her, the tombstone cold beneath her hand.

WE CAN see it through the vapor of our breath—in
the clear night over Newfoundland a brilliant point of
light hanging in Orion, then passing slowly overhead,
a Boeing 747 bucking a hundred-mile-per-hour head
wind westward.

Back in steerage where the package tours go, the
fifty-two members of Old World Fantasy, a tour of
eleven countries in seventeen days, are returning to
Detroit and Windsor, Canada. Shoulder room is twenty
inches. Hip room between armrests is twenty inches.
This is two inches more space than a slave had on the
Middle Passage.

The passengers are being slopped with freezing-cold
sandwiches of slippery meat and processed cheese food,
and are rebreathing the farts and exhalations of others
in economically reprocessed air, a variation on the
ditch-liquor principle established by cattle and pig
merchants in the 1950s.

Dr Hannibal Lecter is in the center of the middle row in steerage with children on both sides of

him and a woman holding an infant at the end of the row. After so many years in cells and restraints, Dr Lecter does not like to be confined. A computer game in the lap of the small boy beside him beeps incessantly.

Like many others scattered throughout the cheapest seats, Dr Lecter wears a bright yellow smiley-face badge with CAN-AM TOURS on it in big red letters, and like the tourists he wears faux athletic warm-ups. His warm-ups bear the insignia of the Toronto Maple Leafs, a hockey team. Beneath his clothing, a considerable amount of cash is strapped to his body.

Dr Lecter has been with the tour three days, having bought his place from a Paris broker of last-minute illness cancellations. The man who should have been in this seat went home to Canada in a box after his heart gave out climbing the dome of St Peter's.

When he reaches Detroit, Dr Lecter must face passport control and customs. He can be sure security and immigration officers at every major airport in the western world have been alerted to watch for him. Where his picture is not taped to the wall of passport control, it is waiting under the hot button of every customs and immigration computer.

In all of this, he thinks that he may enjoy one piece of luck: The pictures the authorities are using could be of his old face. The false passport he used to enter Italy has no corresponding home-country file to provide a current likeness: In Italy, Rinaldo Pazzi had tried to simplify his own life and satisfy Mason Verger by taking the Carabinieri's file, including the photograph and negative used on "Dr Fell's" *permesso di soggiorno* and work permit. Dr Lecter found them in Pazzi's briefcase and destroyed them.

Unless Pazzi took photos of "Dr Fell" from hiding, there is a good chance that no current likeness of Dr Lecter's new face exists in the world. It is not so different from his old face—a little collagen added around the nose and cheeks, changed hair, spectacles— but it is different enough if attention is not called to him. For the scar on the back of his hand, he has found a durable cosmetic and a tanning agent.

He expects that at Detroit Metropolitan Airport the Immigration Service will divide the arrivees into two lines, U.S. Passports and Other. He has chosen a border city so the Other line will be full. This airplane is loaded with Canadians. Dr Lecter thinks he can be swept through with the herd, as long as the herd accepts him. He has toured some historic sites and galleries with these tourists, he has flown in the stews of the airplane with them, but there are limits: He cannot eat this airline swill with them.

Tired and footsore, weary of their clothes and their companions, the tourists root in their supper bags, and from their sandwiches remove the lettuce, black with cold.

Dr Lecter, not wishing to call attention to himself, waits until the other passengers have picked through this sorry fare, waits until they have gone to the bathroom and most have fallen asleep. Far at the front, a stale movie plays. Still he waits with the patience of a python. Beside him the small boy has fallen asleep over his computer game. Up and down the broad airplane, the reading lights wink out.

Then and only then, with a furtive glance around, Dr Lecter takes from beneath the seat in front of him his own lunch in an elegant yellow box trimmed with brown from Fauchon, the Paris caterer. It is tied with two ribbons of silk gauze in complementary colors. Dr Lecter has provisioned himself with wonderfully aromatic truffled pâté de foie gras, and Anatolian figs still weeping from their severed stems. He has a half-bottle of a St Estephe he favors. The silk bow yields with a whisper.

Dr Lecter is about to savor a fig, holds it before his lips, his nostrils flared to its aroma, deciding whether to take all the fig in one glorious bite or just half, when the computer game beside him beeps. It beeps again. Without turning his head, the doctor palms the fig and looks down at the child beside him. The scents of truffle, foie gras and cognac climb from the open box.

The small boy sniffs the air. His narrow eyes, shiny as those of a rodent, slide sideways to Dr Lecter's lunch. He speaks with the piercing voice of a competitive sibling:

"Hey, Mister. Hey, Mister." He's not going to stop.

"What is it?"

"Is that one of those special meals?"

"It is not."

"What've you got in there then?" The child turned his face up to Dr Lecter in a full wheedle. *"Gimme a bite?"*

"I'd very much like to," Dr Lecter replied, noting that beneath the child's big head, his neck was only as big around as a pork tenderloin, "but you wouldn't like it. It's *liver.*"

"Liverwurst! Awesome! Mom won't care, Mooaaaahm!"

Unnatural child, who loves liverwurst and either whines or screams.

The woman holding the baby at the end of the row started awake.

Travelers in the row ahead, their chairs cranked back until Dr Lecter can smell their hair, look back through the crack between seats. "We're trying to sleep up here."

"*Mooooaaaahm, can I have some of his samwich?*"

The baby in Mother's lap awoke and began to cry. Mother dipped a finger into the back of its diaper, came up negative, and gave the baby a pacifier.

"What is it you're trying to *give* him, sir?"

"It's liver, Madame," Dr Lecter said as quietly as possible. "I haven't given—"

"*Liverwurst, my favorite, I want it, he* said *I could have some of it* . . ." The child stretched the last word into a piercing whine.

"Sir, if you're giving something to my *child*, could I see it?"

The stewardess, her face puffed from an interrupted nap, stopped by the woman's seat as the baby howled. "Everything all right here? Could I bring you something? Warm a bottle?"

The woman took out a capped baby bottle and gave it to the stewardess. She turned on her reading light, and while she searched for a nipple, she called to Dr Lecter. "Would you pass it down to me? If you're offering it to my *child*, I want to see it. No offense, but he's got a tricky tummy."

We routinely leave our small children in day care among strangers. At the same time, in our guilt we evince paranoia about strangers and foster fear in children. In times like these, a genuine monster has to watch it, even a monster as indifferent to children as Dr Lecter.

He passed his Fauchon box down to Mother.

"Hey, nice bread," she said, poking it with her diaper finger.

"Madame, you may *have* it."

"I don't want the *liquor*," she said, and looked around for a laugh. "I didn't know they'd let you bring your own. Is this *whiskey*? Do they *allow* you to drink this on the plane? I think I'll keep this ribbon if you don't want it."

"*Sir*, you can't open this alcoholic beverage on the aircraft," the stewardess said. "I'll hold it for you, you can claim it at the gate."

"Of course. Thank you so much," Dr Lecter said.

Dr Lecter could overcome his surroundings. He could make it all go away. The beeping of the computer game, the snores and farts, were nothing compared to the hellish screaming he'd known in the violent wards. The seat was no tighter than restraints. As he had done in his cell so many times, Dr Lecter put his head back, closed his eyes and retired for relief into the quiet of his memory palace, a place that is quite beautiful for the most part.

For this little time, the metal cylinder howling eastward against the wind contains a palace of a thousand rooms.

As once we visited Dr Lecter in the Palazzo of the Capponi, so we will go with him now into the palace of his mind . . .

The foyer is the Norman Chapel in Palermo, severe and beautiful and timeless, with a single reminder of mortality in the skull graven in the floor. Unless he is in a great hurry to retrieve information from the palace, Dr Lecter often pauses here as he does now, to admire the chapel. Beyond it, far and complex, light and dark, is the vast structure of Dr Lecter's making.

The memory palace was a mnemonic system well known to ancient scholars and much information was preserved in them through the Dark Ages while Vandals burned the books. Like scholars before him, Dr Lecter stores an enormous amount of information keyed to objects in his thousand rooms, but unlike the ancients, Dr Lecter has a second purpose for his palace; sometimes he lives there. He has passed years among its exquisite collections, while his body lay bound on a violent ward with screams buzzing the steel bars like hell's own harp.

Hannibal Lecter's palace is vast, even by medieval standards. Translated to the tangible world it would rival the Topkapi Palace in Istanbul for size and complexity.

We catch up to him as the swift slippers of his mind pass from the foyer into the Great Hall of the Seasons. The palace is built according to the rules discovered by Simonides of Ceos and elaborated by Cicero four hundred years later; it is airy, high-ceilinged, furnished with objects and tableaux that are vivid, striking, sometimes shocking and absurd, and often beautiful. The displays are well spaced and well lighted like those of a great museum. But the walls are not the neutral colors of museum walls. Like Giotto, Dr Lecter has frescoed the walls of his mind.

He has decided to pick up Clarice Starling's home address while he is in the palace, but he is in no hurry for it, so he stops at the foot of a great staircase where the Riace bronzes stand. These great bronze warriors attributed to Phidias, raised from the seafloor in our own time, are the centerpiece of a frescoed space that could unspool all of Homer and Sophocles.

Dr Lecter could have the bronze faces speak Meleager if he wished, but today he only wants to look at them.

A thousand rooms, miles of corridors, hundreds of facts attached to each object furnishing each room, a pleasant respite awaiting Dr Lecter whenever he chooses to retire there.

But this we share with the doctor: In the vaults of our hearts and brains, danger waits. All the chambers are not lovely, light and high. There are holes in the floor of the mind, like those in a medieval dungeon floor—the stinking oubliettes, named for forgetting, bottle-shaped cells in solid rock with the trapdoor in the top. Nothing escapes from them quietly to ease us. A quake, some betrayal by our safeguards, and sparks of memory fire the noxious gases—things trapped for years fly free, ready to explode in pain and drive us to dangerous behavior . . .

Fearfully and wonderfully made, we follow as he moves with a swift light stride along the corridor of his own making, through a scent of gardenias, the presence of great sculpture pressing on us, and the light of pictures.

His way leads around to the right past a bust of

Pliny and up the staircase to the Hall of Addresses, a room lined with statuary and paintings in a fixed order, spaced wide apart and well lit, as Cicero recommends.

Ah . . . The third alcove from the door on the right is dominated by a painting of St Francis feeding a moth to a starling. On the floor before the painting is this tableau, life-sized in painted marble:

A parade in Arlington National Cemetery led by Jesus, thirty-three, driving a '27 Model-T Ford truck, a "tin lizzie," with J. Edgar Hoover standing in the truck bed wearing a tutu and waving to an unseen crowd. Marching behind him is Clarice Starling carrying a .308 Enfield rifle at shoulder arms.

Dr Lecter appears pleased to see Starling. Long ago he obtained Starling's home address from the University of Virginia Alumni Association. He stores the address in this tableau, and now, for his own pleasure, he summons the numbers and the name of the street where Starling lives:

3327 Tindal

Arlington, VA 22308

Dr Lecter can move down the vast halls of his memory palace with unnatural speed. With his reflexes and strength, apprehension and speed of mind, Dr Lecter is well armed against the physical world. But there are places within himself that he may not safely go, where Cicero's rules of logic, of ordered space and light do not apply . . .

He has decided to visit his collection of ancient textiles. For a letter he is writing to Mason Verger, he wants to review a text of Ovid on the subject of flavored facial oils which is attached to the weavings.

He proceeds down an interesting flat-weave kilim runner toward the hall of looms and textiles.

In the world of the 747, Dr Lecter's head is pressed back against the seat, his eyes are closed. His head bobs gently as turbulence bumps the airplane.

At the end of the row, the baby has finished its bottle and is not yet asleep. Its face reddens. Mother feels the little body tense within the blanket, then relax. There is no question what has happened. She does not need to dip her finger in the diaper. In the row ahead someone says "Jeeeezus."

To the stale gymnasium reek of the airplane is added another layer of smell. The small boy, seated beside Dr Lecter, inured to the baby's habits, continues to eat the lunch from Fauchon.

Beneath the memory palace, the traps fly up, the oubliettes yawn their ghastly stench . . .

A few animals had managed to survive the artillery and machine-gun fire in the fighting that left Hannibal Lecter's parents dead and the vast forest on their estate scarred and blasted.

The mixed bag of deserters who used the remote hunting lodge ate what they could find. Once they found a miserable little deer, scrawny, with an arrow in it, that had managed to forage beneath the snow and survive. They led it back into the camp to keep from carrying it.

Hannibal Lecter, six, watched through a crack in the barn as they brought it in, pulling and twisting its head against the plowline twisted around its neck. They did not wish to fire a shot and managed to knock it off its spindly legs and hack at its throat with an axe, cursing at one another in several languages to bring a bowl before the blood was wasted.

There was not much meat on the runty deer and in two days, perhaps three, in their long overcoats, their breaths stinking and steaming, the deserters came through the snow from the hunting lodge to unlock the barn and choose again from among the children huddled in the straw. None had frozen, so they took a live one.

They felt Hannibal Lecter's thigh and his upper arm and chest, and instead of him, they chose his sister, Mischa, and led her away. To play, they said. No one who was led away to play ever returned.

Hannibal held on to Mischa so hard, held to Mischa with his wiry grip until they slammed the heavy barn door on him, stunning him and cracking the bone in his upper arm.

They led her away through snow still stained bloody from the deer.

He prayed so hard that he would see Mischa again, the prayer consumed his six-year-old mind, but it did not drown out the sound of the axe. His prayer to see her again did not go entirely unanswered—he did see a few of Mischa's milk teeth in the reeking stool pit his captors used between the lodge where they slept and the barn where they kept the captive children who were their sustenance in 1944 after the Eastern Front collapsed.

Since this partial answer to his prayer, Hannibal Lecter had not been bothered by any considerations of deity, other than to recognize how his own modest predations paled beside those of God, who is in irony matchless, and in wanton malice beyond measure.

In this hurtling aircraft, his head bouncing gently against the head-rest, Dr Lecter is suspended between his last view of Mischa crossing the bloody snow and the sound of the axe. He is held there and he cannot stand it. In the world of the airplane comes a short scream from his sweating face, thin and high, piercing.

Passengers ahead of him turn, some wake from sleep. Some in the row ahead of him are snarling. "Kid, Jesus Christ, what is the *matter* with you? My God!"

Dr Lecter's eyes open, they look straight ahead, a hand is on him. It is the small boy's hand.

"You had a bad dream, huh?" The child is not frightened, nor does he care about the complaints from the forward rows.

"Yes."

"I have bad dreams a lots of times too. I'm not laughing at you."

Dr Lecter took several breaths, his head pressed back against the seat. Then his composure returned as though calm rolled down from his hairline to cover his face. He bent his head to the child and said in a confidential tone, "You're right not to eat this swill, you know. Don't ever eat it."

Airlines no longer provide stationery. Dr Lecter, in perfect command of himself, took some hotel stationery from his breast pocket and began a letter to Clarice Starling. First, he sketched her face. The sketch is now in a private holding at the University of Chicago and available to scholars. In it Starling looks like a child and her hair, like Mischa's, is stuck to her cheek with tears . . .

We can see the airplane through the vapor of our breath, a brilliant point of light in the clear night sky. See it cross the Pole star, well past the point of no return, committed now to a great arc down to tomorrow in the New World.

CHAPTER

49

THE STACKS of paper and files and diskettes in Starling's cubicle reached critical mass. Her request for more space went unanswered. *Enough.* With the recklessness of the damned she commandeered a spacious room in the basement at Quantico. The room was supposed to become Behavioral Science's private darkroom as soon as Congress appropriated some money. It had no windows, but plenty of shelves and, being built for a darkroom, it had double blackout curtains instead of a door.

Some anonymous office neighbor printed a sign in Gothic letters that read HANNIBAL'S HOUSE and pinned it on her curtained entrance. Fearful of losing the room, Starling moved the sign inside.

Almost at once she found a trove of useful personal material at the Columbia College of Criminal Justice Library, where they maintained a Hannibal Lecter Room. The college had original papers from his medical and psychiatric practices and transcripts of his trial and the civil actions against him. On her first visit to the library Starling waited forty-five minutes while custodians hunted for the keys to the Lecter room without success. On the second occasion, she found an indifferent graduate student in charge, and the material uncatalogued.

Starling's patience was not improving in her fourth decade. With Section Chief Jack Crawford backing her at the U.S. Attorney's office, she got a court order to move the entire college collection to her basement room at Quantico. Federal marshals accomplished the move in a single van.

The court order created waves, as she feared it would. Eventually, the waves brought Krendler . . .

At the end of a long two weeks, Starling had most of the library material organized in her makeshift Lecter center. Late on a Friday afternoon she washed her face and hands of the bookdust and grime, turned down the lights and sat on the floor in the corner, looking at the many shelf-feet of books and papers. It is possible that she nodded off for a moment . . .

A smell awakened her, and she was aware that she was not alone. It was the smell of shoe polish.

The room was semidark, and Deputy Assistant Inspector General Paul Krendler moved along the shelves slowly, peering at the books and pictures. He hadn't bothered to knock—there was no place to knock on the curtains and Krendler was not inclined to knocking anyway, especially at subordinate agencies. Here, in this basement at Quantico, he was definitely slumming.

One wall of the room was devoted to Dr Lecter in Italy, with a large photograph posted of Rinaldo

Pazzi hanging with his bowels out from the window at Palazzo Vecchio. The opposite wall was concerned with crimes in the United States, and was dominated by a police photograph of the bow hunter Dr Lecter had killed years ago. The body was hanging on a peg board and bore all the wounds of the medieval Wound Man illustrations. Many case files were stacked on the shelves along with civil records of wrongful death lawsuits filed against Dr Lecter by families of the victims.

Dr Lecter's personal books from his medical practice were here in an order identical to their arrangement in his old psychiatric office. Starling had arranged them by examining police photos of the office with a magnifying glass.

Much of the light in the dim room came through an X ray of the doctor's head and neck which glowed on a light box on the wall. The other light came from a computer workstation at a corner desk. The screen theme was "Dangerous Creatures." Now and then the computer growled.

Piled beside the machine were the results of Starling's gleaning. The painfully gathered scraps of paper, receipts, itemized bills that revealed how Dr Lecter had lived his private life in Italy, and in America before he was sent to the asylum. It was a makeshift catalog of his tastes.

Using a flatbed scanner for a table, Starling had laid a single place setting that survived from his home in Baltimore—china, silver, crystal, napery radiant white, a candlestick—four square feet of elegance against the grotesque hangings of the room.

Krendler picked up the large wineglass and pinged it with his fingernail.

Krendler had never felt the flesh of a criminal, never fought one on the ground, and he thought of Dr Lecter as a sort of media bogeyman and an opportunity. He could see his own photograph in association with a display like this in the FBI museum once Lecter was dead. He could see its enormous campaign value. Krendler had his nose close to the X-ray profile of the doctor's capacious skull, and when Starling spoke to him, he jumped enough to smudge the X ray with nose grease.

"Can I help you, Mr Krendler?"

"Why're you sitting there in the dark?"

"I'm thinking, Mr Krendler."

"People on the Hill want to know what we're doing about Lecter."

"This is what we're doing."

"Brief me, Starling. Bring me up to speed."

"Wouldn't you prefer Mr Crawford—"

"Where *is* Crawford?"

"Mr Crawford's in court."

"I think he's losing it, do you ever feel that way?"

"No, sir, I don't."

"What are you doing here? We got a beef from the college when you seized all this stuff out of their library. It could have been handled better."

"We've gathered everything we can find regarding Dr Lecter here in this place, both objects and records. His weapons are in Firearms and Toolmarks, but we have duplicates. We have what's left of his personal papers."

"What's the point? You catching a crook, or writing a book?" Krendler paused to store this catchy rhyme in his verbal magazine. "If, say, a ranking Republican on Judiciary Oversight should ask me what *you*, Special Agent Starling, are doing to catch Hannibal Lecter, what could I tell him?"

Starling turned on all the lights. She could see that Krendler was still buying expensive suits while saving money on his shirts and ties. The knobs of his hairy wrists poked out of his cuffs.

Starling looked for a moment through the wall, past the wall, out to forever and composed herself. She made herself see Krendler as a police academy class.

"We know Dr Lecter has very good ID," she began. "He must have at least one extra solid identity, maybe more. He's careful that way. He won't make a dumb mistake."

"Get to it."

"He's a man of very cultivated tastes, some of them exotic tastes, in food, in wine, music. If he comes here, he'll want those things. He'll have to get them. He won't deny himself.

"Mr Crawford and I went over the receipts and papers left from Dr Lecter's life in Baltimore before he was first arrested, and what receipts the Italian police were able to furnish, lawsuits from creditors after his arrest. We made a list of some things he likes. You can see here: In the month that Dr Lecter served the flautist Benjamin Raspail's sweetbreads to other members of the Baltimore Philharmonic Orchestra board, he bought two cases of Château Pétrus bordeaux at thirty-six hundred dollars a case. He bought five cases of Bâtard-Montrachet at eleven hundred dollars a case, and a variety of lesser wines.

"He ordered the same wine from room service in St Louis after he escaped, and he ordered it from Vera dal 1926 in Florence. This stuff is pretty rarified. We're checking importers and dealers for case sales.

"From the Iron Gate in New York, he ordered Grade A foie gras at two hundred dollars a kilo, and through the Grand Central Oyster Bar he got green oysters from the Gironde. The meal for the Philharmonic board began with these oysters, followed by sweet-breads, a sorbet, and then, you can read here in *Town & Country* what they had"—she read aloud quickly—"*a notable dark and glossy ragout, the constituents never determined, on saffron rice. Its taste was darkly thrilling with great bass tones that only the vast and careful reduction of the* fond *can give*. No victim's ever been identified as being in the ragout. Da da, it goes on—here it describes his distinctive tableware and stuff in detail. We're cross-checking credit card purchases at the china and crystal suppliers."

Krendler snorted through his nose.

"See, here in this civil suit, he still owes for a Steuben chandelier, and Galeazzo Motor Company of Baltimore sued to get back his Bentley. We're tracking sales of Bentleys, new and used. There aren't that many. And the sales of supercharged Jaguars. We've faxed the restaurant game suppliers asking about purchases of wild boar and we'll do a bulletin the week before the red-legged partridges come in from Scotland." She pecked at her keyboard and consulted a list, then stepped away from the machine when she felt Krendler's breath too close behind her.

"I've put in for funds to buy cooperation from some of the premier scalpers of cultural tickets, the culture vultures, in New York and San Francisco—there are a couple of orchestras and string quartets he particularly likes, he favors the six or seventh row and always sits on the aisle. I've distributed the best likenesses we have to Lincoln Center and Kennedy Center, and most of the philharmonic halls. Maybe you could help us with that out of the DOJ budget, Mr Krendler." When he didn't reply, she went on. "We're cross-checking new subscriptions to some cultural journals he's subscribed to in the past—anthropology, linguistics, *Physical Review*, mathematics, music."

"Does he hire S and M whores, that kind of thing? Male prostitutes?"

Starling could feel Krendler's relish in the question. "Not to our knowledge, Mr Krendler. He was seen at concerts in Baltimore years ago with several attractive women, a couple of them were prominent in Baltimore charity work and stuff. We have their birthdays flagged for gift purchases. None of them was ever harmed to our knowledge, and none has ever agreed to speak about him. We don't know anything about his sexual preferences."

"I've always figured he was a homo-sexual."

"Why would you say that, Mr Krendler?"

"All this artsy-fartsy stuff. Chamber music and tea-party food. I don't mean anything personal, if you've got a lot of sympathy for those people, or friends like that. The main thing, what I'm impressing on you,

Starling: I *better* see cooperation here. There are no little fiefdoms. I want to be copied on every 302, I want every time card, I want every lead. Do you understand me, Starling?"

"Yes, sir."

At the door he said, "Be sure you do. You might have a chance to improve your situation here. Your so-called career could use all the help it can get."

The future darkroom was already equipped with vent fans. Looking him in the face, Starling flipped them on, sucking out the smell of his aftershave and his shoe polish. Krendler pushed through the blackout curtains without saying good-bye.

The air danced in front of Starling like heat shimmer on the gunnery range.

In the hall Krendler heard Starling's voice behind him.

"I'll walk outside with you, Mr Krendler."

Krendler had a car and driver waiting. He was still at the level of executive transport where he made do with a Mercury Grand Marquis sedan.

Before he could get to his car, out in the clear air, she said, "Hold it, Mr Krendler."

Krendler turned to her, wondering. Might be a glimmer of something here. Angry surrender? His antenna went up.

"We're here in the great out-of-doors," Starling said. "No listening devices around, unless you're wearing one." An urge hit her that she could not resist. To work with the dusty books she was wearing a loose denim shirt over a snug tank top.

Shouldn't do this. *Fuck it.*

She popped the snaps on her shirt and pulled it open. "See, I'm not wearing a wire." She wasn't wearing a bra either. "This is maybe the only time we'll ever talk in private, and I want to ask you. For years I've been doing the job and every time you could you've stuck the knife in me. What is it with you, Mr Krendler?"

"You're welcome to come talk about it . . . I'll make time for you, if you want to review . . ."

"We're talking about it now."

"You figure it out, Starling."

"Is it because I wouldn't see you on the side? Was it when I told you to go home to your wife?"

He looked at her again. She really wasn't wearing a wire.

"Don't flatter yourself, Starling . . . this town is full of cornpone country pussy."

He got in beside his driver and tapped on the dash, and the big car moved away. His lips moved, as he wished he had framed it: "Cornpone cunts like you." There was a lot of political speaking in Krendler's future, he believed, and he wanted to sharpen his verbal karate, and get the knack of the sound bite.

"IT COULD work, I'm telling you," Krendler said into the wheezing dark where Mason lay. "Ten years ago, you couldn't have done it, but she can move customer lists through that computer like shit through a goose." He shifted on the couch under the bright lights of the seating area.

Krendler could see Margot silhouetted against the aquarium. He was used to cursing in front of her now, and rather enjoyed it. He bet Margot wished she had a dick. He felt like saying *dick* in front of Margot, and thought of a way: "It's how she's got the fields set up, and paired Lecter's preferences. She could probably tell you which way he carries his dick."

"On that note, Margot, bring in Dr Doemling," Mason said.

Dr Doemling had been waiting out in the playroom among the giant stuffed animals. Mason could see him on video examining the plush scrotum of the big giraffe, much as the Viggerts had orbited the David. On the screen he looked much smaller than

312

the toys, as though he had compressed himself, the better to worm his way into some childhood other than his own.

Seen under the lights of Mason's seating area, the psychologist was a dry person, extremely clean but flaking, with a dry comb-over on his spotted scalp and a Phi Beta Kappa key on his watch chain. He sat down on the opposite side of the coffee table from Krendler and seemed familiar with the room.

There was a worm hole in the apple on his side of the bowl of fruits and nuts. Dr Doemling turned the hole to face the other way. Behind his glasses, his eyes followed Margot with a degree of wonderment bordering on the oafish as she got another pair of walnuts and returned to her place by the aquarium.

"Dr Doemling's head of the psychology department at Baylor University. He holds the Verger Chair," Mason told Krendler. "I've asked him what kind of bond there might be between Dr Lecter and the FBI agent Clarice Starling. Doctor . . ."

Doemling faced forward in his seat as though it were a witness stand and turned his head to Mason as he would to a jury. Krendler could see in him the practiced manner, the careful partisanship of the two-thousand-dollar-a-day expert witness.

"Mr Verger obviously knows my qualifications, would you like to hear them?" Doemling asked.

"No," Krendler said.

"I've reviewed the Starling woman's notes on her interviews with Hannibal Lecter, his letters to her, and the material you provided me on their backgrounds," Doemling began.

Krendler winced at this, and Mason said, "Dr Doemling has signed a confidentiality agreement."

"Cordell will put your slides up on the elmo when you want them, Doctor," Margot said.

"A little background first." Doemling consulted his notes. "We *knooowww* Hannibal Lecter was born in Lithuania. His father was a count, title dating from the tenth century, his mother high-born Italian, a Visconti. During the German retreat from Russia some passing Nazi panzers shelled their estate near Vilnius from the high road and killed both parents and most of the servants. The children disappeared after that. There were two of them, Hannibal and his sister. We don't know what happened to the sister. The point is, Lecter was an orphan, like Clarice Starling."

"Which I told *you*," Mason said impatiently.

"But what did you conclude from it?" Dr Doemling asked. "I'm not proposing a kind of sympathy between two orphans, Mr Verger. This is not about sympathy. Sympathy does not enter here. And mercy is left bleeding in the dust. Listen to me. What a common experience of being an orphan gives Dr Lecter is simply a better ability to understand her, and ultimately control her. This is all about *control*.

"The Starling woman spent her childhood in institutions, and from what you tell me she does not evidence any stable personal relationship with a man. She lives with a former classmate, a young African-American woman."

"That's very likely a sex thing," Krendler said.

The psychiatrist did not even spare Krendler a look— Krendler was automatically overruled. "You can never

314

say to a certainty why someone lives with someone else."

"It is one of the things that is hid, as the Bible says," Mason said.

"Starling looks pretty tasty, if you like whole wheat," Margot offered.

"I think the attraction's from Lecter's end, not hers," Krendler said. "You've seen her—she's a pretty cold fish."

"*Is* she a cold fish, Mr Krendler?" Margot sounded amused.

"You think she's queer, Margot?" Mason asked.

"How the hell would I know? Whatever she is, she treats it as her own damn business—that was my impression. I think she's tough, and she had on her game face, but I wouldn't say she's a cold fish. We didn't talk much, but that's what I took from it. That was before you *needed* me to *help* you, Mason—you ran me out, remember? I'm not going to say she's a cold fish. Girl who looks like Starling has to keep a certain distance in her face because *assholes* are hitting on her all the time."

Here Krendler felt that Margot looked at him a beat too long, though he could only see her in outline.

How curious, the voices in this room. Krendler's careful bureauese, Doemling's pedantic bray, Mason's deep and resonant tones with his badly pruned plosives and leaking sibilants and Margot, her voice rough and low, tough-mouthed as a livery pony and resentful of the bit. Under it all, the gasping machinery that finds Mason breath.

"I have an idea about her private life, regarding her

apparent father fixation," Doemling went on. "I'll get into it shortly. Now, we have three documents of Dr Lecter's concerning Clarice Starling. Two letters and a drawing. The drawing is of the Crucifixion Clock he designed while he was in the asylum." Dr Doemling looked up at the screen. "The slide, please."

From somewhere outside the room, Cordell put up the extraordinary sketch on the elevated monitor. The original is charcoal on butcher paper. Mason's copy was made on a blueprint copier and the lines are the blue of a bruise.

"He tried to patent this," Dr Doemling said. "As you can see, here is Christ crucified on a clock face and His arms revolve to tell the time, just like the Mickey Mouse watches. It's interesting because the face, the head hanging forward, is that of Clarice Starling. He drew it at the time of their interviews. Here's a photograph of the woman, you can see. *Cordell*, is it? Cordell, put up the photo please."

There was no question, the Jesus head was Starling.

"Another anomaly is that the figure is nailed to the cross through the wrists rather than the palms."

"That's accurate," Mason said. "You've *got* to nail them through the wrists and use big wooden washers, otherwise they get loose and start flapping. Idi Amin and I found that out the hard way when we reenacted the whole thing in Uganda at Easter. Our Saviour was actually nailed through the wrists. All the Crucifixion paintings are wrong. It's a mistranslation between the Hebrew and Latin Bibles."

"Thank you," Dr Doemling said without sincerity. "The Crucifixion clearly represents a destroyed object of veneration. Note that the arm that forms the minute hand is at six, modestly covering the pudenda. The hour hand is at nine, or slightly past. Nine is a clear reference to the traditional hour when Jesus was crucified."

"And when you put six and nine together, note that you get sixty-nine, a figure popular in social intercourse," Margot could not help saying. In response to Doemling's sharp glance, she cracked her walnuts and shells rattled to the floor.

"Now let's take up Dr Lecter's letters to Clarice Starling. Cordell, if you'd put them up." Dr Doemling took a laser pointer from his pocket. "You can see that the writing, a fluent copperplate executed with a square-nibbed fountain pen, is machinelike in its regularity. You see that sort of handwriting in medieval papal bulls. It's quite beautiful, but freakishly regular. There is nothing spontaneous here. He's planning. He wrote this first one soon after he had escaped, killing five people in the process. Let's read from the text:

Well, Clarice, have the lambs stopped screaming?

You owe me a piece of information, you know, and that's what I'd like.

An ad in the national edition of the Times *and in the* International Herald-Tribune *on the first of any month will be fine. Better put it in the* China Mail *as well.*

I won't be surprised if the answer is yes and no. The lambs will stop for now. But, Clarice, you judge yourself with all the mercy of the dungeon scales at Threave; you'll have to earn it again and again, the blessed silence. Because it's the plight that drives you, seeing the plight, and the plight will not end, ever.

I have no plans to call on you, Clarice, the world being more interesting with you in it. Be sure you extend me the same courtesy . . .

Dr Doemling pushed his rimless glasses up on his nose and cleared his throat. "This is a classic example of what I have termed in my published work *avunculism*—it's beginning to be referred to broadly in the professional literature as *Doemling's avunculism*. Possibly it will be included in the next *Diagnostic and Statistical Manual*. It may be defined for laymen as the act of posturing as a wise and caring patron to further a private agenda.

"I gather from the case notes that the question about the lambs screaming refers to a childhood experience of Clarice Starling's, the slaughter of the lambs on the ranch in Montana, her foster home," Dr Doemling went on in his dry voice.

"She was trading information with Lecter," Krendler said. "He knew something about the serial killer Buffalo Bill."

"The second letter, seven years later, is on the face of it a letter of condolence and support," Doemling said. "He taunts her with references to her parents, whom she apparently venerates. He calls her father 'the dead night watchman' and her mother 'the chambermaid.' And then he invests them with excellent qualities she can imagine that they had, and further enlists these qualities to excuse her own failings in her career. This is about ingratiation, this is about control.

"I think the woman Starling may have a lasting attachment to her father, an *imago*, that prevents her from easily forming sexual relationships and may incline her to Dr Lecter in some kind of transference, which in his perversity he would seize on at once. In this second letter he again encourages her to contact him with a personal ad, and he provides a code name."

My Christ, the man went on! Restlessness and boredom were torture for Mason because he couldn't fidget. "Right, fine, good, Doctor," Mason interrupted. "Margot, open the window a little. I've got a new source on Lecter, Dr Doemling. Someone who knows both Starling and Lecter and saw them together, and he's been around Lecter more than anyone. I want you to talk to him."

Krendler squirmed on the couch, his bowels beginning to stir as he saw where this was going.

CHAPTER
51

MASON SPOKE into his intercom and a tall figure came into the room. He was as muscular as Margot and dressed in whites.

"This is Barney," Mason said. "He was in charge of the violent ward at the Baltimore State Hospital for the Criminally Insane for six years when Lecter was there. Now he works for me."

Barney preferred to stand in front of the aquarium with Margot, but Dr Doemling wanted him in the light. He took a place beside Krendler.

"*Barney* is it? Now, *Barney*, what is your professional training?"

"I have an LPN."

"You're a *licensed practical nurse*? Good for you. Is that all?"

"I have a bachelor's degree in the humanities from the United States Correspondence College," Barney said, expressionless. "And a certificate of attendance from the Cummins School of Mortuary Science. I'm qualified as a diener. I did that at night during nursing school."

"You worked your way through LPN school as a morgue attendant?"

"Yes, removing bodies from crime scenes and assisting at autopsies."

"Before that."

"Marine Corps."

"I see. And while you were working at the state hospital you saw Clarice Starling and Hannibal Lecter interacting—what I mean is, you saw them talking together?"

"It seemed to me they—"

"Let's start with just exactly *what* you saw, not what you *thought* about what you saw, can we do that?"

Mason interrupted. "He's smart enough to give his opinion. Barney, you know Clarice Starling."

"Yes."

"You knew Hannibal Lecter for six years."

"Yes."

"What was it between them?"

At first Krendler had trouble understanding Barney's high, rough voice, but it was Krendler who asked the pertinent question. "Did Lecter act differently in the Starling interviews, Barney?"

"Yes. Most of the time he didn't respond at all to visitors," Barney said. "Sometimes he would open his eyes long enough to insult some academic who was trying to pick his brain. He made one visiting professor cry. He was tough with Starling, but he answered her more than most. He was interested in her. She intrigued him."

"How?"

Barney shrugged. "He hardly ever got to see women. She's really good-looking—"

321

"I don't need your opinion on that," Krendler said. "Is that all you know?"

Barney did not reply. He looked at Krendler as though the left and right hemispheres of Krendler's brain were two dogs stuck together.

Margot cracked another walnut.

"Go on, Barney," Mason said.

"They were frank with one another. He's disarming that way. You have the feeling that he wouldn't deign to lie."

"Wouldn't do *what* to lie?" Krendler said.

"*Deign*," Barney said.

"D-E-I-G-N," Margot Verger said out of the dark. "To condescend. Or to *stoop*, Mr Krendler."

Barney went on. "Dr Lecter told her some unpleasant things about herself, and then some pleasant ones. She could face the bad things, and then enjoy the good more, knowing it wasn't bullshit. He thought she was charming and amusing."

"*You* can judge what Hannibal Lecter found 'amusing'?" Dr Doemling said. "Just how do you go about that, *Nurse* Barney?"

"By listening to him laugh, Dr *Dumling*. They taught us that in LPN school, a lecture called 'Healing and the Cheerful Outlook.'"

Either Margot snorted or the aquarium behind her made the noise.

"Cool it, Barney. Tell us the rest," Mason said.

"Yes, sir. Sometimes Dr Lecter and I would talk late at night, when it got quiet enough. We talked about courses I was taking, and other things. He—"

"Were you taking some kind of mail-order course in

psychology, by any chance?" Doemling had to say.

"No, sir, I don't consider psychology a science. Neither did Dr Lecter." Barney went on quickly, before Mason's respirator permitted him to utter a rebuke. "I can just repeat what he told me—he could see what she was *becoming*, she was charming the way a cub is charming, a small cub that will grow up to be—like one of the big cats. One you can't play with later. She had the cublike earnestness, he said. She had all the weapons, in miniature and growing, and all she knew so far was how to wrestle with other cubs. That amused him.

"The way it began between them will tell you something. At the beginning he was courteous but he pretty much dismissed her—then as she was leaving another inmate threw some semen in her face. That disturbed Dr Lecter, embarrassed him. It was the only time I ever saw him upset. She saw it too and tried to use it on him. He admired her moxie, I think."

"What was his attitude toward the other inmate—who threw the semen? Did they have any kind of relationship?"

"Not exactly," Barney said. "Dr Lecter just killed him that night."

"They were in separate cells?" Doemling asked. "How did he do it?"

"Three cells apart on opposite sides of the corridor," Barney said. "In the middle of the night Dr Lecter talked to him awhile and then told him to swallow his tongue."

"So Clarice Starling and Hannibal Lecter became . . . friendly?" Mason said.

323

"Inside a kind of formal structure," Barney said. "They exchanged information. Dr Lecter gave her insight on the serial killer she was hunting, and she paid for it with personal information. Dr Lecter told me he thought Starling might have too much nerve for her own good, an 'excess of zeal,' he called it. He thought she might work too close to the edge if she thought her assignment required it. And he said once that she was 'cursed with taste.' I don't know what that means."

"Dr Doemling, does he want to fuck her or kill her, or eat her, or what?" Mason asked, exhausting the possibilities he could see.

"Probably all three," Dr Doemling said. "I wouldn't want to predict the order in which he wants to perform those acts. That's the burden of what I can tell you. No matter how the tabloids—and tabloid mentalities— might want to romanticize it, and try to make it *Beauty and the Beast*, his object is her degradation, her suffering, and her death. He has responded to her twice: when she was insulted with the semen in her face and when she was torn apart in the newspapers after she shot those people. He comes in the guise of a mentor, but it's the *distress* that excites him. When the history of Hannibal Lecter is written, and it will be, this will be recorded as a case of *Doemling's avunculism*. To draw him she needs to be distressed."

A furrow has appeared in the broad rubbery space between Barney's eyes. "May I put something in here, Mr Verger, since you asked me?" He did not wait for permission. "In the asylum, Dr Lecter responded to her when she held on to herself, stood there wiping come off her face and did her job. In the letters he calls her a warrior, and points out that she saved that child in the shoot-out. He admires and respects her courage and her discipline. He says himself he's got no plans to come around. One thing he does *not* do is lie."

"That's exactly the kind of tabloid thinking I was talking about," Doemling said. "Hannibal Lecter does not have emotions like admiration or respect. He feels no warmth or affection. That's a romantic delusion, and it shows the dangers of a little education."

"Dr Doemling, you don't remember me, do you?" Barney said. "I was in charge of the ward when *you* tried to talk to Dr Lecter, a lot of people tried it, but you're the one who left crying as I recall. Then he reviewed your book in the *American Journal of Psychiatry*. I couldn't blame you if the review made you cry."

"That'll do, Barney," Mason said. "See about my lunch."

"A half-baked autodidact, there's nothing worse," Doemling said when Barney was out of the room.

"You didn't tell me you'd interviewed Lecter, Doctor," Mason said.

"He was catatonic at the time, there was nothing to get."

"And that made you cry?"

"That's not true."

"And you discount what Barney says."

"He's as deceived as the girl."

"Barney's probably hot for Starling himself," Krendler said.

Margot laughed to herself, but loudly enough for Krendler to hear.

"If you want to make Clarice Starling attractive to Dr Lecter, let him see her *distressed*," Doemling said. "Let the damage he *sees* suggest the damage he could *do*. Seeing her wounded in any symbolic way will incite him like seeing her play with herself. When the fox hears a rabbit scream, he comes running, but not to help."

CHAPTER

52

"I CAN'T deliver Clarice Starling," Krendler said when Doemling was gone. "I can pretty much tell you where she is and what she's doing, but I can't control Bureau assignments. And if the Bureau puts her out there for bait, they'll cover her, believe me."

Krendler pointed his finger into Mason's darkness to make his point. "You can't move in on that action. You couldn't get outside that coverage and intercept Lecter. The stakeout would spot your people in no time. Second, the Bureau won't initiate proactive unless he contacts her again or there's evidence he's close—he wrote to her before and he never came around. It would take twelve people minimum to stake her out, it's expensive. You'd be better off if you hadn't gotten her off the hot seat in the shooting. It'll be messy, reversing your field and trying to hang her with that again."

"Shoulda, woulda, coulda," Mason said, doing a fair job with the *s*, all things considered. "Margot, look in the Milan paper, *Corriere della Sera*, for Saturday, the day after Pazzi was killed, check the first item in the agony column. Read it to us."

Margot held the dense print up to the light. "It's in English, addressed to A. A. Aaron. Says: *Turn yourself in to the nearest authorities, enemies are close. Hannah.* Who's Hannah?"

"That's the name of the horse Starling had as a kid," Mason said. "It's a warning to Lecter from Starling. He told her in his letter how to contact him."

Krendler was on his feet. "God*dammit*. She couldn't have known about Florence. If she knows about that, she must know I've been showing you the stuff."

Mason sighed and wondered if Krendler was smart enough to be a useful politician. "*She* didn't know anything. I placed the ad, in *La Nazione* and *Corriere della Sera* and in the *International Herald-Tribune*, to run the day *after* we moved on Lecter. That way if we missed, he'd think Starling tried to help him. We'd still have a tie to him through Starling."

"Nobody picked it up."

"No. Except maybe Hannibal Lecter. He may thank her for it—by mail, in person, who knows? Now, listen to me: You've still got her mail covered?"

Krendler nodded. "Absolutely. If he sends her anything, you'll see it before she does."

"Listen carefully to this, Krendler: The way this ad was ordered and paid for, Clarice Starling can never prove she *didn't* place it on her own, and that's a felony. That's crossing the bright line. You can break her with it, Krendler. You know how much the FBI gives a shit about you when you're out. You could be dog meat. She won't even be able to get a concealed weapon permit. Nobody will watch her but me. And Lecter will know she's out there by herself. We'll try some other things first." Mason paused to breathe and then went on. "If they don't work, we'll do like Doemling says and 'distress' her with this ad—*distress* her, hell, you can break her in two with it. Save the half with the pussy, is my advice. The other end is too goddamned earnest. Ouch—I didn't mean to blaspheme."

Clarice Starling running through falling leaves in a Virginia state park an hour from her house, a favorite place, no sign of any other person in the park on this fall weekday, a much-needed day off. She ran a familiar path in the forested hills beside the Shenandoah River. The air was warmed by the early sun on the hilltops, and in the hollows suddenly cool, sometimes the air was warm on her face and cool on her legs at the same time.

The earth these days was not quite still beneath Starling as she walked; it seemed steadier when she ran.

Starling running through the bright day, bright and dancing flares of light through the leaves, the path dappled and in other places striped with the shadows of tree trunks in the low early sun. Ahead of her three deer started, two does and a spike buck clearing the path in a single heart-lifting bound, their raised white flags shining in the gloom of the deep forest as they bounded away. Gladdened, Starling leaped herself.

Still as a figure in a medieval tapestry, Hannibal

Lecter sat among the fallen leaves on the hillside above the river. He could see one hundred fifty yards of the running path, his field glasses proofed against reflection by a homemade cardboard shroud. First he saw the deer start, and bound past him up the hill and then, for the first time in seven years, he saw Clarice Starling whole.

Below the glasses his face did not change expression, but his nostrils flared with a deep intake of breath as though he could catch her scent at this distance.

The breath brought him the smell of dry leaves with a hint of cinnamon in them, the molding leaves beneath, and the gently decaying forest mast, a whiff of rabbit pellets from yards away, the deep wild musk of a shredded squirrel skin beneath the leaves, but not the scent of Starling, which he could have identified anywhere. He saw the deer start ahead of her, saw them bounding long after they had left her sight.

She was in his view for less than a minute, running easily, not fighting the ground. A minimal day pack high on her shoulders with a bottle of water. Backlit, the early light behind her blurring her outline as though she had been dusted with pollen on her skin. Tracking with her, Dr Lecter's binoculars picked up a sun flare off the water beyond her that left him seeing spots for minutes. She disappeared as the path sloped down and away, the back of her head the last thing he saw, the ponytail bouncing like the flag of a white-tail deer.

Dr Lecter remained still, made no attempt to follow her. He had her image running clearly in his head. She would run in his mind for as long as he chose for her to. His first real sight of her in seven years, not counting tabloid pictures, not counting distant glimpses of a head in a car. He lay back in the leaves with his hands behind his head, watching the thinning foliage of a maple above him quiver against the sky, so dark the sky that it was almost purple. Purple, purple, the bunch of wild muscadines he had picked climbing to this spot were purple, beginning to shrivel from the full, dusty grape, and he ate several, and squeezed some in his palm and licked the juice as a child will lick its hand spread wide. Purple, purple.

Purple the eggplant in the garden.

There was no hot water at the high hunting lodge during the middle of the day and Mischa's nurse carried the beaten copper tub into the kitchen garden for the sun to warm the two-year-old's bathwater. Mischa sat in the gleaming tub among the vegetables in the warm sun, white cabbage butterflies around her. The water was only deep enough to cover her chubby legs, but her solemn brother Hannibal and the big dog were strictly set to watch her while the nurse went inside to get a receiving blanket.

Hannibal Lecter was to some of the servants a frightening child, frighteningly intense, preternaturally knowing, but he did not frighten the old nurse, who knew her business, and he did not frighten Mischa, who put her star-shaped baby hands flat on his cheeks and laughed into his face. Mischa reached past him and held out her arms to the eggplant, which she loved to stare at in the sun. Her eyes were not maroon like her brother Hannibal's, but blue, and as she stared at the eggplant, her eyes seemed to draw color from it, to darken with it. Hannibal Lecter knew that the color was her passion. After she was carried back inside and the cook's helper came grumbling to dump the tub in the

garden, Hannibal knelt beside the row of eggplants, the skin
of the bath-soap bubbles swarming with reflections, purple
and green, until they burst on the tilled soil. He took out
his little penknife and cut the stem of an eggplant, polished
it with his handkerchief, the vegetable warm from the sun in
his arms as he carried it, warm like an animal, to Mischa's
nursery and put it where she could see it. Mischa loved dark
purple, loved the color aubergine, as long as she lived.

Hannibal Lecter closed his eyes to see again the deer
bounding ahead of Starling, to see her come bounding
down the path, limned golden with the sun behind her,
but this was the wrong deer, it was the little deer with
the arrow in it pulling, pulling against the rope around
its neck as they led it to the axe, the little deer they
ate before they ate Mischa, and he could not be still
anymore and he got up, his hands and mouth stained
with the purple muscadines, his mouth turned down
like a Greek mask. He looked after Starling down the
path. He took a deep breath through his nose, and took
in the cleansing scent of the forest. He stared at the spot
where Starling disappeared. Her path seemed lighter
than the surrounding woods, as though she had left a
bright place behind her.

He climbed quickly to the ridge and headed downhill
on the other side toward the parking area of a nearby
campsite where he had left his truck. He wanted to
be out of the park before Starling returned to her
automobile, parked two miles away in the main lot
near the ranger booth, now closed for the season.

It would be at least fifteen minutes before she could
run back to her car.

Dr Lecter parked beside the Mustang and left his

motor running. He had had several opportunities to examine her car in the parking lot of a grocery near her house. It was the state park's annual discount admittance sticker on the window of Starling's old Mustang that first alerted Hannibal Lecter to this place, and he had bought maps of the park at once and explored it at his leisure.

The car was locked, hunkered down over its wide wheels as though it were asleep. Her car amused him. It was at once whimsical and terribly efficient. On the chrome door handle, even bending close, he could smell nothing. He unfolded his flat steel slim jim and slid it down into the door above the lock. Alarm? Yes? No? *Click*. No.

Dr Lecter got into the car, into air that was intensely Clarice Starling. The steering wheel was thick and covered with leather. It had the word MOMO on the hub. He looked at the word with his head tilted like that of a parrot and his lips formed the words "MO MO." He sat back in the seat, his eyes closed, breathing, his eyebrows raised, as though he were listening to a concert.

Then, as though it had a mind of its own, the pointed pink tip of his tongue appeared, like a small snake finding its way out of his face. Never altering expression, as though he were unaware of his movements, he leaned forward, found the leather steering wheel by scent, and put around it his curled tongue, cupping with his tongue the finger indentations on the underside of the wheel. He tasted with his mouth the polished two o'clock spot on the wheel where her palm would rest. Then he leaned back in the seat, his tongue back where it lived, and his closed mouth moved as though he savored wine. He took a deep breath and held it while he got out and locked Clarice Starling's Mustang. He did not exhale, he held her in his mouth and lungs until his old truck was out of the park.

CHAPTER
54

IT IS an axiom of behavioral science that vampires are territorial, while cannibals range widely across the country.

The nomadic existence held little appeal for Dr Lecter. His success in avoiding the authorities owed much to the quality of his long-term false identities and the care he took to maintain them, and his ready access to money. Random and frequent movement had nothing to do with it.

With two alternate identities long established, each with excellent credit, plus a third for the management of vehicles, he had no trouble feathering for himself a comfortable nest in the United States within a week of his arrival.

He had chosen Maryland, about an hour's drive south from Mason Verger's Muskrat Farm, and reasonably convenient to the music and theater in Washington and New York.

Nothing about Dr Lecter's visible business attracted attention, and either of his principal identities would have had a good chance of surviving a standard audit. After visiting one of his lockboxes in Miami, he rented from a German lobbyist for one year a pleasant, isolated house on the Chesapeake shore.

With distinct-ring call forwarding from two telephones in a cheap apartment in Philadelphia, he was able to provide himself with glowing references whenever they were required without leaving the comfort of his new home.

Always paying cash, he quickly obtained from scalpers premium tickets for the symphony, and those ballet and opera performances that interested him.

Among his new home's desirable features was a generous double garage with a workshop, and good overhead doors. There Dr Lecter parked his two vehicles, a six-year-old Chevrolet pickup truck with a pipe frame over the bed and a vise attached, which he bought from a plumber and a housepainter, and a supercharged Jaguar sedan leased through a holding company in Delaware. His truck offered a different appearance from day to day. The equipment he could put into the back or onto the pipe frame included a housepainter's ladder, pipe, PVC, a barbecue kettle, and a butane tank.

With his domestic arrangements well in hand, he treated himself to a week of music and museums in New York, and sent catalogs of the most interesting art shows to his cousin, the great painter Balthus, in France.

At Sotheby's in New York, he purchased two excellent musical instruments, rare finds both of them. The first was a late eighteenth-century Flemish harpsichord nearly identical to the Smithsonian's 1745 Dulkin, with an upper manual to accommodate Bach—the instrument was a worthy successor to the *gravicembalo* he had in Florence. His other purchase was an early electronic instrument, a theremin, built in the 1930s by Professor Theremin himself. The theremin had long fascinated Dr Lecter. He had built one as a child. It is played with gestures of the empty hands in an electronic field. By gesture you evoke its voice.

Now he was all settled in and he could entertain himself. . . .

Dr Lecter drove home to this pleasant refuge on the Maryland shore after his morning in the woods. The sight of Clarice Starling running through the falling leaves on the forest path was well established now in the memory palace of his mind. It is a source of pleasure to him, reachable in less than a second starting from the foyer. He sees Starling run and, such is the quality of his visual memory, he can search the scene for new details, he can hear the big, healthy whitetails bounding past him up the slope, see the calluses on their elbows, a grass burr on the belly fur of the nearest. He has stored this memory in a sunny palace room as far as possible from the little wounded deer . . .

Home again, home again, the garage door dropping with a quiet hum behind his pickup truck.

When the door rose again at noon the black Jaguar came out, bearing the doctor dressed for the city.

Dr Lecter very much liked to shop. He drove directly to Hammacher Schlemmer, the purveyor of fine home and sporting accessories and culinary equipment, and there he took his time. Still in his woodsy mood, with a pocket tape measure he checked the dimensions of three major picnic hampers, all of them lacquered wicker with sewn leather straps and solid brass fittings. Finally, he settled on the medium-sized hamper, as it only had to accommodate a place setting for one.

The wicker case had in it a thermos, serviceable tumblers, sturdy china, and stainless-steel cutlery. The case came only with the accessories. You were obliged to buy them.

In successive stops at Tiffany and Christofle, the doctor was able to replace the heavy picnic plates with Gien French china in one of the *chasse* patterns of leaves and upland birds. At Christofle he obtained a place setting of the nineteenth-century silverware he preferred, in a Cardinal pattern, the maker's mark stamped in the bowl of the spoons, the Paris rat tail on the underside of the handles. The forks were deeply curved, the tines widely spaced, and the knives had a pleasing heft far back in the palm. The pieces hang in the hand like a good dueling pistol. In crystal, the doctor was torn between sizes in his aperitif glasses, and chose a chimney *ballon* for brandy, but in wineglasses there was no question. The doctor chose Riedel, which he bought in two sizes with plenty of room for the nose within the rim.

At Christofle he also found place mats in creamy white linen, and some beautiful damask napkins with a tiny damask rose, like a drop of blood, embroidered in the corner. Dr Lecter thought the play on damask droll and bought six napkins, so that he would always be equipped, allowing for laundry turnaround time.

He bought two good 35,000 BTU portable gas burners, of the kind restaurants use to cook at tableside, and an exquisite copper sauté pan and a copper *fait-tout* to make sauces, both made for Dehillerin in Paris, and two whisks. He was not able to find carbon-steel kitchen knives, which he much preferred to stainless steel, nor could he find some of the special-purpose knives he had been forced to leave in Italy.

His last stop was a medical supply company not far from Mercy General Hospital, where he found a bargain in a nearly brand-new Stryker autopsy saw, which strapped down neatly in his picnic hamper where the thermos used to go. It was still under warranty, and came with general-purpose and cranial blades, as well as a skull key, to nearly complete his *batterie de cuisine*.

Dr Lecter's French doors are open to the crisp evening air. The bay lies soot-and-silver under the moon and moving shadows of the clouds. He has poured himself a glass of wine in his new crystal and set it on a candle stand beside the harpsichord. The wine's bouquet mixes with the salt air and Dr Lecter can enjoy it without ever taking his hands from the keyboard.

He has in his time owned clavichords, virginals, and other early keyboard instruments. He prefers the sound and feel of the harpsichord; because it is not possible to control the volume of the quill-plucked strings, the music arrives like experience, sudden and entire.

Dr Lecter looks at the instrument, opening and closing his hands. He approaches his newly acquired harpsichord as he might approach an attractive stranger via an interesting light remark—he plays an air written by Henry VIII, "Green Grows the Holly."

Encouraged, he essays upon Mozart's "Sonata in B Flat Major." He and the harpsichord are not yet intimate, but its responses to his hands tell him they will come together soon. The breeze rises and the candles flare, but Dr Lecter's eyes are closed to the light, his face is lifted and he is playing. Bubbles fly from Mischa's star-shaped hands as she waves them in the breeze above the tub and, as he attacks the third movement, through the forest lightly flying, Clarice Starling is running, running, rustle of the leaves beneath her feet, rustle of the wind high in the turning trees, and the deer start ahead of her, a spike buck and two does, leaping across the path like the heart leaps. The ground is suddenly colder and the ragged men lead the little deer out of the woods, an arrow in it, the deer pulling against the rope twisted around its neck, men pulling it wounded so they will not have to carry it to the axe, and the music clangs to a stop above the bloody snow, Dr Lecter clutching the edges of the piano stool. He breathes deep, breaths deep, puts his hands on the keyboard, forces a phrase, then two that clang to silence.

We hear from him a thin and rising scream that stops as abruptly as the music. He sits for a long time with his head bent above the keyboard. He rises without sound and leaves the room. It is not possible to tell where he is in the dark house. The wind off the Chesapeake gains strength, whips the candle flames until they gutter out, sings through the strings of the harpsichord in the dark—now an accidental tune, now a thin scream from long ago.

CHAPTER

55

THE MID-ATLANTIC Regional Gun and Knife Show in War Memorial Auditorium. Acres of tables, a plain of guns, mostly pistols and assault-style shotguns. The red beams of laser sights flicker on the ceiling.

Few genuine outdoorsmen come to gun shows, as a matter of taste. Guns are black now, and gun shows are bleak, colorless, as joyless as the inner landscape of many who attend them.

Look at this crowd: scruffy, squinty, angry, egg-bound, truly of the resinous heart. They are the main danger to the right of a private citizen to own a firearm.

The guns they fancy are assault weapons designed for mass production, cheaply made of stampings to provide high firepower to ignorant and untrained troops.

Among the beer bellies, the flab and pasty white of the indoor gunmen moved Dr Hannibal Lecter, imperially slim. The guns did not interest him. He went directly to the display of the foremost knife merchant of the show circuit.

The merchant's name is Buck and he weighs three

hundred twenty-five pounds. Buck has a lot of fantasy swords, and copies of medieval and barbarian items, but he has the best real knives and blackjacks too, and Dr Lecter quickly spotted most of the items on his list, things he'd had to leave in Italy.

"Can I hep you?" Buck has friendly cheeks and a friendly mouth, and baleful eyes.

"Yes. I'll have that Harpy, please, and a straight, serrated Spyderco with a four-inch blade, and that drop-point skinner at the back."

Buck gathered the items.

"I want the good game saw. Not that one, the good one. Let me feel that flat leather sap, the black one . . ." Dr Lecter considered the spring in the handle. "I'll take it."

"Anything else?"

"Yes. I'd like a Spyderco Civilian, I don't see it."

"Not a whole lot of folks know about that. I never stock but one."

"I only require one."

"It's regular two hundred and twenty dollars, I could let you have it for one ninety with the case."

"Fine. Do you have carbon-steel kitchen knives?"

Buck shook his massive head. "You'll have to find old ones at a flea market. That's where I get mine at. You can put an edge on one with the bottom of a saucer."

"Make a parcel and I'll be back for it in a few minutes."

Buck had not often been told to make a parcel, and he did it with his eyebrows raised.

Typically, this gun show was not a show at all, it was a bazaar. There were a few tables of dusty World

343

War Two memorabilia, beginning to look ancient. You could buy M-1 rifles, gas masks with the glass crazing in the goggles, canteens. There were the usual Nazi memorabilia booths. You could buy an actual Zyklon B gas canister, if that is to your taste.

There was almost nothing from the Korean or Vietnam wars and nothing at all from Desert Storm.

Many of the shoppers wore camouflage as if they were only briefly back from the front lines to attend the gun show, and more camouflage clothing was for sale, including the complete ghillie suit for total concealment of a sniper or a bow hunter—a major subdivision of the show was archery equipment for bow hunting.

Dr Lecter was examining the ghillie suit when he became aware of uniforms close beside him. He picked up an archery glove. Turning to hold the maker's mark to the light, he could see that the two officers beside him were from the Virginia Department of Game and Inland Fisheries, which maintained a conservation booth at the show.

"Donnie Barber," said the older of the two wardens, pointing with his chin. "If you ever git him in court, let me know. I'd love to git that son of a bitch out of the woods for good." They were watching a man of about thirty at the other end of the archery exhibit. He was facing them, watching a video. Donnie Barber wore camouflage, his blouse tied around his waist by the sleeves. He had on a khaki-colored sleeveless T-shirt to show off his tattoos and a baseball cap reversed on his head.

Dr Lecter moved slowly away from the officers, looking at various items as he went. He paused at a display of laser pistol sights an aisle away and, through a trellis hung with holsters, the doctor watched the flickering video that held Donnie Barber's attention.

It was a video about hunting mule deer with bow and arrow.

Apparently someone off camera was hazing a deer along a fence through a wooded lot, while the hunter drew his bow. The hunter was wired for sound. His breathing grew faster. He whispered into the microphone, "It don't git any better than this."

The deer humped when the arrow hit it and ran into the fence twice before leaping the wire and running away.

Watching, Donnie Barber jerked and grunted at the arrow strike.

Now the video huntsman was about to field-dress the deer. He began at what he called the ANN-us.

Donnie Barber stopped the video and ran it back to the arrow strike again and again, until the concessionaire spoke to him.

"Fuck yourself, asshole," Donnie Barber said. "I wouldn't buy shit from you."

At the next booth, he bought some yellow arrows, broad-heads with a razor fin crosswise in the head. There was a box for a prize drawing and, with his purchase, Donnie Barber received an entry slip. The prize was a two-day deer lease.

Donnie Barber filled out his entry and dropped it through the slot, and kept the merchant's pen as he disappeared with his long parcel into the crowd of young men in camouflage.

*   *   *

As a frog's eyes pick up movement, so the merchant's eyes noted any pause in the passing crowd. The man before him now was utterly still.

"Is that your best crossbow?" Dr Lecter asked the merchant.

"No." The man took a case from under the counter. "This is the best one. I like the recurve better than the compound if you got to tote it. It's got the windlass you can drive off a 'lectric drill or use it manual. You know you can't use a crossbow on deer in Virginia unless you're handicapped?" the man said.

"My brother's lost one arm and he's anxious to kill something with the other one," Dr Lecter said.

"Oh, I gotcha."

In the course of five minutes, the doctor purchased an excellent crossbow and two dozen quarrels, the short, thick arrows used with a crossbow.

"Tie up a parcel," Dr Lecter said.

"Fill out this slip and you might win you a deer hunt. Two days on a good lease," the merchant said.

Dr Lecter filled out his slip for the drawing and dropped it through the slot in the box.

As soon as the merchant was engaged with another customer, Dr Lecter turned back to him.

"Bother!" he said. "I forgot to put my telephone number on my drawing slip. May I?"

"Sure, go ahead."

Dr Lecter took the top off the box and took out the top two slips. He added to the false information on his own, and took a long look at the slip beneath, blinking once, like a camera clicking.

THE GYM at Muskrat Farm is high-tech black and chrome, with the complete Nautilus cycle of machines, free weights, aerobic equipment and a juice bar.

Barney was nearly through with his workout, cooling down on a bike, when he realized he was not alone in the room. Margot Verger was taking off her warm-ups in the corner. She wore elastic shorts and a tank top over a sports bra and now she added a weight-lifting belt. Barney heard weights clank in the corner. He heard her breathing as she did a warm-up set.

Barney was pedaling the bicycle against no resistance, toweling his head, when she came over to him between sets.

She looked at his arms, looked at hers. They were about the same. "How much can you bench-press?" she said.

"I don't know."

"I expect you know, all right."

"Maybe three eighty-five, like that."

"*Three eighty-five?* I don't think so, big boy. I don't

think you can press three eighty-five."

"Maybe you're right."

"I got a hundred dollars that says you can't bench press three eighty-five."

"Against?"

"Against a hundred dollars, the hell you think? And I'll spot you."

Barney looked at her and wrinkled his rubbery forehead. "Okay."

They loaded on the plates. Margot counted the ones on the end of the bar Barney had loaded as though he might cheat her. He responded by counting with elaborate care the ones on Margot's end.

Flat on the bench now, Margot standing above him at his head in her spandex shorts. The juncture of her thighs and abdomen was knurled like a baroque frame and her massive torso seemed to reach almost to the ceiling.

Barney settled himself, feeling the bench against his back. Margot's legs smelled like cool liniment. Her hands were lightly on the bar, nails painted coral, shapely hands to be so strong.

"Ready?"

"Yes." He pushed the weight up toward her face, bent over him.

It wasn't much trouble for Barney. He set the weight back on its bracket ahead of Margot's spot. She got the money from her gym bag.

"Thank you," Barney said.

"I do more squats than you" is all she said.

"I know."

"How do you know that?"

"I can pee standing up."

Her massive neck flushed. "So can I."

"Hundred bucks?" Barney said.

"Make me a smoothie," she said.

There was a bowl of fruit and nuts on the juice bar. While Barney made fruit smoothies in the blender, Margot took two walnuts in her fist and cracked them.

"Can you do just one nut, with nothing to squeeze it against?" Barney said. He cracked two eggs on the rim of the blender and dropped them in.

"Can you?" Margot said, and handed him a walnut.

The nut lay in Barney's open palm. "I don't know." He cleared the space in front of him on the bar and an orange rolled off on Margot's side. "Oops, sorry," Barney said.

She picked it up from the floor and put it back in the bowl.

Barney's big fist clenched. Margot's eyes went from his fist to his face, then back and forth as his neck corded with strain, his face flushed. He began to tremble, from his fist a faint cracking sound, Margot's face falling, he moved his trembling fist over the blender and the cracking came louder. An egg yolk and white plopped into the blender. Barney turned the machine on and licked the tips of his fingers. Margot laughed in spite of herself.

Barney poured the smoothies into glasses. From across the room they might have been wrestlers or power lifters in two weight divisions.

"You feel like you *have* to do everything guys do?" he said.

349

"Not some of the dumb stuff."

"You want to try male bonding?"

Margot's smile went away. "Don't set me up for a dick joke, Barney."

He shook his massive head. "Try me," he said.

CHAPTER
57

IN HANNIBAL'S House the gleanings grew as day by day Clarice Starling felt her way along the corridors of Dr Lecter's taste:

Rachel DuBerry had been somewhat older than Dr Lecter when she was an active patron of the Baltimore Symphony and she was very beautiful, as Starling could see in the *Vogue* pictures from the time. That was two rich husbands ago. She was now Mrs Franz Rosencranz of the textile Rosencranzes. Her social secretary put her on the line:

"Now I just send the orchestra money, dear. We're away far too much for me to be actively involved," Mrs Rosencranz nee DuBerry told Starling. "If it's some sort of tax question, I can give you the number of our accountants."

"Mrs Rosencranz, when you were active on the boards of the Philharmonic and the Westover School you knew Dr Hannibal Lecter."

A considerable silence.

"Mrs Rosencranz?"

"I think I'd better take your number and call you back through the FBI switchboard."

"Certainly."

When the conversation resumed:

"Yes, I knew Hannibal Lecter socially years ago and the press has camped on my doorstep ever since about it. He was an extraordinarily charming man, absolutely singular. Sort of made a girl's *fur crackle*, if you know what I mean. It took me years to believe the other side of him."

"Did he ever give you any gifts, Mrs Rosencranz?"

"I received a note from him on my birthdays usually, even after he was in custody. Sometimes a gift, before he was committed. He gives the *most* exquisite gifts."

"And Dr Lecter gave the famous birthday dinner for you. With the wine vintages keyed to your birth date."

"Yes," she said. "Suzy called it the most remarkable party since Capote's Black and White Ball."

"Mrs Rosencranz, if you should hear from him, would you please call the FBI at the number I'll give you? Another thing I'd like to ask you if I may, do you have any special anniversaries with Dr Lecter? And Mrs Rosencranz, I need to ask you your birth date."

A distinct chill on the phone. "I would think that information was easily available to you."

"Yes, ma'am, but there are some inconsistencies among the dates on your social security, your birth certificate and your driver's license. In fact, none of them are the same. I apologize, but we're keying custom orders on high-end items to the birthdays of Dr Lecter's known acquaintances."

"'Known acquaintances.' I'm a *known acquaintance* now, what an awful term." Mrs Rosencranz chuckled. She was of a cocktail and cigarette generation and her voice was deep. "Agent Starling, how old are you?"

"I'm thirty-two, Mrs Rosencranz. I'll be thirty-three two days before Christmas."

"I'll just say, in all kindness, I hope you'll have a couple of 'known acquaintances' in your life. They do help pass the time."

"Yes, ma'am, and your birth date?"

Mrs Rosencranz at last parted with the correct information, characterizing it as "the date Dr Lecter is familiar with."

"If I may ask, ma'am, I can understand changing the birth year, but why the month and day?"

"I wanted to be a Virgo, it matches better with Mr Rosencranz, we were dating then."

The people Dr Lecter had met while he was living in a cage viewed him somewhat differently:

Starling rescued former U.S. Senator Ruth Martin's daughter, Catherine, from the hellish basement of the serial killer Jame Gumb and, had Senator Martin not been defeated in the next election, she might have done Starling much good. She was warm to Starling on the telephone, gave her news of Catherine, and wanted her news.

"You never asked me for anything, Starling. If you ever want a job—"

"Thank you, Senator Martin."

"About that goddamned Lecter, no, I'd have notified the Bureau of course if I heard from him, and I'll put your number here by the phone. Charlsie knows how to handle mail. I don't expect to hear from him. The last thing that prick said to me in Memphis was '*Love your suit.*' He did the single cruelest thing anybody's ever done to me, do you know what it was?"

"I know he taunted you."

"When Catherine was missing, when we were desperate and he said he had information on Jame Gumb, and I was pleading with him, he asked me, he looked into my face with those snake eyes and asked me if I had nursed Catherine. He wanted to know if I *breast-fed* her. I told him yes. And then he said, 'Thirsty work isn't it?' It just brought it all back suddenly, holding her as a baby, thirsty, waiting for her to get full, it pierced me like nothing I ever felt, and he *just sucked down my pain.*"

"What kind was it, Senator Martin?"

"What kind—I'm sorry?"

"What kind of suit did you have on, that Dr Lecter liked."

"Let me think—a navy Givenchy, very tailored," Senator Martin said, a little piqued at Starling's priorities. "When you've got him back in the slammer, come see me, Starling, we'll ride some horses."

"Thank you, Senator, I'll remember that."

Two phone calls, one on each side of Dr Lecter, one showed his charm, the other his scales. Starling wrote down:

Vintage keyed to birthdays, which was already covered in her little program. She made a note to add *Givenchy* to her list of high-end goods. As an afterthought she wrote down *breast-fed*, for no reason she could say, and there was no time to think about it because her red phone was ringing.

"This is Behavioral Science? I'm trying to get through to Jack Crawford, this is Sheriff Dumas in Clarendon Country, Virginia."

"Sheriff, I'm Jack Crawford's assistant. He's in court today. I can help you. I'm Special Agent Starling."

"I needed to speak to Jack Crawford. We got a fella in the morgue that's been trimmed up for *meat*, have I got the right department?"

"Yes sir, this is the mea—yes, sir, you certainly do. If you'll tell me exactly where you are, I'm on the way, and I'll alert Mr Crawford as soon as he's through testifying."

Starling's Mustang got enough second-gear rubber out of Quantico to make the Marine guard frown at her, and wag his finger, and keep himself from smiling.

THE CLARENDON County Morgue in northern Virginia is attached to the county hospital by a short air lock with an exhaust fan in the ceiling and wide double doors at each end to facilitate access by the dead. A sheriff's deputy stood before these doors to keep out the five reporters and cameramen who crowded around him.

From behind the reporters, Starling stood on her tiptoes and held her badge high. When the deputy spotted it and nodded, she plunged through. Strobe lights flashed and a sun gun flared behind her.

Quiet in the autopsy room, only the clink of instruments put down in a metal tray.

The county morgue has four stainless-steel autopsy tables, each with its scales and sink. Two of the tables were draped, the sheets oddly tented by the remains they covered. A routine hospital postmortem was in progress at the table nearest the windows. The pathologist and his assistant were doing something delicate and did not look up when Starling came in.

The thin shriek of an electric saw filled the room, and

in a moment the pathologist carefully set aside the cap of a skull and lifted in his cupped hands a brain, which he placed on the scales. He whispered the weight into the microphone he wore, examined the organ in the scale pan, poked it with a gloved finger. When he spotted Starling over the shoulder of his assistant, he dumped the brain into the open chest cavity of the corpse, shot his rubber gloves into a bin like a boy shooting rubber bands and came around the table to her.

Starling found shaking his hand a bit crawly.

"Clarice Starling, Special Agent, FBI."

"I'm Dr Hollingsworth—medical examiner, hospital pathologist, chief cook and bottle washer." Hollingsworth has bright blue eyes, shiny as well-peeled eggs. He spoke to his assistant without looking away from Starling. "Marlene, page the sheriff in cardiac ICU, and undrape those remains, please, ma'am."

In Starling's experience medical examiners were usually intelligent but often silly and incautious in casual conversation, and they liked to show off. Hollingsworth followed Starling's eyes. "You're wondering about that brain?"

She nodded and showed him her open hands.

"We're not careless here, Special Agent Starling. It's a favor I do the undertaker, not putting the brain back in the skull. In this case they'll have an open coffin and a lengthy wake, and you can't prevent brain material leaking onto the pillow, so we stuff the skull with Huggies or whatever we have and close it back up, and I put a notch in the skull cap over both ears, so it won't slide. Family gets the whole body back, everybody's happy."

"I understand."

"Tell me if you understand *that*," he said. Behind Starling, Dr Hollingsworth's assistant had removed the covering sheets from the autopsy tables.

Starling turned and saw it all in a single image that would last as long as she lived. Side by side on their stainless-steel tables lay a deer and a man. From the deer projected a yellow arrow. The arrow shaft and the antlers had held up the covering sheet like tent poles.

The man had a shorter, thicker yellow arrow through his head transversely at the tips of his ears. He still wore one garment, a reversed baseball cap, pinned to his head by the arrow.

Looking at him, Starling suffered an absurd burp of laughter, suppressed so fast it might have sounded like dismay. The similar positions of the two bodies, on their sides instead of in the anatomical position, revealed that they had been butchered almost identically, the sirloin and loin removed with neatness and economy along with the small filets that lie beneath the spine.

A deer's fur on stainless steel. Its head elevated by the antlers on the metal pillow block, the head turned and the eye white as though it tried to look back at the bright shaft that killed it—the creature, lying on its side in its own reflection in this place of obsessive order, seemed wilder, more alien to man than a deer ever seemed in the woods.

The man's eyes were open, some blood came from his lachrymal ducts like tears.

"Odd to see them together," Dr Hollingsworth said. "Their hearts weighed exactly the same." He looked at Starling and saw that she was all right. "One difference on the man, you can see here where the short ribs were separated from the spine and the lungs pulled out the back. They almost look like wings, don't they?"

"Bloody Eagle," Starling muttered, after a moment's thought.

"I never saw it before."

"Me either," Starling said.

"There's a term for that? What did you call it?"

"The Bloody Eagle. The literature at Quantico has it. It's a Norse sacrificial custom. Chop through the short ribs and pull the lungs out the back, flatten them out like that to make wings. There was a neo-Viking doing it in Minnesota in the thirties."

"You see a lot of this, I don't mean *this*, but this kind of stuff."

"Sometimes I do, yes."

"It's out of my line a little. We get mostly straight-forward murders—people shot and knifed, but do you want to know what I think?"

"I'd like very much to know, Doctor."

"I think the man, his ID says Donnie Barber, killed the deer illegally yesterday, the day before the season started—I know that's when it died. That arrow's consistent with the rest of his archery equipment. He was butchering it in a hurry. I haven't done the antigens on that blood on his hands, but it's deer blood. He was just going to take what deer hunters call the backstrap, and he started a sloppy job, this short ragged cut here. Then he got a big surprise, like this arrow through his head. Same color, but a different kind of arrow. No notch in the butt. Do you recognize it?"

"It looks like a crossbow quarrel," Starling said.

"A second person, maybe the one with the crossbow, finished dressing the deer, doing a much better job, and then, by God, he did the man too. Look how precisely the hide is reflected here, how *decisive* the incisions are. Nothing spoiled or wasted. Michael DeBakey couldn't do it better. There's no sign of any kind of sexual interference with either of them. They were simply butchered for meat."

Starling touched her lips with her knuckle. For a second the pathologist thought she was kissing an amulet.

"Dr Hollingsworth, were the livers missing?"

A beat of time before he replied, peering at her over his glasses. "The *deer's* liver is missing. Mr Barber's liver apparently wasn't up to standard. It was partly excised and examined, there's an incision just along the portal vein. His liver is cirrhotic and discolored. It remains in the body, would you like to see?"

"No, thank you. What about the thymus?"

"The sweetbreads, yes, missing in both cases. Agent Starling, nobody's said the name yet, have they?"

"No," Starling said. "Not yet."

A puff from the air lock and a lean, weathered man in a tweed sports jacket and khaki pants stood in the doorway.

"Sheriff, how's Carleton?" Hollingsworth said. "Agent Starling, this is Sheriff Dumas. The sheriff's brother is upstairs in cardiac ICU."

"He's holding his own. They say he's stable, he's 'guarded,' whatever that means," the sheriff said. He called outside, "Come on in here, Wilburn."

The sheriff shook Starling's hand and introduced

the other man. "This is Officer Wilburn Moody, he's a game warden."

"Sheriff. If you want to stay close to your brother we could go back upstairs," Starling said.

Sheriff Dumas shook his head. "They won't let me in to see him again for another hour and a half. No offense, Miss, but I called for Jack Crawford. Is he coming?"

"He's stuck in court—he was on the stand when your call came. I expect we'll hear from him very shortly. We really appreciate you calling us so fast."

"Old Crawford taught my National Police Academy Class at Quantico umpteen years ago. Damndest fellow. If he sent you, you must know what you're doing—want to go ahead?"

"Please, Sheriff."

The sheriff took a notebook out of his coat pocket. "The individual here with the arrow through his head is Donnie Leo Barber, WM thirty-two, resides in a trailer at Trail's End Park at Cameron. No employment I can find. General discharge with prejudice from the Air Force four years ago. He's got an airframe and power plant ticket from the FAA. Sometime airplane mechanic. Paid a misdemeanor fine for discharging a firearm in the city limits, paid a fine for criminal trespass last hunting season. Pled guilty to poaching deer in Summit County, when was that, Wilburn?"

"Two seasons ago, he just got his license back. He's known to the department. He don't bother to track nothing after he shoots it. If it don't fall, just wait on another'n . . . one time—"

"Tell what you found today, Wilburn."

"Well, I was coming along on county road forty-seven, about a mile west of the bridge there around seven o'clock this morning when Old Man Peckman flagged me down. He was breathing hard and holding his chest. All he could do was open and shut his mouth and point off in the woods there. I went maybe, oh, not more than a hunderd and fifty yards in the thick woods and there was this Barber here sprawled up against a tree with a arrow through his head and that deer there with a arrow in it. They was stiff from yesterday at least."

"Yesterday morning early, I'd say, cool as it was," Dr Hollingsworth said.

"Now the season just opened *this* morning," the game warden said. "This Donnie Barber had a climbing tree stand with him that he hadn't set up yet. Looked like he went out there yesterday to get ready for today, or else he went to poach. I don't know why else he'd take his bow, if he was just setting up the stand. Here come this nice deer and he just couldn't help himself.—I've saw people do this a lots. This kinda behavior's got common as pig tracks. And then this other 'un come up on him while he was butchering. I couldn't tell nothing from the tracks, a rain come down out there so hard, the bottom just fell out right then—"

"That's why we took a couple of pictures and pulled out the bodies," Sheriff Dumas said. "Old Man Peckman owns the woods. This Donnie had on him a legitimate two-day lease to hunt starting today, with Peckman's signature on it. Peckman always sold one lease a year, and he advertised it and had it farmed out with some brokers. Donnie also had a letter in

362

his back pocket saying *Congratulations you have won a deer lease.* The papers are wet, Miss Starling. Nothing against our fellows, but I'm wondering if you ought to do the fingerprinting at your lab. The arrows too, the whole thing was wet when we got there. We tried not to touch them."

"You want to take these arrows with you, Agent Starling? How would you like me to take 'em out?" Dr Hollingsworth asked.

"If you'd hold them with retractors and saw them in two at the skin line on the feather side and push the rest through, I'll wire them to my board with some twist ties," Starling said, opening her case.

"I don't think he was in a fight, but do you want fingernail scrapings?"

"I'd rather clip them to do DNA. I don't need them ID'd by finger, but separate them hand from hand, if you would, Doctor."

"Can you run PCR-STR?"

"They can in the main lab. We'll have something for you, Sheriff, in three to four days."

"Can you do that deer blood yourself?" Warden Moody asked.

"No, we can just tell it's animal blood," Starling said.

"What if you was to just find the deer meat in somebody's Frigidaire," Warden Moody offered. "You'd want to know whether it come out of that deer, wouldn't you? Sometimes *we* have to be able to tell deer from deer by blood to make a poaching case. Every individual deer is different. You wouldn't think that, would you? We have to send blood off to Portland, Oregon, to the

Oregon Game and Fish, they can tell you if you wait long enough. They come back with 'This is Deer No. One,' they'll say, or just call it 'Deer A,' with a long case number since, you know, a deer don't have any name. That *we* know of."

Starling liked Moody's old weather-beaten face. "We'll call this one 'John Doe,' Warden Moody. That's useful to know about Oregon, we might have to do some business with them, thank you," she said and smiled at him until he blushed and fumbled with his cap.

As she bent her head to rummage in her bag, Dr Hollingsworth considered her for the pleasure it gave him. Her face had lit up for a moment, talking with old Moody. That beauty spot in her cheek looked very much like burnt gunpowder. He wanted to ask, but thought better of it.

"What did you put the papers in, not plastic?" she asked the sheriff.

"Brown paper sacks. A brown paper sack never hurt much of anything." The sheriff rubbed the back of his neck with his hand, and looked up at Starling. "You know why I called your outfit, why I wanted Jack Crawford over here. I'm glad you came, now that I recollect who you are. Nobody's said 'cannibal' outside this room because the press will tromp the woods flat as soon as it's out. All they know is it could be a hunting accident. They heard maybe a body was mutilated. They don't know Donnie Barber was cut for meat. There's not that many cannibals, Agent Starling."

"No, Sheriff. Not that many."

"It's awful neat work."

"Yessir, it is."

"I may be thinking about him because he's been in the paper so much—does this look like that Hannibal Lecter to you?"

Starling watched a daddy longlegs hide in the drain of the vacant autopsy table. "Dr Lecter's sixth victim was a bow hunter," Starling said.

"Did he eat him?"

"That one, no. He left him hanging from a peg board wall with all sorts of wounds in him. He left him looking like a medieval medical illustration called Wound Man. He's interested in medieval things."

The pathologist pointed to the lungs spread across Donnie Barber's back. "You were saying this was an old ritual."

"I think so," Starling said. "I don't know if Dr Lecter did this. If he did it, the mutilation's not a fetish—this arrangement's not a compulsive thing with him."

"What is it then?"

"It's whimsy," she said, looking to see if she put them off with the exact word. "It's *whimsy*, and it's what got him caught last time."

THE DNA lab was new, smelled new, and the personnel were younger than Starling. It was something she'd have to get used to, she thought with a twinge—she'd be a year older very soon.

A young woman with A. BENNING on her name tag signed for the two arrows Starling brought.

A. Benning had had some bad experiences receiving evidence, judging from her evident relief when she saw the two missiles wired carefully to Starling's evidence board with twist ties.

"You don't want to know what I see sometimes when I open these things," A. Benning said. "You have to understand that I can't tell you anything, like in five minutes—"

"No," Starling said. "There's no reference RFLP on Dr Lecter, he escaped too long ago and the artifacts have been polluted, handled by a hundred people."

"Lab time is too valuable to run every sample, like fourteen hairs say from a motel room. If you bring me—"

"Listen to me," Starling said, "then you talk. I've asked the Questura in Italy to send me the toothbrush they think belonged to Dr Lecter. You can get some epithelial cheek cells off it. Do both RFLP and short tandem repeats on them. This crossbow quarrel has been in the rain, I doubt you'll get much off it, but look here—"

"I'm sorry, I didn't think you'd understand—"

Starling managed a smile. "Don't worry, A. Benning, we'll get along fine. See, the arrows are both yellow. The crossbow quarrel is yellow because it's been painted by hand, not a bad job, but a little streaky. Look here, what does that look like under the paint?"

"Maybe a hair off the brush?"

"Maybe. But look how it's curved toward one end and has a little bulb at the end. What if it's an eyelash?"

"If it's got the follicle—"

"Right."

"Look, I can run PCR-STR—three colors at once—in the same line in the gel and get you three DNA sites at a time. It'll take thirteen sites for court, but a couple of days will be enough to know pretty well if it's him."

"A. Benning, I knew you could help me."

"You're Starling. I mean Special Agent Starling. I didn't mean to get off on the wrong foot—I see a lot of real bad evidence the cops send in—it has nothing to do with you."

"I know."

"I thought you'd be older. All the girls—the women know about you, I mean everybody does, but you're kind of"—A. Benning looked away—"kind of special to us." A. Benning held up her chubby little thumb. "Good luck with the Other. If you don't mind my saying so."

60

MASON VERGER's major domo, Cordell, was a large man with exaggerated features who might have been handsome with more animation in his face. He was thirty-seven years old and he could never work in the health industry in Switzerland again, or have any employment there that put him in close contact with children.

Mason paid him a large salary to be in charge of his wing, with responsibility for his care and feeding. He had found Cordell to be absolutely reliable and capable of anything. Cordell had witnessed acts of cruelty on video as Mason interviewed little children that would have moved anyone else to rage or tears.

Today Cordell was a little concerned about the only matter holy to him, money.

He gave his familiar double knock on the door and went into Mason's room. It was completely dark except for the glowing aquarium. The eel knew he was there and rose from his hole, hoping.

"Mr Verger?"

A moment while Mason came awake.

"I need to mention something to you, I have to make an extra payment in Baltimore this week to the same person we spoke about before. It's not any kind of emergency basis, but it would be prudent. That Negro child Franklin ate some rat poison and was in *cridical* condition earlier this week. He's telling his foster mother it was your suggestion he should poison his cat to keep the police from torturing it. So, he gave the cat to a neighbor and took the rat poison himself."

"That's absurd," Mason said. "I had nothing to do with it."

"Of course it's absurd, Mr Verger."

"Who's complaining, the woman you get the kids from?"

"She's the one that has to be paid at once."

"Cordell, you didn't interfere with the little bastard? They didn't find anything in him at the hospital, did they? I'll find out, you know."

"No, sir. In your home? Never, I swear it. You know I'm not a fool. I love my job."

"Where is *Franklin*?"

"Maryland-Misericordia Hospital. When he gets out he'll go to a group home. You know the woman he lived with got kicked off the foster home list for smoking marijuana. She's the one complaining about you. We may have to deal with her."

"Coon doper, shouldn't be much problem."

"She doesn't know anybody to go to with it. I think she needs some careful handling. Kit gloves. The welfare worker wants her to shut up."

"I'll think about that. Go ahead and pay the welfare clerk."

"A thousand dollars?"

"Just make sure she knows that's all she gets."

Lying on Mason's couch in the dark, her cheeks stiff with dried tears, Margot Verger listened to Cordell and Mason talking. She had been trying to reason with Mason when he fell asleep. Obviously Mason thought she had left. She opened her mouth to breathe quietly, trying to time her breaths to the hiss of his respirator. A pulse of gray light in the room as Cordell left. Margot lay flat on the couch. She waited almost twenty minutes, until the pump settled into Mason's sleep rhythm, before she left the room. The eel saw her go, but Mason did not.

61

MARGOT VERGER and Barney had been hanging out together. They did not talk a great deal, but they watched football in the recreation room, and *The Simpsons*, and concerts sometimes on educational TV, and together they followed *I, Claudius*. When Barney's shift made him miss some episodes, they ordered the tape.

Margot liked Barney, she liked the way she was one of the guys with him. He was the only person she'd known who was cool like that. Barney was very smart, and there was something a little other-worldly about him. She liked that too.

Margot had a good liberal arts education as well as her computer science. Barney, self-taught, had opinions that ranged from childish to penetrating. She could provide context for him. Margot's education was a broad and open plain defined by reason. But the plain rested on top of her mentality like the Flat Earther's world rests on a turtle.

Margot Verger made Barney pay for his joke about

squatting to pee. She believed that her legs were stronger than his, and time proved her right. By feigning difficulty at lower weights she lured him into a bet on leg presses and won back her hundred dollars. In addition, using the advantage of her lighter weight, she beat him in one-armed pull-ups, but she would only bet on the right arm, her left being weaker from a childhood injury sustained in a struggle with Mason.

Sometimes at night, after Barney's shift with Mason was over, they worked out together, spotting one another on the bench. It was a serious workout, largely silent except for their breathing. Sometimes they only said good night as she packed her gym bag and disappeared toward the family quarters, off-limits to the staff.

This night she came into the black and chrome gymnasium directly from Mason's room with tears in her eyes.

"Hey, hey," Barney said. "You all right?"

"Just family crap, what can I tell you? I'm all right," Margot said.

She worked out like a fiend, too much weight, too many reps.

Once Barney came and took a barbell from her and shook his head. "You're gonna tear something," he said.

She was still grinding on an exercise bike when he called it quits, and stood under the gym's steaming shower, letting the hot water take the long day down the drain. It was a communal gym shower with four overhead nozzles and some extra nozzles at waist and thigh level. Barney liked to turn on two showers and converge their streams on his big body.

Soon Barney was enveloped in a thick fog that shut out everything but the pounding of the water on his head. Barney liked to reflect in the shower: Clouds of steam. *The Clouds*. Aristophanes. Dr Lecter explaining about the lizard pissing on Socrates. It occurred to him that, before he was peened under the relentless hammer of Dr Lecter's logic, somebody like Doemling could have pushed him around.

When he heard another shower go on, he paid little attention and continued scrubbing himself. Other personnel used the gym, but mostly in the early morning and late afternoon. It is male etiquette to pay little attention to other bathers in a communal athletic shower, but Barney wondered who it was. He hoped it wasn't Cordell, who gave him the creeps. It was rare for anyone else to use this facility at night. Who in the hell *was* that? Barney turned to let the water pound on the back of his neck. Clouds of steam, fragments of the person next to him appear between the billows like fragments of fresco on a plastered wall. Here a massive shoulder, there a leg. A shapely hand scrubbing a muscular neck and shoulder, coral fingernails, that was Margot's hand. Those were painted toes. That was Margot's leg.

Barney put his head back against the pulsing shower stream and took a deep breath. Next door the figure turning, scrubbing in a businesslike way. Washing her hair now. That was Margot's flat ribbed belly, her small breasts standing up on her big pecs, nipples raised to the jetting water, that was Margot's groin, knurled at the juncture of body and thigh, and that's got to be Margot's pussy, framed in a blond trimmed mohawk.

Barney took as deep a breath as he could and held it

. . . he could feel himself developing a problem. She was shining like a horse, pumped to the limit from the hard workout. As Barney's interest grew more apparent, he turned his back to her. Maybe he could just ignore her until she left.

The water went off next door. But now her voice came. "Hey, Barney, what's the spread on the Patriots?"

"With . . . with my guy, you can get Miami and five and a half." He looked over his shoulder.

She was drying herself just beyond the range of Barney's spray. Her hair was plastered down. Her face looked fresh now and the tears were gone. Margot had excellent skin.

"So you gonna take the points?" she said. "The pick 'em pool at Judy's office has got . . ."

Barney couldn't pay attention to the rest. Margot's mohawk, jeweled with droplets, framed pink. Barney's face felt hot and he had a major cockstand. He was puzzled and disturbed. That freezing feeling came over him. He had never felt any attraction to men. But Margot for all her muscles was clearly not a man, and he liked her.

What is this shit of coming in the shower with him anyway?

He turned off his water and faced her wet. Without thinking about it, he put his big hand on her cheek. "For God's sake, Margot," he said, his breath thick in his throat.

She looked down at him. "God*dammit*, Barney. Don't . . ."

Barney stretched his neck and leaned forward, trying

to kiss her gently anywhere on her face without touching her with his member, but touched her anyway, she pulling away, looked down at the catenary strand of crystal fluid that stretched between him and her flat stomach, and she caught him across his broad chest with a forearm worthy of a middle guard, his feet went out from under him and he sat hard on the shower floor.

"You fucking bastard," she hissed, "I might have known it. Faggot! Take that thing and stick it up . . ."

Barney rolled to his feet and was out of the shower, pulling on his clothes wet, and he left the gym without a word.

Barney's quarters were in a building separate from the house, slate-roofed former stables that were garages now with apartments in the gables. Late at night he sat pecking on his laptop, working on a correspondence course on the Internet. He felt the floor tremble as someone solid came up the stairs.

A light knock at the door. When he opened it, Margot stood there, muffled in heavy sweats and a stocking cap.

"Can I come in a minute?"

Barney looked at his feet for a few seconds before he stood back from the door.

"Barney. Hey, I'm sorry about in there," she said. "I kind of panicked. I mean, I screwed up and then I panicked. I liked being friends."

"Me too."

"I thought we could be like, you know, regular buddies."

"Margot, come *on*. I said we'd be friends but I'm not a damn eunuch. You came in the fucking shower with me. You looked good to me, I can't help that. You come in the shower naked and I see two things together I really *like*."

"Me and a pussy," Margot said.

They were surprised to laugh together.

She came and grabbed him in a hug that might have injured a less powerful man. "Listen, if it was gonna be a guy it would have to be you. But that's not my thing. It really is not. Not now, never will be."

Barney nodded. "I know that. It just got away from me."

They stood quiet a minute with their arms around each other.

"You want to try to be friends?" she said.

He thought about it a minute. "Yeah. But you've got to help me a little bit. Here's the deal: I'm going to make this major effort to forget what I saw in the shower, and you don't show it to me anymore. And don't show me any boobs either, while you're at it. How's that?"

"I can be a good friend, Barney. Come to the house tomorrow. Judy cooks, I cook."

"Yeah, but you may not cook any better than I do."

"Try me," Margot said.

CHAPTER

62

DR LECTER held a bottle of Château Pétrus up to the light. He had raised it to the upright position and set it on its bottom a day ago, in case it might have sediment. He looked at his watch and decided it was time to open the wine.

This was what Dr Lecter considered a serious risk, more of a chance than he liked to take. He did not want to be rash. He wanted to enjoy the wine's color in a crystal decanter. What if, after drawing the cork too early, he decided there was none of its holy breath to be lost in decanting? The light revealed a bit of sediment.

He removed the cork as carefully as he might trepan a skull, and placed the wine in his pouring device, which was driven by a crank and screw to tilt the bottle by minute increments. Let the salt air do a bit of work and then he would decide.

He lit a fire of shaggy chunk charcoal and made himself a drink, Lillet and a slice of orange over ice, while he considered the *fond* he had been working on for days. Dr Lecter followed the inspired lead of Alexandre Dumas in fashioning his stock. Only three days ago, upon his return from the deer-lease woods, he had added to the stockpot a fat crow which had been stuffing itself with juniper berries. Small black feathers swam on the calm waters of the bay. The primary feathers he saved to make plectra for his harpsichord.

Now Dr Lecter crushed juniper berries of his own and began to sweat shallots in a copper saucepan. With a neat surgical knot, he tied a piece of cotton string around a fresh bouquet garni and ladled stock over it in the saucepan.

The tenderloin Dr Lecter lifted from his ceramic crock was dark from the marinade, dripping. He patted it dry and turned the pointed end back on itself and tied it to make the diameter constant for the length of the meat.

In time the fire was right, banked with one very hot area and a step in the coals. The tenderloin hissed on the iron and blue smoke whirled across the garden, moving as though to the music on Dr Lecter's speakers. He was playing Henry VIII's moving composition "If True Love Reigned."

Late in the night, his lips stained by the red Château Pétrus, a small crystal glass of honey-colored Château d'Yquem on his candle stand, Dr Lecter plays Bach. In his mind Starling runs through the leaves. The deer start ahead of her, and run up the slope past Dr Lecter, sitting still on the hillside. Running, running, he is into "Variation Two" of the *Goldberg Variations*, the candlelight playing on his moving hands—a stitch in the music, a flash of bloody snow and dirty teeth, this time no more than a flash that disappears with a distinct sound, a solid *thock*, a crossbow bolt driving through a skull—and we have the pleasant woods again, and flowing music and Starling, limned in polleny light runs out of sight, her ponytail bobbing like the flag of a deer, and without further interruption, he plays the movement through to the end and the sweet silence after was as rich as Château d'Yquem.

Dr Lecter held his glass up to the candle. The candle flared behind it as the sun flared on water, and the wine itself was the color of the winter sun on Clarice Starling's skin. Her birthday was coming soon, the doctor reflected. He wondered if there was extant a bottle of Château d'Yquem from her birth year. Perhaps a present was in order for Clarice Starling, who in three weeks would have lived as long as Christ.

AT THE moment Dr Lecter raised his wine to the candle, A. Benning, staying late at the DNA lab, raised her latest gel to the light and looked at the electrophoresis lines dotted with red, blue, and yellow. The sample was epithelial cells from the toothbrush brought over from the Palazzo Capponi in the Italian diplomatic pouch.

"Ummmm umm umm umm," she said and called Starling's number at Quantico.

Eric Pickford answered.

"Hi, may I speak to Clarice Starling please?"

"She's gone for the day and I'm in charge, how can I help you?"

"Do you have a beeper number for her?"

"She's on the other phone. What have you got?"

"Would you please tell her it's Benning from the DNA lab. Please tell her the toothbrush and the eyelash off the arrow are a match. It's Dr Lecter. And ask her to call me."

"Give me your extension number. Sure, I'll tell her right now. Thanks."

Starling was not on the other line. Pickford called Paul Krendler at home.

When Starling did not call A. Benning at the lab, the technician was a little disappointed. A. Benning had put in a lot of extra time. She went home long before Pickford ever called Starling at home.

Mason knew an hour before Starling.

He talked briefly to Paul Krendler, taking his time, letting the breaths come. His mind was very clear.

"It's time to get Starling out, before they start thinking proactive and put her out for bait. It's Friday, you've got the weekend. Get things started, Krendler. Tip the Wops about the ad and get her out of there, it's time for her to go. And Krendler?"

"I wish we could just—"

"Just do it, and when you get that next picture postcard from the Caymans, it'll have a whole new number written under the stamp."

"All right, I'll—" Krendler said, and heard the dial tone.

The short talk was uncommonly tiring for Mason.

Last, before sinking into a broken sleep, he summoned Cordell and said to him, "Send for the pigs."

64

It is more trouble physically to move a semiwild pig against its will than to kidnap a man. Pigs are harder to get hold of than men and big ones are stronger than a man and they cannot be intimidated with a gun. There are the tusks to consider if you want to maintain the integrity of your abdomen and legs.

Tusked pigs instinctively disembowel when fighting the upright species, men and bears. They do not naturally hamstring, but can quickly learn the behavior.

If you need to maintain the animal alive, you cannot haze it with electrical shock, as pigs are prone to fatal coronary fibrillation.

Carlo Deogracias, master of the pigs, had the patience of a crocodile. He had experimented with animal sedation, using the same acepromazine he planned to use on Dr Lecter. Now he knew exactly how much was required to quiet a hundred-kilo wild boar and the intervals of dosage that would keep him quiet for as long as fourteen hours without any lasting aftereffects.

Since the Verger firm was a large-scale importer and

exporter of animals and an established partner of the Department of Agriculture in experimental breeding programs, the way was made smooth for Mason's pigs. The Veterinary Service Form 17–129 was faxed to the Animal and Plant Health Inspection Service at Riverdale, Maryland, as required, along with veterinary affidavits from Sardinia and a $39.50 user's fee for fifty straws of frozen semen Carlo wanted to bring.

The permits for swine and semen came by return fax, along with a waiver of the usual Key West quarantine for swine, and a confirmation that an on-board inspector would clear the animals at Baltimore-Washington International Airport.

Carlo and his helpers, the brothers Piero and Tommaso Falcione, put the crates together. They were excellent crates with sliding doors at each end, sanded inside and padded. At the last minute, they remembered to crate the bordello mirror too. Something about its rococo frame around reflected pigs delighted Mason in photographs.

Carefully, Carlo doped sixteen swine—five boars raised in the same pen and eleven sows, one of them pregnant, none in estrus. When they were unconscious he gave them a close physical examination. He tested their sharp teeth and the tips of their great tusks with his fingers. He held their terrible faces in his hands, looked into the tiny glazed eyes and listened to make sure their airways were clear, and he hobbled their elegant little ankles. Then he dragged them on canvas into the crates and slid the end doors in place.

The trucks groaned down from the Gennargentu Mountains into Cagliari. At the airport waited an airbus jet freighter operated by Count Fleet Airlines, specialists in transporting racehorses. This airplane usually carried American horses back and forth to race meets in Dubai. It carried one horse now, picked up in Rome. The horse would not be still when it scented the wild-smelling pigs, and whinnied and kicked in its close padded stall until the crew had to unload it and leave it behind, causing much expense later for Mason, who had to ship the horse home to its owner and pay compensation to avoid a lawsuit.

Carlo and his helpers rode with the hogs in the pressurized cargo hold. Every half-hour out over the heaving sea, Carlo visited each pig individually, put his hand on its bristled side and felt the thump of its wild heart.

Even if they were good and hungry, sixteen pigs could not be expected to consume Dr Lecter in his entirety at one seating. It had taken them a day to completely consume the filmmaker.

The first day, Mason wanted Dr Lecter to watch them eat his feet. Lecter would be sustained on a saline drip overnight, awaiting the next course.

Mason had promised Carlo an hour with him in the interval.

In the second course, the pigs could eat him all hollow and consume the ventral-side flesh and the face within an hour, as the first shift of the biggest pigs and the pregnant female fell back sated and the second wave came on. By then the fun would be over anyway.

BARNEY HAD never been in the barn before. He came in a side door under the tiers of seats that surrounded an old showring on three sides. Empty and silent except for the muttering of the pigeons in the rafters, the showring still held an air of expectation. Behind the auctioneer's stand stretched the open barn. Big double doors opened into the stable wing and the tack room.

Barney heard voices and called, "Hello."

"In the tack room, Barney, come on in." Margot's deep voice.

The tack room was a cheerful place, hung with harnesses and the graceful shapes of saddlery. Smell of leather. Warm sunlight streaming in through dusty windows just beneath the eaves raised the smell of leather and hay. An open loft along one side opened into the hayloft of the barn.

Margot was putting up the currycombs and some hackamores. Her hair was paler than the hay, her eyes as blue as the inspection stamp on meat.

"Hi," Barney said from the door. He thought the

room was a little stagy, set up for the sake of visiting children. In its height and the slant of light from the high windows it was like a church.

"Hi, Barney. Hang on and we'll eat in about twenty minutes."

Judy Ingram's voice came from the loft above. "Barneeeeeeey. Good morning. Wait till you see what we've got for lunch! Margot, you want to try to eat outside?"

Each Saturday it was Margot and Judy's habit to curry the motley assortment of fat Shetlands kept for the visiting children to ride. They always brought a picnic lunch.

"Let's try on the south side of the barn, in the sun," Margot said.

Everyone seemed a little too chirpy. A person with Barney's hospital experience knows excessive chirpiness does not bode well for the chirpee.

The tack room was dominated by a horse's skull, mounted a little above head height on the wall, with its bridle and blinkers on, and draped with the racing colors of the Vergers.

"That's Fleet Shadow, won the Lodgepole Stakes in '52, the only winner my father ever had," Margot said. "He was too cheap to get him stuffed." She looked up at the skull. "Bears a strong resemblence to Mason, doesn't it?"

There was a forced-draft furnace and bellows in the corner. Margot had built a small coal fire there against the chill. On the fire was a pot of something that smelled like soup.

A complete set of farrier's tools was on a workbench.

She picked up a farrier's hammer, this one with a short handle and a heavy head. With her great arms and chest, Margot might have been a farrier herself, or a blacksmith with particularly pointed pectorals.

"You want to throw me the blankets?" Judy called down.

Margot picked up a bundle of freshly washed saddle blankets and with one scooping move of her great arm, sent it arching up to the loft.

"Okay, I'm gonna wash up and get the stuff out of the Jeep. We'll eat in fifteen, okay?" Judy said, coming down the ladder.

Barney, feeling Margot's scrutiny, did not check out Judy's behind. There were some bales of hay with horse blankets folded on them for seats. Margot and Barney sat.

"You missed the ponies. They're gone to the stable in Lester," Margot said.

"I heard the trucks this morning. How come?"

"Mason's business." A little silence. They had always been easy with silence, but not this one. "Well, Barney. You get to a point where you can't talk anymore, unless you're going to do something. Is that where we are?"

"Like an affair or something," Barney said. The unhappy analogy hung in the air.

"*Affair*," Margot said, "I've got something for you a hell of a lot better than that. You know what we're talking about."

"Pretty much," Barney said.

"But if you decided you *didn't* want to do something, and later it happened anyway, do you understand you could never come back on me about it?" She tapped

388

her palm with the farrier's hammer, absently perhaps, watching him with her blue butcher's eyes.

Barney had seen some countenances in his time and stayed alive by reading them. He saw she was telling the truth.

"I know that."

"Same if we did something. I'll be extremely generous one time, and one time only. But it would be enough. You want to know how much?"

"Margot, nothing's gonna happen on my watch. Not while I'm taking his money to take care of him."

"*Why*, Barney?"

Sitting on the bale, he shrugged his big shoulders. "Deal's a deal."

"You call that a *deal*? This is a *deal*," Margot said. "*Five million dollars, Barney*. The same five Krendler's supposed to get for selling out the FBI, if you want to know."

"We're talking about getting enough semen from Mason to get Judy pregnant."

"We're talking about something else too. You know if you take Mason's jism from him and leave him alive, he'd get you, Barney. You couldn't run far enough. You'd go to the fucking pigs."

"I'd do what?"

"What is it, Barney, *Semper Fi*, like it says on your arm?"

"When I took his money I said I'd take care of him. While I work for him, I won't do him any harm."

"You don't have to . . . *do* anything to him except the medical, after he's dead. I can't touch him there.

Not one more time. You might have to help me with Cordell."

"You kill Mason, you only get one batch," Barney said.

"We get five cc's, even a low-normal sperm count, put extenders in it, we could try five times with insemination, we could do it in vitro—Judy's family's real fertile."

"Did you think about buying Cordell?"

"No. He'd never keep the deal. His word would be crap. Sooner or later he'd come back on me. He'd have to go."

"You've thought about it a lot."

"Yes. Barney, you have to control the nurse station. There's tape backup on the monitors, there's a record of every second. There's live TV, but no videotape running. We—I put my hand down inside the shell of the respirator and immobilize his chest. Monitor shows the respirator still working. By the time his heart rate and blood pressure show a change, you rush in and he's unconscious, you can try to revive him all you want. The only thing is, you don't happen to notice me. I just press on his chest until he's dead. You've worked enough autopsies, Barney. What do they look for when they suspect smothering?"

"Hemorrhages behind the eyelids."

"Mason doesn't have any eyelids."

She had read up, and she was used to buying anything, anybody.

Barney looked her in the face but he fixed the hammer in his peripheral vision as he gave his answer: "No, Margot."

"If I had let you fuck me would you do it?"

"No."

"If I had fucked *you* would you do it?"

"No."

"If you didn't work here, if you didn't have any medical responsibility to him would you do it?"

"Probably not."

"Is it ethics or chickenshit?"

"I don't know."

"Let's find out. You're fired, Barney."

He nodded, not particularly surprised.

"And, Barney?" She raised a finger to her lips. "Shhhh. Give me your word? Do I have to say I could kill you with that prior in California? I don't need to say that do I?"

"You don't have to worry," Barney said. "*I've* got to worry. I don't know how Mason lets people go. Maybe they just disappear."

"You don't have to worry either, I'll tell Mason you've had hepatitis. You don't know a lot about his business except that he's trying to help the law—and he knows we got the prior on you, he'll let you go."

Barney wondered which Dr Lecter had found more interesting in therapy, Mason Verger or his sister.

IT WAS night when the long silver transport pulled up to the barn at Muskrat Farm. They were late and tempers were short.

The arrangements at Baltimore-Washington International Airport had gone well at first, the on-board inspector from the Department of Agriculture rubber-stamped the shipment of sixteen swine. The inspector had an expert's knowledge of swine and he had never seen anything like them.

Then Carlo Deogracias looked inside the truck. It was a livestock transporter and smelled like one, with traces in the cracks of many former occupants. Carlo would not let his pigs be unloaded. The airplane waited while the angry driver, Carlo and Piero Falcione found another livestock truck more suitable to moving crates, located a truck wash with a steam hose and steam-cleaned the cargo area.

Once at the main gate of Muskrat Farm, a last annoyance. The guard checked the tonnage of the truck and refused them entrance, citing a load limit on an ornamental bridge. He redirected them to the service road through the national forest. Tree branches scraped the tall truck as it crept the last two miles.

Carlo liked the big clean barn at Muskrat Farm. He liked the little forklift that gently carried the cages into the pony stalls.

When the driver of the livestock truck brought an electric cattle prod to the cages and offered to zap a pig to see how deeply drugged it was, Carlo snatched the instrument away from him and frightened him so badly he was afraid to ask for it back.

Carlo would let the great rough swine recover from their sedation in the semidarkness, not letting them out of the cages until they were on their feet and alert. He was afraid that those awakening first might take a bite out of a drugged sleeper. Any prone figure attracted them when the herd was not napping together.

Piero and Tommaso had to be doubly careful since the herd ate the filmmaker Oreste, and later his frozen assistant. The men could not be in the pen or the pasture with the pigs. The swine did not threaten, they did not gnash their teeth as wild pigs will, they simply kept watching the men with the terrible single-mindedness of a swine and sidled nearer until they were close enough to charge.

Carlo, equally single-minded, did not rest until he had walked by flashlight the fence enclosing Mason's wooded pasture which adjoined the great national forest.

Carlo dug in the ground with his pocketknife and examined the forest mast under the pasture trees and found acorns. He had heard jays in the last light driving in and thought it likely there would be acorns. Sure enough, white oaks grew here in the enclosed field, but not too many of them. He did not want the pigs to find their meals on the ground, as they could easily do in the great forest.

Mason had built across the open end of the barn a stout barrier with a Dutch gate in it, like Carlo's own gate in Sardinia.

From behind the safety of this barrier, Carlo could feed them, sailing clothing stuffed with dead chickens, legs of lamb and vegetables over the fence into their midst.

They were not tame, but they were not afraid of men or noise. Even Carlo could not go into the pen with them. A pig is not like other animals. There is a spark of intelligence and a terrible practicality in pigs. These were not at all hostile. They just liked to eat men. They were light of foot like a Miura bull and could cut like a sheep-dog, and their movements around their keepers had the sinister quality of premeditation. Piero had a near moment retrieving from a feeding a shirt that they thought they could use again.

There had never been such pigs before, bigger than the European wild boar and just as savage. Carlo felt he had created them. He knew that the thing they would do, the evil they would destroy, would be all the credit he would ever need in the hereafter.

By midnight, all were asleep in the barn: Carlo, Piero and Tommaso slept without dreaming in the tack room loft, the swine snored in their cages where their elegant little feet were beginning to trot in their dreams and one or two stirred on the clean canvas. The skull of the trotting horse, Fleet Shadow, faintly lit by the coal fire in the farrier's furnace, watched over all.

To ATTACK an agent of the Federal Bureau of Investigation with Mason's false evidence was a big leap for Krendler. It left him a little breathless. If the Attorney General caught him, she would crush him like a roach.

Except for his own personal risk, the matter of ruining Clarice Starling did not weigh with Krendler as would breaking a man. A man had a family to support—Krendler supported his own family, as greedy and ungrateful as they were.

And Starling definitely had to go. Left alone, following the threads with the picky, petty homemaking skills of a woman, Clarice Starling would find Hannibal Lecter. If that happened, Mason Verger would not give Krendler anything.

The sooner she was stripped of her resources and put out there as bait, the better.

Krendler had broken careers before, in his own rise to power, first as a state prosecuting attorney active in politics, and later at Justice. He knew from experience that crippling a woman's career is easier than damaging a man. If a woman gets a promotion that women shouldn't have, the most efficient way is to say she won it on her back.

It would be impossible to make that charge stick to Clarice Starling, Krendler thought. In fact, he couldn't think of anyone more in *need* of a grudge-fucking up the dirt road. He sometimes thought of that abrasive act as he twisted his finger in his nose.

Krendler could not have explained his animosity to Starling. It was visceral and it belonged to a place in himself where he could not go. A place with seat covers and a dome light, door handles and window cranks and a girl with Starling's coloring but not her sense and her pants around one ankle asking him what in the hell was the matter with him, and why didn't he come on and do it, was he *some kind of queer? some kind of queer? some kind of queer?*

If you didn't know what a cunt Starling was, Krendler reflected, her performance in black and white was much better than her few promotions would indicate—he had to admit that. Her rewards had been satisfyingly few: By adding the odd drop of poison to her record over the years, Krendler had been able to influence the FBI career board enough to block a number of plum assignments she should have gotten, and her independent attitude and smart mouth had helped his cause.

Mason wouldn't wait for the disposition of Feliciana Fish Market. And there was no guarantee any shit would stick to Starling in a hearing. The shooting of Evelda Drumgo and the others was the result of a security failure, obviously. It was a miracle Starling was able to save that little bastard of a baby. One more for the public to have to feed. Tearing the scab off that ugly event would be easy, but it was an unwieldy way to get at Starling.

Better Mason's way. It would be quick and she would be out of there. The timing was propitious:

One Washington axiom, proved more times than the Pythagorean theorem, states that in the presence of oxygen, one loud fart with an obvious culprit will cover many small emissions in the same room, provided they are nearly simultaneous.

Ergo, the impeachment trial was distracting the Justice Department enough for him to railroad Starling.

Mason wanted some press coverage for Dr Lecter to see. But Krendler must make the coverage seem an unhappy accident. Fortunately an occasion was coming that would serve him well: the very birthday of the FBI.

Krendler maintained a tame conscience with which to shrive himself.

It consoled him now: If Starling lost her job, at worst some goddamned dyke den where Starling lived would have to do without the big TV dish for sports. At worst he was giving a loose cannon a way to roll over the side and threaten nobody anymore.

A "loose cannon" over the side would "stop rocking the boat," he thought, pleased and comforted as though two naval metaphors made a logical equation. That the rocking boat moves the cannon bothered him not at all.

Krendler had the most active fantasy life his imagination would permit. Now, for his pleasure, he pictured

Starling as old, tripping over those tits, those trim legs turned blue-veined and lumpy, trudging up and down the stairs carrying laundry, turning her face away from the stains on the sheets, working for her board at a bed-and-breakfast owned by a couple of goddamned hairy old dykes.

He imagined the next thing he would say to her, coming on the heels of his triumph with "cornpone country pussy."

Armed with Dr Doemling's insights, he wanted to stand close to her after she was disarmed and say without moving his mouth, "You're old to still be fucking your daddy, even for Southern white trash." He repeated the line in his mind, and considered putting it in his notebook.

Krendler had the tool and the time and the venom he needed to smash Starling's career, and as he set about it, he was vastly aided by chance and the Italian mail.

68

THE BATTLE Creek Cemetery outside Hubbard, Texas, is a small scar on the lion-colored hide of central Texas in December. The wind is whistling there at this moment, and it will always whistle there. You cannot wait it out.

The new section of the cemetery has flat markers so it's easy to mow the grass. Today a silver heart balloon dances there over the grave of a birthday girl. In the older part of the cemetery they mow along the paths every time and get between the tombstones with a mower as often as they can. Bits of ribbon, the stalks of dried flowers, are mixed in the soil. At the very back of the cemetery is a compost heap where the old flowers go. Between the dancing heart balloon and the compost heap, a backhoe is idling, a young black man at the controls, another on the ground, cupping a match against the wind as he lights a cigarette . . .

"Mr Closter, I wanted you to be here when we did this so you could see what we're up against. I'm sure you will discourage the loved ones from any viewing," said

Mr Greenlea, director of the Hubbard Funeral Home. "That casket—and I want to compliment you again on your taste—that casket will make a proud presentation, and that's as far as they need to see. I'm happy to give you the professional discount on it. My own father, who is dead at the present time, rests in one just like it."

He nodded to the backhoe operator and the machine's claw took a bite out of the weedy, sunken grave.

"You're positive about the stone, Mr Closter?"

"Yes," Dr Lecter said. "The children are having one stone made for both the mother and the father."

They stood without talking, the wind snapping their trouser cuffs, until the backhoe stopped about two feet down.

"We'd better go with shovels from here," Mr Greenlea said. The two workers dropped into the hole and started moving dirt with an easy, practiced swing.

"Careful," Mr Greenlea said. "That wasn't much of a coffin to start with. Nothing like what he's getting now."

The cheap pressboard coffin had indeed collapsed on its occupant. Greenlea had his diggers clear the dirt around it and slide a canvas under the bottom of the box, which was still intact. The coffin was raised in this canvas sling and swung into the back of a truck.

On a trestle table in the Hubbard Funeral Home garage, the pieces of the sunken lid were lifted away to reveal a sizeable skeleton.

Dr Lecter examined it quickly. A bullet had notched the short rib over the liver and there was a depressed fracture and bullet hole high on the left forehead. The skull, mossy and clogged and only partly exposed, had good, high cheekbones he had seen before.

"The ground don't leave much," Mr Greenlea said.

The rotted remains of trousers and the rags of a cowboy shirt draped the bones. The pearl snaps from the shirt had fallen through the ribs. A cowboy hat, a triple-X beaver with a Fort Worth crease, rested over the chest. There was a notch in the brim and a hole in the crown.

"Did you know the deceased?" Dr Lecter asked.

"We just bought this mortuary and took over this cemetery as an addition to our group in 1989," Mr Greenlea said. "I live locally now, but our firm's headquarters is in St Louis. Do you want to try to preserve the clothing? Or I could let you have a suit, but I don't think—"

"No," Dr Lecter said. "Brush the bones, no clothing except the hat and the buckle and the boots, bag the small bones of the hands and feet, and bundle them in your best silk shroud with the skull and the long bones. You don't have to lay them out, just get them all. Will keeping the stone compensate you for reclosing?"

"Yes, if you'll just sign here, and I'll give you copies of those others," Mr Greenlea said, vastly pleased at the coffin he had sold. Most funeral directors coming for a body would have shipped the bones in a carton and sold the family a coffin of his own.

Dr Lecter's disinterment papers were in perfect accord with the Texas Health and Safety Code Sec. 711.004, as he knew they would be, having made them himself, downloading the requirements and facsimile forms from the Texas Association of Counties Quick Reference Law Library.

The two workmen, grateful for the power tailgate on Dr Lecter's rental truck, rolled the new coffin into place and lashed it down on its dolly beside the only other item in the truck, a cardboard hanging wardrobe.

"That's such a good idea, carrying your own closet. Saves wrinkling your ceremonial attire in a suitcase, doesn't it?" Mr Greenlea said.

In Dallas, the doctor removed from the wardrobe a viola case and put in it his silk-bound bundle of bones, the hat fitting nicely into the lower section, the skull cushioned in it.

He shoved the coffin out the back at the Fish Trap Cemetery and turned in his rental at Dallas—Fort Worth Airport, where he checked the viola case straight through to Philadelpha.

IV

NOTABLE OCCASIONS ON THE CALENDAR OF DREAD

ON MONDAY, Clarice Starling had the weekend exotic purchases to check, and there were glitches in her system that required the help of her computer technician from Engineering. Even with severely pruned lists of two or three of the most special vintages from five vintners, the reduction to two sources for American foie gras, and five specialty grocers, the numbers of purchases were formidable. Call-ins from individual liquor stores using the telephone number on the bulletin had to be entered by hand.

Based on the identification of Dr Lecter in the murder of the deer hunter in Virginia, Starling cut the list to East Coast purchases except for Sonoma foie gras. Fauchon in Paris refused to cooperate. Starling could make no sense of what Vera dal 1926 in Florence said on the telephone, and faxed the Questura for help in case Dr Lecter ordered white truffles.

At the end of the workday on Monday, December 17, Starling had twelve possibilities to follow up. They were combinations of purchases on credit cards. One

405

man had bought a case of Pétrus and a supercharged Jaguar, both on the same American Express.

Another placed an order for a case of Bâtard-Montrachet and a case of green Gironde oysters.

Starling passed each possibility along to the local line bureau for follow-up.

Starling and Eric Pickford worked separate but overlapping shifts in order to have the office manned during store retail hours.

It was Pickford's fourth day on the job and he spent part of it programming his auto-dial telephone. He did not label the buttons.

When he went out for coffee, Starling pushed the top button on his telephone, Paul Krendler himself answered.

She hung up and sat in silence. It was time to go home. Swiveling her chair slowly around and around, she regarded all the objects in Hannibal's House. The X rays, the books, the table set for one. Then she pushed out through the curtains.

Crawford's office was open and empty. The sweater his late wife knitted for him hung on a coat tree in the corner. Starling put her hand out to the sweater, did not quite touch it, slung her coat over her shoulder and started the long walk to her car.

She would never see Quantico again.

ON THE evening of December 17, Clarice Starling's doorbell rang. She could see a federal marshal's car behind the Mustang in her driveway.

The marshal was Bobby, who drove her home from the hospital after the Feliciana shoot-out.

"Hi, Starling."

"Hi, Bobby. Come in."

"I'd like to, but I oughta tell you first. I've got a notice here I've got to serve you."

"Well, hell. Serve me in the house where it's warm," Starling said, numb in the middle.

The notice, on the letterhead of the Inspector General of the Department of Justice, required her to appear at a hearing the next morning, December 18, at nine A.M. in the J. Edgar Hoover Building.

"You want a ride tomorrow?" the marshal asked.

Starling shook her head. "Thanks, Bobby, I'll take my car. Want some coffee?"

"No, thanks. I'm sorry, Starling." The marshal clearly wanted to go. There was an awkward silence.

"Your ear's looking good," he said at last.

She waved to him as he backed out of the drive.

The letter simply told her to report. No reason was given.

Ardelia Mapp, veteran of the Bureau's internecine wars and thorn in the side of the good-old-boy network, immediately brewed her grandmother's strongest medicinal tea, renowned for enhancing the mentality. Starling always dreaded the tea, but there was no way around it.

Mapp tapped the letterhead with her finger. "The Inspector General doesn't *have* to tell you a damn thing," Mapp said between sips. "If our Office of Professional Responsibility had charges, or the OPR-DOJ had something on you, they'd have to tell you, they'd have to serve you with papers. They'd have to give you a damn 645 or a 644 with the charges right there on it, and if it was criminal you'd have a lawyer, full disclosure, everything the crooks get, right?"

"Damn straight."

"Well, this way you get diddly-squat in advance. Inspector General's political, he can take over any case."

"He took over this one."

"With Krendler blowing smoke up his butt. Whatever it is, if you decide you want to go with an Equal Opportunity case, I've got all the numbers. Now, listen to me, Starling, you've got to tell them you want to tape. IG doesn't use signed depositions. Lonnie Gains got into that mess with them over that. They keep a record of what you say, and sometimes it changes after you say it. You don't ever see a transcript."

When Starling called Jack Crawford, he sounded as though he'd been asleep.

"I don't know what it is, Starling," he said. "I'll call around. One thing I do know, I'll be there tomorrow."

MORNING, AND the armored concrete cage of the Hoover Building brooding under a milky overcast.

In this era of the car bomb, the front entrance and the courtyard are closed most days, and the building is ringed by old Bureau automobiles as an improvised crash barrier.

The D.C. police follow a mindless policy, writing tickets on some of the barrier cars day after day, the sheaf building up under the wipers and tearing off in the wind to blow down the street.

A derelict warming himself over a grate in the sidewalk called to Starling and raised his hand as she passed. One side of his face was orange from some emergency room's Betadine. He held out a Styrofoam cup, worn down at the edges. Starling fished in her purse for a dollar, gave him two, leaning in to the warm stale air and the steam.

"Bless your heart," he said.

"I need it," said Starling. "Every little bit helps."

Starling got a large coffee at Au Bon Pain on the

Tenth Street side of the Hoover Building as she had done so many times over the years. She wanted the coffee after a ragged sleep, but she didn't want to need to pee during the hearing. She decided to drink half of it.

She spotted Crawford through the window and caught up with him on the sidewalk. "You want to split this big coffee, Mr Crawford? They'll give me another cup."

"Is it decaf?"

"No."

"I better not, I'll jump out of my skin." He looked peaked and old. A clear drop hung at the end of his nose. They stood out of the foot traffic streaming toward the side entrance of the FBI headquarters.

"I don't know what this meeting is, Starling. Nobody else from the Feliciana shoot-out has been called, that I can find out. I'll be with you." Starling passed him a Kleenex and they entered the steady stream of the arriving day shift.

Starling thought the clerical personnel looked unusually spiffy.

"Ninetieth anniversary of the FBI. Bush is coming to speak today," Crawford reminded her.

There were four TV satellite uplink trucks on the side street.

A camera crew from WFUL-TV was set up on the sidewalk filming a young man with a razor haircut talking into a hand microphone. A production assistant stationed on top of the van saw Starling and Crawford coming in the crowd.

"That's her, that's her in the navy raincoat," he called down.

"Here we go," said Razor Cut. "Rolling."

The crew made a swell in the stream of people to get the camera in Starling's face.

"Special Agent Starling, can you comment on the investigation of the Feliciana Fish Market Massacre? Has the report been submitted? Are you the subject of charges in killing the five—" Crawford took off his rain hat and, pretending to shield his eyes from the lights, managed to block the camera lens for a moment. Only the security door stopped the TV crew.

Sumbitches were tipped.

Once inside Security, they stopped in the hall. The mist outside had covered Starling and Crawford with tiny droplets. Crawford popped a Ginkgo Biloba tablet dry.

"Starling, I think they may have picked today because there's all the stir over the impeachment and the anniversary. Whatever they want to do could slide by in the rush."

"Why tip the press then?"

"Because not everybody in this hearing is singing off the same page. You've got ten minutes, want to powder your nose?"

72

STARLING HAD rarely been up to seven, the executive floor of the J. Edgar Hoover Building. She and the other members of her graduating class gathered there seven years ago to see the director congratulate Ardelia Mapp as valedictorian, and once an assistant director had summoned her to accept her medal as Combat Pistol Champion.

The carpet in Assistant Director Noonan's office was deep beyond her experience. In the clubby atmosphere of leather chairs in his meeting room there was the distinct smell of cigarettes. She wondered if they had flushed the butts and fanned the air before she got there.

Three men stood up when she and Crawford came into the room and one did not. The standees were Starling's former boss, Clint Pearsall of the Washington Field Office, Buzzard's Point; A/DIC Noonan of the FBI, and a tall red-haired man in a raw silk suit. Keeping his seat was Paul Krendler of the Inspector General's Office. Krendler turned his head to her on

413

his long neck as though he were locating her by scent. When he faced her she could see both his round cars at the same time. Oddly, a federal marshal she didn't know stood in the corner of the room.

FBI and Justice personnel customarily are neat in their appearance, but these men were groomed for TV. Starling realized they must be appearing in the ceremonies downstairs with former President Bush later in the day. Otherwise she would have been summoned to the Justice Department rather than the Hoover Building.

Krendler frowned at the sight of Jack Crawford at Starling's side.

"Mr Crawford, I don't think your attendance is required for this procedure."

"I'm Special Agent Starling's immediate supervisor. My place is here."

"I don't think so," Krendler said. He turned to Noonan. "Clint Pearsall is her boss of record, she's just TDY with Crawford. I think Agent Starling should be questioned privately," he said. "If we need additional information, we can ask Section Chief Crawford to stand by where we can reach him."

Noonan nodded. "We certainly would welcome your input, Jack, after we've heard independent testimony by the—by Special Agent Starling. Jack, I want you to stand by. If you want to make it the reading room of the library, make yourself comfortable, I'll call you."

Crawford got to his feet. "Director Noonan, may I say—"

"You *may* leave, is what you *may* do," Krendler said.

Noonan got to his feet. "Hold it please, it's my meeting, Mr Krendler, until I turn it over to you. Jack, you and I go way back. The gentleman from Justice is too recently appointed to understand that. You'll get to say your piece. Now leave us and let Starling talk for herself," Noonan said. He leaned to Krendler and said something in his ear that made his face turn red.

Crawford looked at Starling. All he could do was bitch himself up.

"Thank you for coming, sir," she said.

The marshal let Crawford out.

Hearing the door click shut behind her, Starling straightened her spine and faced the men alone.

From there the proceeding went forward with the dispatch of an eighteenth-century amputation.

Noonan was the highest FBI authority in the room, but the Inspector General could overrule him, and the inspector apparently had sent Krendler as his plenipotentiary.

Noonan picked up the file before him. "Would you identify yourself, please, for the record?"

"Special Agent Clarice Starling. *Is* there a record, Director Noonan? I'd be glad if there was."

When he did not answer, she said, "Do you mind if I tape the proceedings?" She took a tough little Nagra tape recorder from her purse.

Krendler spoke up. "Ordinarily this sort of preliminary meeting would be in the Inspector General's office at Justice. We're doing it here because it's to everybody's convenience with the ceremony today, but the IG rules apply. This is a matter of some diplomatic sensitivity. No tape."

"Tell her the charges, Mr Krendler," Noonan said.

"Agent Starling, you stand accused of unlawful disclosure of sensitive material to a fugitive felon," Krendler said, his face under careful control. "Specifically you are accused of placing this advertisement in two Italian newspapers warning the fugitive Hannibal Lecter that he was in danger of being captured."

The marshal brought Starling a page of smudged newsprint from *La Nazione*. She turned it to the window to read the circled material:

A. A. Aaron—Turn yourself in to the nearest authorities, enemies are close. Hannah.

"How do you respond?"

"I didn't do it. I never saw this before."

"How do you account for the fact that the letter uses a code name 'Hannah' known only to Dr Hannibal Lecter and this Bureau? The code name Lecter asked you to use?"

"I don't know. Who found this?"

"The Document Service at Langley happened to see it in the course of translating *La Nazione*'s coverage on Lecter."

"If the code is a secret within the Bureau, how did Document Service at Langley recognize it in the paper? CIA runs Document Service. Let's ask them who brought 'Hannah' to their attention."

"I'm sure the translator was familiar with the case file."

"*That* familiar? I doubt it. Let's ask him who suggested he watch out for it. How would I have known Dr Lecter was in Florence?"

"You're the one who found the computer query from

416

the Questura in Florence to the Lecter VICAP file,"
Krendler said. "The query came several days prior to
the Pazzi murder. We don't know when you discovered
it. Why else would the Questura in Florence be asking
about Lecter?"

"What possible reason would I have to warn him?
Director Noonan, why is this a matter for the IG?
I'm prepared to take a polygraph examination anytime.
Wheel it in here."

"The Italians registered a diplomatic protest over
the attempted warning of a known felon in their
country," Noonan said. He indicated the red-haired
man beside him. "This is Mr Montenegro from the
Italian Embassy."

"Good morning, sir. And the *Italians* found out
how?" Starling said. "Not from Langley."

"The diplomatic beef puts the ball in our court,"
Krendler said before Montenegro could open his mouth.
"We want this cleaned up to the satisfaction of the
Italian authorities, and to my satisfaction and that of
the IG, and we want it PDQ. It's better for everybody
if we look at all the facts together. What is it with you
and Dr Lecter, Ms Starling?"

"I interrogated Dr Lecter several times on the orders
of Section Chief Crawford. Since Dr Lecter's escape
I've had two letters from him in seven years. You have
both of them," Starling said.

"Actually, we have more," Krendler said. "We got
this yesterday. What else you might have received, we
don't know." He reached behind him to get a cardboard
box, much stamped and much battered by the mails.

Krendler pretended to enjoy the fragrances coming

417

from the box. He indicated the shipping label with his
finger, not bothering to show Starling. "Addressed to
you at your home in Arlington, Special Agent Starling. Mr Montenegro, would you tell us what these
items are?"

The Italian diplomat poked through the tissue-
wrapped items, his cufflinks winking.

"Yes, this are lotions, *sapone di mandorle*, the famous
almond soap of Santa Maria Novella in Florence, from
the Farmacia there, and some perfumes. The sort of
thing people are giving when they felt in love."

"These have been scanned for toxins and irritants,
right, Clint?" Noonan asked Starling's former supervisor.

Pearsall looked ashamed. "Yes," he said. "There's
nothing wrong with them."

"A gift of love," Krendler said with some satisfaction.
"Now we have the mash note." He unfolded the sheet of
parchment from the box and held it up, revealing the
tabloid picture of Starling's face with the winged body
of a lioness. He turned the sheet to read Dr Lecter's
copperplate script: "*Did you ever think, Clarice, why
the Philistines don't understand you? It's because you're
the answer to Samson's riddle: You are the honey in
the lion.*"

"*Il miele dentro la leonessa*, that's nice," Montenegro
said, filing it away for his own use at a later time.

"It's *what*?" Krendler said.

The Italian waved the question away, seeing that
Krendler would never hear the music in Dr Lecter's
metaphor, nor feel its tactile evocations anywhere else.

"The Inspector General wants to take it from here,

418

because of the international ramifications," Krendler said. "Which way it will go, administrative charges or criminal, depends on what we find out in our ongoing probe. If it goes criminal, Special Agent Starling, it'll be turned over to the Public Integrity Section of the Justice Department, and PIS will take it to trial. You'll be informed in plenty of time to prepare. Director Noonan . . ."

Noonan took a deep breath and swung the axe. "Clarice Starling, I'm placing you on administrative leave until such time as this matter is adjudicated. You will surrender weapons and FBI identification. Your access is revoked to all but public federal facilities. You will be escorted from the building. Please surrender your sidearms and ID now to Special Agent Pearsall. Come."

Walking to the table, Starling saw the men for a second as bowling pins at a shooting contest. She could kill the four of them before one could clear his weapon. The moment passed. She took out her .45, looked steadily at Krendler as she dropped the clip into her hand, put the clip on the table and shucked the round out of the pistol's chamber. Krendler caught it in the air and squeezed it until his knuckles turned white.

Badge and ID went next.

"You have a backup sidearm?" Krendler said. "And a shotgun?"

"Starling?" Noonan prompted.

"Locked in my car."

"Other tactical equipment?"

"A helmet and a vest."

"Mr Marshal, you will retrieve those when you escort

Miss Starling to her vehicle," Krendler said. "Do you have an encryption cell phone?"

"Yes."

Krendler raised his eyebrows to Noonan.

"Turn it in," Noonan said.

"I want to say something, I think I'm entitled to that."

Noonan looked at his watch. "Go ahead."

"This is a frame. I think Mason Verger is trying to capture Dr Lecter himself for purposes of personal revenge. I think he just missed him in Florence. I think Mr Krendler may be in collusion with Verger and wants the FBI's effort against Dr Lecter to work for Verger. I think Paul Krendler of the Department of Justice is making money out of this and I think he is willing to destroy me to do it. Mr Krendler has behaved toward me before in an inappropriate manner and is acting now out of spite as well as financial self-interest. Only this week he called me a 'cornpone country pussy.' I would challenge Mr Krendler before this body to take a lie detector test with me on these matters. I'm at your convenience. We could do it now."

"Special Agent Starling, it's a good thing you're not sworn here today—" Krendler began.

"*Swear* me. You swear too."

"I want to assure you, if the evidence is lacking you're entitled to full reinstatement without prejudice," Krendler said in his kindliest voice. "In the meantime you'll receive pay and remain eligible for insurance and medical benefits. The administrative leave is not itself punitive, Agent Starling, use it to your advantage," Krendler said, adopting a confidential tone. "In fact, if you wanted to take this hiatus to have that dirt taken out of your cheek, I'm sure the medical—"

"It's not dirt," Starling said. "It's gunpowder. No wonder you didn't recognize it."

The marshal was waiting, his hand outstretched to her.

"I'm sorry, Starling," Clint Pearsall said, his hands full of her equipment.

She looked at him and looked away. Paul Krendler drifted toward her as the other men waited to let the diplomat, Montenegro, leave the room first. Krendler started to say something between his teeth, he had it ready: "Starling, you're old to still be—"

"Excuse me." It was Montenegro. The tall diplomat had turned away from the door and come to her.

"Excuse me," Montenegro said again, looking into Krendler's face until he went away, his face twisted.

"I am sorry this has happen to you," he said. "I hope you are innocent. I promise I will press the Questura in Florence to find out how the *inserzione*, the ad, was paid for at *La Nazione*. If you think of something in . . . in my sphere of Italy to follow up, please tell me and I will insist on it." Montenegro handed her a card, small and stiff and bumpy with engraving and seemed not to notice Krendler's outstretched hand as he left the room.

Reporters, cleared through the main entrance for the coming anniversary ceremony, thronged in the courtyard. A few seemed to know whom to watch for.

"Do you have to hold my elbow?" Starling asked the marshal.

"No ma'am, I don't," he said, and made a way for her through the boom microphones and the shouted questions.

This time Razor Cut seemed to know the issue. The questions he shouted were "Is it true that you've been suspended from the Hannibal Lecter case? Do you anticipate criminal charges being brought against you? What do you say to the Italian charges?"

In the garage, Starling handed over her protective vest, her helmet, her shotgun and her backup revolver. The marshal waited while she unloaded the little pistol and wiped it down with an oily cloth.

"I saw you shoot at Quantico, Agent Starling," he said. "I got to the quarterfinals myself for the marshal's service. I'll wipe down your .45 before we put it up."

"Thank you, Marshal."

He lingered after she was in the car. He said something over the boom of the Mustang. She rolled down the window and he said it again.

"I hate this happening to you."

"Thank you, sir. I appreciate you saying it."

A press chase car was waiting outside the garage exit. Starling pushed the Mustang to lose him and got a speeding ticket three blocks from the J. Edgar Hoover Building. Photographers took pictures while the D.C. patrolman wrote it out.

Assistant Director Noonan sat at his desk after the

meeting was over, rubbing the spots his glasses left on the sides of his nose.

Getting rid of Starling didn't bother him so much— he believed there was an emotional element in women that often didn't fit in with the Bureau. But it hurt him to see Jack Crawford cut down. Jack had been very much one of the boys. Maybe Jack had a blind spot for the Starling girl, but that happens—Jack's wife was dead and all. Noonan had a week once when he couldn't keep from looking at an attractive stenographer and he had to get rid of her before she caused some trouble.

Noonan put on his glasses and took the elevator down to the library. He found Jack Crawford in the reading area, in a chair with his head back against the wall. Noonan thought he was asleep. Crawford's face was gray and he was sweating. He opened his eyes and gasped.

"Jack?" Noonan patted his shoulder, then touched his clammy face. Noonan's voice then, loud in the library. "You, librarian, call the medics!"

Crawford went to the FBI infirmary, and then to the Jefferson Memorial Intensive Care Cardiac Unit.

KRENDLER COULD not have asked for better coverage.

The ninetieth birthday of the FBI was combined with a tour for newsmen of the new crisis management center. Television news took full advantage of this unaccustomed access to the J. Edgar Hoover Building, C-SPAN carrying former President Bush's remarks in full, along with those of the director, in live programming. CNN excerpted the speeches in running coverage and the networks covered for the evening news. It was as the dignitaries filed off the dais that Krendler had his moment. Young Razor Cut, standing near the stage, posed the question: "Mr Krendler is it true that Special Agent Clarice Starling has been suspended in the Hannibal Lecter investigation?"

"I think it would be premature, and unfair to the agent, to comment on that, at the moment. I'll just say that the Inspector General's office is looking into the Lecter matter. No charges have been filed against anyone."

CNN caught a whiff too. "Mr Krendler, Italian news

sources are saying Dr Lecter may have received information improperly from a government source warning him to flee. Is that the basis of Special Agent Starling's suspension? Is that why the Inspector General's office is involved rather than the internal Office of Professional Responsibility?"

"I can't comment on foreign news reports, Jeff. I *can* say the IG's office is investigating allegations that so far have not been proven. We have as much responsibility toward our own officers as we do our friends overseas," Krendler said, poking his finger into the air like a Kennedy. "The Hannibal Lecter matter is in good hands, not just the hands of Paul Krendler, but experts drawn from all the disciplines of the FBI and the Justice Department. We have a project under way that we can reveal in due time when it has borne fruit."

The German lobbyist who was Dr Lecter's landlord furnished his house with an enormous Grundig television set, and tried to blend it into the décor by putting one of his smaller bronzes of Leda and the Swan on top of the ultramodern cabinet.

Dr Lecter was watching a film called *A Brief History of Time*, about the great astrophysicist Stephen Hawking and his work. He had watched it many times before. This was his favorite part, where the teacup falls off the table and smashes on the floor.

Hawking, twisted in his wheelchair, speaks in his computer-generated voice:

"Where does the difference between the past and the future come from? The laws of science do not distinguish

between the past and the future. Yet there is a big difference between the past and future in ordinary life.

"You may see a cup of tea fall off of a table and break into pieces on the floor. But you will never see the cup gather itself back together and jump back on the table."

The film, run backward, shows the cup reassembling itself on the table. Hawking continues:

"The increase of disorder or entropy is what distinguishes the past from the future, giving a direction to time."

Dr Lecter admired Hawking's work very much and followed it as closely as he could in the mathematical journals. He knew that Hawking had once believed the universe would stop expanding and would shrink again, and entropy might reverse itself. Later Hawking said he was mistaken.

Lecter was quite capable in the area of higher mathematics, but Stephen Hawking is on another plane entirely from the rest of us. For years Lecter had teased the problem, wanting very much for Hawking to be right the first time, for the expanding universe to stop, for entropy to mend itself, for Mischa, eaten, to be whole again.

Time. Dr Lecter stopped his videotape and turned to the news.

Television and news events involving the FBI are listed daily on the FBI's public Web site. Dr Lecter visited the Web site every day to make sure they were still using his old photograph among the Ten Most Wanted. So he learned of the FBI birthday in plenty of time to tune in. He sat in a great armchair in his smoking jacket and ascot and watched Krendler lie. He watched Krendler with his eyes half closed, holding his brandy snifter close under his nose and swirling the contents gently. He had not seen that pale face since Krendler stood outside his cage in Memphis seven years ago, just before his escape.

On the local news from Washington, he saw Starling receive a traffic ticket with microphones stuck in the window of her Mustang. By now the television news had Starling "accused of breaching U.S. security" in the Lecter case.

Dr Lecter's maroon eyes opened wide at the sight of her and in the depths of his pupils sparks flew around his image of her face. He held her countenance whole and perfect in his mind long after she was gone from the screen, and pressed her with another image, Mischa, pressed them together until, from the red plasma core of their fusion, the sparks flew upward, carrying their single image to the east, into the night sky to wheel with the stars above the sea.

Now, should the universe contract, should time reverse and teacups come together, a place could be made for Mischa in the world. The worthiest place that Dr Lecter knew: Starling's place. Mischa could have Starling's place in the world. If it came to that, if that time came round again, Starling's demise would leave a place for Mischa as sparkling and clean as the copper bathtub in the garden.

Dr Lecter parked his pickup a block from Maryland-Misericordia Hospital and wiped his quarters before he put them in the meter. Wearing the quilted jumpsuit workmen wear against the cold, and a long-billed cap against the security cameras, he went in the main entrance.

It had been more than fifteen years since Dr Lecter was in Maryland-Misericordia Hospital, but the basic layout appeared unchanged. Seeing this place where he began his medical practice meant nothing to him. The secure areas upstairs had undergone cosmetic renovation, but should be almost the same as when he practiced here, according to the blueprints at the Department of Buildings.

A visitor's pass from the front desk got him onto the patient floors. He walked along the hall reading the names of patients and doctors on the doors of the rooms. This was the postoperative convalescent unit, where patients came when released from Intensive Care after cardiac or cranial surgery.

Watching Dr Lecter proceed down the hall, you might have thought he read very slowly, as his lips moved soundlessly, and he scratched his head from time to time like a bumpkin. Then he took a seat in the waiting room where he could see the hallway. He waited an hour and half among old women recounting family tragedies, and endured *The Price Is Right* on television. At last he saw what he was waiting for, a surgeon still in surgical greens making rounds alone. This would be . . . the surgeon was going in to see a patient of . . . Dr Silverman. Dr Lecter rose and scratched. He picked up a blowzy newspaper from an end table and walked out of the waiting room. Another room with a Silverman patient was two doors down. Dr Lecter slipped inside. The room was semidark, the patient satisfactorily asleep, his head and the side of his face heavily bandaged. On the monitor screen, a worm of light humped steadily.

Dr Lecter quickly stripped off his insulated coveralls to reveal surgical greens. He pulled on shoe covers and a cap and mask and gloves. He took out of his pocket a white trash bag and unfolded it.

Dr Silverman came in speaking over his shoulder to someone in the hall. *Was a nurse coming with him? No.*

Dr Lecter picked up the wastebasket and began to tip the contents into his trash bag, his back to the door.

"Excuse me, Doctor, I'll get out of your way," Dr Lecter said.

"That's all right," Dr Silverman said, picking up the clipboard at the end of the bed. "Do what you need to do."

"Thank you," Dr Lecter said, and swung the leather

sap against the base of the surgeon's skull, just a flip of the wrist, really, and caught him around the chest as he sagged. It is always surprising to watch Dr Lecter lift a body; size for size he is as strong as an ant. Dr Lecter carried Dr Silverman into the patient's bathroom and pulled down his pants. He set Dr Silverman on the toilet.

The surgeon rested there with his head hanging forward over his knees. Dr Lecter raised him up long enough to peer into his pupils and remove the several ID tags clipped to the front of his surgical greens.

He replaced the doctor's credentials with his own visitor's pass, inverted. He put the surgeon's stethoscope around his own neck in the fashionable boa drape and the doctor's elaborate magnifying surgical glasses went on top of his head. The leather sap went up his sleeve.

Now he was ready to penetrate to the heart of Maryland-Misericordia.

The hospital adheres to strict federal guidelines in handling narcotic drugs. On the patient floors, the drug cabinets on each nurse's station are locked. Two keys, held by the duty nurse and her first assistant, are required to get in. A strict log is kept.

In the operating suites, the most secure area of the hospital, each suite is furnished with drugs for the next procedure a few minutes before the patient is brought in. The drugs for the anesthesiologist are placed near the operating table in a cabinet that has one area refrigerated and one at room temperature.

The stock of drugs is kept in a separate surgical dispensary near the scrub room. It contains a number of preparations that would not be found in the general dispensary downstairs, the powerful sedatives and exotic sedative-hypnotics that make possible open-heart surgery and brain surgery on an aware and responsive patient.

The dispensary is always manned during the working day, and the cabinets are not locked while the pharmacist is in the room. In a heart surgery emergency there is no time to fumble for a key. Dr Lecter, wearing his mask, pushed through the swinging doors to the surgical suites.

In an effort at cheer, the surgery had been painted in several bright color combinations even the dying would find aggravating. Several doctors ahead of Dr Lecter signed in at the desk and proceeded to the scrub room. Dr Lecter picked up the sign-in clipboard and moved a pen over it, signing nothing.

The posted schedule showed a brain tumor removal in Suite B scheduled to start in twenty minutes, the first of the day. In the scrub room, he pulled off his gloves and put them in his pockets, washed up thoroughly, working up to his elbows, dried his hands and powdered them and regloved. Out into the hall now. The dispensary should be the next door on the right. No. A door painted apricot with the sign EMERGENCY GENERATORS and ahead the double doors of Suite B. A nurse paused at his elbow.

"Good morning, Doctor."

Dr Lecter coughed behind his mask and muttered good morning. He turned back toward the scrub room with a mutter as though he had forgotten something. The nurse looked after him for a moment and went on into the operating theater. Dr Lecter stripped off his gloves and shot them into the waste bin. Nobody was paying attention. He got another pair. His body was in the scrub room, but in fact he raced through the foyer of his memory palace, past the bust of Pliny and up the stairs to the Hall of Architecture. In a well-lit area dominated by Christopher Wren's model of St Paul's, the hospital blueprints were waiting on a drawing table. The Maryland-Misericordia surgical suites blueprints line for line from the Baltimore Department of Buildings. He was here. The dispensary was there. No. The drawings were wrong. Plans must have been changed after the blueprints were filed. The generators were shown on the other side in mirror-image space off the corridor to Suite A. Perhaps the labels were reversed. Had to be. He could not afford to poke around.

Dr Lecter came out of the scrub room and started down the corridor to Suite A. Door on the left. The sign said MRI. Keep going. The next door was Dispensary. They had split the space on the plan into a lab for magnetic resonance imaging and a separate drug storage area.

The heavy dispensary door was open, wedged with a doorstop. Dr Lecter ducked quickly into the room and pulled the door closed behind him.

A pudgy male pharmacist was squatting, putting something on a low shelf.

"Can I help you, Doctor?"

"Yes, please."

The young man started to stand, but never made it. Thump of the sap, and the pharmacist broke wind as he folded on the floor.

Dr Lecter raised the tail of his surgical blouse and tucked it behind the gardener's apron he wore beneath.

Up and down the shelves fast, reading labels at lightning speed; *Ambien, amobarbital, Amytal, chloral hydrate, Dalmane, flurazepam, Halcion*, and raking dozens of vials into his pockets. Then he was in the refrigerator, reading and raking, *midazolam, Noctec, scopolamine, Pentothal, quazepam, solzidem*. In less than forty seconds, Dr Lecter was back in the hall, closing the dispensary door behind him.

He passed back through the scrub room and checked himself for lumps in the mirrors. Without haste, back through the swinging doors, his ID tag deliberately twisted upside down, mask on and the glasses down over his eyes, binocular lenses raised, pulse seventy-two, exchanging gruff greetings with other doctors. Down in the elevator, down and down, mask still on, looking at a clipboard he had picked up at random.

Visitors coming in might have thought it odd that he wore his surgical mask until he was well down the steps and away from the security cameras. Idlers on the street might have wondered why a doctor would drive such a ratty old truck.

Back in the surgical suite an anesthesiologist, after pecking impatiently on the door of the dispensary, found the pharmacist still unconscious and it was another fifteen minutes before the drugs were missed.

When Dr Silverman came to, he had slumped to the floor beside the toilet with his pants down. He had no memory of coming into the room and had no idea where he was. He thought he might have had a cerebral event, possibly a strokelet occasioned by the strain of a bowel movement. He was very leery of moving for fear of dislodging a clot. He eased himself along the floor until he could put his hand out into the hall. Examination revealed a mild concussion.

Dr Lecter made two more stops before he went home. He paused at a mail drop in suburban Baltimore long enough to pick up a package he had ordered on the Internet from a funeral supply company. It was a tuxedo with the shirt and tie already installed, and the whole split up the back.

All he needed now was the wine, something truly, truly festive. For that he had to go to Annapolis. It would have been nice to have had the Jaguar for the drive.

75

KRENDLER WAS dressed for jogging in the cold and had to unzip his running suit to keep from overheating when Eric Pickford called him at his Georgetown home.

"Eric, go to the cafeteria and call me on a pay phone."

"Excuse me, Mr Krendler?"

"Just do what I tell you."

Krendler pulled off his headband and gloves and dropped them on the piano in his living room. With one finger he pecked out the theme from *Dragnet* until the conversation resumed: "Starling was a techie, Eric. We don't know how she might have rigged her phones. We'll keep the government's business secure."

"Yes, sir."

"Starling called me, Mr Krendler. She wanted her plant and stuff—that stupid weather bird that drinks out of the glass. But she told me something that worked. She said to discount the last digit on the zip codes for the suspect magazine subscriptions if the difference is three or less. She said Dr Lecter might use

435

several mail drops that were conveniently close to each other."

"And?"

"I got a hit that way. The *Journal of Neurophysiology*'s going to one zip code and *Physica Scripta* and *ICARUS* are going to another. They're about ten miles apart. The subscriptions are in different names, paid with money orders."

"What's *ICARUS*?"

"It's the international journal of solar system studies. He was a charter subscriber twenty years ago. The mail drops are in Baltimore. They usually deliver the journals about the tenth of the month. Got one more thing, a minute ago, a sale on a bottle of Château, what is it, *Yuckum*?"

"Yeah, it's pronounced like EEE-Kim. What about it?"

"High-end wine store in Annapolis. I entered the purchase and it hit on the sensitive dates list Starling put in. The program hit on Starling's birth year. That's the year they made this wine, her birth year. Subject paid three hundred twenty-five dollars cash for it and—"

"This was before or after you talked with Starling?"

"Just after, just a minute ago—"

"So she doesn't know it."

"No. I should call—"

"Are you saying the merchant called you on a single-bottle purchase?"

"Yes, sir. She's got notes here, there are only three bottles like that on the East Coast. She'd notified all three. You've got to admire it."

"Who bought it—what did he look like?"

"White male, medium height with a beard. He was bundled up."

"Has the wine store got a security camera?"

"Yes, sir, that's the first thing I asked. I said we'd send somebody for the tape. I haven't done it yet. The wine store clerk hadn't read the bulletin, but he told the owner because it was such an unusual purchase. Owner ran outside in time to see the subject—he thinks it was the subject—driving away in an old pickup truck. Gray with a vise on the back. If it's Lecter, you think he'll try to deliver it to Starling? We better alert her."

"No," Krendler said. "Don't tell her."

"Can I post the VICAP bulletin board and the Lecter file?"

"*No*," Krendler said, thinking fast. "Have you got a reply from the Questura about Lecter's computer?"

"No, sir."

"Then you can't post VICAP until we can be sure Lecter's not reading it himself. He could have Pazzi's access code. Or Starling could be reading it and tipping him some way like she did in Florence."

"Oh, *right*, I see. Annapolis FO can get the tape."

"Leave it all strictly to me."

Pickford dictated the address of the wine store.

"Keep going on the subscriptions," Krendler instructed. "You can tell Crawford about the subscriptions when he comes back to work. He'll organize coverage on the mail drops after the tenth."

Krendler called Mason's number, and started out running from his Georgetown town house, trotting easily toward Rock Creek Park.

In the gathering gloom only his white Nike headband

437

and his white Nike shoes, and the white stripe down
the side of his dark Nike running suit were visible, as
though there were no man at all among the trademarks.

It was a brisk half-hour run. He heard the blat of
helicopter blades just as he came in sight of the landing
pad near the zoo. He was able to duck under the turning
propeller blades and reach the step without ever breaking stride. The lift of the jet helicopter thrilled him, the
city, the lighted monuments falling away as the aircraft
took him to the heights he deserved, to Annapolis for
the tape and to Mason.

"WILL YOU focus the fucking thing, Cordell?" In Mason's deep radio voice, with its lipless consonants, "focus" and "fucking" sounded more like "hocus" and "hucking."

Krendler stood beside Mason in the dark part of the room, the better to see the elevated monitor. In the heat of Mason's room he had his yuppie running suit pulled down to his waist and the sleeves tied around him, exposing his Princeton T-shirt. His headband and shoes gleamed in the light from the aquarium.

In Margot's opinion Krendler had the shoulders of a chicken. They had barely acknowledged one another when he arrived.

There was no tape or time counter on the liquor store security camera and Christmas business was brisk. Cordell was pushing fast-forward from customer to customer through a lot of purchases. Mason passed the time by being unpleasant.

"What did you say when you went in the liquor store in your running suit and flashed the tin, Krendler?

439

You say you were in the Special Olympics?" Mason was much less respectful since Krendler had been depositing the checks.

Krendler could not be insulted when his interests were at stake. "I said I was undercover. What kind of coverage have you got on Starling now?"

"Margot, tell him." Mason seemed to want to save his own scarce breath for insults.

"We brought in twelve men from our security in Chicago. They're in Washington. Three teams, one member of each is deputized in the state of Illinois. If the police catch them grabbing Dr Lecter, they say they recognized him and it's a citizen's arrest and blah blah. The team that catches turns him over to Carlo. They go back to Chicago and that's all they know."

The tape was running.

"Wait a minute—Cordell, back it up thirty seconds," Mason said. "Look at this."

The liquor store camera covered the area from the front door to the cash register.

In the silent videotape's fuzzy image, a man came in wearing a billed cap, a lumber jacket and mittens. He had full whiskers and wore sunglasses. He turned his back to the camera and carefully closed the door behind him.

It took a moment for the shopper to explain to the clerk what he wanted and he followed the man out of sight into the wine racks.

Three minutes dragged by. At last they came back into camera range. The clerk wiped dust off the bottle and wrapped padding around it before he put it in a bag. The customer pulled off only his right mitten and paid in cash. The clerk's mouth moved as he said "thank you" to the man's back as he was leaving.

A pause of a few seconds, and the clerk called to someone off camera. A heavyset man came into the picture and hurried out the door.

"That's the owner, guy who saw the truck," Krendler said.

"Cordell, can you copy off this tape and enlarge the customer's head?"

"Take a second, Mr Verger. It'll be fuzzy."

"Do it."

"He kept the left mitten on," Mason said. "I may have gotten screwed on that X ray I bought."

"Pazzi said he got his hand fixed, didn't he? Had the extra finger off," Krendler said.

"Pazzi might have had his finger up his butt, I don't know who to believe. You've seen him, Margot, what do you think? Was that Lecter?"

"It's been eighteen years," Margot said. "I just had three sessions with him and he always just stood up behind his desk when I came in, he didn't walk around. He was really still. I remember his voice more than anything else."

Cordell's voice on the intercom. "Mr Verger, Carlo is here."

Carlo smelled of the pigs and more. He came into the room holding his hat over his chest and the rank boar-sausage smell of his head made Krendler blow air out his nose. As a mark of respect, the Sardinian kidnapper withdrew all the way into his mouth the stag's tooth he was chewing.

"Carlo, look at this. Cordell, roll it back and walk him in from the door again."

"That's the *stronzo* son of bitch," Carlo said before the subject on the screen had walked four paces. "The beard is new, but that's the way he moves."

"You saw his hands in *Firenze*, Carlo."

"*Sì.*"

"Five fingers or six on the left?"

". . . Five."

"You hesitated."

"Only to think of *cinque* in English. It's five, I'm sure."

Mason parted his exposed teeth in all he had for a smile. "I love it. He's wearing the mitten trying to keep the six fingers in his description," he said.

Perhaps Carlo's scent had entered the aquarium via the aeration pump. The eel came out to see, and remained out, turning, turning in his infinite Möbius eight, showing his teeth as he breathed.

"Carlo, I think we may finish this soon," Mason said. "You and Piero and Tommaso are my first team. I've got confidence in you, even though he did beat you in Florence. I want you to keep Clarice Starling under surveillance for the day before her birthday, the day itself, and the day after. You'll be relieved while she's asleep in her house. I'll give you a driver and the van."

"*Padrone*," Carlo said.

"Yes."

"I want some private time with the *dottore*, for the sake of my brother, Matteo. You said I could have it." Carlo crossed himself as he mentioned the dead man's name.

"I understand your feelings completely, Carlo. You have my deepest sympathy. Carlo, I want Dr Lecter consumed in two sittings. The first evening, I want the pigs to gnaw off his feet, with him watching through the bars. I want him in good shape for that. You bring him to me in good shape. No blows to the head, no broken bones, no eye damage. Then he can wait overnight without his feet, for the pigs to finish him the next day. I'll talk to him for a while, and then you can have him for an hour before the final sitting. I'll ask you to leave him an eye and leave him conscious so he can see them coming. I want him to see their faces when they eat his face. If you, say, should decide to unman him, it's entirely up to you, but I want Cordell there to manage the bleeding. I want film."

"What if he bleeds to death the first time in the pen?"

"He won't. Nor will he die overnight. What he'll do overnight is wait with his feet eaten off. Cordell will see to that and replace his body fluids, I expect he'll be on an IV drip all night, maybe two drips."

"Or four drips if we have to," said Cordell's disembodied voice on the speakers. "I can do cut-downs on his legs."

"You can spit and piss in his IV at the last, before you roll him into the pen," Mason told Carlo in his most sympathetic voice. "Or you can come in it if you like."

Carlo's face brightened at the thought, then he remembered the muscular *signorina* with a guilty sideways glance. "*Grazie mille, Padrone.* Can you come to see him die?"

443

"I don't know, Carlo. The dust in the barn disturbs me. I may watch on video. Can you bring a pig to me? I want to put my hand on one."

"To this room, *Padrone*?"

"No, they can bring me downstairs briefly, on the power pack."

"I would have to put one to sleep, *Padrone*," Carlo said doubtfully.

"Do one of the sows. Bring her on the lawn outside the elevator. You can run the forklift over the grass."

"You figure on doing this with one van, or a van and a crash car?" Krendler asked.

"Carlo?"

"The van is plenty. Give me a deputy to drive."

"I've got something else for you," Krendler said. "Can we have some light?"

Margot moved the rheostat and Krendler put his backpack on the table beside the bowl of fruit. He put on cotton gloves and took out what appeared to be a small monitor with an antenna and a mounting bracket, along with an external hard drive and a rechargeable battery pack.

"It's awkward covering Starling because she lives in a cul-de-sac with no place to lurk. But she has to come out—Starling's an exercise freak," Krendler said. "She's had to join a private gym since she can't use the FBI stuff anymore. We caught her parked at the gym Thursday and put a beacon under her car. It's Ni-Cad and recharges when the motor's running so she won't find it from a battery drain. The software covers these five contiguous states. Who's going to work this thing?"

444

"Cordell, come in here," Mason said.

Cordell and Margot knelt beside Krendler and Carlo stood over them, his hat held at the height of their nostrils.

"Look here." Krendler switched his monitor on. "It's like a car navigation system except it shows where Starling's car is." An overview of metropolitan Washington appeared on the screen. "Zoom here, move the area with the arrows, got it? Okay, it's not showing any acquisition. A signal from Starling's beacon will light this, and you'll hear a beep. Then you can pick up the source on overview and zoom in. The beep gets faster as you get closer. Here's Starling's neighborhood in street-map scale. You're not getting any blip from her car because we're out of range. Anywhere in metro Washington or Arlington you would. I picked it up from the helicopter coming out. Here's the converter for the AC plug in your van. One thing. You have to guarantee me this thing never gets in the wrong hands. I could get heat from this, it's not in the spy shops yet. Either it's back in my hands or it's in the bottom of the Potomac. You got it?"

"You understand that, Margot?" Mason said. "You, Cordell? Get Mogli to drive and brief him."

A POUND OF FLESH

THE BEAUTY of the pneumatic rifle was that it could be fired with the muzzle inside the van without deafening everyone around it—there was no need to stick the muzzle out the window where the public could see it.

The mirrored window would open a few inches and the small hypodermic projectile would fly, carrying a major load of acepromazine into the muscle mass of Dr Lecter's back or buttocks.

There would be only the crack of the gun's muzzle signature, like a green branch breaking, no bang and no ballistic report from the subsonic missile to draw attention.

The way they had rehearsed it, when Dr Lecter started to collapse, Piero and Tommaso, dressed in white, would "assist" him into the van, assuring any bystanders they were taking him to the hospital. Tommaso's English was best, as he had studied it in seminary, but the *h* in hospital was giving him a fit.

Mason was right in giving the Italians the prime dates for catching Dr Lecter. Despite their failure in Florence, they were by far the most capable at physical man-catching and the most likely to take Dr Lecter alive.

Mason allowed only one gun on the mission other than the tranquilizer rifle—that of the driver, Deputy Johnny Mogli, an off-duty sheriff's deputy from Illinois and long a creature of the Vergers. Mogli grew up speaking Italian at home. He was a person who agreed with everything his victim said before he killed him.

Carlo and the brothers Piero and Tommaso had their net, beanbag gun, Mace, and a variety of restraints. It would be plenty.

They were in position at daylight, five blocks from Starling's house in Arlington, parked in a handicap spot on a commercial street.

The van today was marked with adhesive signs, SENIOR CITIZEN MEDICAL TRANSPORT. It had a handicap tag hanging from the mirror and a false handicap license plate on the bumper. In the glove compartment was a receipt from a body shop for recent replacement of the bumper—they could claim a mix-up at the garage and confuse the issue for the time being if the tag number were questioned. The vehicle identification numbers and registration were legitimate. So were the hundred-dollar bills folded inside them for a bribe.

The monitor, Velcroed to the dashboard and running off the cigarette lighter socket, glowed with a street map of Starling's neighborhood. The same Global Positioning Satellite that now plotted the position of the van also showed Starling's vehicle, a bright dot in front of her house.

At 9:00 A.M., Carlo allowed Piero to eat something.

450

At 10:30 Tommaso could eat. He did not want them both full at the same time, in the event of a long chase on foot. Afternoon meals were staggered too. Tommaso was rummaging in the cooler for a sandwich at midafternoon when they heard the beep.

Carlo's malodorous head swung to the monitor.

"She's moving," Mogli said. He started the van.

Tommaso put the lid back on the cooler.

"Here we go. Here we go . . . Here she goes up Tindal toward the main road." Mogli swung into traffic. He had the great luxury of lying back three blocks where Starling could not possibly see him.

Nor could Mogli see the old gray pickup pull into traffic a block behind Starling, a Christmas tree hanging over the tailgate.

Driving the Mustang was one of the few pleasures Starling could count on. The powerful car, with no ABS and no traction control, was a handful on slick streets for much of the winter. While the roads were clear it was pleasant to wind the V8 out a little in second gear and listen to the pipes.

Mapp, a world-class couponeer, had sent with Starling a thick sheaf of her discount coupons pinned to the grocery list. She and Starling were doing a ham, a pot roast and two casseroles. Others were bringing the turkey.

A holiday dinner on her birthday was the last thing Starling cared about. She had to go along with it because Mapp and a surprising number of female agents, some of whom she only knew slightly and didn't particularly like, were turning out to support her in her misery.

Jack Crawford weighed on her mind. She couldn't visit him in intensive care, nor could she call him. She left notes for him at the nursing station, funny dog pictures with the lightest messages she could compose.

Starling distracted herself in her misery by playing with the Mustang, double-clutching and downshifting, using engine compression to slow for the turn into the Safeway supermarket parking lot, touching her brakes only to flash the brake lights for the drivers behind her.

She had to make four laps of the parking lot before she found a parking place, empty because it was blocked by an abandoned grocery cart. She got out and moved the cart. By the time she parked, another shopper had taken the basket.

She found a grocery cart near the door and rolled it toward the grocery store.

Mogli could see her turn in and stop on the screen of his monitor and in the distance he could see the big Safeway coming up on his right.

"She's going in the grocery store." He turned into the parking lot. It took a few seconds to spot her car. He could see a young woman pushing a cart toward the entrance.

Carlo put the glasses on her. "That's Starling. She looks like her pictures." He handed the glasses to Piero.

"I'd like to take her picture," Piero said. "I got my zoom right here."

There was a handicap parking space across the

parking lane from her car. Mogli pulled into it, ahead of a big Lincoln with handicap plates. The driver honked angrily.

Now they were looking out the back window of the van at the tail of Starling's car.

Perhaps because he was used to looking at American cars, Mogli spotted the old truck first, parked at a distant parking place near the edge of the lot. He could only see the gray tailgate of the pickup.

He pointed the truck out to Carlo. "Has he got a vise on the tail-gate? That what the liquor store guy said? Put the glasses on it, I can't see for the fucking tree. *Carlo, c'è una morsa sul camione?*"

"*Sì.* Yes, it's there, the vise. Nobody inside."

"Should we cover her in the store?" Tommaso did not often question Carlo.

"No, if he does it, he'll do it here," Carlo said.

The dairy items were first. Starling, consulting her coupons, selected cheese for a casserole and some heat 'em and eat 'em rolls. *Damn making scratch rolls for this crowd.* She had reached the meat counter when she realized she had forgotten butter. She left her cart and went back for it.

When she returned to the meat department, her cart was gone. Someone had removed her few purchases and put them on a shelf nearby. They had kept the coupons, and the list.

"God damn it," Starling said, loudly enough for nearby shoppers to hear. She looked around her. Nobody had a thick sheaf of coupons in sight. She took a couple of deep breaths. She could lurk near the cash registers and try to recognize her list, if they still had it clipped to the coupons. What the hell, couple of bucks. Don't let it ruin your day.

There were no free grocery carts near the registers. Starling went outside to find another one in the parking lot.

"*Ecco!*" Carlo saw him coming between the vehicles with his quick, light stride, Dr Hannibal Lecter in a camel's hair overcoat and a fedora, carrying a gift in an act of utter whimsy. "*Madonna!* He's coming to her car." Then the hunter in Carlo took over and he began to control his breathing, getting ready for the shot. The stag's tooth he was chewing appeared briefly through his lips.

The back window of the van did not roll down.

"*Metti in moto!* Back around with your side to him," Carlo said.

Dr Lecter stopped by the passenger side of the Mustang, then changed his mind and went to the driver's side, possibly intending to give the steering wheel a sniff.

He looked around him and slid the slim-jim out of his sleeve.

The van was broadside now. Carlo ready with the rifle. He touched the electric window button. Nothing happened.

Carlo's voice, unnaturally calm now in action. "*Mogli, il finestrino!*"

Had to be the child safety lock, Mogli fumbled for it.

Dr Lecter plunged the slim-jim into the crack beside the window and unlocked the door of Starling's car. He started to get in.

With an oath Carlo slid the side door open a crack and raised the rifle, Piero moving out of his way, the van rocking as the rifle cracked.

The dart flashed in the sunlight and with a small *thock* went through Dr Lecter's starched collar and into his neck. The drug worked fast, a big dose in a critical place. He tried to straighten up, but his knees were going. The package dropped from his hands and rolled under the car. He managed to get a knife out of his pocket and open it as he slumped between the door and the car, the tranquilizer turning his limbs to water. "Mischa," he said as his vision failed.

Piero and Tommaso were on him like big cats, pinning him down between the cars until they were sure he was weak.

Starling, trundling her second grocery cart of the day across the lot, heard the slap of the air rifle and recognized it instantly as a muzzle signature—she ducked by reflex as the people around her shuffled along, oblivious. Hard to tell where it came from. She looked in the direction of her car, saw a man's legs disappearing into a van and thought it was a mugging.

She slapped her side where the gun no longer lived and began to run, dodging through the cars toward the van.

The Lincoln with the elderly driver was back, honking to get in the handicapped spot blocked by the van, drowning out Starling yelling.

"Hold it! Stop! FBI! Stop or I'll shoot!" Maybe she could get a look at the plate.

Piero saw her coming and, moving fast, cut the valve stem off Starling's front tire on the driver's side with Dr Lecter's knife and dived into the van. The van bumped over a parking median and away toward the exit. She could see the plate. She wrote the number in dirt on the hood of a car with her finger.

Starling had her keys out. She heard the hissing of air rushing out the valve stem as she got to her car. She could see the top of the van moving toward the exit.

She tapped on the window of the Lincoln, honking at her now. "Do you have a cell phone? FBI, please, do you have a cell phone?"

"Go on, Noel," the woman in the car said, poking the driver's leg and pinching. "This is just trouble, it's some kind of trick. Don't get involved." The Lincoln pulled away.

Starling ran for a pay phone and called 911.

Deputy Mogli drove the speed limit for fifteen blocks.

Carlo pulled the dart from Dr Lecter's neck, relieved when the hole didn't spurt. There was a hematoma about the size of a quarter under his skin. The injection was supposed to be diffused by a major muscle mass. The son of a bitch might die yet, before the pigs could kill him.

There was no talking in the van, only the heavy breathing of the men and the quacking of the police scanner under the dash. Dr Lecter lay on the floor of the van in his fine overcoat, his hat rolled off his sleek head, one spot of bright blood on his collar, elegant as a pheasant in a butcher's case.

Mogli pulled into a parking garage and drove up to the third level, only pausing long enough to peel the signs off the sides of the van and change the plates.

He needn't have bothered. He laughed to himself when the police scanner picked up the bulletin. The 911 operator, apparently misunderstanding Starling's description of a "gray van or minibus," issued an all-points bulletin for a Greyhound bus. It must be said that 911 got all but one digit of the false license plate right.

"Just like Illinois," Mogli said.

"I saw the knife, I was afraid he'd kill himself to get out of what's coming," Carlo told Piero and Tommaso. "He'll wish he had cut his throat."

When Starling checked her other tires, she saw the package on the ground beneath her car.

A three-hundred-dollar bottle of Château d'Yquem, and the note, written in that familiar hand: *Happy Birthday, Clarice*.

It was then that she understood what she had seen.

STARLING HAD the numbers that she needed in her mind. Drive ten blocks home to her own phone? No, back to the pay phone, taking the sticky receiver from a young woman, apologizing, putting in quarters, the woman summoning a grocery store guard.

Starling called the reactive squad at Washington Field Office, Buzzard's Point.

They knew all about Starling on the squad where she had served so long, and transferred her to Clint Pearsall's office, she digging for more quarters and dealing with the grocery store security guard at the same time, the guard asking again and again for ID.

At last Pearsall's familiar voice on the phone.

"Mr Pearsall, I saw three men, maybe four, kidnap Hannibal Lecter in the Safeway parking lot about five minutes ago. They cut my tire, I couldn't pursue."

"Is this the bus business, the police APB?"

"I don't know about any bus. This was a gray van, handicap plate." Starling gave the number.

"How do you know it was Lecter?"

"He . . . left a gift for me, it was under my car."

"I see . . ." Pearsall paused and Starling jumped into the silence.

"Mr Pearsall, you know Mason Verger's behind it. It has to be. Nobody else would do it. He's a sadist, he'll torture Dr Lecter to death and he'll want to watch. We need to put out a BOLO on all Verger's vehicles and get the U.S. Attorney in Baltimore started on a warrant to search his place."

"Starling . . . Jesus, Starling. Look, I'll ask you one time. Are you sure about what you saw? Think about it a second. Think about every good thing you ever did here. Think about what you swore. There's no going back from here. What did you see?"

What should I say—I'm not a hysteric? That's the first thing hysterics say. She saw in the instant how far she had fallen in Pearsall's trust, and of what cheap material his trust was made.

"I saw three men, maybe four, kidnap a man on the parking lot at Safeway. At the scene I found a gift from Dr Hannibal Lecter, a bottle of Château d'Yquem wine from my birth year with a note in his handwriting. I have described the vehicle. I am reporting it to you, Clint Pearsall, SAC Buzzard's Point."

"I'm going forward with it as kidnapping, Starling."

"I'm coming over there. I could be deputized and go with the reactive squad."

"Don't come, I couldn't let you in."

Too bad Starling didn't get away before the Arlington police arrived in the parking lot. It took fifteen minutes to correct the all-points bulletin on the vehicle. A thick woman officer in heavy patent-leather shoes took Starling's statement. The woman's ticket book and radio, Mace and gun and handcuffs, stood out at angles from her big behind and the vents of her jacket gaped. The officer could not decide whether to enter Starling's place of employment as the FBI, or to put "None." When Starling angered her by anticipating her questions, the officer slowed down. When Starling pointed out the tracks of mud and snow tires where the van bumped over the divider, nobody responding had a camera. She showed the officers how to use hers.

Over and over in her head as she repeated her answers, Starling told herself, *I should have pursued, I should have pursued. I should have snatched his ass out of that Lincoln and pursued.*

KRENDLER CAUGHT the first squeal on the kidnapping. He called around to his sources and then he got Mason on a secure phone.

"Starling saw the snatch, we hadn't counted on that. She's making a flap at the Washington Field Office. Recommending a warrant to search your place."

"Krendler . . ." Mason waited for breath, or perhaps he was exasperated, Krendler couldn't tell. "I've already registered complaints with the local authorities, the sheriff and the U.S. Attorney's office that Starling was harassing me, calling late at night with incoherent threats."

"Has she?"

"Of course not, but she can't prove she didn't and it muddies the water. Now, I can head off a warrant in this county and in this state. But I want you to call the U.S. Attorney over here and remind him this hysterical bitch is after me. I can take care of the locals myself, believe me."

80

FREE AT last from the police, Starling changed her tire and drove home to her own phones and computer. She sorely missed her FBI cell phone and had not yet replaced it.

There was a message from Mapp on the answering machine: "Starling, season the pot roast and put it in the slow cooker. Do *not* put the vegetables in yet. Remember what happened last time. I'll be in a damn exclusion hearing until about five."

Starling fired up her laptop and tried to call up the Violent Criminal Apprehension Program file on Lecter, but was denied admission not only to VICAP, but the entire FBI computer net. She did not have as much access as the most rural constable in America.

The telephone rang.

It was Clint Pearsall. "Starling, have you harassed Mason Verger on the phone?"

"Never, I swear."

"He claims you have. He's invited the sheriff up there to tour his property, actually requested him to

462

come do it, and they're on the way to look around now. So there's no warrant and no warrant forthcoming. We haven't been able to find any other witnesses to the kidnapping. Only you."

"There was a white Lincoln with an old couple in it. Mr Pearsall, how about checking the credit card purchases at Safeway just before it happened. Those sales have a time stamp."

"We'll get to that, but it'll . . ."

". . . it'll take time," Starling finished.

"Starling?"

"Yes, sir?"

"Between us, I'll keep you posted on the big stuff. But you stay out of it. You're not a law officer while you're on suspension, and you're not supposed to have information. You're Joe Blow."

"Yes, sir, I know."

What do you look at while you're making up your mind? Ours is not a reflective culture, we do not raise our eyes up to the hills. Most of the time we decide the critical things while looking at the linoleum floor of an institutional corridor, or whispering hurriedly in a waiting room with a television blatting nonsense.

Starling, seeking something, anything, walked through the kitchen into the quiet and order of Mapp's side of the duplex. She looked at the photograph of Mapp's fierce little grandmother, brewer of the tea. She looked at Grandmother Mapp's insurance policy framed on the wall. Mapp's side looked like Mapp lived there.

Starling went back to her side. It looked to her like

nobody lived there. What did she have framed? Her diploma from the FBI Academy. No photograph of her parents survived. She had been without them for a long time and she had them only in her mind. Sometimes, in the flavors of breakfast or in a scent, a scrap of conversation, a homely expression overheard, she felt their hands on her: She felt it strongest in her sense of right and wrong.

Who the hell was she? Who had ever recognized her?

You are a warrior, Clarice. You can be as strong as you wish to be.

Starling could understand Mason wanting to kill Hannibal Lecter. If he had done it himself or had hired it done, she could have stood it; Mason had a grievance.

But she could not abide the thought of Dr Lecter tortured to death; she shied from it as she had from the slaughter of the lambs and the horses so long ago.

You are a warrior, Clarice.

Almost as ugly as the act itself was the fact that Mason would do this with the tacit agreement of men sworn to uphold the law. It is the way of the world.

With this thought, she made a simple decision:

The world will not be this way within the reach of my arm.

She found herself in her closet, on a stool, reaching high.

She brought down the box John Brigham's attorney had delivered to her in the fall. It seemed forever ago.

*   *   *

There is much tradition and mystique in the bequest of personal weapons to a surviving comrade in arms. It has to do with a continuation of values past individual mortality.

People living in a time made safe for them by others may find this difficult to understand.

The box John Brigham's guns came in was a gift in itself. He must have bought it in the Orient when he was a Marine. A mahogany box with the lid inlaid in mother of pearl. The weapons were pure Brigham, well worn, well maintained and immaculately clean. An M1911A1 Colt .45 pistol, and a Safari Arms cut-down version of the .45 for concealed carry, a boot dagger with one serrated edge. Starling had her own leather. John Brigham's old FBI badge was mounted on a mahogany plaque. His DEA badge was in the box loose.

Starling pried the FBI badge off the plaque and put it in her pocket. The .45 went in her Yaqui slide behind her hip, covered by her jacket.

The short .45 went on one ankle, the knife on the other, inside her boots. She took her diploma out of the frame and folded it for her pocket. In the dark somebody might mistake it for a warrant. As she creased the heavy paper, she knew she was not quite herself, and she was glad.

Another three minutes at her laptop. From the Mapquest Web site she printed out a large-scale map of the Muskrat Farm and the national forest around it. For a moment she looked at Mason's meat kingdom, traced its boundaries with her finger.

The Mustang's big pipes blew the dead grass flat as she pulled out of her driveway to call on Mason Verger.

A HUSH over Muskrat Farm like the quiet of the old Sabbath. Mason excited, terribly proud that he could bring this off. Privately, he compared his accomplishment to the discovery of radium.

Mason's illustrated science text was the best-remembered of his schoolbooks; it was the only book tall enough to allow him to masturbate in class. He often looked at an illustration of Madame Curie while doing this, and he thought of her now and the tons of pitchblende she boiled to get the radium. Her efforts were very much like his, he thought.

Mason imagined Dr Lecter, the product of all his searching and expenditure, glowing in the dark like the vial in Madame Curie's laboratory. He imagined the pigs that would eat him going to sleep afterward in the woods, their bellies glowing like lightbulbs.

It was Friday evening, nearly dark. The maintenance crews were gone. None of the workers had seen the van arrive, as it did not come by the main gate, but by the fire road through the national forest that served as Mason's service road. The sheriff and his crew had completed their cursory search and were well away before the van arrived at the barn. Now the main gate was manned and only a trusted skeleton crew remained at Muskrat:

Cordell was at his station in the playroom—overnight relief for Cordell would drive in at midnight. Margot and Deputy Mogli, still wearing his badge from cozening the sheriff, were with Mason, and the crew of professional kidnappers were busy in the barn.

By the end of Sunday it would all be done, the evidence burnt or roiling in the bowels of the sixteen swine. Mason thought he might feed the eel some delicacy from Dr Lecter, his nose perhaps. Then for years to come Mason could watch the ferocious ribbon, ever circling in its figure eight, and know that the infinity sign it made stood for Lecter dead forever, dead forever.

At the same time, Mason knew that it is dangerous to get exactly what you want. What would he do after he had killed Dr Lecter? He could wreck some foster homes, and torment some children. He could drink martinis made with tears. But where was the hard-core fun coming from?

What a fool he would be to dilute this ecstatic time with fears about the future. He waited for the tiny spray against his eye, waited for his goggle to clear, then puffed his breath into a tube switch: Anytime he liked he could turn on his video monitor and see his prize . . .

THE SMELL of a coal fire in the tack room of Mason's barn and the resident smells of animals and men. Firelight on the trotting horse Fleet Shadow's long skull, empty as Providence, watching it all in blinders.

Red coals in the farrier's furnace flare and brighten with the hiss of the bellows as Carlo heats a strap of iron, already cherry-red.

Dr Hannibal Lecter hangs on the wall beneath the horse skull like a terrible altarpiece. His arms are outstretched straight from his shoulders on either side, well bound with rope to a singletree, a thick oak crosspiece from the pony cart harness. The singletree runs across the doctor's back like a yoke and is fastened to the wall with a shackle of Carlo's manufacture. His legs do not reach the floor. His legs are bound over his trousers like roasts rolled and tied, with many spaced coils, each coil knotted. No chain or handcuffs are used— nothing metal that would damage the teeth of the pigs and discourage them.

When the iron in the furnace reaches white heat,

468

Carlo brings it to the anvil with his tongs and swings his hammer, beating the bright strap into a shackle, red sparks flying in the semidark, bouncing off his chest, bouncing on the hanging figure of Dr Hannibal Lecter.

Mason's TV camera, odd among the ancient tools, peers at Dr Lecter from its spidery metal tripod. On the workbench is a monitor, dark now.

Carlo heats the shackle again, and hurries with it outside to attach it to the forklift while it is glowing and pliable. His hammer echoes in the vast height of the barn, the blow and its echo, *BANG-bang, BANG-bang*.

A scratchy chirping from the loft as Piero finds a rebroadcast of the soccer game on shortwave. His Cagliari team is playing hated Juventus in Rome.

Tommaso sits in a cane chair, the tranquilizer rifle propped against the wall beside him. His dark priest's eyes never leave Dr Lecter's face.

Tommaso detects a change in the stillness of the bound man. It is a subtle change, from unconsciousness to unnatural self-control, perhaps no more than a difference in the sound of his breathing.

Tommaso gets up from his chair and calls out into the barn.

"Si sta svegliando."

Carlo returns to the tack room, the stag's tooth flicking in and out of his mouth. He is carrying a pair of trouser legs stuffed with fruit and greens and chickens. He rubs the trousers against Dr Lecter's body and under his arms.

Keeping his hand carefully away from the face, he seizes Lecter's hair and raises his head.

"Buona sera, Dottore."

A crackle from the speaker on the TV monitor. The monitor lights and Mason's face appears . . .

"Turn on the light over the camera," Mason said. "Good evening, Dr Lecter."

The doctor opened his eyes for the first time.

Carlo thought sparks flew behind the fiend's eyes, but it might have been a reflection of the fire. He crossed himself against the Evil Eye.

"Mason," the doctor said to the camera. Behind Mason, Lecter could see Margot's silhouette, black against the aquarium. "Good evening, Margot," his tone courteous now. "I'm glad to see you again." From the clarity of his speech, Dr Lecter may have been awake for some time.

"Dr Lecter," came Margot's hoarse voice.

Tommaso found the sun gun over the camera and turned it on.

The harsh light blinded them all for a second.

Mason in his rich radio tones: "Doctor, in about twenty minutes we're going to give the pigs their first course, which will be your feet. After that we'll have a little pajama party, you and I. You can wear shorties by then. Cordell's going to keep you alive for a long time—"

Mason was saying something further, Margot leaning forward to see the scene in the barn.

Dr Lecter looked into the monitor to be sure Margot was watching him. Then he whispered to Carlo, his metallic voice urgent in the kidnapper's ear:

"Your brother, Matteo, must smell worse than you by now. He shit when I cut him."

Carlo reached to his back pocket and came out with the electric cattle prod. In the bright light of the TV camera, he whipped it across the side of Lecter's head. Holding the doctor's hair with one hand, he pressed the button on the handle, holding the prod close in front of Lecter's face as the high-voltage current arced in a wicked line between the electrodes on the end.

"Fuck your mother," he said and plunged it arcing into Dr Lecter's eye.

Dr Lecter made no sound—the sound came from the speaker, Mason roaring as his breath permitted him, and Tommaso strained to pull Carlo away. Piero came down from the loft to help. They sat Carlo down in the cane chair. And held him.

"Blind him and there's no money!" they screamed in both his ears at once.

Dr Lecter adjusted the shades in his memory palace to relieve the terrible glare. Ahhhhh. He leaned his face against the cool marble flank of Venus.

Dr Lecter turned his face full to the camera and said clearly: "I'm not taking the chocolate, Mason."

"Sumbitch is crazy. Well, we knew he was crazy," said Deputy Sheriff Mogli. "But Carlo is too."

"Go down there and get between them," Mason said.

"You sure they got no guns?" Mogli said.

"You hired out to be tough, didn't you? No. Just the tranquilizer gun."

"Let me do it," Margot said. "Keep from starting some macho crap between them. The Italians respect their mamas. And Carlo knows I handle the money."

471

"Walk the camera out and show me the pigs," Mason said. "Dinner's at eight!"

"I don't have to stay for that," Margot said.

"Oh, yes you do," Mason said.

MARGOT TOOK a deep breath outside the barn. If she was willing to kill him, she ought to be willing to look at him. She could smell Carlo before she opened the door to the tack room. Piero and Tommaso stood on either side of Lecter. They faced Carlo, seated in the chair.

"*Buona sera, signori*," Margot said. "Your friends are right, Carlo. You ruin him now, no money. And you've come so far and done so well."

Carlo's eyes never left Dr Lecter's face.

Margot took a cell phone from her pocket. She punched numbers on its lighted face and held it out to Carlo. "Take it." She held it in his line of vision. "Read it."

The automatic dialer read BANCO STEUBEN.

"That's your bank in Cagliari, Signore Deogracias. Tomorrow morning, when this is done, when you've made him pay for your brave brother, then I'll call this number and tell your banker my code and say, 'Give Signor Deogracias the rest of the money you hold for him.' Your banker will confirm it to you on the phone.

473

Tomorrow evening you'll be in the air, on your way home, a rich man. Matteo's family will be rich too. You can take them the doctor's cojones in a zip-lock bag to comfort them. But if Dr Lecter can't see his own death, if he can't see the pigs coming to eat his face, you get nothing. Be a man, Carlo. Go get your pigs. I'll sit with the son of a bitch. In half an hour you can hear him scream while they eat his feet."

Carlo threw his head back and took a deep breath. *"Piero, andiamo! Tu, Tommaso, rimani."*

Tommaso took his seat in the cane chair beside the door.

"I've got it under control, Mason," Margot said to the camera.

"I'll want to bring his nose with me back to the house. Tell Carlo," Mason said. The screen went dark. Moving out of his room was a major effort for Mason and the people around him, requiring reconnection of his tubes to containers on his traveling gurney and switching over his hard-shell respirator to an AC power pack.

Margot looked into Dr Lecter's face.

His injured eye was swollen shut between the black burn marks the electrodes had left at each end of his eyebrow.

Dr Lecter opened his good eye. He was able to keep the cool feeling of Venus' marble flank on his face.

"I like the smell of that liniment, it smells cool and lemony," Dr Lecter said. "Thank you for coming, Margot."

"That's exactly what you said to me when the matron brought me into your office the first day. When they were doing presentencing on Mason the first time."

"Is that what I said?" Having just returned from the memory palace where he read over his interviews with Margot, he knew it to be so.

"Yes. I was crying, dreading to tell you about Mason and me. I was dreading having to sit down too. But you never asked me to sit—you knew I had stitches, didn't you? We walked in the garden. Do you remember what you told me?"

"You were no more at fault for what happened to you—"

"'—than if I had been bitten on the behind by a mad dog' was what you said. You made it easy for me then, and the other visits too, and I appreciated it for a while."

"What else did I tell you?"

"You said you were much weirder than I would ever be," she said. "You said it was all right to be weird."

"If you try, you can remember everything we ever said. Remember—"

"Please don't beg me now." It jumped out of her, she didn't mean to say it that way.

Dr Lecter shifted slightly and the ropes creaked.

Tommaso got up and came to check his bonds. "*Attenzione alla bocca, Signorina.* Be careful of the mouth."

She didn't know if Tommaso meant Dr Lecter's mouth or his words.

"Margot, it's been a long time since I treated you, but I want to talk to you about your medical history, just for a moment, privately." He cut his good eye toward Tommaso.

475

Margot thought for a moment. "Tommaso, could you leave us for a moment."

"No, I'm sorry, Signorina, but I stand outside with the door open." Tommaso went with the rifle out into the barn and watched Dr Lecter from a distance.

"I'd never make you uncomfortable by begging, Margot. I would be interested to know *why* you're doing this. Would you tell me that? Have you started taking the chocolate, as Mason likes to say, after you fought him so long? We don't need to pretend you're revenging Mason's face."

She did tell him. About Judy, about wanting the baby. It took her less than three minutes; she was surprised at how easily her troubles summarized.

A distant noise, a screech and half a scream. Outside in the barn, against the fence he had erected across the open end of the barn, Carlo was fiddling with his tape recorder, preparing to summon the pigs from the wooded pasture with recorded cries of anguish from victims long dead or ransomed.

If Dr Lecter heard, he did not show it. "Margot, do you think Mason will just *give* you what he promised? You're begging Mason. Did begging help you when he tore you? It's the same thing as taking his chocolate and letting him have his way. But he'll make Judy eat the cheese. And she's not used to it."

She did not answer, but her jaw set.

"Do you know what would happen if, instead of crawling to Mason, you just stimulated his prostate gland with Carlo's cattle prod? See it there by the workbench?"

Margot started to get up.

"*Listen to me*," the doctor hissed. "Mason will deny you. You know you'll have to kill him, you've known it for twenty years. You've known it since he told you to bite the pillow and not make so much noise."

"Are you saying you'd do it *for* me? I could never trust you."

"No, of course not. But you could trust me *never to deny that I did it*. It would actually be more therapeutic for you to kill him yourself. You'll remember I recommended that when you were a child."

"'Wait until you can get away with it,' you said. I took some comfort from that."

"Professionally, that's the sort of catharsis I had to recommend. You're old enough now. And what difference would one more murder charge make to me? You know you'll have to kill him. And when you do, the law will follow the money—right to you and the new baby. Margot, I'm the only other suspect you've got. *If I'm dead before Mason, who would the suspect be?* You can do it when it suits you and I'll write you a letter gloating about how I enjoyed killing him myself."

"No, Dr Lecter, I'm sorry. It's too late. I've got my arrangements made." She looked into his face with her bright butcher's blue eyes. "I can do this and sleep afterward, and you know I can."

"Yes, I know you can. I always liked that in you. You are much more interesting, more . . . capable than your brother."

She got up to go. "I'm sorry, Dr Lecter, for what that's worth."

Before she reached the door, he said, "Margot, when does Judy ovulate again?"

477

"What? In two days, I think."

"Do you have everything else you need? Extenders, equipment to fast-freeze?"

"I've got all the facilities of a fertilization clinic."

"Do one thing for me."

"Yes?"

"Curse at me and snatch out a piece of my hair, back from the hairline if you don't mind. Get a little skin. Hold it in your hand walking back to the house. Think about putting it in Mason's hand. After he's dead.

"When you get to the house, ask Mason for what you want. See what he says. You've delivered me, your part of the bargain is complete. Hold the hair in your hand and ask him for what you want. See what he says. When he laughs in your face, come back here. All you have to do is take the tranquilizer rifle and shoot the one behind you. Or hit him with the hammer. He has a pocketknife. Just cut the ropes on one arm and give me the knife. And leave. I can do the rest."

"No."

"Margot?"

She put her hand on the door, braced against a plea.

"Can you still crack a walnut?"

She reached in her pocket and brought out two. The muscles of her forearm bunched and the nuts cracked.

The doctor chuckled. "Excellent. With all that strength, walnuts. You can offer Judy walnuts to help her get past the taste of Mason."

Margot walked back to him, her face set. She spat in his face and jerked out a lock of his hair near

478

the top of his head. It was hard to know how she meant it.

She heard him humming as she left the room.

As Margot walked toward the lighted house, the little divot of scalp stuck to the palm of her hand with blood, the hair hanging from her hand and she did not even need to close her fingers around it.

Cordell passed her in a golf cart loaded with medical equipment to prepare the patient.

FROM THE expressway overpass northbound at Exit 30, Starling could see a half-mile away the lighted gatehouse, far outpost of Muskrat Farm. Starling had made up her mind on the drive to Maryland: she would go in the back way. If she went to the front gate with no credentials and no warrant she'd get a sheriff's escort out of the county, or to the county jail. By the time she was free again, it would all be done.

Never mind permission. She drove up to Exit 29, well beyond Muskrat Farm, and came back along the service road. The blacktop road seemed very dark after the expressway lights. It was bounded by the expressway on her right, on the left a ditch and a high chain-link fence separated the roadway from the looming black of the national forest. Starling's map showed a gravel fire road intersecting this blacktop a mile farther along and well out of sight of the gatehouse. It was where she had mistakenly stopped on her first visit. According to her map, the fire road ran through the national forest to Muskrat Farm. She was measuring by her odometer.

The Mustang seemed louder than usual, running just above idle, booming off the trees.

There it was in her headlights, a heavy gate welded of metal pipe and topped with barbed wire. The SERVICE ENTRANCE sign she had seen on her first visit was gone now. Weeds had grown up in front of the gate and over the ditch-crossing with its culvert.

She could see in her headlights that the weeds had recently been pressed down. Where the fine grit and sand had washed off the pavement and made a little sandbar, she could see the tracks of mud-and-snow tires. Were they the same as the van tracks she saw in the parking median at Safeway? She didn't know if they were exactly the same, but they could have been.

A chrome padlock and chain secured the gate. No sweat there. Starling looked up and down the road. Nobody coming. *A little illegal entry here.* It felt like a crime. She checked the gateposts for sensor wires. None. Working with two picks and holding her little flashlight in her teeth, it took her less than fifteen seconds to open the padlock. She drove through the entrance and continued well into the trees before she walked back to close the gate. She draped the chain back on the gate with the padlock on the outside. From a little distance it looked normal. She left the loose ends inside so she could butt it open more easily with the car if she had to.

Measuring on the map with her thumb, it was about two miles through the forest to the farm. She drove through the dark tunnel of the fire road, the night sky sometimes visible overhead, sometimes not, as the branches closed overhead. She eased along in second gear at little over an idle, with just the parking lights, trying to keep the Mustang as quiet as possible, dead weeds brushing the undercarriage. When the odometer said a mile and eight-tenths, she stopped. With the engine off, she could hear a crow calling in the dark. *The crow was pissed at something*. She hoped to God it was a crow.

CORDELL CAME into the tack room brisk as a hangman, intravenous bottles under his arms, tubes dangling from them. "*The* Dr Hannibal Lecter!" he said. "I wanted that mask of yours so badly for our club in Baltimore. My girlfriend and I have a *dungeony* sort of thing, sort of Jay-O and leather."

He put his things down on the anvil stand and put a poker in the fire to heat.

"Good news and bad news," Cordell said in his cheerful nursey voice and faint Swiss accent. "Did Mason tell you the drill? The drill is, in a little while I'll bring Mason down here and the pigs will get to eat your feet. Then you'll wait overnight and tomorrow Carlo and his brothers will feed you through the bars head first, so the pigs can eat your face, just like the dogs ate Mason's. I'll keep you going with IVs and tourniquets until the last. You really *are* done, you know. That's the bad news."

Cordell glanced at the TV camera to be sure it was off. "The *good* news is, it doesn't *have* to be much worse than a trip to the dentist. Check this out, *Doctor*." Cordell held a hypodermic syringe with a long needle in front of Dr Lecter's face. "Let's talk like two medical people. I could get behind you and give you a spinal that would keep you from feeling *anything* down there. You could just close your eyes and try not to listen. You'd just feel some jerking and pulling. And once Mason's got his jollies for the evening and gone to the house I could give you something that would just stop your heart. Want to see it?" Cordell palmed a vial of Pavulon and held it close enough to Dr Lecter's open eye, but not close enough to get bitten.

The firelight played on the side of Cordell's avid face, his eyes were hot and happy. "You've got lots of money, Dr Lecter. Everybody says so. *I* know how this stuff works—I put money around in places too. Take it out, move it, *fuss* with it. I can move mine on the phone and I bet you can too."

Cordell took a cell phone from his pocket. "We'll call your banker, you say him a code, he'll confirm to me and I'll fix you right up." He held up the spinal syringe. "Squirt, squirt. Talk to me."

Dr Lecter mumbled, his head down. "Suitcase" and "locker" were all Cordell could hear.

"Come on, Doctor, and then you can just sleep. Come on."

"Unmarked hundreds," Dr Lecter said, and his voice trailed away.

Cordell leaned closer and Dr Lecter struck to the length of his neck, caught Cordell's eyebrow in his small sharp teeth and ripped a sizeable piece of it out as Cordell leaped backward. Dr Lecter spit the eyebrow like a grape skin into Cordell's face.

Cordell mopped the wound and put a tape butterfly on it that gave him a quizzical expression.

He packed up his syringe. "All that relief, wasted," he said. "You'll look at it differently before daylight. You know I have stimulants to take you quite the other way. And I'll make you wait."

He took the poker from the fire.

"I'm going to hook you up now," Cordell said. "Whenever you resist me I'll burn you. This is what it feels like."

He touched the glowing end of the poker to Dr Lecter's chest and crisped his nipple through his shirt. He had to smother the widening circle of fire on the doctor's shirtfront.

Dr Lecter did not make a sound.

Carlo backed the forklift into the tack room. With Piero and Carlo lifting together, Tommaso ever ready with the tranquilizer rifle, they moved Dr Lecter to the fork and shackled his singletree to the front of the machine. He was seated on the fork, his arms bound to the singletree, with his legs extended, each leg fastened to one tine of the fork.

Cordell inserted an IV needle with a butterfly into the back of each of Dr Lecter's hands. He had to stand on a bale of hay to hang the plasma bottles on the machine on each side of him. Cordell stood back and admired his work. Odd to see the doctor splayed there with an IV in each hand, like a parody of something Cordell couldn't quite remember. Cordell rigged slip-knot tourniquets just above each knee with cords that could be pulled behind the fence to keep the doctor from bleeding to death. They could not be tightened now. Mason would be furious if Lecter's feet were numb.

Time to get Mason downstairs and put him in the van. The vehicle, parked behind the barn, was cold. The Sards had left their lunch in it. Cordell cursed and threw their cooler out on the ground. He'd have to vacuum the fucking thing at the house. He'd have to air it out too. The fucking Sards had been smoking in here too, after he forbade it. They'd replaced the cigarette lighter and left the power cord of the car beacon monitor still swinging from the dash.

STARLING SWITCHED off the Mustang's interior light and pulled the trunk release before she opened the door.

If Dr Lecter was here, if she could get him, maybe she could put him cuffed hand and foot in the trunk and get as far as the county jail. She had four sets of cuffs and enough line to hog-tie him and keep him from kicking. Better not to think about how strong he was.

There was some frost on the gravel when she put her feet out. The old car groaned as her weight came off the springs.

"Got to complain don't you, you old son of a bitch," she said to the car beneath her breath. Suddenly she remembered talking to Hannah, the horse she rode away into the night from the slaughter of the lambs. She did not close the car door all the way. The keys went into a tight trouser pocket so they would not tinkle.

The night was clear under a quarter moon and she could walk without her flashlight as long as there was some open night sky. She tried the edge of the gravel and found it loose and uneven. Quieter to walk in a packed wheel track in the gravel, looking ahead to judge how the road lay with her peripheral vision, her head slightly turned to the side. It was like wading in soft darkness, she could hear her feet crunch the gravel but she couldn't see the ground.

The hard moment came when she was out of sight of the Mustang, but could still feel its loom behind her. She did not want to leave it.

She was suddenly a thirty-three-year-old woman, alone, with a ruined civil service career and no shotgun, standing in a forest at night. She saw herself clearly, saw the crinkles of age beginning in the corners of her eyes. She wanted desperately to go back to her car. Her next step was slower, she stopped and she could hear herself breathing.

The crow called, a breeze rattled the bare branches above her and then the scream split the night. A cry so horrible and hopeless, peaking, falling, ending in a plea for death in a voice so wracked it could have been anyone. "*Uccidimi!*" And the scream again.

The first one froze Starling, the second one had her moving at a trot, wading fast through the dark, the .45 still holstered, one hand holding the dark flashlight, the other extended into the night before her. *No, you don't, Mason. No, you don't. Hurry. Hurry.* She found she could stay in the packed track by listening to her footfalls, and feeling the loose gravel on either side. The road turned and ran along a fence. Good fence, pipe fence, six feet high.

Came sobs of apprehension and pleas, the scream building, and ahead of Starling, beyond the fence, she heard movement through brush, the movement breaking into a trot, lighter than the hoofbeats of a horse, quicker in rhythm. She heard grunting she recognized.

Closer the agonized sounds, clearly human, but distorted, with a single squeal over the cries for a second, and Starling knew she was hearing either a recording or a voice amplified with feedback in the microphone. Light through the trees and the barn looming. Starling pressed her head on the cold iron to look through the fence. Dark shapes rushing, long and hip-high. Across forty yards of clear ground the open end of a barn with the great doors open wide, a barrier across the end of the barn with a Dutch gate in it, and an ornate mirror suspended above the gate, the mirror reflecting the light of the barn in a bright patch on the ground. Standing in the clear pasture outside the barn, a stocky man in a hat with a boom box radio/tape player. He covered one ear with his hand as a series of howls and sobs came from the machine.

Out of the brush now they came, the wild swine with their savage faces, wolflike in their speed, long-legged and deep-chested, shaggy, spiky gray bristles.

Carlo dashed back through the Dutch gate and closed it when they were still thirty yards from him. They stopped in a semicircle waiting, their great curved tusks holding their lips in a permanent snarl. Like linemen anticipating the snap of the ball, they surged forward, stopped, jostled, grunting, clicking their teeth.

Starling had seen livestock in her time, but nothing like these hogs. There was a terrible beauty in them, grace and speed. They watched the doorway, jostling and rushing forward, then backing, always facing the barrier across the open end of the barn.

Carlo said something over his shoulder and disappeared back into the barn.

The van backed into view inside the barn. Starling recognized the gray vehicle at once. It stopped at an angle near the barrier. Cordell got out and opened the sliding side door. Before he turned off the dome light, Starling could see Mason inside in his hard-shell respirator, propped on pillows, his hair coiled on his chest. A ringside seat. Floodlights came on over the doorway.

From the ground beside him, Carlo picked up an object Starling did not recognize at first. It looked like someone's legs, or the lower half of a body. If it was half a body, Carlo was very strong. For a second Starling feared it was the remains of Dr Lecter, but the legs bent wrong, bent in ways the joints would not permit.

They could only be Lecter's legs if he had been wheeled and braided, she thought for a bad moment. Carlo called into the barn behind him. Starling heard a motor start.

The forklift came into Starling's view, Piero driving, Dr Lecter raised high with the fork, his arms spread on the singletree and the IV bottles swaying above his hands with the movement of the vehicle. Held high so that he could see the ravening swine, could see what was coming.

The forklift came at an awful processional speed, Carlo walking beside it and on the other side Johnny Mogli, armed.

Starling fixed on Mogli's deputy badge for an instant. A star, not like the locals' badges. White hair, white shirt, like the driver of the kidnap van.

From the van came Mason's deep voice. He hummed "Pomp and Circumstance" and giggled.

The pigs, raised with noise, were not afraid of the machine, they seemed to welcome it.

The forklift stopped near the barrier. Mason said something to Dr Lecter that Starling could not hear. Dr Lecter did not move his head or give any sign that he had heard. He was higher even than Piero at the controls. Did he look in Starling's direction? She never knew because she was moving fast along the fence line, along the side of the barn, finding the double doors where the van had backed in.

Carlo sailed the stuffed trousers into the pigpen. The hogs leaped forward as one, room for two on each leg, shouldering the others aside. Tearing, snarling, pulling and ripping, dead chickens in the trouser legs coming to pieces, pigs shaking their heads from side to side with chicken guts flailing. A field of tossing bristled backs.

Carlo had only provided the lightest of appetizers, just three chickens and a little salad. In moments the trousers were rags and the slavering pigs turned their avid little eyes back to the barrier.

Piero lowered the fork to just the height above ground level. The upper part of the Dutch gate would keep the pigs away from Dr Lecter's vitals for the time being. Carlo removed the doctor's shoes and socks.

"This little piggy went EEE EEE EEE all the way home," Mason called from the van.

Starling was coming up behind them. All were facing

the other way, facing the pigs. She passed the tack room door, moved out into the center of the barn.

"Now, don't let him bleed out," Cordell said from the van. "Be ready when I tell you to tighten the tourniquets." He was clearing Mason's goggle with a cloth.

"Anything to say, Dr Lecter?" came Mason's deep voice.

The .45 boomed in the enclosure of the barn and Starling's voice: *"Hands up and freeze. Turn off the motor."*

Piero seemed not to understand.

"Fermate il motore," Dr Lecter said helpfully.

Only the impatient squealing of the pigs now.

She could see one gun, on the hip of the white-haired man wearing the star. Holster with a thumb break. *Put the men on the ground first.*

Cordell slid behind the wheel fast, the van moving. Mason yelling at him. Starling swung with the van, caught the white-haired man's movement in the corner of her eye, swung back to him as he pulled his gun to kill her, him yelling *"Police,"* and she shot him twice in the chest, a fast double tap.

His .357 shot two feet of fire toward the ground, he went back a half step and to his knees, looking down at himself, his badge tuliped by the fat .45 slug that had passed through it and tumbled sideways through his heart.

Mogli went over backward and lay still.

In the tack room, Tommaso heard the shots. He grabbed the air rifle and climbed to the hayloft, dropped to his knees in the loose hay and crawled toward the side of the hayloft that overlooked the barn.

"Next," Starling said in a voice she did not know. Do this fast while Mogli's death still had them. "On the ground, *you* head toward the wall. *You* on the ground, head this way. *This way*."

"*Girati dall' altra parte*," Dr Lecter explained from the forklift.

Carlo looked up at Starling, saw that she would kill him and lay still. She cuffed them fast with one hand, their heads in opposite directions, Carlo's wrist to Piero's ankle and Piero's ankle to Carlo's wrist. All the time the cocked .45 behind one of their ears.

She pulled her boot knife and went around the forklift to the doctor.

"Good evening, Clarice," he said when he could see her.

"Can you walk, are your legs working?"

"Yes."

"Can you see all right?"

"Yes."

"I'm going to cut you loose. With all due respect, Doctor, if you fuck with me I'll shoot you dead, here and now. Do you understand that?"

"Perfectly."

"Do right and you'll live through this."

"Spoken like a Protestant."

She was working all the time. The boot knife was sharp. She found the serrated edge worked fastest on the slick new rope.

His right arm was free.

"I can do the rest if you give me the knife."

She hesitated. Backed to the length of his arm and gave him the short dagger. "My car's a couple of

493

hundred yards down the fire road." She had to watch him and the men on the ground.

He had a leg free. He was working on the other, having to cut each coil separately. Dr Lecter could not see behind him where Carlo and Piero were lying facedown.

"When you're loose, don't try to run. You'll never make the door. I'll give you two pairs of cuffs," Starling said. "There's two guys cuffed on the ground behind you. Make 'em crawl to the forklift and cuff them to it so they can't get a phone. Then cuff yourself."

"*Two?*" he said. "*Watch it, there ought to be three.*"

As he spoke the dart from Tommaso's rifle flew, a silver streak under the floodlights, and quivered in the center of Starling's back. She spun, instantly dizzy, vision going dark, trying to spot a target, saw the barrel at the edge of the loft and fired, fired, fired, fired. Tommaso rolling back from the edge, splinters stinging him, blue gun smoke rolling up into the lights. She fired once more as her vision failed, reached behind her hip for a magazine even as her knees gave way.

The noise seemed to further animate the pigs and seeing the men in their inviting position on the ground, they squealed and grunted, pressing against the barrier.

Starling pitched forward on her face, the empty pistol bouncing away the breech locked open. Carlo and Piero raised their heads to look and they were scrambling, crawling awkwardly together as a bat crawls, toward Mogli's body and his pistol and handcuff keys. Sound of Tommaso pumping the tranquilizer rifle in the loft. He had a dart left. He rose now and came to the edge, looking over the barrel, seeking Dr Lecter on the other side of the forklift.

Here came Tommaso walking along the edge of the loft, there would be no place to hide.

Dr Lecter lifted Starling in his arms and backed fast toward the Dutch gate, trying to keep the forklift between him and Tommaso, advancing carefully, watching his footing at the edge of the loft. Tommaso fired and the dart, aimed at Lecter's chest, hit bone in Starling's shin. Dr Lecter pulled the bolts on the Dutch gate.

Piero snatched Mogli's key chain, frantic, Carlo scrambling for the gun, and came the pigs in a rush to the meal that was struggling to get up. Carlo managed to fire the .357 once, and a pig collapsed, the others climbing over the dead pig and onto Carlo and Piero, and the body of Mogli. More rushed on through the barn and into the night.

Dr Lecter, holding Starling, was behind the gate when the pigs rushed through.

Tommaso from the loft could see his brother's face down in the pack and then it was only a bloody dish. He dropped the rifle in the hay. Dr Lecter, erect as a dancer and carrying Starling in his arms, came out from behind the gate, walked barefoot out of the barn, through the pigs. Dr Lecter walked through the sea of tossing backs and blood spray in the barn. A couple of the great swine, one of them the pregnant sow, squared their feet to him, lowered their heads to charge.

When he faced them and they smelled no fear, they trotted back to the easy pickings on the ground.

Dr Lecter saw no reinforcements coming from the house. Once under the trees of the fire road, he stopped to pull the darts out of Starling and suck the wounds. The needle in her shin had bent on the bone.

Pigs crashed through the brush nearby.

He pulled off Starling's boots and put them on his own bare feet. They were a little tight. He left the .45 on her ankle so that, carrying her, he could reach it.

Ten minutes later, the guard at the main gatehouse looked up from his newspaper toward a distant sound, a ripping noise like a piston-engined fighter on a strafing run. It was a 5.0-liter Mustang turning 5800 rpm across the interstate overpass.

MASON WHINING and crying to get back in his room, crying as he had when some of the smaller boys and girls fought him at camp and managed to get in a few licks before he could crush them under his weight.

Margot and Cordell took him up in the elevator on his wing and secured him in his bed, hooked up to his permanent sources of power.

Mason was as angry as Margot had ever seen him, the blood vessels pulsing over the exposed bones of his face.

"I better give him something," Cordell said when they were out in the playroom.

"Not yet. He's got to think for a little while. Give me the keys to your Honda."

"Why?"

"Somebody's got to go down there and see if anybody's alive. Do you want to go?"

"No, but—"

"I can drive your car into the tack room, the van won't go through the door, now give me the fucking keys."

Downstairs now, out in the drive. Tommaso coming across the field from the woods, trotting, looking behind him. *Think, Margot.* She looked at her watch. 8:20. *At midnight, Cordell's relief would come. There was time to bring men from Washington in the helicopter to clean up.* She drove to Tommaso across the grass.

"I try to catch up them, a pig knock me. He"— Tommaso pantomimed Dr Lecter carrying Starling— "the woman. They go in the loud car. She have *due*"—he held up two fingers—"*freccette*." He pointed to his back and leg. *Freccette. Dardi.* Stick 'em. Bam. *"Due freccette."* He pantomimed shooting.

"Darts," Margot said.

"Darts, maybe too much *narcotico*. She's maybe dead."

"Get in," Margot said. "We've got to go see."

Margot drove into the double side doors, where Starling had entered the barn. Squeals and grunts and tossing bristled backs. Margot drove forward honking and drove the pigs back enough to see there were three human remains, none recognizable anymore.

They drove into the tack room and closed the doors behind them.

Margot considered that Tommaso was the only one left alive who had ever seen her at the barn, not counting Cordell.

This may have occurred to Tommaso too. He stood a cautious distance from her, his dark intelligent eyes on her face. There were tears on his cheeks.

Think, Margot. You don't want any shit from the

Sards. They know on their end that you handle the money. They'll dime you out in a second.

Tommaso's eyes followed her hand as it went into her pocket.

The cell phone. She punched up Sardinia, the Steuben banker at home at two-thirty in the morning. She spoke to him briefly and passed the telephone to Tommaso. He nodded, replied, nodded again and gave her back the phone. The money was his. He scrambled to the loft and got his satchel, along with Dr Lecter's overcoat and hat. While he was getting his things, Margot picked up the cattle prod, tested the current and slid it up her sleeve. She took the farrier's hammer too.

Tommaso, driving Cordell's car, dropped Margot off
at the house. He would leave the Honda in long-term
parking at Dulles International Airport. Margot promised him she would bury what was left of Piero and
Carlo as well as she could.

There was something he felt he should say to her
and he gathered himself and got his English together.
"Signorina, the pigs, you must know, the pigs help the
Dottore. They stand back from him, circle him. They
kill my brother, kill Carlo, but they stand back from Dr
Lecter. I think they worship him." Tommaso crossed
himself. "You should not chase him anymore."

And throughout his long life in Sardinia, Tommaso
would tell it that way. By the time Tommaso was
in his sixties, he was saying that Dr Lecter, carrying the woman, had left the barn borne on a drift
of pigs.

After the car was gone down the fire road, Margot
stood for minutes looking up at Mason's lighted windows. She saw the shadow of Cordell moving on

the walls as he fussed around Mason, replacing the monitors on her brother's breath and pulse.

She slipped the handle of the farrier's hammer down the back of her pants and settled the tail of her jacket over the head.

Cordell was coming out of Mason's room with some pillows when Margot got off the elevator.

"Cordell, fix him a martini."

"I don't know—"

"*I* know. Fix him a martini."

Cordell put the pillows on the love seat and knelt in front of the bar refrigerator.

"Is there any juice in there?" said Margot, coming close behind him. She swung the farrier's hammer hard against the base of his skull and heard a popping sound. His head smashed into the refrigerator, rebounded, and he fell over backward off his haunches looking at the ceiling with his eyes open, one pupil dilating, the other not. She turned his head sideways against the floor and came down with the hammer, depressing his temple an inch, and thick blood came out his ears.

She did not feel anything.

Mason heard the door of his room open and he rolled his goggled eye. He had been asleep for a few moments, the lights soft. The eel was also asleep beneath its rock.

Margot's great frame filled the doorway. She closed the door behind her.

"Hi, Mason."

"What happened down there? What took you so fucking long?"

"They're all dead down there, Mason." Margot came

to his bedside and unclipped the telephone line from Mason's phone and dropped it on the floor.

"Piero and Carlo and Johnny Mogli are all dead. Dr Lecter got away and he carried the Starling woman with him."

Froth appeared between Mason's teeth as he cursed.

"I sent Tommaso home with his money."

"You *what*???? You fucking idiot bitch, now listen, we're going to clean this up and start over. We've got the weekend. We don't have to worry about what Starling saw. If Lecter's got her, she's good as dead."

Margot shrugged. "She never saw *me*."

"Get on the horn to Washington and get four of those bastards up here. Send the helicopter. Show them the backhoe—show them—Cordell! Get in here." Mason whistled into his panpipes. Margot pushed the pipes aside and leaned over him, so that she could see his face.

"Cordell's not coming, Mason. Cordell's dead."

"What?"

"I killed him in the playroom. Now. Mason, you're going to give me what you owe me." She put up the side rails on his bed and, lifting the great coil of his plaited hair, she stripped the cover off his body. His little legs were no bigger around than rolls of cookie dough. His hand, the only extremity he could move, fluttered at the phone. His hard-shell respirator puffed up and down in its regular rhythm.

From her pocket Margot took a nonspermicidal condom and held it up for him to see. From her sleeve she took the cattle prod.

"Remember, Mason, how you used to spit on your

cock for lubrication? Think you could work up some spit? No? Maybe I can."

Mason bellowed when his breath permitted, a series of donkeylike brays, but it was over in half a minute, and very successfully too.

"You're dead, Margot." It sounded more like "Nargot."

"Oh, Mason, we all are. Didn't you know? But these aren't," she said, securing her blouse over her warm container. "They're wiggling. I'll show you how. I'll show you how they wiggle—show-and-tell."

Margot picked up the spiky fish-handling gloves beside the aquarium.

"I could adopt Judy," Mason said. "She could be my heir, and we could do a trust."

"We certainly could," Margot said, lifting a carp out of the holding tank. She brought a chair from the seating area, and standing on it, took the lid off the big aquarium. "But we won't."

She bent over the aquarium with her great arms down in the water. She held the carp by the tail down close to the grotto and when the eel came out she grabbed it behind the head with her powerful hand and lifted it clear out of the water, over her head. The mighty eel thrashing, as long as Margot and thick, its festive skin flashing. She gripped the eel with the other hand too and when it flexed it was all she could do to hold on with the spiky gloves imbedded in its hide.

Careful down off the chair and she came to Mason carrying the flexing eel, its head shaped like a bolt cutter, teeth clicking together with a sound like a telegraph key, the back-curved teeth no fish ever escaped. She flopped the eel on top of his chest, on the respirator and holding it with one hand, she lashed his pigtail around and around and around it.

"Wiggle, wiggle, Mason," she said.

She held the eel behind the head with one hand and with the other she forced down Mason's jaw, forced it down, putting her weight on his chin, him straining with what strength he had, and with a creaking, cracking sound his mouth opened.

"You should have taken the chocolate," Margot said, and stuffed the eel's maw into Mason's mouth, it seizing his tongue with its razor-sharp teeth as it would a fish and not letting go, never letting go, its body thrashing tangled in Mason's pigtail. Blood blew out Mason's nose hole and he was drowning.

Margot left them together, Mason and the eel, the carp circling alone in the aquarium. She composed herself at Cordell's desk and watched the monitors until Mason flat-lined.

The eel was still moving when she went back into Mason's room. The respirator went up and down, inflating the eel's air bladder as it pumped bloody froth out of Mason's lungs. Margot rinsed the cattle prod in the aquarium and put it in her pocket.

Margot took from a baggie in her pocket the bit of Dr Lecter's scalp and the lock of his hair. She scraped blood from the scalp with Mason's fingernails, unsteady work with the eel still moving, and entwined the hair in his fingers. Last, she stuffed a single hair into one of the fish gloves.

Margot walked out without looking at the dead Cordell and went home to Judy with her warm prize, tucked where it would stay warm.

504

VI

A LONG SPOON

Therefore bihoveth hire a ful long spoon
That shal ete with a feend.

—*Geoffrey Chaucer*,
FROM *THE CANTERBURY TALES*,
"THE MERCHANT'S TALE"

CLARICE STARLING lies unconscious in a large bed beneath a linen sheet and a comforter. Her arms, covered by the sleeves of silk pajamas, are on top of the covers and they are restrained with silk scarves, only enough to keep her hands away from her face and to protect the IV butterfly in the back of her hand.

There are three points of light in the room, the low shaded lamp and the red pinpoints in the center of Dr Lecter's pupils as he watches her.

He is sitting in an armchair, his fingers steepled under his chin. After a time he rises and takes her blood pressure. With a small flash-light he examines her pupils. He reaches beneath the covers and finds her foot, brings it out from under the covers and, watching her closely, stimulates the sole with the tip of a key. He stands for a moment, apparently lost in thought, holding her foot gently as though it were a small animal in his hand.

From the manufacturer of the tranquilizer dart, he has learned its content. Because the second dart that struck Starling hit bone in her shin, he believes she did not get a full double dose. He is administering stimulant countermeasures with infinite care.

Between ministrations to Starling, he sits in his armchair with a big pad of butcher paper doing calculations. The pages are filled with the symbols both of astrophysics and particle physics. There are repeated efforts with the symbols of string theory. The few mathematicians who could follow him might say his equations begin brilliantly and then decline, doomed by wishful thinking: Dr Lecter wants time to reverse— no longer should increasing entropy mark the direction of time. He wants increasing order to point the way. He wants Mischa's baby teeth back out of the stool pit. Behind his fevered calculations is the desperate wish to make a place for Mischa in the world, perhaps the place now occupied by Clarice Starling.

Morning and yellow sunlight in the playroom at Muskrat Farm. The great stuffed animals with their button eyes regard the body of Cordell, covered now.

Even in the middle of winter, a bluebottle fly has found the body and is walking over the covering sheet where blood has soaked through.

Had Margot Verger known the raw ablative tension suffered by the principals in a media-ridden homicide, she might never have stuffed the eel down her brother's throat.

Her decision not to try to clean up the mess at Muskrat Farm and to simply duck until the storm was over was a wise one. No one living saw her at Muskrat when Mason and the others were killed.

Her story was that the first frantic call from the midnight relief nurse wakened her in the house she shared with Judy. She came to the scene and arrived shortly after the first sheriff's officers.

The lead investigator for the sheriff's department, Detective Clarence Franks, was a youngish man with eyes a bit too close together, but he was not stupid as Margot had hoped he would be.

"Can't just anybody come up here in that elevator, it takes a key to get in, right?" Franks asked her. The detective and Margot sat awkwardly side by side on the love seat.

"I suppose so, if that's the way they came."

"'They,' Ms Verger? Do you think there might be more than one?"

"I have no idea, Mr Franks."

She had seen her brother's body still joined to the eel and covered by a sheet. Someone had unplugged the respirator. The criminalists were taking samples of aquarium water and taking swipes of blood from the floor. She could see in Mason's hand the piece of Dr Lecter's scalp. They hadn't found it yet. The criminalists looked to Margot like Tweedledum and Tweedledee.

Detective Franks was busy scribbling in his notebook.

"Do they know who those other poor people are?" Margot said. "Did they have families?"

"We're working it out," Franks said. "There were three weapons we can trace."

In fact, the sheriff's department was not sure how many persons had died in the barn, as the pigs had disappeared into the deep woods dragging with them the depleted remains for later.

"In the course of this investigation, we might have to ask you and your—your *longtime companion* to undergo a polygraph examination, that's a lie detector, would you consent to that, Ms Verger?"

"Mr Franks, I'll do anything to catch these people. To specifically answer your question, ask me and Judy when you need us. Should I talk to the family lawyer?"

"Not if you don't have anything to hide, Ms Verger."

"Hide?" Margot managed tears.

"Please, I have to do this, Ms Verger." Franks started to put his hand on her massive shoulder and thought better of it.

STARLING WOKE in the fresh-smelling semidark, knowing in some primal way that she was near the sea. She moved slightly on the bed. She felt a deep soreness all over, and then she fell away from consciousness again. When next she woke, a voice was talking quietly to her, offering a warm cup. She drank from it, and the taste was similar to the herbal tea Mapp's grandmother sent her.

Day and evening again, the smell of fresh flowers in the house, and once the faint sting of a needle. Like the thud and crackle of distant fireworks, the remnants of fear and pain popped on the horizon, but not close, never close. She was in the garden of the hurricane's eye.

"Waking. Waking, calm. Waking in a pleasant room," a voice said. She heard faint chamber music.

She felt very clean and her skin was scented with mint, some ointment that gave a deep comforting warmth.

Starling opened her eyes wide.

Dr Lecter stood at a distance from her, very still, as he had stood in his cell when she first saw him. We are accustomed to seeing him unfettered now. It is not shocking to see him in open space with another mortal creature.

"Good evening, Clarice."

"Good evening, Dr Lecter," she said, responding in kind with no real idea of the time.

"If you feel uncomfortable, it's just bruises you suffered in a fall. You'll be all right. I'd just like to be positive about something though, could you please look into this light?" He approached her with a small flashlight. Dr Lecter smelled like fresh broadcloth.

She forced herself to keep her eyes open as he examined her pupils, then he stepped away again.

"Thank you. There's a very comfortable bathroom, just in there. Want to try your feet? Slippers are beside your bed, I'm afraid I had to borrow your boots."

She was awake and not awake. The bathroom was indeed comfortable and furnished with every amenity. In the following days she enjoyed long baths there, but she did not bother with her reflection in the mirror, so far was she from herself.

DAYS OF talk, sometimes hearing herself and wondering who was speaking with such intimate knowledge of her thoughts. Days of sleep and strong broth and omelettes.

And one day Dr Lecter said, "Clarice, you must be tired of your robes and pajamas. There are some things in the closet you might like—only if you want to wear them." And in the same tone, "I put your personal things, your purse and your gun and your wallet, in the top drawer of the chest, if you want any of that."

"Thank you, Dr Lecter."

In the closet were a variety of clothes, dresses, pants suits, a shimmery long gown with a beaded top. There were cashmere pants and pullovers that appealed to her. She chose tan cashmere, and moccasins.

In the drawer was her belt and Yaqui slide, empty of the lost .45, but her ankle holster was there beside her purse, and in it was the cut-down .45 automatic. The clip was full of fat cartridges, nothing in the chamber, the way she wore it on her leg. And her boot

514

knife was there, in its scabbard. Her car keys were in her purse.

Starling was herself and not herself. When she wondered about events it was as though she saw them from the side, saw herself from a distance.

She was happy to see her car in the garage when Dr Lecter took her out to it. She looked at the wipers and decided to replace them.

"Clarice, how do you think Mason's men followed us to the grocery store?"

She looked up at the garage ceiling for a moment, thinking.

It took her less than two minutes to find the antenna running crosswise between the backseat and the package shelf, and she followed the antenna wire to the hidden beacon.

She turned it off and carried it into the house by the antenna as she might carry a rat by the tail.

"Very nice," she said. "Very new. Decent installation too. I'm sure it's got Mr Krendler's prints on it. May I have a plastic bag?"

"Could they search for it with aircraft?"

"It's off now. They couldn't search with aircraft unless Krendler admitted he used it. You know he didn't do that. Mason could sweep with his helicopter."

"Mason is dead."

"Ummmm," Starling said. "Would you play for me?"

CHAPTER

93

PAUL KRENDLER swung between tedium and rising fear in the first days after the murders. He arranged for direct reports from the FBI local field office in Maryland.

He felt reasonably safe from any audit of Mason's books because the passage of money from Mason to his own numbered account had a fairly foolproof cutout in the Cayman Islands. But with Mason gone, he had big plans and no patron. Margot Verger knew about his money, and she knew he had compromised the security of the FBI files on Lecter. Margot had to keep her mouth shut.

The monitor for the auto beacon worried him. He had taken it from the Engineering building at Quantico without signing it out, but he was on the entry log at Engineering for that day.

Dr Doemling and the big nurse, Barney, had seen him at Muskrat, but only in a legitimate role, talking with Mason Verger about how to catch Hannibal Lecter.

General relief came to everyone on the fourth afternoon after the murders when Margot Verger was able to play for the sheriff's investigators a newly taped message on her answering machine.

The policemen stood rapt in the bedroom, staring at the bed she shared with Judy and listening to the voice of the fiend. Dr Lecter gloated over the death of Mason and assured Margot that it was extremely painful and prolonged. She sobbed into her hand, and Judy held her. Finally Franks led her from the room, saying "No need for you to hear it again."

With the prodding of Krendler, the answering machine tape was brought to Washington and a voiceprint confirmed the caller was Dr Lecter.

But the greatest relief for Krendler came in a telephone call on the evening of the fourth day.

The caller was none other than U.S. Representative Parton Vellmore of Illinois.

Krendler had only spoken to the congressman on a few occasions, but his voice was familiar from television. Just the fact of the call was a reassurance; Vellmore was on the House Judiciary Subcommittee and a notable shitepoke; he would fly from Krendler in an instant if Krendler was hot.

"Mr Krendler, I know you were well acquainted with Mason Verger."

"Yes, sir."

"Well, it's just a goddamned shame. That sadistic son of a bitch ruined Mason's life, mutilated him and then came back and killed him. I don't know if you're aware of it, but one of my constituents also died in that tragedy. Johnny Mogli, served the people of Illinois for years in law enforcement."

"No, sir, I wasn't aware of that. I'm sorry."

"The point is, Krendler, we have to go on. The Vergers' legacy of philanthropy and their keen interest in public policy will continue. It's bigger than the death of one man. I've been talking to several people in the twenty-seventh district and to the Verger people. Margot Verger has made me aware of your interest in public service. Extraordinary woman. Has a real practical side. We're getting together very soon, real informal and quiet, and talk about what we can do next November. We want you on board. Think you could make the meeting?"

"Yes, Congressman. Definitely."

"Margot will call you with the details, it'll be in the next few days."

Krendler put the phone down, relief washing over him.

The discovery in the barn of the .45 Colt registered to the late John Brigham, now known to be the property of Clarice Starling, was a considerable embarrassment to the Bureau.

Starling was listed as missing, but the case was not carried as a kidnapping, as no living person saw her abducted. She was not even an agent missing from active duty. Starling was an agent on suspension, whose whereabouts were unknown. A bulletin was issued for her vehicle with the VIN number and the license plate, but with no special emphasis on the owner's identity.

Kidnapping commands much more effort from law enforcement than a missing persons case. The classification made Ardelia Mapp so angry she wrote her letter of resignation to the Bureau, then thought it better to wait and work from within. Again and again Mapp found herself going to Starling's side of the duplex to look for her.

Mapp found the Lecter VICAP file and National Crime Information Center files maddeningly static, with only trivial additions: The Italian police had managed to find Dr Lecter's computer at last—the Carabinieri were playing Super Mario on it in their recreation room. The machine had purged itself the moment investigators hit the first key.

Mapp badgered everyone of influence she could reach in the Bureau since Starling disappeared.

Her repeated calls to Jack Crawford's home were unanswered.

She called Behavioral Science and was told Crawford remained in Jefferson Memorial Hospital with chest pains.

She did not call him there. In the Bureau, he was Starling's last angel.

STARLING HAD no sense of time. Over the days and nights there were the conversations. She heard herself speaking for minutes on end, and she listened.

Sometimes she laughed at herself, hearing artless revelations that normally would have mortified her. The things she told Dr Lecter were often surprising to her, sometimes distasteful to a normal sensibility, but what she said was always true. And Dr Lecter spoke as well. In a low, even voice. He expressed interest and encouragement, but never surprise or censure.

He told her about his childhood, about Mischa.

Sometimes they looked at a single bright object together to begin their talks, almost always there was but a single light source in the room. From day to day the bright object changed.

Today, they began with the single highlight on the side of a teapot, but as their talk progressed, Dr Lecter seemed to sense their arrival at an unexplored gallery in her mind. Perhaps he heard trolls fighting on the other side of a wall. He replaced the teapot with a silver belt buckle.

"That's my daddy's," Starling said. She clapped her hands together like a child.

"Yes," Dr Lecter said. "Clarice, would you like to talk with your father? Your father is here. Would you like to talk with him?"

"My daddy's here! Hey! All right!"

Dr Lecter put his hands on the sides of Starling's head, over her temporal lobes, which could supply her with all of her father she would ever need. He looked deep, deep into her eyes.

"I know you'll want to talk privately. I'll go now. You can watch the buckle, and in a few minutes, you'll hear him knock. All right?"

"Yes! Super!"

"Good. You'll just have to wait a few minutes."

Tiny sting of the finest needle—Starling did not even look down—and Dr Lecter left the room.

She watched the buckle until the knock came, two firm knocks, and her father came in as she remembered him, tall in the doorway, carrying his hat, his hair slicked down with water the way he came to the supper table.

"Hey, Baby! What time do you eat around here?"

He had not held her in the twenty-five years since his death, but when he gathered her to him, the western snaps on his shirtfront felt the very same, he smelled of strong soap and tobacco, and she sensed against her the great volume of his heart.

"Hey, Baby. Hey, Baby. Did you fall down?" It was the same as when he gathered her up in the yard after she tried to ride a big goat on a dare. "You was doing pretty good 'til she swapped ends so fast. Come on in the kitchen and let's see what we can find."

Two things on the table in the spare kitchen of her childhood home, a cellophane package of SNO BALLS, and a bag of oranges.

Starling's father opened his Barlow knife with the blade broken off square and peeled a couple of oranges, the peelings curling on the oilcloth. They sat in ladder-back kitchen chairs and he freed the sections by quarters and alternately he ate one, and he gave one to Starling. She spit the seeds in her hand and held them in her lap. He was long in a chair, like John Brigham.

Her father chewed more on one side than the other and one of his lateral incisors was capped with white metal in the fashion of forties army dentistry. It gleamed when he laughed. They ate two oranges and a SNO BALL apiece and told a few knock-knock jokes. Starling had forgotten that wonderful squirmy feeling of springy icing under the coconut. The kitchen dissolved and they were talking as grown people.

"How you doin', Baby?" It was a serious question.

"They're pretty down on me at work."

"I know about that. That's that courthouse crowd, Sugar. Sorrier bunch never—never drew breath. You never shot nobody you didn't have to."

"I believe that. There's other stuff."

"You never told a lie about it."

"No, sir."

"You saved that little baby."

"He came out all right."

"I was real proud of that."

"Thank you, sir."

"Sugar, I got to take off. We'll talk."

"You can't stay."

He put his hand on her head. "We can't never stay, Baby. Can't nobody stay like they want to."

He kissed her forehead and walked out of the room. She could see the bullet hole in his hat as he waved to her, tall in the doorway.

CLEARLY STARLING loved her father as much as we love anybody, and she would have fought in an instant over a slur on his memory. Yet, in conversation with Dr Lecter, under the influence of a major hypnotic drug and deep hypnosis, this is what she said:

"I'm really mad at him, though. I mean, come on, how come he had to be behind a goddamned drugstore in the middle of the night going up against those two pissants that killed him. He short-shucked that old pump shotgun and they had him. They were nothing and they had him. He didn't know what he was doing. He never learned anything."

She would have slapped the face of anybody else saying that.

The monster settled back a micron in his chair. *Ahh, at last we've come to it. These schoolgirl recollections were becoming tedious.*

Starling tried to swing her legs beneath the chair like a child, but her legs were too long. "See, he had that job, he went and did what they told him, went around with that damned watchman's clock and then he was dead. And Mama was washing the blood out of his hat to bury it with him. Who came home to *us*? Nobody. Damn few SNO BALLS after that, I can tell you. Mama and me, cleaning up motel rooms. People leaving wet Trojans on the nightstand. He got killed and left us because he was too goddamned stupid. He should have told those town jackasses to stuff the job."

Things she would never have said, things banned from her higher brain.

From the beginning of their acquaintance, Dr Lecter had needled her about her father, calling him a night watchman. Now he became Lecter the Protector of her father's memory.

"Clarice, he never wished for anything but your happiness and well-being."

"Wish in one hand and shit in the other one and see which one gets full the first," said Starling. This adage of the orphans' home should have been particularly distasteful coming from that attractive face, but Dr Lecter seemed pleased, even encouraged.

"Clarice, I'm going to ask you to come with me to another room," Dr Lecter said. "Your father visited you, as best you could manage. You saw that, despite your intense wish to keep him with you, he couldn't stay. He visited you. Now it's time for you to visit him."

Down a hall to a guest bedroom. The door was closed.

"Wait a moment, Clarice." He went inside.

She stood in the hall with her hand on the knob and heard a match struck.

Dr Lecter opened the door.

"Clarice, you know your father is dead. You know that better than anyone."

"Yes."

"Come in and see him."

Her father's bones were composed on a twin bed, the long bones and rib cage covered by a sheet. The remains were in low relief beneath the white cover, like a child's snow angel.

Her father's skull, cleaned by the tiny ocean scavengers off Dr Lecter's beach, dried and bleached, rested on the pillow.

"Where was his star, Clarice?"

"The village took it back. They said it cost seven dollars."

"This is what he is, this is all of him now. This is what time has reduced him to."

Starling looked at the bones. She turned and quickly left the room. It was not a retreat and Lecter did not follow her. He waited in the semidark. He was not afraid, but he heard her coming back with ears as keen as those of a staked-out goat. Something bright metal in her hand. A badge, John Brigham's shield. She put it on the sheet.

"What could a badge mean to you, Clarice? You shot a hole through one in the barn."

"It meant everything to him. That's how much he knewww." The last word distorted and her mouth turned down. She picked up her father's skull and sat on the other bed, hot tears springing in her eyes and pouring down her cheeks.

Like a toddler she caught up the tail of her pullover

and held it to her cheek and sobbed, bitter tears falling with a hollow *tap tap* on the dome of her father's skull resting in her lap, its capped tooth gleaming. "I *love* my Daddy, he was as good to me as he knew how to be. It was the best time I ever had." And it was true, and no less true than before she let the anger out.

When Dr Lecter gave her a tissue she simply gripped it in her fist and he cleaned her face himself.

"Clarice, I'm going to leave you here with these remains. Remains, Clarice. Scream your plight into his eyeholes and no reply will come." He put his hands on the sides of her head. "What you need of your father is here, in your head, and subject to your judgment, not his. I'll leave you now. Do you want the candles?"

"Yes, please."

"When you come out, bring only what you need."

He waited in the drawing room, before the fire. He passed the time playing his theremin, moving his empty hands in its electronic field to create the music, moving the hands he had placed on Clarice Starling's head as though he now directed the music. He was aware of Starling standing behind him for some time before he finished his piece.

When he turned to her, her smile was soft and sad and her hands were empty.

Ever, Dr Lecter sought pattern.

He knew that, like every sentient being, Starling formed from her early experience matrices, frameworks by which later perceptions were understood.

Speaking to her through the asylum bars so many

527

years ago, he had found an important one for Starling, the slaughter of lambs and horses on the ranch that was her foster home. She was imprinted by their plight.

Her obsessive and successful hunt for Jame Gumb was driven by the plight of his captive.

She had saved him from torture for the same reason.

Fine. Patterned behavior.

Ever looking for situational sets, Dr Lecter believed that Starling saw in John Brigham her father's good qualities—and with her father's virtues the unfortunate Brigham was also assigned the incestual taboo. Brigham, and probably Crawford, had her father's good qualities. Where were the bad?

Dr Lecter searched for the rest of this split matrix. Using hypnotic drugs and hypnotic techniques much modified from cameral therapy, he was finding in Clarice Starling's personality hard and stubborn nodes, like knots in wood, and old resentments still flammable as resin.

He came upon tableaux of pitiless brightness, years old but well tended and detailed, that sent limbic anger flashing through Starling's brain like lightning in a thunderhead.

Most of them involved Paul Krendler. Her resentment of the very real injustices she had suffered at Krendler's hands was charged with the anger at her father that she could never, never acknowledge. She could not forgive her father for dying. He had left the family, he had stopped peeling oranges in the kitchen. He had doomed her mother to the commode brush and the pail. He had stopped holding Starling close, his great heart booming like Hannah's heart as they rode into the night.

Krendler was the icon of failure and frustration. He could be blamed. But could he be defied? Or was Krendler, and every other authority and taboo, empowered to box Starling into what was, in Dr Lecter's view, her little low-ceiling life?

To him one hopeful sign: Though she was imprinted with the badge, she could still shoot a hole through one and kill the wearer. Why? Because she had committed to action, identified the wearer as a criminal and made the judgment ahead of time, overruling the imprinted icon of the star. Potential flexibility. The cerebral cortex rules. Did that mean room for Mischa *within* Starling? Or was it simply another good quality of the place Starling must vacate?

BARNEY, BACK in his apartment in Baltimore, back in the round of working at Misericordia, had the three to eleven shift. He stopped for a bowl of soup at the coffee shop on his way home and it was nearly midnight when he let himself into his apartment and turned on the light.

Ardelia Mapp sat at his kitchen table. She was pointing a black semiautomatic pistol at the center of his face. From the size of the hole in the muzzle, Barney judged it was a .40 caliber.

"Sit down, Nursey," Mapp said. Her voice was hoarse and around her dark pupils her eyes were orange. "Pull your chair over there and tip back against the wall."

What scared him more than the big stopper in her hand was the other pistol on the place mat before her. It was a Colt Woodsman .22 with a plastic pop bottle taped to the muzzle as a silencer.

The chair groaned under Barney's weight. "If the chair legs break don't shoot me, I can't help it," he said.

"Do you know anything about Clarice Starling?"

"No."

Mapp picked up the small-caliber gun. "I'm not fucking around with you, Barney. The second I think you're lying, Nursey, I'm gonna darken your stool, do you believe me?"

"Yes." Barney knew it was true.

"I'm going to ask you again. Do you know anything that would help me find Clarice Starling? The post office says you had your mail forwarded to Mason Verger's place for a month. *What the fuck, Barney?*"

"I worked up there. I was taking care of Mason Verger, and he asked me all about Lecter. I didn't like it up there and I quit. Mason was pretty much of a bastard."

"Starling's gone away."

"I know."

"Maybe Lecter took her, maybe the pigs got her. If he took her what would he do with her?"

"I'm being honest with you—I don't know. I'd help Starling if I could. Why wouldn't I? I kind of liked her and she was getting me expunged. Look in her reports or notes or—"

"I have. I want you to understand something, Barney. This is a one-time-only offer. If you know anything you better tell me now. If I *ever* find out, no matter how long from now, that you held out something that might have helped, I will come back here and this gun will be the last thing you ever see. I will kill your big ugly ass. Do you believe me?"

"Yes."

"Do you know anything?"

"No." The longest silence he could ever remember. "Just sit still there until I'm gone."

It took Barney an hour and a half to go to sleep. He lay in his bed looking at the ceiling, his brow, broad as a dolphin's, now sweaty, now dry. Barney thought about callers to come. Just before he turned out his light, he went into his bathroom and took from his DOP kit a stainless-steel shaving mirror, Marine Corps issue.

He padded into the kitchen, opened an electrical switch box in the wall and taped the mirror inside the switch box door.

It was all he could do. He twitched in his sleep like a dog.

After his next shift, he brought a rape kit home from the hospital.

THERE WAS only so much Dr Lecter could do to the German's house while retaining the furnishings. Flowers and screens helped. Color was interesting to see against the massive furniture and high darkness; it was an ancient, compelling contrast, like a butterfly lit on an armored fist.

His absentee landlord apparently had a fixation on Leda and the Swan. The interspecies coupling was represented in no less than four bronzes of varying quality, the best a reproduction of Donatello, and eight paintings. One painting delighted Dr Lecter, an Anne Shingleton with its genius anatomical articulation and some real heat in the fucking. The others he draped. The landlord's ghastly collection of hunting bronzes was draped as well.

Early in the morning the doctor laid his table carefully for three, studying it from different angles with the tip of his finger beside his nose, changed candlesticks twice and went from his damask place mats to a gathered tablecloth to reduce to more manageable size the oval dining table.

The dark and forbidding sideboard looked less like an aircraft carrier when high service pieces and bright copper warmers stood on it. In fact, Dr Lecter pulled out several of the drawers and put flowers in them, in a kind of hanging gardens effect.

He could see that he had too many flowers in the room, and must add more to make it come back right again. Too many was too many, but way too many was just right. He settled on two flower arrangements for the table: a low mound of peonies in a silver dish, white as SNO BALLS, and a large, high arrangement of massed Bells of Ireland, Dutch iris, orchids and parrot tulips that screened away much of the table's expanse and created an intimate space.

A small ice storm of crystal stood before the service plates, but the flat silver was in a warmer to be laid at the last moment.

The first course would be prepared at table, and accordingly he organized his alcohol burners, with his copper *fait-tout*, his saucepan and sauté pan, his condiments and his autopsy saw.

He could get more flowers when he went out. Clarice Starling was not disturbed when he told her he was going. He suggested she might like to sleep.

In the afternoon of the fifth day after the murders, Barney had finished shaving and was patting alcohol on his cheeks when he heard the footsteps on the stairs. It was almost time for him to go to work.

A firm knock. Margot Verger stood at his door. She carried a big purse and a small satchel.

"Hi, Barney." She looked tired.

"Hi, Margot. Come in."

He offered her a seat at the kitchen table. "Want a Coke?" Then he remembered that Cordell's head was driven into a refrigerator and he regretted the offer.

"No thanks," she said.

He sat down across the table from her. She looked over his arms as a rival bodybuilder, then back to his face.

"You okay, Margot?"

"I think so," she said.

"Looks like you don't have any worries, I mean from what I read."

"Sometimes I think about the talks we had, Barney. I kind of thought I might hear from you sometime."

535

He wondered if she had the hammer in the purse or the satchel.

"Only way you hear from me, maybe I'd like to see how you're doing sometime, if that was okay. Never asking for anything. Margot, you're cool with me."

"It's just, you know, you worry about loose ends. Not that I've got anything to hide."

He knew then she had the semen. It was when the pregnancy was announced, if they managed one, that she'd be worried about Barney.

"I mean, it was a godsend, his death, I'm not going to lie about that."

The speed of her talk told Barney she was building momentum.

"Maybe I would like a Coke," she said.

"Before I get it for you, let me show you something I've got for you. Believe me, I can put your mind at rest and it'll cost you nothing. Take a second. Hold on."

He picked a screwdriver out of a canister of tools on the counter. He could do that with his side to Margot.

In the kitchen wall were what appeared to be two circuit breaker boxes. Actually one box had replaced the other in the old building, and only the one on the right was in service.

At the electrical boxes, Barney had to turn his back to Margot. Quickly he opened the one on the left. Now he could watch her in the mirror taped inside the switchbox door. She put her hand inside the big purse. Put it in, didn't take it out.

By removing four screws, he was able to lift out of the box the disconnected panel of circuit breakers. Behind the panel was the space within the hollow wall.

Reaching carefully inside, Barney removed a plastic bag.

He heard a hitch in Margot's breathing when he took out the object the bag contained. It was a famous brutish visage—the mask Dr Lecter had been forced to wear in the Baltimore State Hospital for the Criminally Insane to prevent him from biting. This was the last and most valuable item in Barney's cache of Lecter memorabilia.

"Whoa!" Margot said.

Barney placed the mask facedown on the table on a piece of waxed paper under the bright kitchen light. He knew Dr Lecter had never been allowed to clean his mask. Dried saliva was crusted inside the mouth opening. Where the straps attached to the mask were three hairs, caught in the fastenings and pulled out by their roots.

A glance at Margot told him she was okay for the moment.

Barney took from his kitchen cabinet the rape kit. The small plastic box contained Q-tips, sterile water, swatches and clean pill bottles.

With infinite care he swabbed up the saliva flakes with a moistened Q-tip. He put the Q-tip into a pill bottle. The hairs he pulled loose from the mask and put them in a second bottle.

He touched his thumb to the sticky sides of two pieces of scotch tape, leaving a clear fingerprint each time, and taped the lids on the bottles. He gave the two containers to Margot in a baggie.

"Let's say I got in some trouble and I lost my mind and I tried to roll over on you—say I tried to tell the police some story on you to beat some charges of my own. You have proof there that I was at least an accomplice in the death of Mason Verger and maybe did the whole thing myself. At the least I supplied you with the DNA."

"You'd get immunity before you ratted."

"For conspiring maybe, but not for physically taking part in a big-publicity murder. They'd promise me use-immunity on conspiracy and then fuck me when they figured I helped. I'd be screwed forever. It's right there in your hands."

Barney was not positive of this, but he thought it sounded pretty good.

She could also plant the Lecter DNA on Barney's still form anytime she needed to, and they both knew it.

She looked at him for what seemed like a very long time with her bright blue butcher's eyes.

She put the satchel on the table. "Lot of money in there," she said. "Enough to see every Vermeer in the world. Once." She seemed a little giddy, and oddly happy. "I've got Franklin's cat in the car, I've got to go. Franklin and his stepmother and his sister Shirley and some guy named Stringbean and God knows who else are coming out to Muskrat when Franklin gets out of the hospital. Cost me fifty dollars to get that fucking cat. It was living next door to Franklin's old house under an alias."

She did not put the plastic bag in her purse. She carried it in her free hand. Barney guessed she didn't want him to see her other option in the purse.

At the door he said, "Think I could have a kiss?"

She stood on tiptoe and gave him a quick kiss on the lips.

"That will have to do," she said primly. The stairs creaked under her weight going down.

Barney locked his door and stood for minutes with his forehead against the cool refrigerator.

STARLING WOKE to distant chamber music, and the tangy aromas of cooking. She felt wonderfully refreshed and very hungry. A tap at her door and Dr Lecter came in wearing dark trousers, a white shirt and an ascot. He carried a long suit bag and a hot cappuccino for her.

"Did you sleep well?"

"Great, thank you."

"The chef tells me we'll dine in an hour and a half. Cocktails in an hour, is that all right? I thought you might like this—see if it suits you." He hung the bag in the closet and left without another sound.

She did not look in her closet until after a long bath, and when she did look she was pleased. She found a long dinner gown in cream silk, narrowly but deeply décolleté beneath an exquisite beaded jacket.

On the dresser were a pair of earrings with pendant cabochon emeralds. The stones had a lot of fire for an unfaceted cut.

Her hair was always easy for her. Physically, she felt very comfortable in the clothes. Even unaccustomed as she was to this level of dress, she did not examine herself long in the mirror, only looking to see if everything was in place.

The German landlord built his fireplaces oversized. In the drawing room, Starling found a good-sized log blazing. She approached the warm hearth in a whisper of silk.

Music from the harpsichord in the corner. Seated at the instrument, Dr Lecter in white tie.

He looked up and saw her and his breath stopped in his throat. His hands stopped too, still spread above the keyboard. Harpsichord notes do not carry, and in the sudden quiet of the drawing room, they both heard him take his next breath.

Two drinks waited before the fire. He occupied himself with them. Lillet with a slice of orange. Dr Lecter handed one to Clarice Starling.

"If I saw you every day, forever, I'd remember this time." His dark eyes held her whole.

"How many times have you seen me? That I don't know about?"

"Only three."

"But here—"

"Is outside of time, and what I may see taking care of you does not compromise your privacy. That's kept in its own place with your medical records. I'll confess it *is* pleasant to look at you asleep. You're quite beautiful, Clarice."

"Looks are an accident, Dr Lecter."

"If comeliness were earned, you'd still be beautiful."

"Thanks."

"Do not say '*Thanks*.'" A fractional turn of his head was enough to dash his annoyance like a glass thrown in the fireplace.

"I say what I mean," Starling said. "Would you like it better if I said 'I'm glad you find me so.' That would be a little fancier, and equally true."

She raised her glass beneath her level prairie gaze, taking back nothing.

It occurred to Dr Lecter in the moment that with all his knowledge and intrusion, he could never entirely predict her, or own her at all. He could feed the caterpillar, he could whisper through the chrysalis; what hatched out followed its own nature and was beyond him. He wondered if she had the .45 on her leg beneath the gown.

Clarice Starling smiled at him then, the cabochons caught the firelight and the monster was lost in self-congratulation at his own exquisite taste and cunning.

"Clarice, dinner appeals to taste and smell, the oldest senses and the closest to the center of the mind. Taste and smell are housed in parts of the mind that precede pity, and pity has no place at my table. At the same time, playing in the dome of the cortex like miracles illumined on the ceiling of a church are the ceremonies and sights and exchanges of dinner. It can be far more engaging than theater." He brought his face close to hers, taking some reading in her eyes. "I want you to understand what riches you bring to it, Clarice, and what your *entitlements* are. Clarice, have you studied your reflection lately? I think not. I doubt that you ever do. Come into the hall, stand in front of the pier glass."

Dr Lecter brought a candelabrum from the mantel. The tall mirror was one of the good eighteenth-century antiques, but slightly smoky and crazed. It was out of Château Vaux-le-Vicomte and God knows what it has seen.

"Look, Clarice. That delicious vision is what you are. This evening you will see yourself from a distance for a while. You will see what is just, you will say what is true. You've never lacked the courage to say what you think, but you've been hampered by constraints. I will tell you again, pity has no place at this table.

"If remarks are passed that are unpleasant in the instant, you will see that context can make them something between droll and riotously funny. If things are said that are painfully true, then it is only passing truth and will change." He took a sip of his drink. "If you feel pain bloom inside you, it will soon blossom into relief. Do you understand me?"

"No, Dr Lecter, but I remember what you said. Damn a bunch of self-improvement. I want a pleasant dinner."

"That I promise you." He smiled, a sight that frightens some.

Neither looked at her reflection now in the clouded glass; they watched each other through the burning tapers of the candelabrum and the mirror watched them both.

"Look, Clarice."

She watched the red sparks pinwheel deep in his eyes and felt the excitement of a child approaching a distant fair.

From his jacket pocket Dr Lecter took a syringe, the

needle fine as a hair and, never looking, only feeling, he slipped the needle into her arm. When he withdrew it, the tiny wound did not even bleed.

"What were you playing when I came in?" she asked.

"'If Love Now Reigned.'"

"It's very old?"

"Henry the Eighth composed it about 1510."

"Would you play for me?" she said. "Would you finish it now?"

THE BREEZE of their entry into the dining room stirred the flames of the candles and the warmers. Starling had only seen the dining room in passage and it was wonderful to see the room transformed. Bright, inviting. Tall crystal repeating the candle flames above the creamy napery at their places and the space reduced to intimate size with a screen of flowers shutting off the rest of the table.

Dr Lecter had brought his flat silver from the warmer at the last minute and when Starling explored her place setting, she felt in the handle of her knife an almost feverish heat.

Dr Lecter poured wine and gave her only a tiny *amuse-gueule* to eat for starters, a single Belon oyster and a morsel of sausage, as he had to sit over half a glass of wine and admire her in the context of his table.

The height of his candlesticks was exactly right. The flames lit the deeps of her décolleté and he did not have to be vigilant about her sleeves.

"What are we having?"

He raised his finger to his lips. "You never ask, it spoils the surprise."

They talked about the trimming of crow quills and their effect on the voice of a harpsichord, and only for a moment did she recall a crow robbing her mother's service cart on a motel balcony long ago. From a distance she judged the memory irrelevant to this pleasant time and she deliberately set it aside.

"Hungry?"

"Yes!"

"Then we'll have our first course."

Dr Lecter moved a single tray from the sideboard to a space beside his place at the table and rolled a service cart to tableside. Here were his pans, his burners, and his condiments in little crystal bowls.

He fired up his burners and began with a goodly knob of Charante butter in his copper *fait-tout* saucepan, swirling the melting butter and browning the butterfat to make *beurre-noisette*. When it was the brown of a hazelnut, he set the butter aside on a trivet.

He smiled at Starling, his teeth very white.

"Clarice, do you recall what we said about pleasant and unpleasant remarks, and things being very funny in context?"

"That butter smells wonderful. Yes, I remember."

"And do you remember who you saw in the mirror, how splendid she was?"

"Dr Lecter, if you don't mind my saying so this is getting a little *Dick and Jane*. I remember perfectly."

"Good. Mr Krendler is joining us for our first course."

Dr Lecter moved the large flower arrangement from the table to the sideboard.

Deputy Assistant Inspector General Paul Krendler, in the flesh, sat at the table in a stout oak armchair. Krendler opened his eyes wide and looked about. He wore his runner's headband and a very nice funeral tuxedo, with integral shirt and tie. The garment being split up the back, Dr Lecter had been able to sort of tuck it around him, covering the yards of duct tape that held him to the chair.

Starling's eyelids might have lowered a fraction and her lips slightly pursed as they sometimes did on the firing range.

Now Dr Lecter took a pair of silver tongs from the sideboard and peeled off the tape covering Krendler's mouth.

"Good evening, again, Mr Krendler."

"Good evening." Krendler did not seem to be quite himself. His place was set with a small tureen.

"Would you like to say good evening to Ms Starling?"

"Hello, Starling." He seemed to brighten. "I always wanted to watch you eat."

Starling took him in from a distance, as though she were the wise old pier glass watching. "Hello, Mr Krendler." She raised her face to Dr Lecter, busy with his pans. "How did you ever catch him?"

"Mr Krendler is on his way to an important conference about his future in politics," Dr Lecter said. "Margot Verger invited him as a favor to me. Sort of a quid pro quo. Mr Krendler jogged up to the pad in Rock Creek Park to meet the Verger helicopter. But he caught a ride with me instead. Would you like to say grace before our meal, Mr Krendler. Mr *Krendler*?"

"Grace? Yes." Krendler closed his eyes. "Father, we thank thee for the blessings we are about to receive and we dedicate them to Thy service. Starling is a big girl to be fucking her daddy even if she is southern. Please forgive her for that and bring her to my service. In Jesus' name, amen."

Starling noted that Dr Lecter kept his eyes piously closed throughout the prayer.

She felt quick and calm. "*Paul*, I have to tell you, the Apostle *Paul*, couldn't have done better. He hated women too. He should have been named *Appall*."

"You really blew it this time, Starling. You'll never be reinstated."

"Was that a *job* offer you worked into the blessing? I never saw such tact."

"I'm going to Congress." Krendler smiled unpleasantly. "Come around the campaign headquarters, I might find something for you to do. You could be an office girl. Can you type and file?"

"Certainly."

"Can you take dictation?"

"I use voice-recognition software," Starling said. She continued in a judicious tone. "If you'll excuse me for talking shop at the table, you aren't fast enough to steal in Congress. You can't make up for a second-rate intelligence just by playing dirty. You'd last longer as a big crook's gofer."

"Don't wait on us, Mr Krendler," Dr Lecter urged. "Have some of your broth while it's hot." He raised the covered *potager* and straw to Krendler's lips.

Krendler made a face. "That soup's not very good."

"Actually, it's more of a parsley and thyme infusion," the doctor said, "and more for our sake than yours. Have another few swallows, and let it circulate."

Starling apparently was weighing an issue, using her palms like the Scales of Justice. "You know, Mr Krendler, every time you ever leered at me, I had the nagging feeling I had done something to deserve it." She moved her palms up and down judiciously, a motion similar to passing a Slinky back and forth. "I *didn't* deserve it. Every time you wrote something negative in my personnel folder, I resented it, but still I searched myself. I doubted myself for a moment, and tried to scratch this tiny itch that said Daddy knows best.

"You *don't* know best, Mr Krendler. In fact, you don't know anything." Starling had a sip of her splendid white Burgundy and said to Dr Lecter, "I *love* this. But I think we should take it off the ice." She turned again, attentive hostess, to her guest. "You are forever an . . . an *oaf*, and beneath notice," she said in a pleasant tone. "And that's enough about you at this lovely table. Since you are Dr Lecter's guest, I hope you enjoy the meal."

"*Who are you anyway?*" Krendler said. "You're not Starling. You've got the spot on your face, but you're not Starling."

Dr Lecter added shallots to his hot browned butter and at the instant their perfume rose, he put in minced caper berries. He set the saucepan off the fire, and set his sauté pan on the heat. From the sideboard he took a large crystal bowl of ice cold water and a silver salver and put them beside Paul Krendler.

"I had some plans for that smart mouth," Krendler said, "but I'd *never* hire you now. Who gave you an appointment anyway?"

"I don't expect you to change your attitude entirely as the other Paul did, Mr Krendler," Dr Lecter said. "You are not on the road to Damascus, or even on the road to the Verger helicopter."

Dr Lecter took off Krendler's runner's headband as you would remove the rubber band from a tin of caviar.

"All we ask is that you keep an open mind." Carefully, using both hands, Dr Lecter lifted off the top of Krendler's head, put it on the salver and removed it to the sideboard. Hardly a drop of blood fell from the clean incision, the major blood vessels having been tied and the others neatly sealed under a local anesthetic, and the skull sawn around in the kitchen a half-hour before the meal.

Dr Lecter's method in removing the top of Krendler's skull was as old as Egyptian medicine, except that he had the advantage of an autopsy saw with cranial blade, a skull key and better anesthetics. The brain itself feels no pain.

The pinky-gray dome of Krendler's brain was visible above his truncated skull.

Standing over Krendler with an instrument resembling a tonsil spoon, Dr Lecter removed a slice of Krendler's prefrontal lobe, then another, until he had four. Krendler's eyes looked up as though he were following what was going on. Dr Lecter placed the slices in the bowl of ice water, the water acidulated with the juice of a lemon, in order to firm them.

"Would you like to swing on a star," Krendler sang abruptly. *"Carry moonbeams home in a jar."*

In classic cuisine, brains are soaked and then pressed and chilled overnight to firm them. In dealing with the item absolutely fresh, the challenge is to prevent the material from simply disintegrating into a handful of lumpy gelatin.

With splendid dexterity, the doctor brought the firmed slices to a plate, dredged them lightly in seasoned flour, and then in fresh brioche crumbs.

He grated a fresh black truffle into his sauce and finished it with a squeeze of lemon juice.

Quickly he sautéed the slices until they were just brown on each side.

"Smells great!" Krendler said.

Dr Lecter placed the browned brains on broad croutons on the warmed plates, and dressed them with the sauce and truffle slices. A garnish of parsley and whole caper berries with their stems, and a single nasturtium blossom on watercress to achieve a little height, completed his presentation.

"How is it?" Krendler asked, once again behind the flowers and speaking immoderately loud, as persons with lobotomies are prone to do.

"Really excellent," Starling said. "I've never had caper berries before."

Dr Lecter found the shine of butter sauce on her lip intensely moving.

Krendler sang behind the greens, mostly day-care songs, and he invited requests.

Oblivious to him, Dr Lecter and Starling discussed Mischa. Starling knew of the doctor's sister's fate from their conversations about loss, but now the doctor spoke in a hopeful way about her possible return. It did not seem unreasonable to Starling on this evening that Mischa might return.

She expressed the hope that she might meet Mischa.

"You could never answer the phone in my office. You sound like a cornbread country cunt," Krendler yelled through the flowers.

"See if I sound like Oliver Twist when I ask for *MORE*," Starling replied, releasing in Dr Lecter glee he could scarcely contain.

A second helping consumed most of the frontal lobe, back nearly to the premotor cortex. Krendler was reduced to irrelevant observations about things in his immediate vision and the tuneless recitation behind the flowers of a lengthy lewd verse called "Shine."

Absorbed in their talk, Starling and Lecter were no more disturbed than they would have been by the singing of happy birthday at another table in a restaurant, but when Krendler's volume became intrusive, Dr Lecter retrieved his crossbow from a corner.

"I want you to listen to the sound of this stringed instrument, Clarice."

He waited for a moment of silence from Krendler and shot a bolt across the table through the tall flowers.

"That particular frequency of the crossbow string, should you hear it again in any context, means only your complete freedom and peace and self-sufficiency," Dr Lecter said.

The feathers and part of the shaft remained on the visible side of the flower arrangement and moved at more or less the pace of a baton directing a heart.

Krendler's voice stopped at once and in a few beats the baton stopped too.

"It's about a D below middle C?" Starling said.

"Exactly."

A moment later Krendler made a gargling sound behind the flowers. It was only a spasm in his voice box caused by the increasing acidity of his blood, he being newly dead.

"Let's have our next course," the doctor said, "a little sorbet to refresh our palates before the quail. No, no, don't get up. Mr Krendler will help me clear, if you'll excuse him."

It was all quickly done. Behind the screen of the flowers, Dr Lecter simply scraped the plates into Krendler's skull and stacked them in his lap. He replaced the top of Krendler's head and, picking up the rope attached to a dolly beneath his chair, towed him away to the kitchen.

There Dr Lecter rewound his crossbow. Conveniently it used the same battery pack as his autopsy saw.

The quails' skins were crisp and they were stuffed with foie gras. Dr Lecter talked about Henry VIII as composer and Starling told him about computer-aided design in engine sounds, the replication of pleasing frequencies.

Dessert would be in the drawing room, Dr Lecter announced.

CHAPTER

101

A SOUFFLÉ and glasses of Château d'Yquem before the fire in the drawing room, coffee ready on a side table at Starling's elbow.

Fire dancing in the golden wine, its perfume over the deep tones of the burning log.

They talked about teacups and time, and the rule of disorder.

"And so I came to believe," Dr Lecter was saying, "that there had to be a place in the world for Mischa, a prime place vacated for her, and I came to think, Clarice, that the best place in the world was yours."

The firelight did not plumb the depths of her bodice as satisfactorily as the candlelight had done, but it was wonderful playing on the bones of her face.

She considered a moment. "Let me ask you this, Dr Lecter. If a prime place in the world is required for Mischa, and I'm not saying it isn't, what's the matter with *your* place? It's well occupied and I know you would never deny her. She and I could be like sisters.

553

And if, as you say, there's room in me for my father, why is there not room in you for Mischa?"

Dr Lecter seemed pleased, whether with the idea, or with Starling's resource is impossible to say. Perhaps he felt a vague concern that he had built better than he knew.

When she replaced her glass on the table beside her, she pushed off her coffee cup and it shattered on the hearth. She did not look down at it.

Dr Lecter watched the shards, and they were still.

"I don't think you have to make up your mind right this minute," Starling said. Her eyes and the cabochons shone in the firelight. A sigh from the fire, the warmth of the fire through her gown, and there came to Starling a passing memory—*Dr Lecter, so long ago, asking Senator Martin if she breast-fed her daughter*. A jeweled movement turning in Starling's unnatural calm: For an instant many windows in her mind aligned and she saw far across her own experience. She said, "Hannibal Lecter, did your mother feed you at her breast?"

"Yes."

"Did you ever feel that you had to relinquish the breast to Mischa? Did you ever feel you were required to give it up for her?"

A beat. "I don't recall that, Clarice. If I gave it up, I did it gladly."

Clarice Starling reached her cupped hand into the deep neckline of her gown and freed her breast, quickly peaky in the open air. "You don't have to give up this one," she said. Looking always into his eyes, with her trigger finger she took warm Château d'Yquem from

554

her mouth and a thick sweet drop suspended from her nipple like a golden cabochon and trembled with her breathing.

He came swiftly from his chair to her, went on a knee before her chair, and bent to her coral and cream in the firelight his dark sleek head.

Buenos Aires, Argentina, three years later:

Barney and Lillian Hersh walked near the Obelisk on the Avenida 9 de Julio in the early evening. Ms Hersh is a lecturer at London University, on sabbatical. She and Barney met in the anthropology museum in Mexico City. They like each other and have been traveling together two weeks, trying it a day at a time, and it is getting to be more and more fun. They are not getting tired of one another.

They had arrived in Buenos Aires too late in the afternoon to go to the Museo Nacional, where a Vermeer was on loan. Barney's mission to see every Vermeer in the world amused Lillian Hersh and it did not get in the way of a good time. He had seen a quarter of the Vermeers already, and there were plenty to go.

They were looking for a pleasant café where they could eat outside.

Limousines were backed up at the Teatro Colón, Buenos Aires' spectacular opera house. They stopped to watch the opera lovers go in.

556

Tamerlane was playing with an excellent cast, and a Buenos Aires opening night crowd is worth seeing.

"Barney, you up for the opera? I think you'd like it. I'll spring."

It amused him when she used American slang. "If you'll walk me through it, *I'll* spring," Barney said. "You think they'll let us in?"

At that moment a Mercedes Maybach, deep blue and silver, whispered up to the curb. A doorman hurried to open the car.

A man, slender and elegant in white tie, got out and handed out a woman. The sight of her raised an admiring murmur in the crowd around the entrance. Her hair was a shapely platinum helmet and she wore a soft sheath of coral frosted with an overlayer of tulle. Emeralds flashed green at her throat. Barney saw her only briefly, through the heads of the crowd, and she and her gentleman were swept inside.

Barney saw the man better. His head was sleek as an otter and his nose had an imperious arch like that of Perón. His carriage made him seem taller than he was.

"Barney? Oh, Barney," Lillian was saying, "when you come back to yourself, if you ever do, tell me if you'd like to go to the opera. If they'll let us in *in mufti*. There, I said it, even if it's not precisely apt— I've always wanted to say I was *in mufti*."

When Barney did not ask what mufti was, she glanced at him sidelong. He always asked everything.

"Yes," Barney said absently. "*I'll* spring." Barney had plenty of money. He was careful with it, but not cheap. Still, the only tickets available were in the rafters among the students.

Anticipating the altitude of his seats, he rented field glasses in the lobby.

The enormous theater is a mix of Italian Renaissance, Greek and French styles, lavish with brass and gilt and red plush. Jewels winked in the crowd like flashbulbs at a ball game.

Lillian explained the plot before the overture began, talking in his ear quietly.

Just before the houselights went down, sweeping the house from the cheap seats, Barney found them, the platinum blond lady and her escort. They had just come through the gold curtains into their ornate box beside the stage. The emeralds at her throat glittered in the brilliant houselights as she took her seat.

Barney had only glimpsed her right profile as she entered the opera. He could see the left one now.

The students around them, veterans of the high-altitude seats, had brought all manner of viewing aids. One student had a powerful spotting scope so long that it disturbed the hair of the person in front of him. Barney traded glasses with him to look at the distant box. It was hard to find the box again in the long tube's limited field of vision, but when he found it, the couple was startlingly close.

The woman's cheek had a beauty spot on it, in the position the French call "Courage." Her eyes swept over the house, swept over his section and moved on. She seemed animated and in expert control of her coral mouth. She leaned to her escort and said something, and they laughed together. She put her hand on his hand and held his thumb.

"*Starling*," Barney said under his breath.

"What?" Lillian whispered.

Barney had a lot of trouble following the first act of the opera. As soon as the lights came up for the first intermission, he raised his glass to the box again. The gentleman took a champagne flute from a waiter's tray and handed it to the lady, and took a glass himself. Barney zoomed in on his profile, the shape of his ears.

He traced the length of the woman's exposed arms. They were bare and unmarked and had muscle tone, in his experienced eye.

As Barney watched, the gentleman's head turned as though to catch a distant sound, turned in Barney's direction. The gentleman raised opera glasses to his eyes. Barney could have sworn the glasses were aimed at him. He held his program in front of his face and hunkered down in his seat to try to be about average height.

"Lillian," he said. "I want you to do me a great big favor."

"Um," she said. "If it's like some of the others, I'd better hear it first."

"We're leaving when the lights go down. Fly with me to Rio tonight. No questions asked."

The Vermeer in Buenos Aires is the only one Barney never saw.

FOLLOW THIS handsome couple from the opera? All right, but very carefully . . .

At the millennium, Buenos Aires is possessed by the tango and the night has a pulse. The Mercedes, windows down to let in the music from the dance clubs, purrs through the Recoleta district to the Avenida Alvear and disappears into the courtyard of an exquisite Beaux Arts building near the French Embassy.

The air is soft and a late supper is laid on the terrace of the top floor, but the servants are gone.

Morale is high among the servants in this house, but there is an iron discipline among them. They are forbidden to enter the top floor of the mansion before noon. Or after service of the first course at dinner.

Dr Lecter and Clarice Starling often talk at dinner in languages other than Starling's native English. She had college French and Spanish to build on, and she has found she has a good ear. They speak Italian a lot at mealtimes; she finds a curious freedom in the visual nuances of the language.

Sometimes our couple dances at dinnertime. Sometimes they do not finish dinner.

Their relationship has a great deal to do with the penetration of Clarice Starling, which she avidly welcomes and encourages. It has much to do with the envelopment of Hannibal Lecter, far beyond the bounds of his experience. It is possible that Clarice Starling could frighten him. Sex is a splendid structure they add to every day.

Clarice Starling's memory palace is building as well. It shares some rooms with Dr Lecter's own memory palace—he has discovered her in there several times—but her own palace grows on its own. It is full of new things. She can visit her father there. Hannah is at pasture there. Jack Crawford is there, when she chooses to see him bent over his desk—after Crawford was home for a month from the hospital, the chest pains came again in the night. Instead of calling an ambulance and going through it all again, he chose simply to roll over to the solace of his late wife's side of the bed.

Starling learned of Crawford's death during one of Dr Lecter's regular visits to the FBI public Web site to admire his likeness among the Ten Most Wanted. The picture the Bureau is using of Dr Lecter remains a comfortable two faces behind.

After Starling read Jack Crawford's obituary, she walked by herself for most of a day, and she was glad to come home at evening.

A year ago she had one of her own emeralds set in a ring. It is engraved inside with AM-CS. Ardelia Mapp received it in an untraceable wrapper with a note. *Dear Ardelia, I'm fine and better than fine. Don't*

look for me. I love you. I'm sorry I scared you. Burn this.
Starling.

Mapp took the ring to the Shenandoah River where Starling used to run. She walked a long way with it clutched in her hand, angry, hot-eyed, ready to throw the ring in the water, imagining it flashing in the air and the small plop. In the end she put it on her finger and shoved her fist in her pocket. Mapp doesn't cry much. She walked a long way, until she could be quiet. It was dark when she got back to her car.

It is hard to know what Starling remembers of the old life, what she chooses to keep. The drugs that held her in the first days have had no part in their lives for a long time. Nor the long talks with a single light source in the room.

Occasionally, on purpose, Dr Lecter drops a teacup to shatter on the floor. He is satisfied when it does not gather itself together. For many months now, he has not seen Mischa in his dreams.

Someday perhaps a cup will come together. Or somewhere Starling may hear a crossbow string and come to some unwilled awakening, if indeed she even sleeps.

We'll withdraw now, while they are dancing on the terrace—the wise Barney has already left town and we must follow his example. For either of them to discover us would be fatal.

We can only learn so much and live.

Acknowledgments

In trying to understand the structure of Dr Lecter's memory palace, I was aided by Frances A. Yates's remarkable book *The Art of Memory*, as well as Jonathan D. Spence's *The Memory Palace of Matteo Ricci*.

Robert Pinsky's translation of *Dante's Inferno* was a boon and a pleasure to use, as were the annotations of Nicole Pinsky. The term "festive skin" is Pinsky's translation of Dante.

"In the garden of the hurricane's eye" is John Ciardi's phrase and the title of one of his poems.

The first lines of poetry Clarice Starling recalls in the asylum are from T.S. Eliot's "Burnt Norton," *Four Quartets*.

My thanks to Pace Barnes for her encouragement, support and wise counsel.

Carole Baron, my publisher, editor and friend, helped me make this a better book.

Athena Varounis and Bill Trible in the United States and Ruggero Perugini in Italy showed me the best

563

and brightest in law enforcement. None of them is a character in this book, nor is any other living person. The wickedness herein I took from my own stock.

Niccolo Capponi shared with me his deep knowledge of Florence and its art and allowed Dr Lecter to use his family palazzo. My thanks also to Robert Held for his scholarship and to Caroline Michahelles for much Florentine insight.

The staff of Carnegie Public Library in Coahoma County, Mississippi, looked up things for years. Thank you.

I owe a lot to Marguerite Schmitt: With one white truffle and the magic in her heart and hands, she introduced us to the wonders of Florence. It is too late to thank Marguerite; in this moment of completion I want to say her name.